SEVEN TEARS FOR
APOLLO

SEVEN TEARS

By Phyllis A. Whitney—SEVEN TEARS FOR
APOLLO—WINDOW ON THE SQUARE—BLUE
FIRE—THUNDER HEIGHTS—THE MOONFLOWER
—SKYE CAMERON—THE TREMBLING HILLS—
THE QUICKSILVER POOL—RED IS FOR MURDER

APPLETON-CENTURY-CROFTS

FOR APOLLO

PHYLLIS A.
WHITNEY

NEW YORK

Affiliate of
MEREDITH PRESS
Des Moines & New York

All the characters and incidents in this story are a product of the author's imagination. But the Isle of Rhodes prevails and any claims made herewith for its beauty and fascination are sure to fall short of the enchanting reality.

SEVEN TEARS FOR
APOLLO

1

THE MUSEUM'S statue of Apollo was a copy. The original held a place of honor in Olympia in the faraway Peloponnese. On his pedestal the god stood unclothed in the full magnificence of male youth. A scant drapery broke the line of shoulder and outstretched arm, drawn casually across the back to hang downward in marble folds above the left wrist. Stylized ringlets rimmed his brow and curled upward at the nape of his neck. The hand was gone from the outstretched arm, but his eyes, blank now in marble sockets, followed the direction of the lifted arm in its gesture of command. There seemed at first glance a feminine softness in the rounded curve of cheek and chin, the fullness of lip. But muscular strength underlay the rounding to lend, perhaps, a hint of cruelty that befitted a god who had blazed across the Grecian firmament with all the fiery splendor of the sun.

The girl who stood before the statue, staring upward through swimming tears, had something of the same classic beauty of the age to which the figure of the god belonged. She was in her early twenties, tall, with a slender column of neck supporting the heavy coil of blond hair she wore upon its nape. There was a grace of modeling to the line of her forehead and nose, although here was no chill marble but warm flesh that could feel the flicking lash of pain. Behind gray eyes, fully lidded, was a human brain, and where there is mind there is memory and anguish.

Seven times she must weep for Apollo, he had said, before she would shake free of the bonds that held her—whatever that meant. Gino Nikkaris had loved to speak like the Delphic oracle, mouthing fine, mystical phrases upon which many interpretations might be placed. She had stood weeping before this very statue five years ago when she had seen Gino for the first time. She had been seventeen then, and the presence of the statue had been incidental. It was her father's death, three months before, that caused her tears, and she had faced Apollo so that her back would be to the Sunday crowds thronging this place where her father had been a curator for so long that it seemed a second home to her.

Gino, knowing every line of the original by heart, had given the statue no second glance. He had looked at Dorcas Brandt and seen in her face, for all her fairness, the mark of Greece— a mark rightfully descended from a long-ago great-grandmother whose name had also been Dorcas. Gino was ten years older than she, but ten years were hardly more to him than to Apollo, and her very youth had appealed to him. The seeming helplessness of youth, the lack of experience had spoken to him strongly, had even played into his hands. What chance had she, lonely and too ready to trust, to resist the dark fascination that was Gino?

There had been no look of Greece about him for all that his father came from Rhodes. His family resemblance had been outwardly on the side of his Italian mother. But the hot mixture of the two countries in his blood had given him a storminess of impulse, a volatility, a leaning toward violence that made him as compelling to behold in his opposite way as was this calm and wholly Greek statue of the Olympia Apollo before which she stood these several years later.

A voice spoke behind her and she turned in quick dismay—as though the past could repeat itself. But it was only a museum guard who had known her father and herself as a little girl.

"Dorcas, isn't it?" he asked. "Mrs. Nikkaris, I should say. I was sorry to hear about the plane crash . . . your husband . . ."

He had seen her tears and misinterpreted them, but she had no wish to explain.

"Thank you," she said, and then brightly, blinking away the grief that could not be for Gino, but was only for the girl Dorcas Brandt had been and would never be again. "I'm going away soon. On a trip to Greece. It's a job, really. I'll be acting as Miss Farrar's secretary. But it will be a change and—and very interesting, I'm sure."

How lame that sounded. But there could be no putting into easy words all this trip meant to her. Partly because of a longing to renew herself and shake off the last vestige of her illness in the golden light of Greece. Partly as a pilgrimage—something she owed in spirit to those who were gone. And partly because of her need to find the wife of Markos Dimitriou; her desperate need to see the woman, talk with her, discover, if it was possible, the truth of what had happened.

The guard shook hands warmly and wished her a good trip. As Dorcas watched him move away, she thought of Markos, who had also worked in this museum, and had been her most trusted friend after the death of her father. Especially her friend during the last miserable year of her marriage to Gino.

[5]

Markos had been near retirement when he died. Remembering, she stiffened herself against this particular anguish.

Gino, in a sense, had paid in retribution for any violent action he might have taken, dying himself in violence. Yet what he had set in motion had not ended with his death. She could defend herself only with the truth and she must find it without allowing herself to be destroyed in the process. There must not be another breakdown of the sort she had so recently suffered, no return to that place of nurses and doctors that fell just short of being an institution. As Fernanda Farrar had said, somewhat doubtfully, she must start anew.

There was young Beth to think of. Her daughter—and Gino's. Beth, who must never know what her father had truly been, who must not grow up to resemble him.

Dorcas looked up at the statue, and now her eyes were dry. "I've cried for you twice," she said softly. "They say that Rhodes was your favorite island, so if I must weep again, I'll do it there."

The whimsy cheered her a little. She left the museum and took a bus down the avenue for home. In the spring dusk street lamps were coming on and the great buildings marched in a shimmer of light down the length of their narrow island.

The building in which she and Gino had lived was an old one and no modern skyscraper. But it was high enough to give Fernanda Farrar the penthouse she occupied and into which Dorcas and Beth had moved after Gino's death. Dorcas had been willing enough to get out of rooms that bore Gino's stamp, glad to accept Fernanda's invitation to move upstairs. Fernanda had been something of a foster mother to Gino, but Dorcas had been fond of her in spite of that close relationship. Perhaps more than anyone else Fernanda had been blinded, dazzled, subjugated by Gino. Perhaps more than anyone else

[6]

she grieved for his loss, although being Fernanda she would never give ground to a show of weakness. Until she was strong again, Dorcas would accept the sheltering wing she offered. Until the trip to Greece had been made and what must be done had been done, she could feel reasonably safe in Fernanda's penthouse. Nothing could touch her there.

The self-service elevator stopped at the fourth floor and she left it to pick up Beth, who was visiting a playmate downstairs. Beth was nearly four. She had Gino's dark coloring, but there, for the most part, all resemblance ended. Beth's was a quiet nature, imaginative and rather shy, except on those occasions when she lost her temper. Then she was alarmingly like Gino. He had loved Beth too well, too lavishly, too possessively. That, too, was ended. And better so.

The bow had pulled off Beth's silky-dark pony tail, her face bore a trace of currant jam, and she had a slightly doggy smell about her from playing with her friend's spaniel. When she saw Dorcas in the doorway, she left the dog to run to her mother.

"Mommy!" she cried with the warmth that always made Dorcas's heart turn over and reminded her painfully of the months when her illness had put her so far out of Beth's reach. She caught the little girl up and hugged her, doggy smell and all. They went upstairs together with Beth's hand in hers, and she unlocked the door to Fernanda's penthouse without presentiment.

At her touch a creamy-shaded light came on in the vestibule. In the living room beyond, dusk pressed against high windows. Clearly Fernanda was not yet home from her afternoon lecture. When Fernanda Farrar entered a room she automatically shed gloves and coat, hat and handbag as she crossed its width, even kicking off her spike-heeled shoes if her feet were tormenting

[7]

her. But while the galley sheets of her new book lay spread upon the sofa where she had left them, and her pencil had rolled to the floor, the room was innocent of strewn possessions, the apartment empty of sound. The eminent Miss Farrar lived with an exuberance that did not tend toward so hushed a quiet as this. Since Hilda had taken the afternoon off, even the kitchen quarters were still.

Beth chattered happily about the spaniel and Dorcas walked, still without premonition, to the door of the guest room Fernanda had turned over to her and Beth. She flicked on the overhead light and stood transfixed in the doorway, her grasp tightening on Beth's hand.

It had happened again.

Although it was impossible for this to have occurred in a penthouse, high on the roof, the pattern had been repeated. The other time had been in the old apartment downstairs, with a balcony easy to the street. That was one reason why she had moved in with Fernanda, where she would be up here, far out of reach. Yet the evidence lay everywhere.

Drawers in her desk had been pulled open, her papers scattered. The bureau had been dumped free of its contents, hatboxes pulled from the closet, her traveling case opened.

"Look!" Beth cried in bewilderment.

Dorcas fought against the faintness that was a remnant of those terrible months when she could scarcely raise her head for lack of strength. That dreaded feeling must not come again, and she thrust the wave of vertigo back.

Last time there had been one strange touch in the confusion that had been left behind. An eerie touch that had been more frightening, somehow, than the mere disturbance of her physical possessions. Now she left Beth in the doorway and stepped into the room, reluctant, yet drawn by her own need to be sure. There was no marking on the bureau as there had been before. But she had no time to feel relief, for as she turned toward the beds, she saw the two chalked circles upon the dark wood of one—almost like disembodied eyes that watched her without blinking.

Fear ran sickly through her. This was deliberate. No chance prowler had been in this room. There was ugly purpose here.

Leaving the light burning, she turned from the bedroom and saw the open french doors in the living room—doors that gave onto the roof and garden that made this place so desirable. She did not need to step outside to remember the closeness of the next roof. A man who was not afraid of a good leap could make the distance easily. Yet such a possibility had seemed remote, unlikely, and Fernanda had assured her it could not happen here.

So let Fernanda find this, she thought. Let Fernanda decide what to do. Since nothing had been taken that other time, Fernanda had rather pooh-poohed its importance. She had said the chalk marks were the work of some zany prowler, and the police had also put them down to a nut. Dorcas had no desire to call the police now and deal with their further questioning. Let Fernanda handle this.

But she could not wait here for Fernanda or Hilda to return. She could not remain in the apartment with those two chalked circles staring at her. Yet she did not want to frighten Beth.

"Come," she said to the child. "Let's go down to the drugstore and have hot chocolates with marshmallows on top."

Beth regarded her solemnly. Her small, dark-eyed face with its cleft chin that was like Dorcas's own wore the stamp of awareness. A child seemed to have antennae that sensed falseness of tone and action. She was not fooled by this sudden

[9]

cheery plan. Fear had touched her with its contagion, and Dorcas could not bear to see it in her face.

"We'll come back in a little while," she promised.

"When Aunt Fern is here to take care of us?" Beth asked.

"*I* can take care of you!" Dorcas said, too quickly.

Beth had grown all too accustomed to turning to Fernanda rather than to her mother. She could not be blamed, but this must change.

"Come along," Dorcas said more gently, and held out her hand. There was a second's hesitation before Beth took it and they went out of the apartment together.

The elevator carried them down, its elderly machinery creaking in the empty silence of the shaft. The dark wood of the lobby floor echoed to the sound of their feet as they hurried toward the door. Not until the cool air of early evening struck her cheeks did the faintness fade and a healthy lacing of anger sweep through Dorcas.

Gino was gone, but his hand still lay heavily upon her life. That slender, long-fingered hand that could nevertheless wield a force she would never forget. There was nothing definite in these two occurrences to point to Gino's friends, yet, instinctively, she knew. There was her experience of the past. Whenever he went away on a trip, he set one or another of his cronies to watch over her. For her protection, he said. But she'd always had a sense of being spied upon. Now, although Gino was two months dead, his friends had not left her alone. And there was the matter of the letter.

A few days after the air crash a man she had never seen before had called on her, asking for a letter that might have come for Gino from Greece after his death. In spite of his rather unpleasant persistence, Dorcas had dealt summarily with him. She wanted nothing to do with Gino's unsavory

"When we retire, when we can get away . . ." Always that was the refrain: "When we can make it, we will go together to Greece." Once Dorcas had slipped out of bed and run to the kitchen in her pajamas to make sure they were not leaving without her. "I want to go with you!" she had cried in sudden fear. Her father had laughed and said that of course she would go with them. Did she not have the face of a Grecian *korai*? Markos had taken her on his knee and told her those wonderful stories about his own beautiful island of Rhodes.

All through her growing-up years Greece had been the load-stone pulling her. Though Gino would never take her there—indeed he had forbidden it. He had wanted her on none of his trips. Now she would go, not only for herself, but for Markos and her father. She would stand in sacred places and look for the three of them; she would feel what they would have felt. It was a debt she owed them, for all that Fernanda thought her sentimental.

"Mommy, I'm through," said Beth, and Dorcas glanced at the clock with a start.

The half-hour was gone and she paid their check, walking back to the building with Beth's hand once more tightly in hers. Surely Fernanda would be home by now.

When Dorcas opened the penthouse door she could hear the kitchen sounds that meant Hilda was at work. A trail of flowered hat and navy shoes, handbag and fur stole led across the living room. Large blue-and-white earrings had been dropped into an ash tray. The door of Dorcas's bedroom stood open. From inside came a rustling of sounds.

"Run to the kitchen and help Hilda," Dorcas said, and gave Beth a little shove. Then she went to the door and looked into the bedroom.

A good deal of the disorder had been cleared away. Hatboxes

[13]

and traveling bag had gone back to the closet. The desk had been righted. Fernanda knelt upon the floor before an open bureau drawer working swiftly, neatly, efficiently.

"What on earth are you doing?" Dorcas asked.

Fernanda's blue-tinged hair, usually so smartly coifed, had slipped a little with her efforts and a lock of it trembled over guileless blue eyes as she looked at Dorcas.

"Oh, dear," she said. "I thought I might have everything put back before you came. You've caught me red-handed, haven't you?"

Dorcas went to the foot of the bed where the markings had been. The circles of chalk were gone. Not so much as a white smudge remained. For a moment she was shaken, almost doubting the evidence of her own eyes, as she had so often come to doubt in that place where they had put her. But she would not accept that now.

"I was here earlier," she told Fernanda. "I saw what had happened. I thought you'd better find it for yourself this time. Why didn't you leave everything as it was and call the police?"

Fernanda was not a small woman, and it took a considerable heave and the help of a corner of the bureau to get her to her feet. She tucked in her blouse, brushed wrinkles from her navy wool skirt, and avoided Dorcas's eyes.

"I didn't want you to know," she said. "I didn't want you to be upset all over again."

In exasperation Dorcas went to the desk and sat down before it. "I'm not made of glass, but I think it's probably normal to be upset with two housebreakings in less than two months."

"I know," Fernanda said, unusually meek. "I'm upset, too. But I had to think of you first, and then of our trip. We're off to Greece in a week, dear. If we call the police now there will be all sorts of questions and delays. Is it really worth it?"

"Because this has something to do with what Gino was last involved in? Because you're afraid to dig too deeply?"

Fernanda went off on a tangent. "I never approved of all Gino's friends. But in his business he had to meet a lot of odd people. Goodness knows what some of them were up to. May still be up to. As soon as we're out of the country this will stop. No need to upset ourselves and worry needlessly. There's been no real harm done."

Gino's business—Gino's nebulous and at times quite profitable business! Dorcas could almost laugh aloud at the proper term. Could you call it a business to be a sort of unethical middleman between wealthy buyers of the world's art treasures and the objects they longed to possess? A purchaser for those collectors who seemed to have few scruples about how they acquired an art treasure they might covet. About his "business" she had come to know a little and had suspected more. Early in her marriage she had discovered the inadvisability of asking questions. Gino's displeasure could readily take a course she did not want to remember.

She gave in suddenly. Once she was out of reach in Greece this persecution would stop. Fernanda was right about that, at least.

"All right," she said. "Let it go."

Fernanda had been watching her anxiously and she gave her approval in hearty relief.

"That's the best way I'm sure, dear. We don't want anything to interfere with our trip." She paused significantly. "And, Dorcas, let's soft pedal this with Beth, shall we? She asked me a few questions just now and I told her things were out in your room because I was helping you to pack."

"I don't like to tell her what isn't true," Dorcas said.

Fernanda dismissed such an objection firmly. "Perhaps

[17]

you'd better trust my judgment on this, dear. Beth and I got along beautifully while you were ill. No tantrums at all. Do cheer up and come along to dinner. We're keeping Hilda waiting."

Dorcas followed her soberly, troubled by the course Fernanda had taken. It was true that Beth must be protected from concerns beyond her years, but lately it had seemed that Fernanda grew more and more highhanded and possessive in her relationship with the child. Of course that was typical of Fernanda, to start with. For all her basic kindliness and good nature, she had the instincts of a steam roller. It was sometimes better to get out of her way than to offer opposition and find oneself flattened in the process. But getting out of her way would not be easy on this trip. Besides, the voice of self-doubt whispered in her mind, Fernanda might be right in her handling of Beth.

By the time Dorcas reached the dinner table Beth had been set in her chair, her napkin pinned on. There was the sort of picnic gaiety in the air that Fernanda could create with children. Was it true, as Fernanda sometimes implied, and Gino had claimed outright, that Beth's mother was not good for the child?

At once she rejected this treachery to her own confidence. This was a pit Gino had dug for her deliberately. She was well now and she could refuse to harbor such thoughts. All mothers made mistakes in the handling of their children. She was no different and no worse than the others. In her devotion to Beth she was undoubtedly better than some.

She smiled at Beth as she picked up her soup spoon.

2 𝗟𝗟𝗟𝗟𝗟𝗟𝗟𝗟𝗟𝗟𝗟𝗟𝗟𝗟𝗟𝗟𝗟𝗟𝗟𝗟𝗟𝗟𝗟𝗟𝗟𝗟𝗟𝗟𝗟𝗟𝗟𝗟

DURING DINNER Fernanda talked a little about her afternoon at the club. Then, overriding interruptions from Beth, she went into a reminiscent account of the way she had come to help Gino and his family get from Italy to Rhodes at the start of the war. It was a story Dorcas had heard many times, yet she found herself tensing as she listened.

Gino's Italian mother had worked in the small house Fernanda had taken for a few months in Milano. Her loyalty lay with her Greek husband who had long wanted to return to Rhodes. True, the island was in Italian hands, but he felt matters would be better there. Fernanda had used her own money to make that return possible, and the little family had left the country of Gino's mother. In Rhodes they had found themselves caught by the Italian military occupation of the island and Fernanda had lost touch with them for a while. But she did not forget the boy Gino.

Even as a child Gino had known what he wanted and been able to turn others to his purpose with those winning ways that were in evidence as long as one gave in to him. And he had possessed a drive, a determination that matched Fernanda's own.

"I'll never forget," she recalled wistfully, "that last talk we had in my sunny Milano garden before I left for home. Gino was tall for his age even then, and as quick and graceful on his feet as a dancer. I sat on a bench near a marble fountain and told him about America. While he listened he was up on the fountain, balancing on the rim, or down on the grass turning handsprings as likely as not. He was never one to be quiet. Do you remember, Dorcas?"

She remembered. In the man the sense of restlessness, of disquiet, both inner and outer, had sometimes been difficult to live with. There had been no repose in Gino, but always movement. His eyes turning, seeking, his hands nervous and never still. She did not want to remember, but Fernanda went on.

"It was he who announced that he would come to America. He told me that he would come because I would be there and because I would undoubtedly need him. Who else would there be to bring my morning coffee and run my errands and advise me on the problems of my life? Who could do these things better for me than my devoted Gino?"

She smiled, and there was a mistiness in her eyes. Beth started to talk, but Fernanda touched her hand and she was silent.

"I knew he had to have the chance I could give him. I promised him that day that I would send for him when it was possible. As I'd never married, and had no children of my own, Gino was like a son to me."

She had kept her promise when the war was over. Gino had never again lived in Greece, although until his parents died he returned to Rhodes now and then to visit them. His brothers and sisters were older and already scattered when the war began. Fernanda had met none of them. It was upon Gino alone that her attention focused.

As Dorcas had reason to know, Greece had fascinated Gino and drawn him strongly. With his devotion to art, his love for the very feel of marble, he should have been a sculptor, Fernanda said. But somehow a willingness to perform the drudgery of learning a craft until it could become an art was not in him. He wanted too much too easily, too quickly. Or perhaps his real talent was for appreciation rather than creation. Had he been wealthy he would have been a collector himself. As it was, he had turned to a line of work that enabled him to handle the treasures he could not possess.

Perhaps it eased Fernanda's heart to speak of Gino now, to bring him back as if to their midst. Perhaps, too, she wanted to remind his wife of her loss. It had been difficult to pretend with Fernanda.

When there was a pause in the narrative, Dorcas asked a question that had puzzled her more than once.

"Why did you never marry? You should have had a big family to mother, Fernanda, a husband to take up all your attention."

"As if any one person or thing could do that!" Fernanda laughed. But she went on without resentment. "I suppose I've always attracted the wrong kind of man—the man who wants someone to lean on and thinks I'd make a good prop, when what I really wanted was a man strong enough to manage *me*. There aren't many of those."

So, not finding a husband, she had settled for a son, Dorcas thought—a son who could govern her with the imperative will of Gino Nikkaris. Strangely enough, Gino had loved her in return. He had used her, yes, but he had given her devotion and tenderness in return. Fortunately for her, the years between them saved her from the physical attraction that roused in Gino something the older woman did not suspect was there.

Fernanda ate her ice cream in dreamy sadness, yearning over her lost son. Dorcas ached for her a little. The Gino in whom Fernanda believed was only a small part of the whole. Real for Fernanda, but for no one else. Yet even after Gino's death, she was still taking imaginary orders from him and that might prove difficult where Beth was concerned.

When dinner was over, Fernanda went to work on the galley proofs that must be returned to her publisher before she left on the trip. Dorcas read Beth a story and put her to bed, then she slipped into a coat and went out upon the penthouse roof. From behind a row of bleak and empty flower boxes she looked down into the one-way cross street where traffic flowed endlessly from east to west.

In a week, she reminded herself, she would be in Greece. There was still an unreality about the fact, even though she knew all the plans by heart. A man named Johnny Orion was to meet them in Athens and go with them to Rhodes. He was a young American high-school teacher who liked to spend his summers abroad whenever it was possible. Fernanda had met him at a lecture some years ago in Chicago and he had offered his services as a guide and driver for a previous trip to Greece. The arrangement had been successful and Fernanda had sent Johnny ahead to make plans for this trip also. Thus there would be no concern about those details of travel that Fernanda hated to bother with. Johnny Orion, to all accounts, also served another use for Fernanda, allowing her to get into just enough trouble to make for lively reading in her books, but not into anything disastrously serious.

What sort of man would be willing to take on such a job

and put up with Fernanda's autocratic ways, Dorcas was not sure. Perhaps he was one of the useful ones who made good errand boys, dancing willing attendance to whatever tune Fernanda whistled. It didn't matter to Dorcas, providing he got things done.

She thrust her hands into her coat pockets and stared unseeingly at the flow of traffic below. The muted roar of the city after dark hemmed her in. The sky glowed orange with the reflection of light. City skies were never truly dark, and she could see no stars. Only one more week until Rhodes. She shivered in a gust of wind that cut through the corridor of the street, yet her shiver was not because of any physical chill. Its origin lay in the past.

With a quiet lift of her shoulders she steadied herself. In Rhodes she would not be the wife of Gino Nikkaris, not even by name. In spite of Fernanda's shocked opposition, she had taken steps immediately after Gino's death to regain the use of her father's name. There had been something of a cleansing for her in the gesture. She had not wanted Beth to grow up with Nikkaris for her last name, even though it belonged to the beloved Greece of Dorcas's own father. Brandt was a good name, a sound, sturdy name—they would be called by it from now on. All had been done that was possible to build toward a new future. Or would be, once she had found the wife of Markos Dimitriou.

The remembrance she had been fighting all day surged back like the rolling of a dark tide. She put her hands upon the rough edge of a flower box and braced herself. Let it come then. She was well now, and being well meant being able to face the past without running from it in that weakness and terror that had come to be part of her illness. But her legs continued to tremble as she stood there. She could not always follow her doctor's instructions to face her own fears and then dismiss them. With Gino gone there was surely no real reason to fear. Yet in a certain sense he would not die. Fernanda kept him alive. Her own memories brought him back and would not be quiet. Sometimes he lived in Beth, frighteningly.

There were many reasons why life with Gino had become intolerable soon after her marriage. Her suspicion that some of the art objects he handled had not come legitimately into his hands had been accidentally confirmed. She could remember vividly the scene when she had confronted him with her innocent indignation. He had come home late in the evening while she was getting ready for bed. When he entered the room she had flung her discovery at him recklessly and he had stood behind her at her dressing table and laughed his enjoyment of her shock and indignation.

Now her fingers gripped the flower box in pain, but she let the memories come.

In the mirrored reflection Gino's eyes had been aware of a beauty come to life in the heat of anger—an awareness all too easily whetted by opposition. She had come to know that he loved her best when she was angry with him and ready to fight him, when there was something in her for him to conquer and subdue.

In the mirror she had seen his hand flash out in a gesture she'd come to dread—a gesture that was both a mockery of affection and a prelude to an excitement in him that made her skin crawl in memory. His hand came swiftly from behind to touch her chin, the fingers following the line of her jaw, her throat—lightly, delicately, almost as she had seen him touch the smooth surface of marble. But with a difference. When he touched flesh with that particular gesture, he made a promise that he always kept.

[24]

She was not a cold woman. She had never been. In the early months of marriage she had given herself eagerly, willingly, expecting to be his partner in the matter of love. He had not wanted a partner. He had wanted from her an exquisite terror that he knew very well how to arouse. Toward the end that terror had begun with the first movement of his hand toward her chin.

Once, before they were married, she had seen him step on a dog's foot. She had thought the incident an accident. Later she had known better. If only she had read it aright, what had happened was a clue to all that Gino Nikkaris was when it came to anything weaker than himself.

There were only two people he never deliberately hurt—Fernanda and Beth. From the first he had been a possessive father toward his baby daughter. And he had found new ways of hurting Dorcas through her love for Beth. The first time she had tried to run away, Beth had been only a year old. She had taken from the bank the small sum of money her father had left her and caught a train out of the city. But it had not been difficult to follow a mother with a baby in her arms. Gino had not troubled to come after her himself, but had sent one of his men.

Again memory quickened, flooding her mind with painful pictures.

Two days after she had run away, she'd opened her hotel room door one morning expecting the maid and had found a lean, sad-looking man in dark glasses standing there. He had stepped quickly into the room and closed the door behind him. She had known at once that her flight was up.

"I will take you back to him," he said. He had spoken with an accent, she recalled, and he had never once mentioned Gino's name.

[25]

She had not surrendered without an effort. She had tried to bribe him, offering the little money she had, promising more.

He had neither laughed nor grown angry. "It is no use to run," he told her. "Perhaps I myself would escape if I knew the way. I find it better to stay alive."

Whether or not he was threatening her she could not tell, but the last of her courage had seeped away. She went to the bed where the baby lay sleeping and picked her up.

The stranger had taken her back to Gino. He had been neither kind nor unkind, but she had been afraid of him. He had not talked to her beyond necessity, or even told her his name. In her terrified despair she had not thought much about him at the time, though once or twice later she had wondered if Gino's death had enabled him to "escape." Or was he still bound in some strange way to Gino and still serving him? Could it be this same cold, sad man who had entered her room today and left those eerie chalk marks by way of warning? She would be more afraid of him than of a total stranger.

All this, however, was pure speculation, and without purpose.

Gino had been cruelly pleased to have her back after that first attempt at flight. He had told Fernanda that she was mentally unstable and that Beth must be taken from her if she grew worse. Frighteningly, he had caught her up at every turn that seemed to indicate emotional imbalance, until she had begun to doubt herself and question her own fears uneasily. She had not tried to run away again for a long while, lest she lose Beth entirely.

In the meantime there were, of course, other women, and proof enough of the fact. She had not cared. Such interest on Gino's part gave her a respite to a degree, though not wholly.

She was safe only when she was numb, blank, indifferent. And not always, even then, for the whim might seize him to arouse her from lethargy and leave her once more in trembling terror.

The girl of seventeen who had stood before the statue of Apollo in the museum that day had not dreamed there were such men.

It was not until Beth was old enough to speak and understand that Gino began in subtle ways to turn the child against her mother. Dorcas had known then that she must take Beth away, and this time she must make good her escape. She must succeed, not only for the sake of her own life and sanity, but for all Beth's future. In no way was Gino good for the child.

She had gone to her old friend Markos Dimitriou for help. He still worked at the museum and he had been delighted to see her. Early in their marriage Gino had interfered with their friendship. Perhaps he had not wanted careless remarks about his work made in the presence of Markos, who was simple and good and given to speaking the truth without fear.

How kind Markos had been when she had told her story and asked for his advice. He had said simply, "Come, we will go for a walk." He had left his work at the museum, taken her to a bank, and drawn out the savings for a trip to Greece he and his wife planned to make as soon as he retired. The sum was not large, for his wife had known illness and been in the hospital. There was a thousand dollars and he had drawn it out in cash and placed it in her hands.

"It is a loan," he said. "You are as good as any bank for money, my young friend. With this you will go away. At once. You must not wait. I have seen this coming. He is not a good man, this Gino Nikkaris. I think both Italy and Greece would be ashamed to own him. Take Beth and go to Chicago,

or anywhere. You have your typing skill—you will find work and make a new life. Let me know, and we will be in touch. Do not worry that this is right or wrong. It is right. I think there is danger if you stay."

She had embraced him warmly at parting and gone home to make hasty preparations. That was the last time she had seen him alive. If only she had left that same night. But she had waited for a morning train. Gino had been away on one of his many trips and she did not expect him home for another week. In the morning, as she went to the door with her suitcase in one hand and Beth by the other, he had walked into the apartment.

Not even Beth's presence had held him in check. At a glance he realized her intent and pulled her handbag from her arm to open it. The money had been there, and he had taken in his hand the wad of bills.

"Where did you get this?" he demanded.

How well she remembered the look of him at that moment. Tall and slender, his angry vitality lending a flash to dark eyes, fury to winged brows.

Her throat had closed so completely that she could not answer, even to lie. But he needed no answer. He knew well enough the only person to whom she could have turned.

When he flung out of the room, taking the money with him, Dorcas had phoned the museum at once. Markos was not yet at work, but they would have him call her as soon as he came in.

How dreadful the waiting had been all that long morning. How frightening the silent telephone. Markos was not at home either, though she spoke briefly to his wife, trying not to alarm her. Beth had sensed her fear and was frightened,

too. Trying to distract the child had been something to occupy her.

An eleven o'clock a news broadcast gave her the answer. A worker at the museum, Markos Dimitriou, had been struck down by a hit-and-run driver that morning on his way to work and had died in the hospital. The driver had been at the wheel of a green car. Gino had no green car, but she knew he would stop at nothing and he would behave with sharp intelligence, concealing his traces skilfully.

What had happened afterward was more difficult to recall in detail because it flowed into the blanketing fog and misery of her illness. She had confronted Gino, accused him, stood up to him. That she could remember. And she could remember his laughter and the cunning of the torment he'd begun to practice. Beth was whisked out of her hands and sent upstairs to stay with a loving, sympathetic Fernanda. It must have been easy for him to convince Fernanda of her breakdown and need for professional care. Anything Dorcas had tried to tell her was used as a pitiful affirmation of an unbalanced state. A nursing home was the only answer, Gino said.

She had gone to the home in near hysteria, beating against the wall of lies that surrounded her, weeping for her child and for Markos. They had treated her kindly in the home, listened to her without belief, fed her, rested her, soothed her. At last she, too, began to learn cunning. If she was to get out, if she was to return to Beth, she must fool everyone, including Gino. Her "improvement" consisted of an apparent acceptance of her illness with all the supposed delusions that had been part of it. Her nerves and hysteria had been no delusion and they had increased her own doubts, given her cause to fear that all that was said about her might be true. Yet somehow she managed to learn an acquiescence that hid both her rage and her fear. She presented to the world a meekness of demeanor that won her release. "Well" again, she was allowed to go home. Beth had missed her, and the joy of their reunion had been her reward. Beth had not been won away completely. Indeed, she seemed a little afraid of her father.

For months only Beth's welfare had mattered to Dorcas. Still emotionally shattered, she managed, nevertheless, to offer Gino a blind submission that served her well, turning him from her in distaste. Biding her time, she waited until he was away on a trip, then she gave possible watchers the slip and went to the house of Markos Dimitriou.

Strangers occupied his home. Neighbors said his wife had returned to Rhodes. Newspaper reports had said she was in the hospital at her husband's side when he died. But if she knew or suspected anything, she had not spoken out. The neighbors had no knowledge of her exact whereabouts, had heard nothing from her. A door seemed to have closed upon her.

Except for this one fruitless expedition, Dorcas had been exceedingly careful in those first months out of the home. That something new was in the wind with Gino, she was aware. She had learned to recognize his moods of dark excitement, his secret exultation when someone was being tricked, when a coup was in the making. There had been correspondence from Rhodes, even a transatlantic telephone call or two. Then Gino had decided upon a trip to San Francisco. She had kept her own council and hidden the fact that she watched him and waited—waited for the time when he would make a mistake and give himself into her hands. Her demeanor had continued to be mild, deceptively sweet, a little vacant. She suspected that he thought her slightly addled by erased those chalk marks from the end of the bed," she said quietly.

Fernanda was working on her proofs again, pencil poised disapprovingly over a word. She did not look up. "What are you talking about, dear? What chalk marks?"

This, Dorcas thought, was why she had held back. She had seen the marks. And then they were gone. If Fernanda disclaimed any knowledge of them, what was she to believe? That Fernanda was lying? Or that her own mind was playing tricks on her? That she had seen the circles only because of the other time, only because she feared to see them?

By sheer effort of will she kept her voice low, unstrained. "When I found that upheaval in my room, I noticed something else. Two circles had been drawn in white chalk on the end of one bed. Why did you rub them out?"

Fernanda looked up from her work, less guilelessly now. "Oh, dear, you are upset about something. Dorcas, I don't know a thing about any chalk marks. Are you certain—"

"I'm certain," Dorcas said. But how could she be certain if Fernanda claimed she had never seen the marks?

Abruptly Fernanda flung down her pencil. "Oh, all right! I never was any good as a liar. I did see the marks and I erased them on purpose. I knew how upset you'd be if you found them, and of course I didn't know that you'd been in the room. I suppose I'm really thinking of Beth and the upsetting effect you have on her when something frightens you. I meant well, dear. So you might as well forgive me. And now I'm going to put you to work and keep you busy until we leave. Then you'll have no time for this brooding. You'll feel fine once we're on our way."

Relief as well as fear could make one feel weak, Dorcas discovered. The marks had been real. There was no use being angry with Fernanda. The lights that guided her were her own and like no one else's.

Neither of them mentioned the chalk marks again in the days that remained before leaving. Fernanda's antidote for worry helped, and Dorcas was thankful to find herself assigned to one task after another, with no time at all to think about past or future. Except when she lay in bed at night and could not sleep. Or when she fell asleep and dreamed endlessly of white eyes staring.

3

WHEN THE day of their departure came, Fernanda's promise that Dorcas would feel better proved only half true. Even after they were on their way to the airport, Dorcas was ridden by uneasiness. She could imagine a car following them. In the crowds at the terminal she found herself wondering if this man, or perhaps that one, was a friend of Gino. A tall man in dark glasses made her grasp Beth's hand more tightly. This was nonsense, she knew, and the result of nerves not wholly healed from laceration. Once the baggage was checked through and passport matters completed, she began to feel a little better. The limbo of the overseas waiting room in which they were isolated from the rest of the terminal gave her some sensation of security. And once aboard the plane, with Beth strapped into the window seat beside her and Fernanda across the aisle, the sense of being watched fell away. At last she could lean back in her seat and give herself up to the luxury of feeling safe.

With release came exhaustion. She slept a good part of the flight, rousing herself only for meals and when the jet set down in London and Rome and they had to leave the plane in transit. The sense of suspension stayed with her and was oddly enervating, draining her of energy. Fernanda took over with Beth, and Dorcas had no desire to oppose her.

When the plane landed at the Athens airport, she still felt as though she had not slept for months, experiencing nothing but weary indifference at this arrival in Greece.

"Put on your dark glasses right away," Fernanda advised. "The light will be blinding."

Both her father and Markos had spoken with longing of the marvelous light of Greece which she must behold with the naked eye to savor fully. But Dorcas put on her glasses and went groggily down the steps to soil that was Greek, feeling nothing of bright spring warmth, nothing of homecoming. She knew Fernanda watched her with concern, but she was past caring. Deep within herself she was lying fallow, recovering. She did not want to waken. Not just yet. It was better to remain indifferent.

Customs for an American was a matter of form. Beyond the barrier Johnny Orion awaited them. He was a young man in his late twenties, with a cheerful American voice, a near-crew cut of reddish hair, and a wide grin. Fernanda gave him a hug of affection and introduced Dorcas Brandt as her "sleepy young friend." Johnny said, "I know how you must feel," and when she could rouse herself for no fitting response, he paid no further attention. After a smile and a "hi" for Beth, he talked cheerfully to Fernanda.

Vaguely, Dorcas heard the plans he had made. They would have the afternoon in Athens. The plane for Rhodes did not leave until six-thirty in the evening. He had borrowed a car from a Greek friend, since Fernanda would not pick up her rented car until they reached Rhodes. If they liked, he would drive them around Athens, or even out to Sounion.

Fernanda shook her head. She knew Athens and she had other fish to fry. Dorcas was relieved. She was not yet ready for Greece. All she wanted was a place where she might curl up and give herself over to continued lassitude. Here, where she was to have felt safe and once more alive, she knew instead the growing fear that her exhaustion would go on forever, that she was, as Gino had always said, never going to get better. He had told her in no uncertain terms that he thought her hopelessly unbalanced. And how was she to disprove the echo of those words, even with Gino gone, unless she could rouse herself to feel something?

On and on droned the voices, and Dorcas caught the words of a suggestion Fernanda was making.

"I've made appointments to see several people at the Grande Bretagne," she told Johnny. "So suppose you drop me there and then take Beth and Dorcas for a drive."

The thought of effort was dismaying. "Please," Dorcas said, "let Beth and me stay here at the airport until it's time to leave for Rhodes. I don't want to do anything."

Fernanda made up her mind without hesitation. "Beth needs a change, if you don't. Run along with Johnny and breathe some fresh air. There's not much but cigarette smoke here in this waiting room. Take her in tow and give her your favorite test, Johnny. See if she passes it better than I did."

It was true that Beth had turned as lively as a puppy, and since opposition would take even more energy, Dorcas gave in and went with them to the car.

In the front seat, with Johnny driving, Fernanda talked about arrangements and plans all the way into Athens. Beth bounced beside her mother in the back seat and filled the

[37]

air with questions and exclamations. Her silky dark hair escaped beneath a blue-flowered hat and flew in wisps across her cheeks as she turned eagerly from one side of the car to the other.

At the Grande Bretagne they dropped Fernanda, set a time for picking her up for the trip back, and then Dorcas and Beth moved up with Johnny.

The roar of a big city surrounded them, and the inescapable odors of gasoline and exhaust fumes, the noise, the dust. Behind dark glasses Dorcas closed her eyes and resisted both clamor and smells. This was not the Greece of her father. It meant nothing to her.

Waiting for a traffic light, Johnny turned to look at her frankly. "I keep thinking I've met you somewhere. Do you suppose we've crossed paths?"

Dorcas roused herself to answer. "You've probably met me on a frieze somewhere in Greece. I can't help it. I had a great-grandmother from the Peloponnese. I'm named for her."

Johnny nodded. "That's probably the answer. It's funny how it is. They'll tell you that present-day Greeks are a different breed. Then you walk down a street and find Hermes playing in an Athens alley, or you turn a corner and meet Athena on the back of a donkey."

He was a friendly enough young man, with a casual manner that made him easy company, yet she felt too lethargic to respond.

"Lean back and relax," he said. "Nobody can keep up with Fernanda day and night. I'll wake you when the time comes."

It was pleasant to be with someone who asked nothing of her. She leaned back and closed her eyes. Beth's chatter and Johnny's answers dimmed in her ears and seemed far away as she drowsed. Then she was aware that the car had turned and was winding upward around the curve of a hill.

"It's time now," Johnny said. "This is where we get out."

The car had come to a stop beside other cars drawn up in a parking area. She had no desire to leave the comfortable seat, but when he came around and opened the door, she handed Beth to him and slipped out. Her body felt cramped and stiff, and she stretched as if she might send energy flowing through her with the movement of her blood. They were just below the crest of a small hill rising from the city. She could see Athens spread out below with its busy avenues of traffic, but she did not know why he had brought her here.

Johnny nodded toward the sloping rise of hill ahead. "The top's our objective. It's only a little way—you can make it. Go ahead and I'll take charge of this young lady."

Obediently, since that was still the way of least effort, Dorcas went up the pathway. Over the hill a few sight-seers were busy with cameras, posing with one another against the view, exclaiming and pointing.

Dorcas stepped out into the open and stood for a moment in the blowing wind. Then she took off the protective glasses. Light poured down from a sky unbelievably blue. It beat upward blindingly from the white houses of Athens. Yet she, who had begun to flinch from everything, did not flinch from its brilliance. Out across the rooftops rose another hill, and her first glimpse of it was like the rolling up of a curtain, like the signal for a drama to begin.

How marvelously white were the columns that topped that high, steep rock, how perfect, how complete they seemed, riding the centuries as they had done for more than two thousand years. To the left of the great main temple and well below it a width of entrance steps led up toward farther columns. Here, in long lines that zigzagged back and forth in mounting diagonals, came—surely!—the men and women of ancient Athens climbing toward the great temple above. Distance robbed the tiny figures of definition, showing only the throng as it ascended in slow ritual, back and forth along the wide flight of steps.

This was as it must always have been, with the great flat-topped rock pitching steeply upward into a vast sky, the city fanning out at its foot, the blue sea beyond, and worshipers climbing to the temple.

Johnny came up behind her and lifted Beth so that she, too, could see the high rock. It was a long while before he spoke, and Dorcas was hardly aware of them.

"Come along," he said at length. "Now that you're awake, we're going up there."

It was true that the sight had renewed her, but she still held back. "I'm not sure I want to see it close up. Not right away. From here it's still perfect."

Johnny laughed, and she found she liked the sound. "I'll teach you a trick when we get up there that will spare you all pain."

He set Beth down and Dorcas took the child's hand as they started toward the car on their way to that other hill.

"At least you passed the test," Johnny said. "You kept still and looked. You didn't jabber or reach for a camera right away. Do you know what Fernanda said the first time I brought her up here? She said it made her homesick because it looked just like the First National back in her home town."

Dorcas found herself laughing with him. Her step was lighter than it had been in a long time as she went down the hill at his side. Darkness and terror had retreated. Perhaps the warmth of golden light had begun its healing.

When they reached the rock of the Acropolis they left the car and started up the broken steps on foot. Figures that might have worn the robes of ancient Greece turned into tourists with cameras, into guides commanding their separate groups and jealous of wandering attention as they uttered well-rehearsed pronouncements.

The zigzag lines, Dorcas found, were caused by cement ramps winding back and forth across the rubble that had once been splendid steps. They climbed between the never-completed columns of the Propylaea, with Johnny lifting Beth over rough stone. Then they were in the open again, out in the dust and the wind. On every hand lay great tumbled rocks that had once been smooth paving. Prone blocks of marble for the continuous work of renovation lay all about, with spaces of dusty earth between. Once more it was the Parthenon that commanded the eye, but now it was too close for the illusion to be as perfect as it had seemed from afar.

"You promised me a charm," Dorcas said. "I didn't want to see it like this."

He set Beth upon a low boulder. "Close your eyes," he said to Dorcas. "Remember that the Greeks used color in their work. When this was completed there was crimson and gold and blue. But now you can see it as it was in the beginning. You can see the clean lines, the very bones of the marble as it was four hundred years before Christ when all of this was in the making."

She opened her eyes and forgot the broken pavement, the voices of the guides. Already the groups were scattering, losing themselves in a space so vast that thousands could scarcely have crowded it. Now she could see the wide marble steps, the columns, the sloping roof with the frieze beneath its peak, the figures so wonderfully alive. All was as it might have been

[41]

at the time of the building. It was a place not ruined, but unfinished—its coming perfection already prophesied in lines that carried the eye to soaring grace. The stone was not white, as it seemed from a distance, but aglow with the warm, creamy tones of Grecian marble.

"Thank you, Johnny Orion," Dorcas said. Renewal was a deepening reality. She was truly coming to life.

As they moved around the great central building, the wind that whipped over Athens appeared to be blowing the Acropolis away in swirls of wheat-colored dust. Beth spread her arms as though she were about to take wing and Johnny lifted her down from a prone marble column before she tried to fly. The ease of new companionship did not seem strange to Dorcas.

They found steps not too steep and broken to be climbed and went inside. There was no roof, no sides, only tall columns casting violet-dark shadows, framing glimpses of Athens far below. The floor had been repaired in part, but there were pockets and hollows in the marble and Johnny lifted Beth over the broken places.

Dorcas left them and stood alone where columns framed the view of an Athenian hillside. Once more she took off her glasses and submitted to the full blaze of light. It seemed to fall out of that improbable sky and wash across all this rock, to spread out in dazzling waves beyond, where the roofs of Athens caught and flung it back. Beyond the pillars the wind went by in a great rushing of sound, but here she was sheltered from all but the light. She raised her face to it, let the bright flood of it pour over her its healing rays.

Johnny must have guessed what she was feeling, for he stood silent and let her be. Once she turned back to him in apology and he smiled at her.

[42]

"I know," he said. "It's happened to me up here, too."

He could not know it all. He could not know that she stood here not only for herself, but for her father and for her father's friend as well. Yet she had never met anyone with whom she had felt so quickly at ease, so easily comfortable. She had known Johnny only a few hours, but she liked him very much. There was something about him that gave her a confidence she had not felt in another human being for a long time.

When she turned at last from the wash of light and went back to them, Johnny was telling Beth a story of the king whose name had been given to the Aegean. Here on this rock Aegeus had stood watching the horizon for the ships of Theseus, his son and heir. Theseus had killed the Minotaur, but he had forgotten to change black sails to white as his signal of victory. The old king saw black sails come over the horizon and flung himself in grief over the sides of this very rock.

Beth's eyes were wide as she listened, and Dorcas watched her for a moment. Beth had accepted Johnny, too.

He put the child on her feet and rose from the block of marble. "There's more to see. You're not tired?" he asked Dorcas.

"How could I be—up here?"

"It's been known to happen," he said dryly. "Fernanda says you've been ill and you mustn't overdo."

How much had Fernanda revealed? she wondered, and answered him quickly. "I've been ill, but I'm well now. Completely well. I'm looking forward to Rhodes."

"Of course you are," he said.

As they left the Parthenon and walked toward the Porch of the Maidens, Dorcas quickened her steps, moving more lightly and freely than she had before. She reached the Porch ahead of Johnny and he laughed as he and Beth caught up with her.

"It's a gazelle you are indeed," he said. "You do honor to your name."

So he knew what the name Dorcas meant, she thought, and was somehow pleased.

Above them the caryatides—here the priestesses of Athena herself—stood guard with their baskets upon their heads— baskets in which sharp knives were reputedly hidden, for all the serenity of the faces below. There was a hint of oriental splendor in the ornamentation of the Erechtheion. Here Athena had put away her warrior garb for more feminine robes, ruling from this sacred place as a goddess of the light.

"We'll leave before too long," Johnny said. "But first there's something you must see."

The rock of the Acropolis was like a long ship riding high on a sea of air and light. Now it was toward the stern he led her, carrying Beth for a while, since a four-year-old's legs were not made for Acropolis climbing.

Steps ran steeply down to the entrance of a small building, and as they descended Dorcas realized where they led. This was the little museum of the Acropolis. The halls were cool and had the familiar echoing ring she knew so well. Johnny led the way past marble figures that had once adorned the buildings outside, past miniature reproductions of the frieze Lord Elgin had taken away to England and that Greece wanted back.

The farthest room was his goal. Dorcas crossed its threshold and saw the semicircle of *korai* watching her—damsels out of an archaic past. Their chitons hung in graceful folds, the robes held up by the left hand of each lady. Traces of color remained in embroidered shawl and elaborate hairdress. The

[44]

sculptors had done justice to both beauty and character so that one had a sense of the individuality of each. All but one of them smiled—a polite smile that lifted rounded cheeks and gave softness to the curve of chin.

Johnny said nothing. He waited for her to find out for herself. It was the lady who did not smile who drew her. She was lovely and undoubtedly very old, belonging to an earlier time than the golden century of Pericles. Her eyes looked down upon Dorcas as if in calm recognition, as if she thought, "My sister, you have come." This was the one. This was the face that had somehow come to her through the ages. The face Gino had seen that day in another museum far away.

Suddenly, and without warning, she was crying. She covered her face with her hands and her shoulders shook with the force of her weeping. She had not meant to do this. It was dreadful, yet she could not help herself.

"There's a bench here. Come and sit down." She knew by Johnny's tone that she had alarmed him, but she could not explain.

The overwhelming emotion that so suddenly enveloped her had risen without warning out of the past. It stemmed from her love for her father and for Markos, both of whom had longed to stand in this very place and behold all that she was now beholding. It grew from the talk of Greece she had heard since she was a child, even from the love she had felt in the beginning for Gino—a love that had lost itself in terror and come to nothing—with Gino dead in the funeral pyre of a crashed plane. All this she felt and could not explain to Johnny Orion.

He waited and let her cry. Beth, frightened, tugged at her sleeve and drew her back to the present. Dorcas sat up on the bench, attempting a smile that was not, she suspected, the firm, polite smile of the *korai* on their pedestals.

When she'd wiped her eyes, she kissed Beth's cheek. "I'm all right, darling."

There was concern in Johnny's look, and she saw how very deep a brown his eyes were beneath the irregular line of reddish brows. Gino's had been an opaque black, and somehow impenetrable. Johnny gave something of himself in his look, and his eyes held no secrets.

She did not want him to think her tears were owing to any remnant of emotional instability. Resolutely she stood up.

"That's better," he approved. With a gesture free of self-consciousness he put out a finger and gently touched away one last tear on her cheek.

"A gazelle in more ways than one," he said. "An affrighted creature, the gazelle. I've felt it about you from the first. But there's nothing to trouble you here."

She looked at him without concealment or subterfuge, the growing liking she felt for him in her eyes. There was an instant of oddly charged silence between them. It had been so long since such a feeling had come over her that she did not want to let it go. There was something strengthening in feeling almost painfully alive.

Johnny broke the silence, although he did not step back from whatever he saw in her face. He merely moved on, drawing her with him, as though he knew better than to crowd so new and tentative a response in this moment of first awareness.

He looked at the damp tip of his forefinger and grinned. "You remind me of the sculpture they call the Weeping Boy. The boy with one tear on his marble cheek. We'll see it in the Rhodes Museum."

[46]

A picture of the sculptured head had been in a book of her father's that she had loved as a child and Johnny's whimsy pleased her.

They left the building and returned to the open, moving toward the entrance stairs to the Acropolis. Beth clung to her mother's hand, still disturbed by her tears.

"Fernanda told me that you'd lost your husband recently," Johnny said matter-of-factly as they walked along. "I can understand how you must feel coming here without him."

It was as if he offered her a way out should she wish to take it, a way to step back. It was as if he had said, "I understand your loneliness, your need to reach for any hand."

He did not understand, of course, and there was no way to explain. She could hardly tell him that she was far from being a bereaved and grieving wife. Yet out here in the wind and the great pure sea of light she longed to be done with pretense. She wanted Johnny for a friend. Nothing built on early deception could have solid ground beneath it. At least she could bring one thing into the open. It would be a step toward the truth.

"My married name isn't Brandt," she said. "That was my father's name and I've taken it back. Nikkaris was my married name. My husband was half Greek."

She knew by the quick look he gave her that she had startled him, that Fernanda had not told him this.

"Nikkaris?" he repeated. "I once knew a man by that name. A man named Gino Nikkaris."

That he should have known Gino was somehow disturbing. "He was my husband," she said quietly.

They walked on, carefully picking their way over uneven ground in the shadow of the Parthenon. There was no difference in the pace of their steps, or in the way Johnny kept

Beth from stumbling, or offered a hand to Dorcas. Yet with all her senses she was aware of the change in him. There had been an inner withdrawal, as if he had turned abruptly out of the path they had been taking together in the direction of friendship. His sympathy, his kindness, that moment of something more—all had slipped through her fingers at the mention of Gino's name. Yet though she regretted this, there was a certain satisfaction in it, too. She was glad that however it was he had known Gino, he'd had no liking for him. While she could say nothing now, there would be time in the future. In Rhodes there would be plenty of time. Someday perhaps she would tell him all the truth. For the moment, in spite of the new stiffness between them, she felt not altogether discontented.

At the Grande Bretagne Fernanda was ready for them. During the drive back to the airport Dorcas sat again in the back seat, with Beth dozing in her arms. She could drift now, allow herself to be borne along once more, grateful that she need make no moves for herself. While she was now willing to be part of the current that carried her along, she was not yet ready to strike out and swim for herself.

On the smaller plane of Athenian Airways Johnny quietly took Beth in charge, leaving her free. Dorcas leaned her forehead against the cool window glass beside her seat and watched Greece slip away beneath the wing. Before long the white columns of Sounion on the lower tip of the mainland came into view. Then they were out over the deeply blue Aegean. Almost at once islands began to appear—many of them like dragons crouching in the sea, stretching out claws and jagged tails. Clouds closed in beneath the plane, but now and then a rift showed an island gleaming golden far below in the light of the setting sun. Quickly the sea darkened and lights began to come on here and there, glimpsed far below in the islands of Greece.

The flight was only an hour and a half and there was no meal served on the plane, since no Greek thought of dining before nine o'clock at the earliest. She sipped the coffee the stewardess brought her in a paper cup, and waited for Rhodes, which held the secret of her future.

She knew from studying maps how Rhodes would look. It was a larger island than most, though not nearly so big as Crete. It lay upon the sea in the shape of a great fish, its nose pointed northeast at a diagonal toward the mainland of Turkey. The city of Rhodes was at that northeast tip, on the very nose of the fish.

The plane began to drop toward a lighted runway and the brief last leg of their journey was over. The man from the car agency awaited them at the little airport—a voluble Greek whose name was Mr. Donada. He found a porter for their bags and led the way to the car that would be at Fernanda's disposal for the length of her stay in Rhodes. Johnny sat up front and learned about its workings as they left the airport for the town of Rhodes—"Rodos," as the signs called it at every turn.

Fernanda sat in the back seat and asked questions as fast as Mr. Donada could answer them. The airport was inland, was it not? So now they must be heading for the sea?

This was true, said Mr. Donada. In fact, in Rhodes one could not travel very far at any time without either following the sea or coming in sight of one coast or another.

Fernanda gestured toward a huge dark patch on their right that stood out against the sky—a long mountain that seemed to run beside them. Wasn't that Philerimos? she asked. Mr. Donada agreed that it was, delighted with her knowledge of his island.

[49]

Dorcas held Beth's warm, sleepy body in her arms and was comforted by the feeling of it. With her eyes closed, she no longer listened to voices, but only to the rush of air past the open window of the car. The spring night was cold, but she did not mind. Philerimos, she thought, remembering Markos and his proud talk of the three ancient cities of Rhodes. On Mount Philerimos there was an old monastery, and there was also what little remained of the ruins of one of those cities— Iyalisos. This would be one of the places they would visit, of course.

The car had turned. "There is now the sea," said Mr. Donada, and waved a hand toward the left.

Dorcas could smell the fresh, salty odor on the wind, even though she could not glimpse the water in the darkness or hear its voice above the rush of the car. That was the Aegean out there, she told herself. At last she was in Rhodes. But the sense of reality was still lacking.

They left the sea road and turned into narrow twisting streets where houses were set beyond garden walls and there was a scent of flowers.

"You will like the hotel," Mr. Donada told them. "It is not, of course, the Roses, but it is more new. More small and friendly."

Fernanda had refused to stay at the famous Hotel des Roses because she wanted something intimate where the unexpected was more likely to happen and she would have more to write about. The Olympus had been Johnny's choice when he had flown down to investigate.

They turned into a wide street with a row of palm trees growing down its center and drew up to the curb before the hotel. The glass front of the Olympus revealed a brightly modern lounge with a few people sitting about. Mr. Donada

"I—I rubbed out the marks with my handkerchief," Dorcas said a little sheepishly.

Fernanda set the lamp down and closed the doors against the cool night air. Her look was one of disbelief.

"The marks *were* there," Dorcas insisted. "Made by a child playing with chalk, I suppose. I didn't want to be reminded—"

"You're tired," Fernanda said. "Johnny tells me you had a bit of a weeping spell up on the Acropolis this afternoon. That was natural enough. Now that we're in Rhodes you can rest for a few days and get your bearings."

She did not want to be soothed and quieted—and disbelieved. "I'm all right," she said. "I don't want to rest. I'm here with work to do and I expect to start in on it as soon as you're ready for me."

Fernanda leaned to drop a quick kiss of approval on her cheek. "That's my girl! Hurry now and get ready for dinner."

She went off, and Dorcas was thankful for the never-ceasing demands of a four-year-old. She answered questions and persuaded Beth to stand still long enough to have her hair combed. Then she washed the clinging feel of chalk dust from her hands. There *had* been chalk upon the rail. If she had not smudged it, if she had seen it quickly enough, would she have found two circled chalk eyes staring at her from the flat metal surface?

In the bathroom mirror her face looked pale, and there was a hint of terror in her eyes. "Stop it!" she said to her reflection. "This is Greece. No one has followed you here. No one here knows about what happened at home." But her own look of pale fright was alarming. Was she looking into the face of a woman who skated on the thin edge of reality?

[53]

A woman who did not always know the difference between the real and the unreal?

She splashed cold water over her face, patted her cheeks angrily until the blood flowed and the look of fear faded. It was better to be angry than to be afraid. She did not thank Johnny Orion for having told Fernanda about her tears that afternoon. Evidently they both regarded her as a semi-invalid to be cared for gently, with any upsets allowed for and tolerated. She would have to teach them as quickly as possible that she was nothing of the kind. Teach them—and herself.

A natural color had returned to her face by the time she went downstairs to join Fernanda and Johnny, and she made a special effort to seem carefree and interested as they all went out to dine alfresco in the windy courtyard of a small restaurant whose specialty—which came as no surprise—was fish.

Beth fell asleep while she was eating, and when they went back to the hotel, Johnny carried her up to bed. The thought of chalk marks had been firmly dismissed from Dorcas's mind, and to prove her own good sense and balance, she left the balcony doors ajar when she went to bed.

In the morning Dorcas wakened gradually and lay for a while staring up at the white ceiling with its white-painted beam cutting across the center. She felt more rested than she had in months. Beth was still asleep in the other bed and there was sun beyond the shutters of the balcony. The small room had no window, but only the double doors.

Dorcas got out of bed, slipped into a robe, and went out upon the balcony. The flat rail shone in the light of morning, innocent of smudges. She leaned upon it with confidence, dismissing notions that had their source in last night's weariness.

[54]

The town of Rodos lay across the rounded nose of the fish as it swam toward Turkey. The blue mountains of Anatolia could be no more than forty miles away at this nearest point. The hotel was on the northwest side of the nose, where sunset would be more clearly seen than sunrise. The balcony still lay in shadow, and in the street below palm trees cast their shaggy pattern in exaggerated lengths across the pavement. The sun, rising out of Turkey, had just begun to warm the islands of Greece and the wind was cold and bracing. Beyond low roofs the sea was visible, its waves shimmering with gilt in the early-morning light.

Fernanda heard her and came to her own balcony door to report that she was ravenous.

"Do let's hurry down," she said. "I'm bursting with plans."

It was easy to catch something of Fernanda's excitement on such a morning in such a place. If she were to be disturbed by chalk marks for the rest of her life, she would find herself fainting over hopscotch patterns on the sidewalk, Dorcas thought. Last night's vagaries belonged to someone else. Today she would not be so ridiculous.

She went inside to bathe while Beth was still asleep, came tingling from a shower that was more cold than hot, and rubbed herself into a glow with an oversized bath towel. This was going to be a good day—she had no doubt about it.

Beth was out of bed now and running about in her pajamas. Dorcas helped her to wash and dress, and they both went eagerly down to the lobby, ignoring the single small elevator, taking the two flights of stairs hand in hand.

The lobby was a long room with glass doors down one side overlooking a flagged terrace above the street. The Rhodes fish motif had been given modern treatment in wall mosaics and color was used with a cheerful and liberal hand. There

[55]

was much dusky rose and an Aegean blue, laced with touches of warm yellow. At one end of the lobby small tables had been set with brightly colored cloths and matching napkins that bore the fish design.

Fernanda was ahead of them, a pot of instant coffee on the table before her. She was studying one of her interminable lists, ticking off check marks with a silver pencil. This morning she wore a suit of good gray tweed and had wound a blue scarf around hair that was only slightly less blue in its color. She looked up at Dorcas through blue-rimmed glasses of the particularly piquant slant she liked to affect.

"You look like yourself again," she said cheerfully. "When you've ordered your breakfast, I'll tell you my surprise. Johnny's a sleepyhead, as usual. I'll send a boy to wake him if he doesn't come down soon."

One of the bellhops, doubling as waiter, hurried to fetch cushions for Beth's chair and lifted her onto them. When Dorcas had given their order, Fernanda pushed her lists aside and took off her glasses.

"I must tell you what I've arranged. I thought it would be a help if I found someone to take care of Beth while we're in Rhodes. That way you'll feel less burdened, and you'll be able to run around more with Johnny and me."

This was a sensible move, of course, yet Dorcas experienced a prickling of resistance.

"You've already found someone?" she asked.

"A woman named Vanda Petrus. She comes to us highly recommended and I think she'll be just the person to give you some freedom here in Rhodes."

It was not the plan itself that she instinctively resisted, Dorcas thought, but Fernanda's apparent belief that such decisions were wholly up to her and Beth's mother did not need to be consulted. Still, this was always Fernanda's way, and Dorcas said nothing.

"I haven't seen Mrs. Petrus yet," Fernanda went on, "but she's coming here this morning. The woman who owns this hotel vouches for her and knows her personally. She works at various jobs—sometimes in one of the tourist shops here, sometimes taking care of children when visitors want them off their hands. I understand she lost her own family during the war, so she's quite alone."

The arrangement would be convenient, Dorcas told herself. Yet she could not help her continued stiffening of resistance. Fernanda might at least have discussed the plan ahead of time and given her some choice in the matter of who would care for Beth.

Fernanda sensed her resistance and sighed. "I suppose I've been highhanded again. One has to treat you with gloves, dear. You're so edgy about everything. And that isn't right for Beth. It will do both of you good to be apart a little more."

The accusation was not unjustified. Fernanda was right and she must overcome this tendency to wince from anything that might part her from Beth. The feeling, she knew, was an aftermath of the separation Gino had forced upon her.

"It will be fine, of course," she said with an effort. "What are you planning for this morning?"

"First a trip to the old walled city," Fernanda told her. "I want to get behind those walls before I do anything else."

The "old city," as Dorcas well knew, belonged to the time of the Crusaders, when the Knights of Saint John of Jerusalem had bought the island. They'd ruled it for more than a hundred years, only to be besieged and at last defeated by the Turks in the sixteenth century. Markos had grown nearly as lyrical in his description of the fortress town as he had in speaking of the beauties of the more ancient cities of Rhodes.

Breakfast arrived, with orange juice, warmed rusks in lieu of toast, scrambled eggs, and more coffee. Beth was hungry enough to eat her eggs without objection, and Dorcas found that her own appetite had suddenly come to life. While they ate, a boy from the desk summoned Fernanda to a lobby telephone booth where a call was being held for her.

More breakfasters were coming down to occupy other tables, and Dorcas heard the sound of German and Italian being spoken. Fernanda had said they were the only Americans here. Rhodes was a great vacation spot for Europeans. American tourists were just beginning to discover all the island offered.

Before she returned, Johnny joined them at their table, his short, reddish hair damply on end.

"Hi, toots," he greeted Beth, and gave Dorcas a cheerful "good morning." He had been as pleasant to Dorcas as to Fernanda, but with a faint difference since yesterday when he had learned that she had been Gino Nikkaris's wife. She sensed an edge of something not quite comfortable or easy between them. It would pass, she told herself. A long sleep had rested her and taken away much of her tautness, but it had not changed her feeling of strong liking for Johnny Orion.

Fernanda returned to the table, her cheeks pink with pleasure as she dropped into her place.

"Morning, Johnny. What do you think? There was a piece about me in the local paper last week and it apparently set a few people agog. The woman who just called me is a Madame Xenia Katalonos—apparently a lady of some consequence in Rhodes. I'm not sure exactly what she wants, but I think it's to give me the keys of the city. At least! We're invited to tea day after tomorrow, Dorcas. Me and my secretary. Whatever she knows about Rhodes is to be placed at my disposal. She's going to provide introductions, open sesames, and what-have you."

Johnny laughed. "You'll be a surprise to her, I expect."

His teasing never ruffled Fernanda. She paid no attention. "Katalonos—Katalonos? I wonder why it sounds vaguely familiar?"

"Until our American ears get tuned in, one Greek name sounds just like the next," Johnny said.

Dorcas, following a thought of her own, spoke it aloud. "If she knows Rhodes well, perhaps I can ask her about Mrs. Dimitriou."

Fernanda set down her coffee cup. "Mrs. Dmitriou? What do you mean?"

This was something Dorcas had not told Fernanda. But she must explain her plan sooner or later.

"You remember Markos Dimitriou, who worked at the museum at home?" she said carefully. "This is his widow. I understand she came home to Greece after her husband died. I want to find her in order to pay a debt I owe."

There was rising doubt in Fernanda's eyes, a flicker of concern. Dorcas knew she was remembering a time when Markos Dimitriou's name had been often on Dorcas's lips. It was a name connected with the time of her illness and Fernanda would fear any recurrence.

"You needn't worry," she added quickly. "It's just a small errand I've assigned myself. If she's here, she shouldn't be hard to find."

Fernanda did not look reassured, but she let the matter pass.

"What's our program to be in the old city this morning?" Johnny asked.

"The usual look around," said Fernanda. "You can drive us over and come along, if you will. We'll park the car and walk about inside the walls. I want to see the Street of the Knights and the Palace of the Grand Masters among other things."

"With Italian trimmings," Johnny said. "I understand Mussolini did the palace over to suit himself when it was restored. I suppose you'll also make the usual side excursions?"

Fernanda smiled at him. "My voices will speak to me. They always know where the good stories are. Don't stick to me too closely, you and Dorcas. Things happen better when I'm alone."

"I know," Johnny said dryly, and grinned at Dorcas. "Have you ever gone on a story-hunting expedition with Fernanda? You'll be surprised at what can happen."

Fernanda wrinkled her nose. "We'll have a look at the museum, of course. There are several famous treasures there. Besides, it used to be the Hospital of the Knights, so I must see it. Though I can't do much with museums, as a rule."

"Too many guards around," Johnny said. "For real excitement you need a free hand."

Dorcas listened to his banter with amusement. For all that Johnny teased outrageously, it was clear that a strong affection for Fernanda underlay his words and she suspected that he would give her his solid support in any real pinch. She was beginning to sense something in Johnny Orion that she had not been immediately aware of, because of his easy, casual manner. There was a toughness in him, she suspected. Some basic stubborn tenacity—a sort of dogged strength. It was this, perhaps, that enabled him to work so well with Fernanda. While he made no attempt to manage her, he did not permit her to blow him down and it was clear that she respected this

[60]

very quality of toughness in him. Sensing this made Dorcas curious, and she wondered what sort of world he had grown up in. Where was he going? What did he want from life?

Yesterday in Athens she had felt the beginning of a first tentative movement between herself and Johnny—a step toward something that might vanish at a breath. She wasn't sure she wanted this to grow into something stronger. She wasn't ready yet. But at the same time she regretted the breaking of that tenuous strand.

Fernanda was still talking about the museum they were to visit, sounding as though it was more a chore to go through it than anything else. Dorcas, on the contrary, looked forward to visiting this particular collection. Among other pieces would be the head of the boy with a tear on his cheek that Johnny had mentioned yesterday on the Acropolis. She remembered his finger touching away a tear on her own cheek. The head of the weeping boy was tied up with happy recollections of her own and it would be pleasant to see it in the company of someone like Johnny.

As they were finishing breakfast Mrs. Petrus arrived. She waited by the desk at the far end of the lobby while a boy came to summon Fernanda.

"Let me talk to her first," Fernanda said to Dorcas. "I'll call you over in a moment."

From the distance of her table Dorcas watched the woman who was to care for Beth. She was past her youth, probably in her mid-forties, and leanly built. The bones showed beneath the strong framework of her body. Her dark eyes were set deeply in their sockets, and heavy-lidded. Short-cropped black hair grew close and curly about her head. She was neatly dressed in a dark sweater and dark green skirt with black walking shoes on her feet.

Fernanda bore down upon her with outstretched hand and her usual hearty greeting. Mrs. Petrus allowed her hand to be grasped and shaken, but her response was clearly more restrained. A somber-looking woman, Dorcas thought. Too serious, perhaps? Too stern for the care of a child?

Fernanda spoke with her animatedly for a few moments and then beckoned Dorcas and Beth. Johnny lifted Beth down from her chair and the little girl ran across the lobby to Aunt Fern. Dorcas moved more slowly, watching to see what would happen. Her own peace of mind during their stay in Rhodes would depend a great deal on this woman.

The child ran to Fernanda and clung to her hand, holding back shyly from Mrs. Petrus. She returned the child's stare as if she, too, measured, judged, and waited to be convinced. Then, surprisingly, she went down on her knees to meet Beth at her own level and took something from her handbag and held it out to the little girl.

For a moment longer Beth hesitated, then reached for the toy. Dorcas, coming to her side, saw that it was a carved wooden donkey with olive barrels panniered across his back. Beth held it up to her mother.

"Look, Mommy—a horse! The lady gave me a horse."

"Not horse," Mrs. Petrus corrected gravely. "This is a Greek donkey. A boy in my village makes it for me to bring to the American little girl."

Beth fondled the wooden toy. "I like it. Can I keep it for me?"

"Is for you," Mrs. Petrus said.

Beth smiled at her shyly and for the first time the woman's eyes brightened and lips accustomed to severity softened. Still on her knees, she put a hand lightly on Beth's shoulder.

"We will be friends, I think."

slightest opportunity for Dorcas to object or resist what was being done.

She kissed Beth and told her to mind Vanda and have fun. When she met the woman's eyes again she had the same awareness of an instinctive disliking. It seemed to be mutual. She did not like Vanda and the woman did not like her.

"Thank you for coming to take care of Beth," she said stiffly. "I hope this will work out well."

The woman made her gesture of acquiescence with bowed head, but she did not speak. Dorcas went downstairs with a sense of uneasiness following her like a shadow she could not escape.

Fernanda and Johnny were outside near the car, discussing the workings of Fernanda's camera. Fernanda took pictures constantly, but not with the avid enthusiasm of the usual sight-seer. Her purpose was to make visual records that would recall details at a later date when she sat down to her typewriter to bring the scene to life for her readers.

Waiting for the other two, Dorcas glanced up at the long, low façade of the hotel, not sure which stretch of third-floor balcony was hers. Neither Beth nor Vanda Petrus was in sight. The palm trees down the middle of the street whipped shaggy heads in the breeze and the sound of the sea reached her clearly.

The car was a medium-sized English model that made three in the front seat a crush, so Dorcas got into the back. Determinedly she thrust away all uncertainties and gave her attention to this first real look at the town of Rhodes.

Winding streets led past the greenery of gardens and there were flowers everywhere. Scarlet hibiscus blossoms challenged the eye and rich purple-red bougainvillaea spilled over stone walls, while jasmine warmed sweetly in early-morning sunshine.

In a few blocks they reached Mandraki, a wide promenade along the water front. Here there were modern buildings of concrete, often decorated with Turkish design and with overhanging Turkish balconies and latticework.

No one paid the slightest attention to automobiles in the downtown streets. Johnny stopped for bicycles and for donkeys. He slowed to a crawl for pedestrians. Everyone walked leisurely in the middle of the road and stepped out from curbs without warning. Gesticulating gentlemen argued on the pavement, unwilling to interrupt their discussions for the importunity of a horn. The Greeks were a wonderfully gregarious and friendly people. They liked one another's company and they welcomed the company of the stranger. But Rhodes had been here long before the automobile, and a man had a right to the roadway he had set down for his own convenience.

As the car inched along the plan of the town grew clear. From Mandraki Harbor and the water-front drive Rhodes climbed its gentle hills to a summit that Johnny said was called by the unlikely name of Monte Smith. Up there were the ruins of what had once been the acropolis of Rhodes.

On their left, as they drove toward the huge masonry of walls and towers, was the famous harbor—a small harbor, nearly enclosed by two slender arms of land that all but met at the entry. Out there, facing each other, stood a bronze stag and a doe, symbolizing the deer that had once roamed forested mountains. The medieval fortress of Saint Nicholas guarded the entrance, squat and low, and on the opposite wedge of land three windmills turned arms covered with heavy cloth, like the sails of a ship.

Sounding like a guide, Fernanda gestured toward the fortress. "They say the Colossus of Rhodes stood out there at the entrance to the harbor. Poor sun-god! An earthquake shook him down. He lay there in broken chunks for centuries until an enterprising merchant bought him and carried the pieces away on nine hundred camels. Or so the story goes."

Dorcas hardly listened, her attention focused upon the walls of the Crusaders' city running close beside them now. At intervals the great enclosure of stone was broken by huge towers that guarded every entrance. The whole was Gothic and medieval, ruled over by the great palace up the hill, its towers and castled ramparts visible almost anywhere in the town of Rhodes.

Fernanda ceased to talk and began scribbling hasty notes in the plump, loose-leaf notebook that was always at hand. Once she glanced around at Dorcas.

"Remember what you see, dear. Make notes when anything strikes you. I'll be counting on you to take off my hands the chore of summarizing everything and getting a record down at the end of the day. It's hard to catch details at first because the whole thing seems overwhelming. But you'll learn to look for them, and the ones you see may be different from the ones that catch my eye."

"What detail strikes you most now?" Johnny asked Dorcas.

She spoke her thought aloud. "From a distance all that stone looks dull and gray. But when you get close it's not gray at all, though I'm not sure why."

"It's partly the stone itself," Johnny said. "There's an apricot touch in the sandstone of Rhodes. It always seems alive and warm. The sun helps, of course—the light from sky and water. It can go gray enough when you see it in the shadow."

They drove slowly beside the high wall until Fernanda

[67]

called to Johnny to stop. Along the water a stone wall, low on the land side, dropped steeply to a rocky beach below. Scattered among stones and big boulders were curious stone balls, some of them as large as a man's head, some of them smaller. All had been shaped and rounded by the hand of man.

"What can they be?" Fernanda puzzled. "They don't look like cannon balls—they're too big."

Johnny knew the answer. "Rhodes was a city often besieged in the old days. Those balls were thrown by catapult when Turks and Saracens and pirates tried to breech the walls. I suppose the Knights of Saint John used them, too, in defense. You'll see them everywhere around the town. Out there in the harbor a good many lie where they must have fallen and no one bothers about them."

"Fascinating," Fernanda said thoughtfully, tapping a tooth with the end of her silver pencil.

Johnny laughed and spoke over his shoulder to Dorcas. "We have to watch her when she sounds like that. It means she's cooking something up. If we don't watch her, she'll try to take one of those balls home for a pocket piece."

The stone catapult balls, perhaps more than anything else, Dorcas thought, gave a sense of the past as it hung over Rhodes. Down on the beach the stones shone in the sun, wet and brown and pock marked from long weathering, lying where they had fallen short of the wall they were intended to breech. She could almost hear an echo of the crashing and the tumult.

The car had reached two massively rounded towers with a deep, arched gateway between, offering entry into the walled town. Above the gate still hung the marble buckler of a knight. As they drove through with other traffic, the great masses of stone dwarfed the car.

Once inside, Johnny found an open square where they could park and they got out to walk over ancient cobblestones. Stone buildings two or three stories high closed around them, almost every window bearing the mark of a cross in wood strips that separated the panes. For all that the town within the walls offered shops to draw the tourists, it was a town in its own right. People lived here in houses that were not greatly different from what they had been in the days of the knights.

As they crossed the square, Dorcas was again reminded of Beth's absence. There was no small hand tugging at her own, no demands made upon her attention. She hoped all was going well back at the hotel. She must not worry.

Consulting her map, Fernanda located the Hospital of the Knights, which was now a museum. Again there was a deeply arched doorway set into the face of a great stone building. They went through it to pay the small entry fee and were at once in a medieval world. An intricacy of stone arches ran foursquare about a large, stone-flagged court, open to the sky and the galleries that surrounded the upper floor. Across this stone expanse the figure of a rather improbable lion reclined on a pedestal, watching them with hollow eyes. Nearby were piled more of the rough stone balls.

"Makes you wonder," Johnny said, "if the sculptors who were always making lions as a symbol of courage ever saw one in real life."

Here in the shadows stone had turned once more lifeless and gray and the golden apricot of the outdoor walls was gone. The stone exuded chill, and a cold wind blew through the arches.

The three mounted wide, railless steps and found their way along a gallery lined with pottery jars—the amphorae of Greece that had once held wine or other liquids, wide-mouthed

[69]

storage jars, oil jugs, and ointment jars. Fernanda breezed past these with hardly a second glance, but Johnny lingered and Dorcas saw him stop absorbed before a large jar with a red-figure painting of the ships of Odysseus. As Dorcas had sensed in Athens, Johnny's interest in Greece was far more real than that of Fernanda, who saw mainly the end result of the book she meant to write.

The museum's most valued treasures were kept in small rooms upstairs off one of the main corridors. Here shelves along the walls held small heads and fragments of figurines. In the farthest of these honeycomb rooms they came upon the slender, virginal figure of the Venus of Rhodes. The marble body had been worn by sea waves for centuries before she had been recovered from the water, and her contours had blurred and softened, the very curls of her head smoothed in their undulations. Her features were barely discernible, and over her heart she bore a rusty stain.

Dorcas found herself moved to tenderness before the slight and lovely form. She knew how her father would have stood enthralled before the figure. Fernanda's interest, however, was not to be held by one piece for more than a few moments. She turned to the better-preserved statue of the kneeling Aphrodite drying her hair.

The little nymph was exquisite as she lifted long ringlets of hair in each plump hand, spreading them to the sun. The gentle curves of breast and thigh, the dimpled knees, seemed untouched by the years that had flowed over them. The face was secretive—a young girl's face wearing a half-smile, the lids lowered, hiding her thoughts.

"Let's get on with it," Fernanda said, cheerfully shattering the spell. "What else must we see while we're here? I hardly ever do a museum twice."

Dorcas had been looking about, but she had not found the marble head with the single tear rolling down one cheek. Johnny glanced at her and smiled, and she knew he remembered.

"We haven't seen the weeping boy yet," he reminded Fernanda.

The boy, however, was not to be easily found. The guard they questioned spoke only Greek and their pantomime drew a blank. To thwart Fernanda was to increase her determination. What should be seen must be seen.

"It's surely around somewhere," she said. "Let's find someone who can speak English."

A woman accompanied by several children heard her. "I speak English a little," she offered. "If I can help—"

Fernanda described the head, and the woman knew it at once. "Ah, yes. It has been in this room. One moment—I will ask the guard."

A conversation in Greek went on for several minutes. There was arm waving on the part of the guard and a good deal of head shaking as well. At last the woman turned back to them.

"He is very sorry, but the head is not on exhibit just now. It is removed to the director's office for some reason I do not understand."

Fernanda's own head with its bluish hair and bright blue scarf came up like a steed that sniffs the fray.

"Then let's find the director," she said. "I always believe in going to the top. And when someone says 'no' to me, I insist on following through. Quite often it means a story."

The woman looked somewhat bewildered, but she spoke again to the guard, and they were waved out of the room and toward a distant door. Fernanda had the effect of making one feel part of a large force ready to scale the bastions of authority. Her persistence might seem a little absurd at times, but it made things interesting. Dorcas found that her own curiosity had been whetted. Now she wanted doubly to see the sculpture of the weeping boy.

4

IN THE small office an official was found who spoke English. Fernanda explained her mission to Rhodes and was treated with smiling courtesy. But when she explained that she might not be able to return to the museum later, and wished to see the famous marble head now, there was evidence of reluctance.

"It has been retired from view for the time being," the official explained. "We regret greatly, but it is not on exhibit at the present time."

"Why not?" Fernanda was blunt.

The official gestured vaguely. "We are most sorry, but what you ask is not possible."

Fernanda tapped a tooth with her pencil and Johnny began to whistle softly, as though to call her back to an acceptance of authority.

"May I use your telephone?" she asked the official. "I would like to speak to the governor."

"The—ah—governor?" the man echoed blankly.

"Yes, of course. The governor of the Dodecanese Islands.

Rhodes is the capital, is it not? I have an introduction to the governor and I presume he is in residence now. I'm sure he will use his influence—"

"Madame, the governor is a busy man." The official sounded less cordial now.

"I believe the governor will be interested in assisting me," Fernanda said somewhat grandly. "Do you have this marble piece on the premises?"

The official threw up his hands. "But of course. Perhaps if it is of so great importance that you see it, an exception may be permitted."

He moved toward a closed cabinet in a corner of the room and Fernanda followed on his heels, perhaps a bit disappointed at so easy a victory.

Johnny stopped whistling and winked at Dorcas. "She'll find a better adversary yet—give her time."

The official took out a ring of keys and unlocked the corner cabinet. From its shadowy depths he took something heavy and solid into both hands and brought it to the blotting pad in the center of his desk, setting it down gently.

"There you are, madame," he said. "This is one of the great treasures of Rhodes. It is believed to be part of a figure made by the great Phidias himself."

Dorcas stepped closer to the desk. There was only the head and a broken indication of neck. The boy was young—perhaps seven or eight, and the head was life-size. From the cool, creamy white of the marble he looked up at them, his head turned slightly on the tracing of a neck that afforded a supporting base. Tenderly, sadly, he regarded them, so that the single tear poised on one cheek seemed to tremble as if about to fall. One could almost sense a quiver in the softly turned chin.

Their somewhat unwilling host made a little speech. "Our story tells that this boy is son of the nymph, Rhoda, beloved of Apollo. Perhaps he weeps for his father who rides the sky in his fiery chariot."

Dorcas found herself studying the marble head intently. It was perfection itself, and yet there seemed some spell in the marble that disturbed her, reached out to her—though she did not know why.

Fernanda announced that she was satisfied, and the man put the head away. He bowed politely at their thanks and saw them to the door. Dorcas suspected that he was glad to see them go without a summons to the governor.

"I'm sure I don't know what that was all about," Fernanda said, her voice echoing cheerfully through stone corridors. "Anyway, let's get on to the Street of the Knights. That's what I want to see next."

Dorcas would have liked to stay longer in this ancient building. There were rooms they had not seen. And she had caught a tantalizing glimpse of a vast hall with arched columns down its center—perhaps where the Knights Hospitalers had kept their patients. However, she could return another time and bring Beth along. Beth was accustomed to museums and liked wandering in them. Again the hint of worry about Beth was insistent at the back of her mind, and again she thrust it away. She must refuse to give in to vague anxieties.

When they reached the entrance gate on their way out, Fernanda stopped to look at postcards and booklets for sale. She collected such material by the ton for future reference —especially in museums, where cameras were not allowed. Quickly she sorted through the display and then spoke to the man behind the desk. She wanted a picture of that marble head of a boy crying. The man spoke little English.

"All is here," he said, indicating his stock. "There is nothing more."

Dorcas, too, ran through the cards, but found no photograph of the boy with the tear on his cheek. The omission seemed odd, since other famous pieces were represented by a number of views.

"I'd like to have a picture of the head, too," Dorcas said, thinking of her fondness for the photograph she had known as a child.

"There are sure to be pictures of it around town—I'll find some for you and Fernanda," Johnny promised.

Fernanda, however, had moved on to experiences still ahead, and there was a quickening of eagerness as she put the museum behind her. They left gray walls and went into the bright sunshine of the square.

"Now for the original Street of the Knights," she said. "Something ought to happen there—something I can use."

The street was a short distance from the museum. When they reached its foot Fernanda stopped to take a picture of the narrow, climbing passage that ran between tight stone buildings. Uphill it went beneath an overpass and through an arched gateway at the top. The houses of the knights were built flat against the street, with no spaces between. Again each window bore the marking of a cross. Set into stone over a number of doorways were coats of arms, signifying, among other things, the tongue that each knight had spoken.

As the three climbed the narrow sidewalk in single file, Dorcas had an occasional glimpse through an open doorway of courtyards beyond, where flowers bloomed and interior stone steps mounted beneath more Gothic archways to rooms above.

Before one of these vistas Fernanda paused in delight. "Run

[76]

along, you two. I want to see this. Maybe I'll turn up something interesting if I go in by myself. I'll meet you in a little while in front of the Grand Masters' Palace at the top of the street."

"We'll wait for you," said Johnny. "Take care. And don't go phoning the governor."

Dorcas went ahead up the sidewalk. Alone with Johnny, and without Beth's presence to furnish a focus, there seemed little to say. She was conscious once more of the change that had come over him when he'd learned that she was Gino Nikkaris's widow.

Part way up he led her across the cobblestones to an alleyway so narrow that it made the Knights' Street seem wide by comparison. Here there were more crowding gray stone houses with little sunlight reaching through. Walls hemmed them in and there were unexpected turns, arches, and overpasses on every hand.

"I spent some time in here when I came to Rhodes to make arrangements for Fernanda," Johnny said. "It's a rabbit warren, with crooked streets going every which way, but enormously interesting and alive."

They walked on, pausing beneath a statue of the Virgin in a canopied stone niche high above the street. Johnny spoke knowledgeably of its age and origin, and Dorcas found herself wondering about him again, about his interest in such things.

At the top of the Knights' Street they emerged upon an open courtyard where a huge plane tree grew in a center enclosure. At one side rose the formidable entrance towers of the Palace. Beyond were the ramparts and further towers they had seen from below.

"Are you tired?" Johnny asked. "Let's sit down for a while on the steps over there."

She was not tired at all, but she sat beside him on a wide flight of stone. The thought of Beth was with her again. The tug of anxiety had grown stronger. It would not be quieted by the reproaches of a more reasonable part of her mind.

"How long do you suppose we'll be away from the hotel?" she asked.

Johnny shrugged. "Who knows? I suppose we'll do the Palace when Fernanda joins us, and that may take a while. She's getting oriented today."

Dorcas glanced at her watch and Johnny saw the gesture. "You're not worrying about Beth, are you?" He sounded faintly impatient. "She's perfectly all right, you know."

She did not want him to guess how much she was worrying. The pulse of anxiety had begun a steady beating, almost like the ticking of an alarm clock that marked each passing moment. She had an unhappy feeling that when the alarm went off, she would rush headlong back to the hotel and that no calm reassurances from anyone would keep her from reasonless flight. The knowledge in itself was alarming. She must not prove Fernanda right about her emotional state.

She answered him stiffly. "I don't know anything about this woman Fernanda has brought in to take care of Beth. I don't want to be away too long. I have a queer feeling that she doesn't like me. It makes me uncomfortable."

Johnny moved restlessly on the steps beside her, as though he wished he were doing something else. "You're going to have a hard time if you worry about Beth all the way through this trip. Kids are fairly tough and I doubt that this woman will let her get into trouble. It isn't important whether or not she likes you, so long as she likes Beth. Isn't that true?"

Dorcas had again that sense of inner toughness about Johnny. He would be sympathetic if he saw cause for anxiety, but impatient otherwise. She suspected that he would not be polite about it if he thought her foolish, and she tried to take his attention, and her own, from this unrealistic anxiety.

"Yesterday you mentioned that you knew my husband," she said.

He nodded, and she was aware of the way he stiffened.

She persisted. "How did you happen to meet him?"

"The first time Fernanda came to Greece I helped out with her trip." His voice was expressionless and he answered reluctantly. "We drove through the Peloponnese that time. Nikkaris joined us in Athens and went along."

"You didn't like him, did you?"

"What do you expect me to say?" he demanded.

"I'd like to know what you thought of him."

He did not reply at once, but watched a girl who came out of a nearby doorway and ran across the courtyard to greet a young soldier waiting there. The two walked away hand in hand, and one knew there was affection between them.

"I didn't like him," Johnny admitted when the two were gone.

"Tell me why you didn't."

He looked at her as though he resented the question and did not answer.

"I want to know," she said. "What did Gino do on that trip that made you dislike him?"

"I disliked him from scratch." Johnny was curt. "We rubbed each other the wrong way the first time we met."

"But there was more to it than that?"

"The man is dead." Johnny's impatience was rising. "Supposedly you're his grieving widow. But since you insist, I'll tell you. He was using Fernanda for a bit of petty, and perhaps not so petty, smuggling. She thought he could do no wrong and she swallowed the story he fed her without question. I found out what he was up to and told him to lay off or I'd tell her the truth. The way he reacted made me think I might wake up with a knife in my ribs. He didn't take it very well. If you want to know, I thought him a dangerous man. But he surprised me by paying attention to my warning. And a few days later he bowed out of the trip. I guess he thought it was no use, once I was on to him."

"Gino was like that," Dorcas said. "He used people whenever he could get away with it."

Again Johnny glanced at her, but he made no comment. Undoubtedly he thought her a disloyal wife for not springing to Gino's defense. She could not help that. The time for the truth had not yet come. Because she could not talk to him about Gino, she began, instead, to speak of her father and of his long interest in Greece. She wanted very much to break past the critical resistance Johnny was showing toward her today.

"My father was here only once as a young man," she told him. "He came before he had a family to care for, and he always wanted to return. He had planned a trip when he retired, but he didn't live that long. He wanted to come to Rhodes especially. He said it was a neglected island in many ways."

Johnny was listening now, and something of his impatience with her had faded. "I've felt that. Perhaps because Rhodes is off the beaten path, not so many people come here as might. The travel accounts usually settle for the other islands—for Crete and Delos and the rest. Novel writers do the same. But Rhodes waits with all it has to offer, and those of us who come are glad we did. I was more than happy when Fernanda said she wanted me for this trip."

Dorcas nodded. "In a way, I feel I'm making a sort of pil-

[80]

grimage here for my father, and for a good friend of his who worked at the museum. I keep trying to see everything through their eyes and imagine what they would be thinking. In order to—to bring them here with me."

"You can overdo that," Johnny said dryly.

She gave him a quick look. For a moment she had thought there was sympathy between them again, but she had been wrong. Johnny Orion had a habit of turning unexpected corners that led away from her, putting himself in opposition when she least expected it.

"I don't know what you mean," she said.

He picked up a pebble from the step beside him and tossed it idly in one hand. "What are *you* getting out of this trip? If you spend all your time in a—well, frankly, in a sentimental haze, what is Greece going to do for you? And for Beth?"

It was her turn to be angry. She did not like having the deep love she felt for her father and for Markos called "sentimental." Johnny had not understood at all, and it was clear that they were poles apart.

She did not try to talk to him further, but gave herself fully to the thought of Beth. It was not unreasonable to be concerned about her daughter, she thought rebelliously. Again—this was something Johnny did not understand. This morning Fernanda had left her both resentful and a little frightened by taking Beth deliberately out of her hands. There had been something of a warning in Fernanda's action—as though it was the beginning of a removal of Beth from her care. But of course Fernanda couldn't do that. It wasn't possible. Nevertheless, Dorcas began to wonder more urgently than before about what might be happening at the hotel with Beth in the hands of a stranger. Abruptly her concern was upon her again,

[81]

closing out everything else so that she might listen to the ticking of the alarm.

They sat in silence until Fernanda appeared in the archway and called to Johnny to help her. In her arms she carried a large wood-framed picture.

He ran across the cobblestones to take the burden out of her hands. "More struggling artists?" he asked, holding it up for a look. "I suppose I'm to be pack donkey again?"

"You don't mind," Fernanda told him cheerfully. "And it really was exciting. A lovely little story for my book. Such a talented young man!"

Johnny turned the canvas for Dorcas to see. The artist had a sense of color, at least. There were bold splashes of yellow and blue, a dash of green, and one great gob of scarlet—all rather indiscriminately arranged.

"Clearly the work of genius," said Johnny. "Would you mind telling me if it's supposed to represent anything?"

Fernanda remained unperturbed. "It's the walled city and the harbor, of course. The artist explained it to me. Of course this is just his feeling about old Rhodes. He was most hospitable. He gave me a cup of Turkish coffee and let me pet his cat."

"How much money did he take away from you?" Johnny asked.

Fernanda lifted expressive shoulders. "I paid him more than he asked. The sum he wanted was ridiculous." She looked up at the twin towers of the entrance to the Palace. "Probably we can check the picture in there for now. I must see what dreadful things Mussolini did in his restorations. Are you ready?"

No, Dorcas thought, she could not stay away any longer. She must get back to the hotel and make sure that everything was all right. It would be better to go now before she panicked completely.

"I'm—I'm sorry, Fernanda, but would you mind—" she began.

Fernanda was all sympathetic concern. "We've tired you, haven't we? And that won't do at all."

"She's worried about Beth," Johnny put in. "There's nothing to be done about an anxious mother. I've had to deal with them at school."

Fernanda patted her arm soothingly. "Darling, you mustn't worry. You mustn't let small, imaginary things upset you. Last night you were seeing chalk marks on the balcony. If you're not tired, the sensible thing to do is come along with us and see the Palace."

"Not now, please," Dorcas said. "I want to go back to the hotel."

"Let her go," Johnny said. "If you like, I can drive her to the hotel, leave this masterpiece in the car, and be back for you in twenty minutes."

Fernanda was not pleased, but she gave in with reasonable grace. "We mustn't keep humoring her in these notions," she told Johnny. "But perhaps for this time your solution will do. I don't want to feel hurried going through the Palace. Come and look for me inside when you get back."

She waved them off and walked resolutely toward the twin-towered doorway. Johnny tucked the painting under one arm and took Dorcas's elbow.

"Come along—it's downhill back to the car. We can make it fast."

He had helped her to get away, but she did not feel particularly grateful. She wanted to say, "It's not imaginary. I've perfectly good reasons for being worried." But she was afraid

[83]

he would discount the whole thing just as Fernanda had done. The rapport she had felt with him when they had talked about Rhodes had disappeared as though it had never been.

The drive back to the hotel was maddeningly slow because the streets were filled with people. The market was open and a boat had docked. Rodos was wide-awake and going about its business. Dorcas forced herself to sit quietly for the length of the trip and Johnny made no attempt at cheery conversation. She was glad of that, indifferent now to his silent disapproval.

In front of the hotel he came around and opened the door. "I'll go inside with you and make sure everything is all right."

"Please don't trouble," she told him. "I can manage nicely, now that I'm here."

She tried to slide out of the car, but he stood on the sidewalk, his hands on the door, blocking her way.

"All right, if that's what you want," he said. "But first you'll listen to Uncle Johnny for a minute." He grinned at the look she gave him and went right on. "There's no use telling me to mind my own business. I seldom do. I've brought you home because you showed signs of flying apart in all directions. In a moment I'll let you go in and you'll march right upstairs and find everything just as it should be. Then maybe you'll stop and have a good look at this exaggerated course you've been steering in your worry about Beth. Fernanda's right about the need for you to stop it. She tells me you've been in a nursing home and she doesn't want you back in one. Yet if you keep seeing ominous chalk marks that aren't there and—"

Dorcas pushed his hands from the door and thrust herself out of the car. "The chalk marks *were* there! It was I who erased them. Maybe she didn't tell you that!"

He stood aside, looking sorry—not for his own words, but

for her. She ran up the steps to the hotel, close to tears because not even Johnny Orion believed in her, and desperate, besides, with anxiety for Beth.

The key was not at the desk, so Vanda must be upstairs with Beth. She ran up to the third floor, to arrive at her door painfully out of breath. The knob turned at her touch and she burst abruptly into the room. The shutters to the balcony were closed and the room was shadowed, orderly. A maid had been in to make the beds, but there was more to the orderliness than that—though Dorcas did not stop to note exactly what it was. Only the fact that the room was empty seemed important. Vanda's door stood ajar and a look inside told her that neither Beth nor the woman was there. If they had gone out, what was she to do? How was she to find them quickly? How could she bear to wait, not knowing where they had gone?

The sound of voices reached her and she ran to the balcony doors and pulled them open. In the warm morning sunshine Vanda Petrus sat in a low chair with Beth on her lap. She was telling her a story of old Greece, and the scene could hardly have been more peaceful.

Panic and anxiety died sickly. Johnny's words echoed through her mind as he had promised they would, and behind them sounded Fernanda's words—and Gino's! Had Gino been right from the beginning? Had she lost all sense of balance, all normal self-control? Was she too far gone down this road to self-destruction to turn back?

But there had been chalk marks on the balcony last night. Meaningless, perhaps, but real. And other things had been real, too.

Beth, at least, had not noticed her panic, though Vanda was watching her warily. Having greeted her with a ready, "hi!" Beth demanded that Vanda go on with the story. The woman made a move to set Beth down, but Dorcas stopped her.

"Don't get up, please. Go on with your story. I—I came back ahead of the others."

She returned to the dim room and stood looking around, thoroughly sick and shaken. They said that a person who was ill in this particular way was the last to know. The most irrational behavior could seem logical and the world wholly wrong. But this was what she had come to Greece to disprove —that she had ever been irrational in the first place. She must listen to Johnny and regain control of herself. About that he had been right. And she must seek out Markos Dimitriou's widow at the earliest opportunity because only she could support the truth about Gino. Surely the woman would know something.

Dorcas sat on her bed to still the trembling and stared at the small white room. She saw now why it looked so orderly. Someone had unpacked all her things. Articles she had not taken out last night stood on the dressing table. Suitcases had been thrust under the bed. She felt one against her heel and pulled it out. It had been entirely emptied.

Moving quickly now, she went to the closet. Her dresses and blouses, as well as Beth's things, had been neatly placed on hangers. Shoes stood in a row on the floor of the closet. Even Beth's toys had been unpacked and put away. Her canvas tote bag stood in the closet, empty and collapsed upon its own sides. It was obvious that Vanda had gone through all her things. No hotel maid would take such a task upon herself.

A new throbbing had started at her temples. This was the time to summon reason and self-control. She must not think in terms of "searching." All that was over back in the States.

In Rhodes she was not even Mrs. Nikkaris. Vanda had done a kind, sensible thing—something beyond her line of duty that Dorcas must be grateful for.

She heard a movement from the balcony and Beth's voice objecting. Then Vanda came in and stood just behind her.

"I hope you do not mind that I unpack the clothes," she said.

Listening to the sound of the words without turning to see the woman's face, Dorcas was aware of a not unpleasant cadence, a depth of tone that was quiet and well under command. *Control,* she thought. She must not fling herself around and cry, "What were you looking for? Why did you go through my things?"

As she turned toward Vanda she spoke, and was relieved to hear the normal, unrevealing sound of her own voice. "It was good of you to help. I came home early to take care of this myself. Why don't you go now and bring back your own things, Mrs. Petrus?"

The woman nodded unsmiling agreement and left with a certain quiet dispatch, promising Beth that she would finish the story later.

When she had gone, Dorcas stepped out upon the balcony and looked down at the palm-lined street below. In a few moments Vanda Petrus emerged from the hotel entrance and walked to the corner. She moved with a proud, straight carriage, a free stride. Dorcas watched until she turned the corner out of sight.

"You made her stop the story," Beth accused, and drew dark brows down in an expression that was a reminder of Gino.

"I'll read you a story," Dorcas said. "Let's get one of your books."

Together they pulled open a lower drawer of the bureau where Vanda had packed Beth's things. The little girl made a choice and Dorcas sat in the room's easy chair and switched on a lamp. The sunlight of Rhodes was a little too bright on the balcony. Besides, she liked the seclusion of the room just now. It held her safely in its quiet space. It threatened nothing when she was alone in it with Beth. The child climbed on her lap and they paged through the book. It was a collection of stories and Beth found one she wanted to hear.

As always, it was comforting to have her daughter's small, warm person leaning against her in the complete trust only a young child could give. Her face was gently rapt as the words were read aloud, and the angry quirk was gone from her brows. Yet even as Dorcas read with all the proper dramatic inflections, a part of her mind was busy elsewhere. She could think more quietly now of the problem of herself and her own emotions. Both Fernanda's concern for her and Johnny's impatience had been justified. She had behaved badly, and it would have to stop.

The exciting moment of the story's climax was reached, and as Dorcas turned a page something fell out of the book. She read on, glancing at the envelope in her lap. It was an air-mail envelope with Greek stamps across its face. The handwriting in which it was addressed was unfamiliar, but the name it bore was that of Gino Nikkaris.

She finished the story and set Beth down. "Play with your things for a little while, dear. Mommy has something to do."

The envelope had already been opened. She herself had opened it when it had come to the apartment soon after Gino's death. She had made no sense of the note within at the time. Now she read the strange words once more.

The bride of Apollo mourns her loss. Done is the fearful deed. Gone the Princess from her Castle. At the hour of devils shadow lies upon the grave. Dolorosa, dolorosa, dolorosa.

That was all, and there was no more meaning in the words as she read them now than there had been the first time. Yet now they seemed charged with frightening significance—as if they might be a key to some mystery that would hang over her head until she knew the answer to it. The words had a rhythm to them as though they had been carefully composed, rather than dashed off in haste.

She felt certain that she held in her hand the letter for which her possessions had twice been searched at home—the letter for which a friend of Gino had come looking soon after his death. Had it been this that Vanda Petrus searched for also in her unpacking? But that was something she must not think. There was no reason to be suspicious of Vanda and she must not jump impulsively to conclusions. Acting on intuition got her into nothing but trouble.

She held out the envelope to Beth. "Do you remember seeing this before, darling?"

Beth looked at the bright stamps. "That's mine! I found it in the black-and-gold box on the bookcase at home."

Which was where it had been placed originally, Dorcas thought. It was Beth who had removed it, drawn by the stamps. Beth who had slipped it between the pages of a picture book, so that it had not come to light until this moment.

"It wasn't in the box for you to take, dear," Dorcas said. "Next time you must ask me first. I'll keep it for now."

She returned the message to its envelope and glanced about

the room for a suitable hiding place. In the end she opened her handbag and slipped the envelope into the green leather folder that held her passport. It would be safe there, and in her possession every moment. She was not sure at this point what might be done with the letter. She would have to think about it a while longer.

Now there was a next step she could take. She called to Beth and they went downstairs together to the hotel desk where she spoke to the clerk.

"I would like to know if there is a Mrs. Markos Dimitriou living in Rhodes at this time."

Obligingly he brought the telephone book and ran down the Greek lettering. Twice his finger made a journey before he shook his head.

"I am sorry, madame, but we do not have the Markos Dimitriou. Perhaps there is no telephone?"

"Perhaps not," Dorcas said. She thanked him and took Beth upstairs. When she and Fernanda accepted Madame Xenia Katalonos's invitation to tea, she would push her inquiries further.

Back in the room, she took out the letter and read the cryptic message through. The words seemed like some knell of warning. A warning of death, perhaps? But of death to come, or death already transpired?

There was something here—something she could not put her finger on. She wished she could discuss this with Johnny Orion, but after his warning that she had become too emotional and overwrought, she could not bring herself to open the subject with him. She must keep her own counsel for now and avoid blurting out what might only be regarded as further evidence of an unbalanced state. In a sense the letter reassured

[90]

her. It told her there was something here that had not been created wholly out of her imagination.

She studied the paper in her hands. What had Gino been involved in before his death? What machinery of complicated events might he have set in motion which others must carry out now that he was gone? These others could well be the faceless enemy she sometimes sensed about her.

Quiet was all she asked of Rhodes. This letter belonged to the past. Let it stay where it belonged. Yet she could not bring herself to destroy it. As she returned it to its hiding place, she noted something she had not seen before. In the lower right-hand corner, very small and neat, so that it was hardly noticeable, was drawn a small figure. She studied it closely, and saw that it seemed to be a tiny caricature of an owl—an owl with large round eyes.

Had not the owl belonged to Pallas Athena, as did the olive tree? Had it not been a symbol . . . her fingers tightened on the paper. Suddenly she was seeing only the eyes of the owl. Two exaggerated circles staring up at her from a corner of the letter. Circles such as she had seen twice before. Perhaps even a third time in those chalk marks last night.

Again she was confirmed in her belief that what was happening was no mere figment of an unbalanced imagination. Some stranger, some messenger of her dead husband still pursued her, believing that she possessed something that Gino's friends needed. Some knowledge, perhaps, contained in this coded letter? Even in death Gino continued to torment her.

5 𓃾𓃾𓃾𓃾𓃾𓃾𓃾𓃾𓃾𓃾𓃾𓃾𓃾𓃾𓃾𓃾𓃾𓃾𓃾𓃾𓃾𓃾𓃾𓃾𓃾𓃾

BY THE time Fernanda and Johnny returned to the hotel Vanda Petrus was back as well, bringing with her a cheap suitcase containing things for her stay with Beth.

Fernanda tapped on Dorcas's door to ask if she had found everything in order, and across the hall Johnny came to his own door to hear her answer.

"I suppose it's all right," Dorcas said. "I'm not really sure."

Let them make of that what they pleased!

Fernanda cocked an eyebrow at Johnny and he grinned. Dorcas knew they were silently agreeing that their notions about her behavior that morning had been correct. She did not mind so much now. There was more justification for her concern than they knew.

Fernanda suggested that they go out for lunch. Mrs. Petrus and Beth were to come to the Roses with them for this meal. Dinner would be too late for Beth, and she explained that an arrangement had been made at the hotel so that Vanda might fix a simple supper for herself and the child in the hotel's small, unofficial kitchen. Again all had been arranged without consulting Beth's mother.

Johnny drove them the few blocks to the Hotel des Roses because Fernanda had put on high heels and would not walk. The hotel stood on the water front, with its own private beach—an unadorned monster of a palace built of the yellow stone of Rhodes. Foursquare and solid it loomed, guarded by an iron fence and iron gateway. Into a block of stone beside the doorway was carved the Rose of Rhodes.

A "rose," Fernanda said, that was probably a hibiscus— that most ubiquitous flower of the island, and one the shape in the stone more nearly resembled.

Inside, the halls and salons were old-fashioned and high-ceilinged, giving evidence of an elegant past. The dining room had been divided into two sections, one separate and enclosed, the other open to a terrace that fronted on the sea. Since the day was reasonably balmy, they chose to sit in the open. A head waiter led them to a table which Fernanda promptly rejected, indicating a spot she regarded as choicer. Wisely, the head waiter gave in.

A chair suitable for Beth was brought, and Vanda pinned a napkin around her neck. It was clear that Beth and Vanda were on excellent terms by now, but also that the child was faintly in awe of the Greek woman who had become her nurse.

Just as Vanda was about to seat herself at the round table next to Beth, something strange happened. She hesitated with her hands on the back of her chair, looking toward the dining-room entrance where the head waiter was ushering in a party of three. Suddenly she bent toward Fernanda.

"If you please, madame, I have forgotten something. Something of importance. You will forgive if I do not have luncheon with you now. I will be at the hotel when you return."

She did not wait for Fernanda's assent, and she made no apology to Beth's mother. With her strong, graceful walk,

[94]

she slipped through the room in the direction of the terrace and disappeared outside.

"My goodness, that was sudden!" Fernanda said.

Dorcas was staring at the two women who had just entered the dining room, accompanied by a man. The head waiter was showing the three considerable attention.

"I think she ran away," Dorcas said quietly. "I think she didn't want to be seen by those people who are coming in."

Fernanda looked around as the three moved toward a table. The man was middle-aged and undistinguished in appearance. One of the women, his wife apparently, was dumpy and without elegance. Once one had noted the third of the party the first two were forgotten. This woman came into the dining room with the air of someone who knew that every eye would be upon her and every deference paid her. She was well into middle age, but still beautiful. Her large dark eyes, so typical among Greek women, were lustrous and flashing as she gazed about the room. Her nose was perfectly sculptured, her mouth strong in its modeling. She carried her dark head high, the long hair wound into a coil in the fashion of old Greece. Her black frock spoke of fashion and wealth, as did her jewels. Large links of heavy gold placed a gold locket upon her decidedly majestic breast. There was a gleam of diamonds in its setting and on her hands. She was a large woman, with the frame to carry her weight.

"Medea," Johnny murmured softly.

He was right, Dorcas thought. This was a face made for high tragedy in the Greek manner. There was little humor to lighten it.

The woman had paused beside her companions, accepting with accomplished poise the looks turned her way. She swept the room with a glance that missed nothing, bowing gravely

[95]

here and there to an acquaintance. Fernanda, who always gave her curiosity full rein, remained turned in her chair to watch this grand entrance. The woman's glance fell upon her and the dark, dramatic eyes lighted with recognition. She gestured her companions toward the table where waiters had sprung to attention. Then she came straight across the room to Fernanda and held out a cordial hand.

"You are Miss Farrar, yes? The picture of you in the paper is very like. I am Madame Katalonos. You will do me the great honor by coming to tea at my house on the day after next."

"I am delighted, of course," Fernanda said, and gave Xenia Katalonos her warmest smile. "It is very kind of you."

She introduced Dorcas and Johnny, who had risen, but the woman seemed hardly aware of them except for a brief acknowledgment. All her attention was for Fernanda, and there was an intensity in her look that seemed out of proportion to the cause.

"I will send my car for you at four o'clock," Madame Katalonos said. "This will be my great pleasure. You will excuse me now?"

She swept away, and Fernanda turned back to the table. "Now there, if ever I saw one," she murmured with interest, "is a woman who wants something."

Johnny nodded as he sat down. "She ought to be good for a whole chapter in her own right."

A waiter who hovered waiting for their orders promptly offered information with typical Greek informality. "Madame Xenia is famous actress long time back. She marries man who is very rich and it is the loss of Greece that she leaves our theater. Very sad, her life. First husband drowns from yacht in a storm. Now it is supposed second husband is also dead. Very sad."

This would explain the mark of tragedy in the woman's face, in her eyes. That she had been an actress came as no surprise—her very manner of crossing a room betrayed the fact. The question still remained as to why Vanda Petrus had fled when Madame Katalonos entered the dining room. All through lunch the question remained at the back of Dorcas's mind. It might be interesting to pursue a few questions of her own where Mrs. Petrus was concerned—and when Fernanda was not present to discount them.

During lunch Fernanda bubbled over to Dorcas about her visit that morning to the Palace of the Grand Master. It might be that the restoration was not in the best of taste, and one suspected that the knights would have lived more simply. But it was certainly gorgeous, from the handsome floors to the elaborate hangings and furniture.

"The structure itself is magnificent," she said. "And what a view of the town from its windows! It might make quite a story if someone got locked into the place after dark and had to spend the night with all those ghosts."

Johnny shook his head. "They'd be recent Italian ghosts. The notion isn't up to your usual standards, Fernanda."

"Maybe you're right," Fernanda admitted. "I'll undoubtedly think of something better."

When they returned to the hotel, Dorcas, Beth, and Fernanda went upstairs together. Dorcas suggested transcribing Fernanda's notes and putting down a record of the morning's experiences while they were still fresh in her mind.

"I'm pretty good at dictation," she told Fernanda. "If you want to talk a bit about the Palace or anything else, perhaps I can help by getting down your impressions."

[97]

Fernanda shook her head. "Let it wait till tomorrow, dear. I know you need to rest and recover your strength. You were pretty upset this morning and I don't want to tax you needlessly."

"I'd rather get to work," Dorcas said. "I'm reserving judgment about Mrs. Petrus, but that has nothing to do with my working."

They had reached the third-floor hall and Fernanda stopped before her door. "Thank you, my dear, but I'm going to do as the Greeks do and have a long nap. I'm sure that's the way they manage to keep such late hours. I advise you to do the same. Johnny's going to drive me downtown later this afternoon for an official appointment. So the afternoon is yours."

She went into her room and Dorcas opened her own door, suppressing a slight irritation. She had behaved badly and Fernanda's attitude was understandable to some extent, but still she didn't want to be pampered.

In the room Vanda awaited them calmly. She offered no explanation for her precipitate flight, and whether she had managed to have lunch or not she did not state. The closed look on her face did not encourage questioning. Nevertheless, Dorcas meant to ask questions when the opportunity offered. A plan was beginning to form in her mind.

It was not, after all, hard to accept the period of rest. Beth and she fell asleep quickly in the quiet, shadowed room. Whether or not Vanda slept in her adjoining room beyond the closed door there was no knowing. She was very quiet. Dorcas could imagine her sitting there in silence, guarded and alert— waiting. The picture was not a reassuring one.

Beth awakened first, and when she called to her mother, Dorcas got up feeling fresh and rested. She dressed quickly and then helped Beth into corduroy overalls and sweater.

Vanda heard them moving and tapped at the door. "Miss Farrar tells me I am to take Beth for the rest of the afternoon. So that you may rest."

"I don't need to rest any longer," Dorcas said. She wanted to make it clear that she and Beth were not governed solely by Fernanda. "I'd like to go for a walk. Perhaps you can show us something of the neighborhood. Is there a park nearby?"

The woman considered. "There is a place. I will show you."

Dorcas opened her handbag to make sure of passport and money, then swung the strap over her shoulder. It was good to feel the firm slap of the bag against her hip as they went downstairs. The letter was there. No one had touched it while she slept.

Outside, Vanda took Beth's hand as a matter of course. They turned into one of the narrow streets that wound irregularly through this "new" part of Rhodes. While this was not the "old city," it was no longer as young as the word "new" implied. The houses were large and old-fashioned, unlike the bright little cube houses of modern Rhodes, whose white exteriors were inset with splashes of color. Such houses had spread out upon the hillsides and into suburbs along the sea. But here there were old gardens and the pleasant insistence of flowers that one felt everywhere in Greece. A woman with a bouquet in her arms passed them on the sidewalk. A young gardener worked beyond a low wall with a red blossom stuck jauntily behind one ear.

Vanda led the way toward a gate that opened into a parklike area where thick clumps of rhododendron grew, and an even deeper thicket of blooming oleanders. Beyond, a wide empty space of earth and sparse grass opened beneath tall eucalyptus trees. Nearby was a small enclosure of headstones.

[99]

"This place is Turkish cemetery," Vanda said. "They do not mind if we come inside. Is very old, very quiet."

The narrow headstones tipped crazily now, though once they had all faced neatly toward Mecca. They were set close together and each was topped with a marble turban. It was indeed quiet here beside the stones, with only the faint crunching of leaves beneath their feet to break the afternoon stillness. Vanda spoke softly as she showed Beth that the shape and size of each turban indicated the importance of the man who was buried there.

As she stood listening, Dorcas could hear the sound of waves rolling in on a stony beach not far away—the rush and the sucking back, the rush again, endlessly. Overhead a constant wind blew through the treetops and sent leaves, like neatly turned new moons, drifting down upon them. There was peace here as well as quiet, the sounds of living all gently removed from this grove. She wanted to give herself to the enveloping peace, to think of nothing that would disturb or distress. But she had come with Vanda for a reason and she could not yet relax her watchfulness.

Beth ran about contentedly, picking up small stones and leaves, busy with her own make-believe. Dorcas sat cross-legged on the grassy earth and thought of the questions she wanted to ask Vanda. Leaning against the gray, peeling trunk of a eucalyptus, the woman waited in silence as though she sensed purpose in their being here.

When the first question came, Dorcas gave it no preliminary softening. "Why did you run away from the hotel dining room today?" she asked bluntly.

The words and movements of Vanda Petrus were always deliberate. Even when she had fled from the Hotel des Roses, she had moved with smooth certainty. Now her face was as somber and aloof in its expression as ever and she did not answer quickly. When she spoke, her tone was unhurried, cool.

"There is a woman I do not like. When she comes into the dining room—I go. She does not like me. It is better if we do not meet."

"Madame Katalonos?" Dorcas asked.

There was a hint of surprise in Vanda's eyes. "You know this woman?"

"She came to our table and introduced herself to Miss Farrar," Dorcas said. "We are to have tea with her day after tomorrow."

Vanda absorbed this information, considering it well before she spoke. "She wishes something if she does this," she said finally. "It is better that you watch."

"She's interested in what Miss Farrar will write about Rhodes," Dorcas explained. "She has offered to help in any way she can."

Vanda said nothing.

"Was she really a famous actress? That's what the waiter at the hotel told us."

"She is a woman of Rhodes, and Rhodians are proud of their own," said Vanda with a shrug. "She is more famous after she marries rich husband."

"Was her second husband rich, too?" Dorcas asked.

The faintest animation stirred in Vanda's face. She held out strong, hard-working hands. "Constantine Katalonos is rich—he has these. Only these. But that can be enough—if Madame Xenia does not swallow him up to feed her own ambition."

"Does not?" Dorcas echoed. "I understand that he is dead."

Vanda's eyes flashed sudden startling scorn. "This is what Madame tells to all. She does not want to tell that her

[101]

husband runs away. She puts about him chains and walls. She says, 'Do this, do that.' She tells that it is for the glory of Greece, for her beloved Rhodes. Through Constantine she will bring back the great art of Greece. She eats him—his talent dies."

"What is his talent?" Dorcas asked.

Vanda made a motion of modeling with her strong hands, as if she shaped clay in the air. "He is greatest sculptor in Greece. But no one knows because she swallows him whole. She kills what is in him to do." Vanda's hands came together sharply, flattening the air between them. "One time he makes a head of me. He would pay for me to come to model, but I do this for nothing because he is very great man. Madame Xenia does not like what he does. This head she does not permit to be shown in Athens exhibit. He marries her for freedom to work. She gives him only prison."

Dorcas listened in some astonishment. She had suspected that there might be banked fires behind Vanda Petrus's careful lack of expression. She had not expected to find them burning so angrily hot, but now that she had sensed this heat, she wanted to keep the woman talking.

"Then you believe he's not dead, but has only run away?"

Vanda let her hands fall back against the tree trunk. Her guard was up again. She pushed herself from the tree and went to Beth.

"No—this you do not eat," she said, and withdrew the eucalyptus leaf Beth was nibbling experimentally.

The chance to probe further was gone. All Vanda's attention was now for Beth and it seemed affectionate, as if she had already given something of herself to the child. She looked up from wiping Beth's mouth and hands and saw

Dorcas watching her. Her gaze did not fall, and there was in it a smoldering of anger.

"Once I have daughter—small like this. It is in time of war. We live in the north, where my husband works our small farm. Petrus is not a Greek name, but my husband's mother was Greek and he grew up a Greek. The bandits take my babies— my son, my daughter. They take across border into Bulgaria. My husband they shoot."

She spoke almost defiantly, and Dorcas heard her in shocked dismay. She knew of the thousands of Greeks who had lost their children to the Communists and had never seen them again, but this angry revelation brought home the sharp horror of that massive kidnaping.

"I can feel what you tell me," Dorcas said sorrowfully, touching a hand to her heart. "I can feel it inside me here."

"I do not ask others to suffer for me," Vanda said coldly. "This is not yours to suffer. You have husband. You have child."

"I have no husband," Dorcas said. "Didn't Miss Farrar tell you that I am a widow?"

"She tells me—yes," said Vanda. "Your husband is dead only two months. You are not like the widows of Greece."

She was not like any other widow, Dorcas thought. How could she pretend to grieve for Gino? There was no answer she could make this woman in the face of her veiled contempt.

She stood up and brushed leaves and earth from her skirt. "Let's go back to the hotel. Perhaps Miss Farrar will want me when she returns from her appointment. I'm glad you told me about Madame Katalonos. This may be helpful when we go to see her."

Vanda held out a hand to Beth, who came readily to take it. As they walked through the quiet, shaded grounds of the old cemetery, Vanda returned voluntarily to the subject that seemed to interest her most—Constantine Katalonos.

"You will see a painting of Madame Katalonos's husband in that house. It is very much like him. Always he laughs. He likes to be happy, to be gay. But that woman—she spoils all this. She makes it so he cannot laugh."

Expressively Vanda drew down her dark brows, drew down the corners of her mouth to show how Constantine's wife chose to look. It was the mask of tragedy to perfection, and Dorcas smiled.

"Yes, she looked like that today at the Roses. Very dramatic and—and overwhelming. I can imagine that she might be good at smothering those around her."

For once Vanda was in agreement with something Dorcas had said. She appeared to like the word "smothering" and muttered it once or twice as they walked along. Just before they reached the hotel, Dorcas remembered the unsatisfactory answer she'd had from the desk clerk on the subject of her search. Vanda might know more than he did.

"Tell me," she said, "do you know of a woman—a Greek woman—who has come here from America within the last year? Her name is Mrs. Markos Dimitriou."

Vanda seemed to deliberate guardedly. "There are many called by that name. I do not know. You are looking for her?"

"Yes," Dorcas said, "I'm looking for a woman by that name. It's very important that I find her."

"I will ask," said Vanda.

They reached the hotel just as Fernanda's car drew up to the curb. Johnny was nowhere in sight and Fernanda sat at the wheel. She beckoned to Dorcas with a conspirator's air. Vanda took Beth up the steps and Dorcas went to the car door.

"From the moment I saw them, I knew I had to take one

home!" Fernanda announced triumphantly. "I sent Johnny on an errand to get him out of the way because I was afraid he'd try to stop me. And I went into your room from our balcony and borrowed that canvas bag you use for Beth's toys. I hope you don't mind."

"I don't mind, but what are you talking about?"

Fernanda gestured toward the back of the car. "Open the door and look. I'm really pleased with myself."

Dorcas did as she was bidden. Beth's strong canvas bag sat on the floor of the car, its sides bulging, its mouth zippered shut.

"Look inside," Fernanda urged. "Go ahead and open it."

Dorcas slid the zipper back and spread open the top of the bag. The moment she touched it, she knew. The thing inside was hard and cold and rough to her touch.

"You've stolen one of the catapult balls," she accused.

Fernanda laughed. "In broad daylight, too! Believe me, those things are heavy, even though I picked one of the smaller ones. No one paid the slightest attention. Of course I chose one that was outdoors and in a convenient place. I simply rolled it into the bag and carried it to the car."

Fernanda looked thoroughly smug and pleased with herself.

"Johnny will make you put it back," Dorcas said. "You'll land us all in jail and there'll be an international incident. What are you going to do—take it up to your room? Keep it in a hatbox, perhaps?"

"And have the maids report me? No, indeed. I'll leave it right where it is. Johnny never rides in the back seat. I'll drape this old jacket of mine over the bag and he'll never notice it."

"How are you going to get a thing like that through customs and out of the country?" Dorcas asked. "What do you want it for, anyway?"

[105]

Fernanda took the key from the ignition and got out of the car. "I'll think of something," she said, joining Dorcas on the sidewalk. "It's not as if it were really valuable. Those balls are all over the place. There must be hundreds of them. It will make a lovely doorstop at home."

"Perhaps the authorities would give you one if you asked," Dorcas suggested.

"And spoil my story?" Fernanda was indignant. "Don't you dare tell Johnny—" She broke off, looking up at Beth and Vanda on the terrace above. "Beth seems to have made a friend."

Beth knelt on the flagged terrace petting a yellow tiger cat, while Vanda stood by without objection. The look on the Greek woman's face arrested Dorcas's attention. It was a soft, mothering look—almost a look of possession, as though Beth had begun to belong to Vanda Petrus.

The pang Dorcas felt took her by surprise. Intent upon Vanda, she ran up the flight of steps with a suddenness that frightened the cat. It scratched at Beth, escaped from her grasp, and sprang from the terrace to scoot off down the street.

Angrily, Beth held out her scratched arm for Dorcas to see. "You scared the cat away!" she accused. "It wouldn't have hurt me if you hadn't scared it like that."

At once Vanda knelt beside the little girl, tenderly examining the faint oozing of blood. Her eyes when she looked up at Dorcas were as resentful and accusing as Beth's.

Fernanda had seen the incident. She came up the steps, speaking with authority to Vanda.

"There's a bottle of antiseptic in my medicine bag. Take Beth upstairs and fix that scratch. Here's the key."

Beth had begun to cry, more in frustration over loss of the cat than because of any hurt. She allowed Vanda to pick her up and carry her away without a backward glance for her mother.

"I could have taken care of the scratch," Dorcas said.

Fernanda ignored her protest. "You've got to stop this. I can understand these upsets of yours, but you mustn't let them disturb Beth. This is something I won't have."

"You won't have?" Dorcas flung the words back in a challenge. "Sometimes I think you forget that Beth is my daughter."

All Fernanda's easy good nature had fallen away. The determination that could drive and govern her was in the set of her chin, in the far from guileless look in her eyes.

"That you're Beth's mother is something I never forget," she said. "I hope you'll not make me regret the fact. Gino isn't here to watch over her, but I have a responsibility to Beth."

The thing Dorcas had feared was in the open. The threat she had more than once been aware of in Fernanda had been put into words.

But even as she recognized it, the other woman softened. "I'm sorry if I was sharp, Dorcas. But you must get yourself in hand. You mustn't be the sort of mother who is bad for her own child. If you hadn't rushed up the steps just now without a particle of forethought, nothing would have happened. You behaved as though you were jealous of Vanda's liking for Beth. And that won't do. Now let's forget it. I'll take you up on your offer to do some work for me this afternoon. Perhaps what you need is more to occupy you and take your thoughts off yourself."

Dorcas had to admit that there was justification in Fernanda's words. She had once more behaved without discipline or self-control, put on instinctive guard by the look

[107]

on Vanda's face, and responding with the single desire to break up that scene.

She followed Fernanda upstairs and for the rest of the afternoon worked on the portable typewriter in Fernanda's room. There were copious scribbled notes to set in order, and the adding of her own impressions that Fernanda felt would be useful later. Vanda was sent out for a walk with Beth and there was an obvious effort on the part of both women to keep the child away from her mother.

In a sense the work for Fernanda was calming, yet Dorcas could not give her entire mind to it. At the back of her thoughts questions grew insistently.

Was Fernanda the wise, sensible one, the balance Beth needed against the emotional vagaries of her own mother? Or was Fernanda's blind determination so bent on separating Dorcas from Beth that she was ready to seize upon any excuse that came her way?

Once, when Fernanda went out and left her alone at the typewriter, Dorcas rested her elbows on the keys and pressed her face into her hands. No one else could help her in this. She must help herself. She must stop leaping in fright at every shadow. That was Gino's influence upon her reaching out from the past. She must learn to distinguish the real from the unreal. She must recognize where danger might truly lie, and where the threat was only part of her own lively and fearful imagination.

There was no good reason as yet not to accept Vanda's interest in Beth and he grateful for it. The woman had suffered terribly in the past. The very sight of other women's children must prod old wounds she carried. It was to her credit that she could give affection to a child not her own and from whom she must be parted before long.

This was the only reasonable attitude, Dorcas told herself. There was nothing wrong with her ability to reason and she must give Fernanda no further excuse for taking over with Beth.

Her fingers busied themselves on the typewriter keys and she forced her attention upon Fernanda's notes. Yet at the back of her mind voices whispered, accusing, defending, and would not be quiet. The old voices of self-doubt.

6

THAT EVENING when she went out to a late dinner with Fernanda and Johnny, nothing more was said about what had happened. Fernanda was full of a gay account of her first encounter with officialdom. Apparently the Greeks were proving themselves a match for Fernanda and could themselves take off down some pretty unexpected roads.

It was ten-thirty by the time they returned to the hotel and Dorcas went directly to her room. Beth lay asleep and the room was dark except for a shaft of light coming through the adjoining door to Vanda's room. Dorcas looked in to say she was home and found the woman sitting in a straight chair with her hands in her lap, her eyes staring into space. She recognized Dorcas's presence with a start and said good night to her gravely. Dorcas closed the door between the two rooms, suppressing an urge to lock it.

When she had turned on a lamp, she stood beside Beth's bed, looking down at the sleeping child. One young arm had been thrust above the covers and to Dorcas's touch its soft flesh was warm with sleep. Beth's lips were parted, the other hand curved beneath her cheek. The sight of her sleeping daughter was heart turning. She covered the exposed arm and knelt beside the bed, studying with love the delicate contours, the fine soft tendrils of dark hair. She wanted so much for Beth. She had to make up to her for so many things. She could not afford to fail. Not Fernanda or anyone else could do more for the child than she—granted wisdom and balance and a healthy mind. For Beth's sake she must find in herself all these things.

Later, when she was in her nightgown and had switched off the lamp, she stood for a few moments in the balcony door. The quarter moon had risen and the mountains of Anatolia looked black against the deep dark blue of the sky. The Aegean was faintly gilded, its surface aswell with moving light. Across intervening roofs came the usual soft rush of wind and always the sound of the sea washing over pebbled beaches.

There were few sounds from the hotel. It was early for the tourist season and the rooms were not yet full. This was a quiet, residential street, with little traffic. Lights gleamed and vanished and gleamed again among trees ruffled by the wind. Somewhere a voice was raised in a minor key that cried of heart's loneliness. A song that must surely have its origin in the Orient—a heritage of Turkey's four hundred years in the isle of Rhodes.

She turned at last from the cool touch of the wind, purposefully leaving the balcony doors ajar. Chalk marks on a rail had meant nothing and she must begin at once to prove her ability to distinguish between reality and foolish make-believe. She slipped between the covers gratefully, feeling more at peace with herself than she had in a long while.

When she fell asleep she did not know, or when the moon

rose high and bright and the narrow light pattern from the balcony doors widened, spreading a bar of gold across the floor. She awakened with a start that set her heart thudding and knew that the pattern of light and shadow in the room had changed disturbingly. The sense of peace was gone.

She sat up in bed and stared at the double doors of the balcony. Where she had left the aperture narrow, it was flung wide. Both doors stood open. The open half at the foot of her bed blocked her view of the balcony, but she could see the expanse of floor where a long shadow stretched part way across the room—a shadow that wore the shape of a human figure.

She cried out in soft terror and there was movement at once. The shadow vanished and the band of moonlight lay unmarred upon the floor. Thinking only of danger to Beth, she slipped out of bed and ran barefooted to the balcony. There was no one before the door, and she dared not step outside. She slammed the doors shut and fastened the catch with fingers that fumbled clumsily. Then she ran to the door into Vanda's room and pulled it open without knocking.

The woman sat up in bed as Dorcas called her name, reaching at once for the switch on the bed table lamp. She seemed wide-awake and completely alert as she got out of bed in her coarse, old-fashioned nightgown. She brought her own flannel robe to wrap about Dorcas's bare shoulders.

"What is it, madame? What has happened?" she asked.

Dorcas could scarcely still the chattering of her teeth. "There was s-s-someone on the balcony. A man, I think. He'd opened the doors into my room. He was going to come in when I woke up and frightened him away."

Vanda did not hesitate. She went at once to her own closed balcony doors, pulled them open, and stepped outside.

"There is no one," she said. "It is a dream, perhaps."

Dorcas did not wait to answer her. "Stay with Beth!" she ordered, and ran into the hall from Vanda's room. There had been someone on the balcony—someone who meant her harm.

The hall was empty, but she went to the door of Johnny's room and rapped. He came sleepily to open it, and she told him in a breathless whisper what had happened. At once he did as Vanda had done. He ran through Vanda's open door and out upon the balcony. Then he stepped to the portion of balcony opposite Fernanda's room and called to her softly. She answered at once, and a moment later she had come along the narrow gallery and through into Vanda's room. She was enveloped in layers of blue nylon in a matching gown and peignoir, her face aglow with cream, her hair bound in a silken net that tied under her chin.

As always, Fernanda's enormous vitality was instantly alive. She tooked charge with hardly a pause for questions. After a quick look into Dorcas's room, where Beth lay asleep and Vanda, a tall, thin figure in her long nightgown, stood guard beside the child's bed, she motioned to Dorcas to sit down in the one comfortable chair in Vanda's room. She took the straight one, and Johnny, in pajamas, and as barefooted as Dorcas, stood beside Fernanda, watching.

"Tell me just what you think you saw," Fernanda said.

"There was someone on the balcony outside the doors to my room," Dorcas repeated. "It could have been either a man or a woman, but I think it was a man."

"What do you mean—could have been either? Did you see this person? Don't you know how he looked?"

"I only saw his shadow," Dorcas said. "I left my doors almost closed, and when I awakened they were wide open and there was a shadow across the floor."

Fernanda and Johnny exchanged a look. Fernanda went to Vanda's balcony doors and set them ajar. In a few moments the wind had blown them wide open.

"There was a shadow," Dorcas said, and her voice trembled into an indignant quaver. "I didn't dream this. I saw the shadow of whoever was out on that balcony. I think he was coming into my room."

Fernanda sighed. "If there was someone there, where could he have gone? He's not out there now."

"Through one of the other rooms, I suppose," Dorcas said. "There are probably empty rooms through which he could have escaped. Perhaps he's hiding in one of them now."

"Would you like me to call the desk clerk and have all the rooms on the balcony side searched?" Fernanda asked with an edge of exasperation in her voice. "We've probably waked half the hotel by now, so we might as well wake the other half."

Dorcas looked at Johnny and saw pity in his eyes. He was not impatient with her now, but merely pitying in his disbelief. None of them believed her. Not Johnny Orion, or Fernanda, or even Vanda Petrus, who had come to the adjoining door to listen and add her own attitude of doubt to the feeling in the room. There was an almost tangible reproach in the air, a rejection of her claims. This same feeling had been in evidence so many times at the nursing home where Gino had sent her. Then the only way to allay it had been to pretend surrender. Pretend that reality was not real, that the things she knew and believed had no validity. But this was Rhodes. This was Greece. Her new life was to be born here and she would not give in to this coercion of disbelief that tried to force her in a false direction.

"If I hadn't cried out, he would have come into the room,"

[115]

she repeated stubbornly. "If I hadn't awakened, I don't know what would have happened."

"But you did awaken and everything's all right," Johnny said.

Fernanda shook her head. "There's no use trying to reassure her when she gets into one of these tizzies. They were common when she was ill. Gino often told me about them."

Dorcas put her hands over her face and held herself very still, very quiet. She tightened the very muscles of her stomach to keep them from quivering, and planted her two feet firmly on the floor, pressing down hard. She must not lash out in frustration. She breathed deeply, long, slow breaths, until the quivering died and the impulse to fling futile, angry words at them subsided. She was under control again.

Johnny came to her and drew her hands from before her face. She saw in his eyes that same pity that she would not accept, had no use for. He put a hand beneath her chin to tilt up her head, and she winced away from his touch in sudden revulsion. Her very skin remembered the touch of Gino's hand in just such a gesture, and her rejection was instinctive.

Johnny drew back his hand at once. "I'm sorry," he said, his tone cool.

She could not explain that her revulsion had not been for him. Always that gesture had been a prelude to a mockery of love and the beginning of shame and terror.

"If it would help," Johnny said, "I could fix a bed for myself on the balcony outside your room. Would you feel better if someone was there?"

He was treating her like a child who'd had a bad dream and she shook her head firmly. "I'll be all right. I'm sorry I disturbed everyone."

"That's a good girl," said Fernanda with a sigh of relief.

[116]

"Lock yourself in and never mind the fresh air. It was probably the sense of that open door that upset you."

Vanda returned silently to her room and Fernanda to hers. Johnny checked the clasp on the balcony doors and saw them secured before he went across the hall to his own room. When Dorcas had locked the hall door after Johnny, she went to Vanda's door and turned the key. Then she hurried to pull out the bureau drawer where she had left her handbag. Swiftly she opened it and felt for her passport case. The folded envelope and the letter within were still in their hiding place.

She bent over Beth for a moment, listening to her soft breathing. Then she got into bed and pulled up the covers. She was shivering again but she could not help it.

If only Johnny believed. If only he had not been sorry for her—sorry and unconvinced. She would rather have his impatience than his pity. Impatience meant he thought her capable of control. Pity told her he was looking at someone ill and helpless.

When she fell asleep at last, it was to struggle against some smothering dream that she could not remember in detail when she awoke. She knew only that she dreamed of weeping and that there had been a voice speaking to her, words that commanded. "Give up the letter! Give up the letter!" the voice had said over and over.

She awoke drenched in cold perspiration, the words repeating themselves in her mind. To whom was she to give up the letter? Perhaps she had only to leave it upon her dressing table when she went out of the room in the morning. Leave it there until the hidden watchers found it and took it away. Then they would leave her in peace and there need be no more dreams of weeping.

The light of a bright gold dawn pressed against the balcony

shutters and she lay quietly watching it. The sense of nightmare began to fade, and courage seeped back with the coming of the sun. What had happened last night had been real enough. She, at least, knew that, even though no one else believed her.

She arose to watch the day breaking over Grecian sea and Turkish mountains. Beth got up early, too, and Vanda. When it was time to go downstairs for breakfast, Dorcas flung the strap of her handbag over her shoulder and did not leave the letter behind.

The morning began without hurry. Except to ask how she felt, no one mentioned the occurrence of the night before and Dorcas kept her own counsel. If Fernanda watched her now and then, she pretended not to see. Johnny made no further gestures of sympathy. He behaved with something of the reserve that had begun with the mention of Gino's name.

During the morning he drove Fernanda around Rhodes, while Dorcas sat in the back seat, her feet upon the catapult ball in its canvas bag. They visited Rodini Park, then followed the road that wound up Monte Smith—that hill above the town which had been named for a British naval officer. Here stood the broken columns and chunks of fallen stone that had once been the Acropolis of Rhodes. There was a hippodrome where games had been played, too fully rebuilt to preserve a sense of ancient activity.

During the morning's drive Dorcas strove to put all worry about Beth and Vanda from her mind. Today her emphasis must be upon balance and calm self-possession. Not by the slightest degree must she edge toward the distraught state in which Fernanda and Johnny had seen her more than once yesterday. She could not confide, where she would meet only disbelief, but she could resist being treated like an invalid.

Tomorrow she and Fernanda would have tea with Madame Katalonos and she would ask again about the wife of Markos Dimitriou. If Markos had lived until his wife got to the hospital, if he had seen the face of the man driving the car which cut him down, he would have spoken. Even though the chance was not certain, there was the real possibility that Mrs. Dimitriou would know something. And when the truth was known, then Dorcas would have, not only reassurance about herself, but a weapon to use against Fernanda if it became necessary. If Fernanda tried to take Beth away from her, she would cease to protect her from the truth about Gino. What had happened yesterday had indicated that it might be necessary to fight not only for her own well-being and sanity, but for Beth as well. She would not have Beth placed in the same hands that had raised Gino to what he had become. Yet she knew the trouble Fernanda would make if she tried to remove Beth from her entirely.

On Monte Smith they stood between the columns and looked down upon the town of Rhodes. From here the very quality of the old city was visible, packed as it was within climbing, wandering walls, its rooftops and chimneys crowded together in so tight a maze one could hardly mark the narrow streets twisting between. Here and there the domes and needles of mosque and minaret broke the line of flat roofs. The Turkish occupation had endured until fairly recent times and the mark of the sultans and of Turkish culture was everywhere. There was still a considerable population of Turks living rather reservedly among the exuberant Greeks they had never been able to assimilate.

Outside the Gothic walled city lay the newer Rhodes, more spaciously set among its trees and gardens, with wide avenues and modern civic buildings. Rimming all, beyond the harbor, lay the deeply blue Aegean.

Fernanda wrote off the ruins on Monte Smith with a careless wave of her hand. "This isn't one of the really important places. There's not much left here, and even less at Iyalisos, I understand. It's Camiros and Lindos I want to see. We must arrange a drive to Camiros soon, Johnny."

Johnny had begun whistling plaintively as he stared at the crowded town at their feet. He nodded without answering, and Dorcas wondered what he was thinking. Once this place had been tremendously alive. Fine sculpture had stood on every hand, crowning a city so great that the three older ones had lost their eminence and power and given way to Rhodes.

They left the heights because Fernanda wanted to be on the move and antiquity meant little to her.

Later, during the quiet, warm hours of midday when Rhodes went to sleep, Dorcas found herself unable to rest. When Beth was in bed for her nap and Vanda in the next room, she went idly downstairs in order to move about, feeling as restless as Fernanda.

Outside, it was as if an enchantment lay upon the town. The streets were empty, the market stalls closed, the stores locked and deserted. Nothing stirred. She walked about for a little while then returned to the hotel. Johnny Orion was the only occupant in the lobby. He sat at a table writing a letter. When he saw her, he looked up and beckoned.

"Come and sit down. You've been out in the terrors of noon, I see."

She seated herself somewhat hesitantly and rested her arms on the table between them. She was never sure what she might expect from Johnny. If he was going to be either critical or pitying, she wanted none of his company.

"What do you mean—terrors of noon?" she asked.

"Greeks are never afraid of moonlight or the hours after midnight," he said. "Pan—he's known as a Kaous in Rhodes —and the local nereides choose the hour when the sun is high for their mischief. It's safer to be inside and asleep at that time. Did you know that if you meet a nereid in the sunlight you may lose your power of speech forever? It's well known in every village that this is what has happened to the addled and foolish."

She found herself catching up his last words. "Fernanda thinks I am addled and foolish, though I've met no nereids at noonday. And you thought so, too, last night."

"But you've recovered," he said, not denying her words.

She shook her head. "No—I'm just growing a little stronger every day. I'll learn to dissemble properly in time. But I can't manage it yet. Johnny, there was someone on the balcony last night. There was a shadow."

"Clouds cast shadows," he said. "They can fool you. Don't think about it any more."

There was no reaching him, but today she did not mind so much. With a sense of returning strength, she felt more confident. She must not go on being fearful. If she showed the watchers a bold and indifferent front, they would think she knew of no letter and they would let her be.

"I'm keeping you from your writing," she said, and moved to rise.

He pushed the sheet of paper aside. "It can wait till later. It's to a boy who was in one of my classes back home."

She noted his frown. "A boy in trouble?"

"Maybe. That age can be a time for trouble when you get off on the wrong foot."

"Are you trying to counsel him?"

[121]

"Not exactly." His sudden grin was engaging. "I'm just giving him a little hell. If he trusts me enough, maybe he'll listen."

She found herself suddenly curious—not about the unknown boy, but about Johnny Orion.

"Where did you grow up?" she asked.

"In Chicago," he told her. "A pretty drab part of the West Side, I guess. Only I didn't know it was drab at the time. My father was a cop. A good one. He believed in an old-fashioned principle called responsibility and he believed in kids." Johnny smiled faintly, remembering.

"Tell me about him," Dorcas said.

"There's not much to tell. He did his job every day and in his free time he took on the kids around our neighborhood. He used to make me help him with them. What I didn't know was that he was helping me at the same time. He found things for us to do that we could believe were important. He set me talking to the kids who wouldn't open up with him. He was tough and kind and he believed in right and wrong without any confusion in his own mind. At the same time he knew that nobody was all good or all bad. It was a fine life for me. I didn't know about being underprivileged, though we never had much. I never thought about people not understanding me. He kept me too busy. Besides, we had a public library on the next block and that's where I began to find out about the world. That's where I first got interested in Greece. I've been reading and learning about it ever since. I didn't see why I shouldn't grow up and have a look at it. So here I am. Not very dramatic, I'm afraid."

"Those kids who wouldn't open up—could you do anything about them?"

"Sometimes. Pop was no psychiatrist. He thought there were

a few rotten apples. But he said you could never be sure, so you had to keep trying as long as you could. Not by coddling and easy-going. Many's the walloping he gave me, but it was always deserved, and the big thing was we knew he liked us and thought we could amount to something. I seem to carry no scars on my soul as a result."

"You're tough, too," she said. "Tough in a good way. I've felt it. You must be like him."

"Maybe," he said. "I'd like to be like him."

There was an unexpected easiness between them. Not harmony, exactly, not understanding, but at least a lack of strain.

"Orion?" She spoke the name aloud. "It sounds like a Greek name. Is it?"

He laughed. "It came to me by way of Ireland in the beginning. But it had a sojourn in South America and a few other places and there was a sea change. I like it this way."

"Orion was the hunter slain by jealous Artemis," Dorcas said. "I can't see you as a hunter. O'Ryan goes better with the color of your hair."

"I could hunt if I had to," he said.

Because there was easiness between them, she could ask him a question straight out—a question that brought them back to the present.

"What do you think of Vanda Petrus?"

He considered her words soberly. "Fernanda has told me her story. I expect we're seeing what's left of a broken woman. Some people fight back and save themselves no matter what happens. With others the vital thing inside dies before the body does. This woman seems like one of those."

"I'm not so sure," Dorcas said. "When she looks at Beth, she seems altogether alive. It frightens me a little."

"You worry too much," he said, and she winced from the words. She had opened herself to them and the sense of easiness was gone.

He glanced at his watch and folded the letter. "Things should be opening up soon. I'd better be on my way before Fernanda catches me."

"Catches you?"

The look of Ireland was in his eyes, bright with impudence. "I've got to find the proper parties and get permission for us to smuggle a stone catapult ball out of the country. Fernanda wants a story, not a scandal. There's a law against the removal of archaeological objects—which this might be considered."

"She told you?" Dorcas asked.

Johnny shook his head. "Not Fernanda. She thinks her secret is safe in that canvas bag. This morning I tossed my sweater into the back seat. When I went after it, I saw the bag and being the curious type I investigated. Fortunately, most Greeks have a sense of humor—unless you rub them the wrong way. I've got to make this a very funny story. Wish me luck."

She was laughing as she walked with him to the door. He went down the steps whistling cheerfully, and she suspected that he would make it a very good story indeed. It would be rather nice to have Johnny Orion on her side—not pitying, not disbelieving, not impatient.

7

AT FOUR o'clock the following afternoon Madame Katalonos's chauffeur arrived at the hotel to take them to her house for tea. For all his uniform and smart cap, the man who drove them had the look of a pirate about him, fierce mustachios and all. He spoke no English, but he had his orders and he could open a car door with a huge slab of a hand, making an impressive flourish. And he could drive three blocks like a madman.

The house where Xenia Katalonos lived was nearby—an old house, very large, with a high wall around the property and a well-cared-for garden within. The jingling bell at the gate was answered by a young Greek maid who came to show them in.

Paved walks led through the garden to the house, and the area immediately before the steps was paved with small black and white pebbles arranged in a neat Turkish design. Fernanda paused to admire the geometric pattern.

"Typical of Rhodes," she said. "Both the Turkish touch and the pebbles. Did you know that all those pebbles in the

Children's Fountain at the United Nations were gathered and sent there by the children of Rhodes?"

The maid, waiting politely, led them into the house and left them in a vast, high-ceilinged drawing room carpeted with an oriental rug, its rich colors softened by the years that had made it doubly precious. The furnishings were elegant, chosen with taste and an eye to the blending of soft, deep colors. A tall samovar of burnished copper had been placed upon a low brass-topped table drawn before a sofa of blue brocade.

Madame Xenia did not keep them waiting. She appeared in the doorway almost at once and flowed through it toward them. "Flowed" was the very word, Dorcas thought. Today she had discarded modern fashion for a long, drifting gown of blue and white that draped her fine figure to good effect and stirred gracefully about her knees as she moved. Dorcas remembered the name Johnny had given her. Today she was Medea to the hilt—the boldly shaped bones of her face, her flashing dark eyes and tragic mouth, the strength of will that charged and moved her, all bespoke Greek tragedy.

She greeted Fernanda with a strong clasp of the hand and bowed politely to Dorcas. There was no doubt as to which of the two she knew to be important.

"It is good of you to come, to give me your time," she said, gesturing them toward the sofa and flowing into a chair with the same grace that had marked her entry. "You must tell me all that you have seen, all that you have done. I wish to know everything—so I may help. It is my great regret that my husband is not here to greet you as well. Most unfortunately, he is away."

So that was how Constantine Katalonos's wife meant to play it, Dorcas thought. She was glad to be little noticed since this gave her a better opportunity to study their hostess and her surroundings.

The woman raised dark, handsome eyes to a place on the wall just out of Dorcas's view. "That is a portrait of my husband. A very fine likeness."

Remembering Vanda's words. Dorcas turned with interest to look at the picture that hung in a place of honor. Her first reaction was one of unpleasant shock. The striking, sardonic face of the portrait was urgently familiar. Yet she could not place it in her memory. It was an ageless face, though clearly Constantine had been younger than his wife. The artist had exaggerated the narrowness of the cheeks, emphasized the pointed chin. The eyes were an indefinable color beneath brows that lifted at the outer corners, and they looked at the observer with mocking intent. Surely she would remember such eyes if she had seen them before. It was a dreamer's face, as if the man knew some inner vision. The lips, both sensitive and sensual, smiled, but their expression was derisive, and somehow she knew it well.

Where could she have encountered this man that she should feel faintly ill at the sight of his picture? The sensation was physically disturbing, and she was appalled by her own intense reaction. There seemed so little cause. If she could feel ill at the mere sight of a picture, how was she to reject Fernanda's concern about her? She was beginning to dread these lapses into a state of anxiety she remembered all too well. They seemed to come without warning and to be prompted by anything, or nothing. Even by the picture of a stranger!

Madame Xenia sighed deeply and turned her attention to the samovar. The tea came scalding hot from the spout into glasses set on delicate china saucers adorned with small silver teaspoons. There was a sticky cake of honey and nuts, which their hostess announced she had made herself.

Dorcas sipped hot tea and tried to take strength from the brew as she listened to the two women.

"I am a very good cook," Madame Xenia admitted. "Sometimes I send the servants from my kitchen and make everything myself. Constantine, my husband, has said that no one in all Greece is a better cook than I. But when one talent is sacrificed, it is necessary to find another, yes?"

Fernanda praised the cake and told of their visit to the Hospital of the Knights, which was now a museum. Madame Xenia's interest quickened.

"I am something of a patroness of this museum. Too much has been lost of ancient Rhodes. We try now to preserve whatever we can. And of course there are new discoveries being made. Perhaps in my husband there is a rebirth of our ancient art. It has been my privilege to encourage and help him in his work. The creative artist is not always practical. Myself, I have a practical nature. I am very good for Constantine. I have done all—" She broke off, suddenly overcome by her own emotions.

Dorcas glanced again at the disturbingly familiar face of the man in the picture and thought of Vanda's hints that Constantine had run away from this wife who tried to "eat him up." What was the association that left this sickness of despair in the very pit of her stomach?

Fernanda was speaking of the three ancient cities she had yet to visit—Iyalisos, Camiros, and Lindos, and Dorcas tried to listen. Madame Xenia recovered her poise and spoke of these places with enthusiasm. Camiros had great beauty and was only a short drive from Rhodes. At Iyalisos the ruins were few, but the monastery of Philerimos was there, and an exceptional view. It was a place to which her husband was devoted. He went there often for inspiration. Again not too far from Rhodes. Lindos was a longer drive, but the most beautiful place in all Greece.

"Not even the Acropolis in Athens is more beautiful than the acropolis of Athena Lindia," Madame Xenia told them fervently. "In the village of Lindos I have a small house. It is yours whenever you wish to visit. You must not go and return the same day like a tourist. You must stay in my house and learn to know the beauty of Lindos."

Fernanda accepted with alacrity and Dorcas could see her mentally scooping up everything their hostess said. Xenia would be good for a story in her own right, as Johnny had suggested. Dorcas drank her tea in silence. At least the feeling of illness had passed. Indeed, her first sense of shocked recognition had begun to pass, and in the artist's interpretation she could now find nothing to alarm her. Yet the feeling had been there. Why?

When they had finished tea, their hostess rose. "You must see my husband's work," she announced. "I will be proud to show it to you. If you will wait one moment, please."

She swept out of the room to prepare the way for their pilgrimage and Dorcas seized the opportunity to follow the puzzle of the picture.

"Have you ever seen the man in that portrait before?" she asked Fernanda.

"Why—I don't think so," Fernanda said. "Though I'll admit he looks vaguely familiar."

They both regarded the portrait in silence for a moment and then Fernanda exclaimed aloud.

"Of course, dear! It's our old friend Pan. How could we mistake that face? You'll find him chasing reluctant maidens

[129]

around half the vases of old Greece. I can see why Madame X might worry about that one. Ssh—here she comes."

The man in the picture did look like Pan, Dorcas thought. Perhaps the artist had even stressed the resemblance. Yet she did not feel wholly satisfied. No mere interpretation of Pan would have the power to upset her like this. Her memory was of something real.

"If you will come with me, please," said Madame Xenia from the doorway.

The wide hallway had no rug to hide the highly polished luster of the floor. On a carved table near the foot of wide, uncarpeted stairs was a magnificent head of bronze. It was a little larger than life-size, the head of an old man with wide-set eyes, bushy eyebrows, a scraggly mustache, the marks of life and sorrow grooving his cheeks. Madame Xenia paused beside the head.

"This is an early piece by Constantine Katalonos. He brought it here from Athens when we were married. I am from Rhodes, but my husband is not. This is his father. A good man. He died three years ago. One day we will give this bronze to our museum in Rhodes."

They left the old man to his memories and went on to a closed door that Madame Xenia flung open dramatically. She motioned them ahead and Dorcas found herself in what was surely as fine a studio as any sculptor could hope for.

The light was all that could be desired, although, as Madame Xenia explained, the type of light was less important for the sculptor than for the painter. The floor was of some composition easily cleaned and it gleamed reddish-brown from recent waxing. All about stood wooden pedestal stands, sturdily built for holding heavy blocks of stone or marble. Finished pieces rested on two or three of the stands, two bore covered work still in progress, while the others were empty. Shelves had been built along one long wall, but these, too, showed a sparsity of finished work. A big drawing table with a tilted board held a sketching block, pencils, calipers, all arranged in neat order. Nearby an armature for a miniature human figure waited for the clay. There was no powdering of plaster dust about the room, no traces of clay. What tools were in evidence—a rasp, a gouge, a few chisels, lay upon a stand. The studio was wholly orderly and without life.

Madame Xenia lifted both arms widely, the gesture despairing. "Here he can do his finest work. He has only to ask and I give him what he wishes."

Dorcas thought of the portrait's visionary eyes and wondered how Constantine Katalonos had felt when all this perfection and order were pressed upon him and he was shut in with it, told to create—for the glory of Rhodes, and of his wife.

Their guide led them about the room, showing them the lovely marble figure of a dancing girl, the head of a horse in pinkish terra cotta. In passing a stand she touched something wrapped in wet sacking and the wooden structure rolled upon its casters.

"I am posing for this," she announced. "But I am a difficult subject and he has not finished the head. He is never satisfied. Three times he breaks up the clay and throws it away. I must encourage him to try again. Now I keep the clay wet for when my husband returns."

Dorcas had paused beside a stand on which there was a piece draped with a square of brown cloth. Madame Xenia saw her interest and drew her away at once.

"This is not good. This one I do not like." She turned Dorcas with firm hands toward a large mahogany desk in a corner of the room. Her touch brooked no resistance. She took hold solidly and one moved as she directed.

The desk represented Constantine's "office." Here he sometimes worked at the composing of poetry, his wife explained. Another of his many gifts. Some of his verse had been published in Greek magazines and sometimes when he could not work in clay he translated his poetry into English.

"My husband wished to publish a book of his poems in England or America," she said.

"Wished?" Fernanda repeated the past tense.

The mask of tragedy fell suddenly into place and all pretense was gone. The woman turned her back on the desk and faced Fernanda.

"It is not true, what I say—that my husband is away. He is not away. He is dead. He must be dead because he leaves—and that is the end. I do not know where he has gone. I hear nothing—nothing! But this he would not do. Always he is devoted to me. If he lived, he would tell me where to reach him." She flung a gesture in the direction of the clay head of herself, kept moist for the return of the sculptor. "That I keep to give me hope. But I do not hope any more. Constantine is dead—this I know."

"My goodness!" Fernanda said, taken aback. "I'm terribly sorry that—"

Madame Xenia broke in with a sudden question. "Tell me —you have done a great deal for the man named Gino Nikkaris? Is this not so?"

Dorcas, still lost in her own puzzling, came suddenly alert.

"Why, yes," said Fernanda, startled. "Gino was almost a son to me. Did you know him?"

"Come," the woman said. "We cannot talk in this place." She led them back to the elegant drawing room. The tea

[132]

things had been removed and once more Madame Xenia sat where she could easily raise her eyes to the portrait on the wall.

Dorcas glanced again at that sardonic face—a face out of time immemorial—that of the eternal Pan.

"Please believe me," Madame Katalonos began earnestly, "it is my wish to help you in your work however I can, Miss Farrar. But there is another reason why I must speak with you. Before Constantine went away, he told me he would see his friend Gino Nikkaris in America. He said he would be gone a month, perhaps two months. I did not approve, but my husband would not always take my best advice. And he had gone to America in the past, so I was not at first concerned. But I have heard no word from him at all, and time passes. I know only that he went to see Gino. Can you tell me what has happened? Perhaps you know whether he came to Gino's home?"

The slight feeling of illness was upon Dorcas again. If Constantine's connection was with Gino, then she did not want to remember where she might have seen him, or under what unpleasant circumstances.

Fernanda had listened to her hostess in obvious dismay. Now she shook her head. "I'm sorry. I never learned much about Gino's friends or his business affairs. You know of the plane crash, of course?"

Madame Xenia bowed her head. "Yes. It is this which defeats me. I do not know where to turn since I cannot ask Gino for help. When I see your picture in the paper and learn you are coming to Rhodes, I determine to seek your assistance. I remember that Constantine tells me of Gino's American friend, Miss Fern Farrar. If you know nothing, perhaps you can tell me where I may find Gino's widow. I have put

[133]

through long-distance calls to Gino's home in America, but his widow is no longer there."

Fernanda cleared her throat and threw a bright glance at Dorcas. Dorcas stared at her hands and said nothing. She knew no more of Gino's affairs than Fernanda did. The name of Constantine Katalonos meant nothing to her. She did not want to admit to this woman that she was Gino's widow.

Madame Xenia sat forward earnestly on the edge of her chair. It was possible that in another moment she would slip to her knees in dramatic supplication.

"Perhaps you can intercede for me," she pleaded of Fernanda. "If you can reach the widow of Gino Nikkaris and speak for me, I will go to America. I will do anything. You must help me, please."

"Oh, dear," Fernanda said. "I really don't know what to do." She looked again at Dorcas.

There was no choice, Dorcas realized, reluctant though she was to confess her identity.

"Gino Nikkaris was my husband," she said.

Madame Xenia had paid very little attention to her since their arrival. She had steered her about now and then, but she had not really looked at her. Now she fixed her splendid dark eyes upon Dorcas as though she would draw the very secrets from her soul.

"You are Gino's widow?"

Dorcas nodded. "I am, yes. But I assure you that I know nothing at all about your husband. As far as I know he never came to our apartment. If Gino saw him elsewhere—as he often did with business acquaintances, I know nothing about it. I'm sorry that I'm unable to help you."

This was all perfectly true. There was no point in saying,

"I remember something about your husband that makes me ill, but I don't know what it is."

For a few moments Madame Xenia Katalonos stared at her fixedly. Then she turned to Fernanda.

"I understand that Mrs. Brandt—Mrs. Nikkaris—is your secretary for this trip? She must be very busy working for you?"

"Dorcas has not been well," Fernanda said. "I'm not working her that hard. I want her to rest a good deal. Her work for me is invaluable, but it can be fitted into very little time."

Their hostess's eyes had begun to shine with new inspiration. "In this case, I would like to ask a very large favor of you, Miss Farrar. Would you be so generous as to loan your secretary to me? Perhaps for one afternoon next week?"

Fernanda was clearly surprised and not altogether pleased. "I'm not sure I understand—" she began.

The compelling gaze fixed Dorcas with its bright demand and she did not wait for Fernanda's assent. "You will come, please? For one afternoon only—next week?"

"What is it you want me to do?" Dorcas asked uneasily.

"My husband's poems!" Madame Xenia plunged in, improvising as she went, Dorcas felt sure. "Those he has translated into English. It is necessary for someone to read them, to put them in suitable form to offer for publication in America. You will do this for me? It is a—a memorial for my husband."

"I doubt that Dorcas would be the right person for such an assignment," Fernanda put in quickly. "I really don't think her strength should be taxed with such extra work."

Once more Fernanda was managing her life, Dorcas saw, and resistance stiffened in her. She had no wish to see Madame Xenia again, but she could not afford to give in to Fer-

[135]

nanda's autocratic rulings at every turn. She must start at once to take a stand and make her own decisions.

"I can at least go through this material," she offered. "I could do it at a time when Miss Farrar doesn't need me. There would be nothing taxing about it, I'm sure."

Fernanda, finding herself neatly caught, gave in somewhat doubtfully and Madame Xenia clasped her hands in triumph. Her purpose, undoubtedly, was to see Dorcas again and prod for some remembrance of her husband, and she was ready to pin new hope upon this flight of fancy.

"Then it is arranged," she said. "I will telephone to see when it will be convenient for Miss Farrar to spare you. You must do me the honor to come to luncheon. I will make it for you with my own hands."

She had been promoted, Dorcas found, from a position of no consequence to that of someone to be wooed with elaborate wiles.

Fernanda made little movements of departure, of picking up her gloves and handbag. "We've enjoyed this visit, Madame Katalonos. And I shall remember about the kind offer of your house in Lindos. Are you ready, Dorcas?"

The moment had come for her own request. Even as Dorcas swung the strap of her bag across her shoulder and stood up, the words formed in her mind and she spoke them aloud.

"There is a woman I would like to find here in Rhodes. She is the wife of an old friend of my father. Her name is Mrs. Markos Dimitriou. Do you know of such a person living in the island?"

"Mrs. Markos Dimitriou?" Their hostess repeated the name thoughtfully. "I do not know of such a woman. But if you wish, I can inquire. My servants can ask in the market, in the shops. In Rhodes everyone knows everyone. If it is important, I will find this woman for you."

Dorcas could see that Fernanda was growing uneasy at mention of the Dimitriou name, connecting it, as she did, with the time of Dorcas's illness. Before Fernanda could say anything, Dorcas thanked Madame Xenia.

"If you will find Mrs. Dimitriou for me, I will be glad to come whenever you wish and see if I can help with your husband's poems."

The bargain was made. As they were shown to the door, Madame Xenia promised heartily that if the woman existed in Rhodes she would be found. Fernanda's attempt at an objection was brushed aside. For once Fern Farrar had met her match in a managing female.

The chauffeur drove them furiously back to the hotel and Fernanda let the matter go. In any event, she was more interested in the subject of Constantine.

"It's obvious that Madame Katalonos wants to pump you when I'm not around," she said. "I was trying to get you out of a difficult spot, dear, but you insisted on jumping in anyway."

Dorcas did not altogether trust the large, listening ears of the mustachioed Greek in the front seat. He might not speak English, but there was no telling what he could understand.

"I don't mind helping with the poems if I can," she said mildly.

Fernanda said nothing more. She was frowning somewhat absently and Dorcas wondered why she had opposed a further visit to Madame Xenia's. Was it because the name Constantine had rung some bell so that Fernanda was anxious to back away from a connection that might lead tortuously into Gino's "business"?

She thought of the picture again, and suddenly, without

[137]

warning, memory surged back fully, sickeningly. She knew now the identity of the man in the portrait. In memory she was again a young mother in terrified flight. Again she was opening the door of her hotel room hiding place to a thin man in dark glasses who had come to take her back to Gino. She knew very well now why the sight of Constantine's face had brought upon her the nausea of physical illness. The man whose name she had never known was Constantine Katalonos.

If there were those who took an interest in Dorcas's presence on the island, they made no further moves in the next few days. There were no markings of chalk, no intruder on her balcony. The quiet was welcome, though she could not be reassured. The matter, whatever it was, had not been finished. Her identification of Constantine told her that.

Once she had placed the man in the picture, she could not put him wholly from her mind. She had gone over all she could recall about him again and again. There was little to remember. Her own state at the time had been so frantic and distraught that he had been to her only the figure of a jailor. Yet she could remember an air of sadness that the artist had not put into the picture. She had seen Constantine Katalonos at a time when he himself had been thrown into some deep despair. Because of his thralldom to his wife? Or because of Gino? He had told her that she could not escape, that he himself would escape if he could. While he had not treated her unkindly, she had been afraid of him. She had sensed in him a certain ruthless quality that might show her no mercy if she tried to escape. There had been something else, too—a sense that this man followed no prescribed pattern and was capable of unexpected action. She had dared to put him to no test.

Where Constantine might fit into her present picture she did not know, but she dreaded the thought of meeting him again. Wherever she went, she carried her passport with her and she waited anxiously for the word of Mrs. Dimitriou that did not come from Madame Katalonos.

Fernanda's work was going at its lively best and as usual she was having the time of her life. She made friends wherever she found English spoken, and sometimes without it. Dorcas was kept busy listening to accounts of her impressions and getting them down into a detailed form that Fernanda could use later.

Johnny took Fernanda about and ran strange errands for her. He might tease her a good deal, but he gave her good measure in loyalty and effort. Toward Dorcas he remained kind, but had somehow removed himself from the occasionally easy friendship that had seemed to exist between them.

Almost imperceptibly the care of Beth was slipping from her hands. She was aware of an increasing determination on Fernanda's part to keep the child away from her mother a good part of the time. She checked her own desire to fight this openly and bent herself instead on an effort to prove to Fernanda that she was all that might be desired in a mother for Beth.

Beth liked Vanda, and since the woman's care seemed dependable and she was watchful of the child's safety, there was nothing to complain about. Yet Dorcas's uneasiness about the woman did not subside. Here, too, she had a sense of waiting—for what she did not know.

One afternoon, when everything had reopened for business after the long rest period, Dorcas walked downtown to the market by herself. She left Vanda in a shady part of the hotel terrace cutting out paper dolls for Beth. Fernanda was writing letters. Johnny was absent, having been sent to take pictures inside the old city.

The market was a place Dorcas enjoyed. Along Mandraki its front was a long low building of stone, culminating in a clock tower that could be seen from all over the town of Rhodes. Its modern architecture had been combined with a touch of the Turkish in the shape of windows and the decoration of the façade. A long row of arched doorways opened upon the market square beyond.

Moving by now like a typical Rhodian, Dorcas let three motor scooters and an automobile wait for her as she crossed the street. She stepped through one of the arches into the open square. In its center stood a small building that looked like a large bandstand. That was where meat was sold, and there was a great uproar of discussion and argument going on in the vicinity every morning when the buyers gathered.

Market stalls and small shops ran around the sides of the square and she started past them. The scene was far quieter than it was in the early morning when shoppers were out in force. Dorcas wandered idly until she found the fruit she was looking for. When she'd paid her drachmas, she returned to Mandraki, carrying her purchases in a string bag.

Now she moved in the direction of the walled town, wondering if she might run into Johnny returning from his picture-taking expedition. If he had the car, he might have gone in through the same twin-towered gate they had taken on their first visit to that part of town. She crossed to the sidewalk along the harbor, her skirt whipping in the wind. On the outer rim the three windmills turned in unison and a gentle swell of waves washed within the enclosure. She walked along, watching the anchored fishing boats and a boy on the stony beach sorting octopus in a tentacled heap.

Opposite the towers she turned toward the street again. As she reached the curb a car passed close to her, making the turn into the old city. Dorcas stared after it in surprise. The car was Fernanda's, and Vanda Petrus was behind the wheel. Beside her, with just the top of her small head visible, sat Beth.

There was no time to prepare herself. No time to resist the surge of alarm that flashed through her. Something in her had known that the quiet days of waiting would come to a sudden end. She had been lulled until her guard was down and those who had waited were ready to strike. Vanda, whether she was with them or not, was playing into their hands—with Beth as a hostage. The conviction was terrifying in its force. It brooked no calm reasoning or contradiction.

Dorcas darted across the street and began to run toward the entrance in the great walls. Already the car had gone through and out of sight. Although Vanda had given no sign, Dorcas had a feeling that the woman had seen her at the instant of turning the car.

Beneath the stone arches of the gate she paused to catch her breath, pressing back against the wall so she would not be knocked down by a car coming out of the walled city. There was a policeman inside, waving traffic through the narrow way and into the proper turn.

It had taken her no more than five minutes from the moment when she had seen Vanda and Beth to reach this point. As she went inside, she saw that this had been time enough for Vanda to park the car near the museum and get out. Neither she nor Beth was in sight.

There was a choice of several street openings off the little square and Dorcas stood looking about, her alarm heightening. How was she to find them if they escaped her in this maze? She hurried to an opening where she could look up one of the streets and was barely in time to see Beth whisked around a corner a block or so away. Again Dorcas began to run, ducking past a bicycle, slipping on rough cobblestones. When she turned the corner where she had glimpsed Beth, the child was nowhere in sight, and Dorcas chose a narrow archway and hurried through it.

The street was empty. It ran only a block and then branched off into crooked alleyways. She was sure now that Vanda had seen her and taken flight. If she called out, the sound would only warn her further. It would be better to come upon her without warning—that was the only way. Fear was tight in her throat. Always she had known Vanda was not to be trusted. She should never have listened to Fernanda, or to Johnny's soothing words.

The alleys about her were a maze of narrow stone passage-ways and closely leaning stone buildings. The stone seemed to absorb all sound and it was very quiet. The streets turned and twisted without reason and she knew quickly enough that she had taken the wrong way. She must return to the car and start over.

Breathless now, she went back along the last street she had followed and found that it ran uphill instead of down. She wasn't lost. You couldn't get lost in a place like this, for all that high stone walls and ancient houses cut off the horizon and offered no recognizable landmark. She had only to start downhill and take every turn down thereafter to find herself on the water front. But the old city was too big for someone on foot and she might come out at some distant entrance far from where Vanda had left the car.

Nothing looked familiar now. Each street had its own dark-some character. She passed an open-fronted *taverna* where men sat talking and laughing. They stared at her with friendly interest, but she could not ask them what she wanted to know and she hurried on.

Suddenly the maze opened upon a Turkish fountain with stone steps all around. Not a fountain for decorative purposes, but a source of water for everyday use. In three directions from the central point of the fountain streets opened and she knew she was hopelessly confused so far as finding her way quickly was concerned.

Wearily she sat upon a stone step and pushed wisps of damp hair back from her forehead. Bougainvillaea hung over a nearby wall, blanketing it with unexpected purple, and there was the cheerful sound of birds singing in a garden beyond. A woman watched her from an open doorway. After a moment she went inside and brought out a folding wooden chair, offering it with smiling courtesy. Dorcas sat upon it to please her and tried to make motions that would indicate tall, thin Vanda and small Beth. In a few moments other women joined the first, curious and interested, but concerned, too, because here was someone who appeared to be in trouble. No one spoke a word of English.

She had given up all attempts at explanation by the time the two police officers in dark-green uniforms walked into the square. They came at once to speak to the crowd around her and ask questions in Greek. Again Dorcas went through her motions, but though the two listened earnestly, there was no getting through the barrier of a strange tongue. They invited her to go with them—at least that gesture was plain, offering a way out of the maze.

The two set her courteously between them and it was thus that she went down the hill and around this turn and that until they came upon Johnny Orion taking pictures. Never had she been so glad to see anyone.

The police officers, now that she had found a friend, took polite leave of her, pleased, no doubt, to have her problems so easily solved.

"What's this all about?" Johnny demanded. "I thought for a minute that you'd been arrested."

She tried to explain logically and clearly, but her tongue would not slow to coherence until he took her by the shoulders and gave her a brief shake.

"Stop it!" he ordered. "Just give me words—not whole pages in one breath."

She slowed the urgent flow and managed to explain what had happened. Stated thus, baldly and quietly to Johnny, it no longer seemed an impressive story. It was filled with impulse and alarm without due motivation. Her actions had been based on hunch and emotion and they betrayed the fact that she had taken off in a completely futile pursuit. At least that was the way it must seem to Johnny.

He made no comment, but suggested that they return to the place where Vanda had left the car. Slinging his camera equipment over one shoulder, he drew Dorcas's hand through the crook of his arm, holding her steady as they walked along. She was relieved and a little angry at the same time. Angry with herself as well as with Johnny, because she had not made him understand that there was due cause for her fright.

Johnny said nothing until they reached the open space near the museum. The spot was empty. Fernanda's car was gone.

"Vanda knew I saw her," Dorcas said. "She knew I was trying to follow. She must have slipped back here when I took the wrong turning and now she's got away."

"First of all," Johnny said, "let's get out from behind these walls."

He took her through the towered gateway and across Mandraki to the low stone wall above the harbor. There he made her sit quietly, with the bright sunlight of Rhodes upon her and the walls glowing with their touch of warm gold in reflection of sea and sun.

"You can't go on like this, you know," he told her soberly. "If you see threats in the movement of every shadow, if you let your imagination constantly run away with you, you'll wind up in a hospital again."

"Do you think it's only my imagination?" she demanded.

He looked away, and she knew the answer. The helplessness of defeat enveloped her. There was nothing more she could say to Johnny Orion.

"Let's go back to the hotel," she said.

"We'll take a cab," he agreed. "And when we get there, try to soft pedal what's happened until you find out the reason behind Vanda's trip. She and Beth are probably at the hotel by now. If you burst in with a wild-eyed look and recriminations, only to have it turn out that the trip was legitimate, it will look all the worse for you. Fernanda's worried about you now. What do you say we play it down?"

She did not argue with him, nor did she promise anything. In silence she walked with him to the taxi stand and rode beside him back to the hotel. All that really mattered was to find Beth, to know that she was safe.

The cab pulled up in front of the Olympus and she saw that Fernanda's car was at the curb ahead of them. Fernanda sat at a table on the terrace and Beth was there, playing with the yellow cat, while Vanda watched her.

"Take it easy," Johnny reminded as she thrust open the

[145]

door of the car and got out without waiting. She scarcely heard him. All her attention was on Beth in a flooding of relief that washed away fear. She ran up the steps to the terrace.

"Where did you take her?" she demanded of Vanda. "Where did you go with her in the car?"

The woman stared at her blankly and Fernanda put a quick hand on Dorcas's arm. "Darling, what's the matter? You're clammy with perspiration."

Dorcas drew away from her touch. "What was Vanda doing out with the car? Why did she drive Beth to the old city?"

"Good gracious, why shouldn't she?" Fernanda asked mildly. "I sent her there on an errand. What are you so upset about? What's happened?"

The conviction that had driven her for the last hour was still strong. Dorcas dropped to her knees beside Beth. "Where did you go with Vanda? Where did she take you?"

The little girl answered with cheerful excitement. "We went to see a cat, Mommy. A bigger cat than this one. Its name is Cleo and it let me pet it."

Dorcas stood up, aware that the others were watching her—Fernanda, Johnny, Vanda. Vanda's expression was carefully blank, Fernanda looked concerned, and Johnny was pitying again. She turned her back on them and went into the hotel. She ran up the two flights to her room, locked the door, and flung herself on her bed. Her head was throbbing and she felt a little sick. Were they right—all of them? Was she close to another breakdown, where the most normal happenings took on an aura of evil?

After a time she got up and went into the bathroom to put cold cloths on her forehead. As she reached for the cold-water faucet she looked into the mirror. Her fingers tightened on the knob and she did not turn it. From the square of glass two white circles stared back at her blankly—like the exaggerated eyes of an owl.

She leaned on the basin and fought the dizziness that swept through her. When she could move without swaying, she put out a finger to touch the markings. Someone had used her own cake of white soap—blunted, she saw, at one corner—to draw the circles on the glass. But why? Were these markings being used to frighten her into giving up the letter? There seemed a more ominous purpose behind them than that.

After a moment she turned from the mirror and went to sit on the edge of the bed, her face in her hands. Now that the first shock had died, she was growing angry. If she went to summon Fernanda and Johnny, brought them to look at those marks, they would have to believe that something very wrong was going on. Or would they? Might they not think she had drawn the circles herself with her own cake of soap— perhaps in order to justify earlier erratic behavior? If that were the case, they would soothe and calm her, and they would show how sorry for her they felt. She would be helpless in the face of such disbelief and she would have further hurt her own cause. No, she would leave the marks where they were and she would show them to no one until she could decide calmly, quietly, sensibly, what to do.

At the moment she felt neither calm nor quiet, but thoroughly angry. Anger now was a healthy emotion, one to overcome fear. The markings were meant to frighten her, this she knew. But as long as she refused to remain frightened, she was stronger than those who wished to threaten and torment.

The telephone rang suddenly beside her. There was no one

she wanted to talk to just now and she let it ring. The sound persisted, and there was something compelling about the ringing. She picked up the receiver and managed to keep anger in leash as she said, "Hello."

The voice was Johnny's, and her hands began to perspire in relief, although she was not sure what she had expected from the telephone.

"I've just found that Fernanda is going to be on her own tonight," Johnny said. "Will you have dinner with me, Dorcas? We can have the car and I've found a small place I think you'll like."

She wanted to accept, but if she went with him, it would mean leaving Beth alone with Vanda. Vanda, who had perhaps drawn circles in soap upon her mirror?

He sensed her hesitation. "You were wrong this afternoon, you know. Fernanda's errand was a perfectly natural one. I looked into it. You can't sit guard over Beth every moment. And I don't believe there's any real need for that."

Perhaps he was right. Even if Vanda was behind the markings, she would not harm Beth. And the time had come to talk to Johnny alone.

"Thank you," she said before her new resolution could falter. "I'd love to have dinner with you."

She put down the telephone and lay back on the bed. He was being kind and pitying—and mistaken. She would go to dinner with him tonight and she would show him the letter and tell him all that had happened—back home and here. Somehow she would get through his disbelief.

If only she knew what the owl stood for, what the symbols meant and why they followed her. At least her anger held, and she knew she must find a way to fight.

That night she dressed for dinner with special care. She

[148]

wore a sleeveless sheath of lime-green linen, simply cut. A strand of gold beads made a contrast of color at her throat, and she wore gold earrings of a design that suggested Greece. Her head was bare, and she caught up a lacy gold scarf for her shoulders.

Just before she left the room she did what she had not done for a long time. She smiled at herself in the dressing-table mirror—the delicate smile of a maiden of old Greece. And she went out of the room without another glance at the soaped circles, leaving them there upon the mirror in the bathroom.

8

ᘕᘕᘕᘕᘕᘕᘕᘕᘕᘕᘕᘕᘕᘕᘕᘕᘕᘕᘕᘕᘕᘕᘕᘕᘕᘕᘕᘕᘕᘕᘕᘕ

THE SMALL restaurant was out upon the sea road. They found a place to leave the car and walked up steps to a gravel-strewn courtyard roofed over with matting. Tables stood about on the gravel, empty at this early hour, and the winds of Greece whipped at tablecloths that had been clamped into place at each corner.

"Let's go inside," Johnny said.

There were no more than eight tables in the narrow inner room, all bright with checked cloths. A curved wooden counter with glass sides exhibited cheeses and fruit, and beyond was an open kitchen where it was possible to see one's dinner being cooked. Lights glowed softly golden against walls of split bamboo and candles flickered in plump glasses on each table. Upon a shelf that ran along one wall were displayed plates in the designs of ancient Rhodes, with leaping dolphins and small vessels, their plump sails filled with wind.

A waiter in a white jacket let them make their choice of a table by the wall and Dorcas slipped into her chair and looked around with pleasure. This was not the usual bare and echoing Greek dining room, nor was it one of the overdone modern places.

One other couple sat two tables away—a middle-aged German pair who ate with concentration and wasted no time on conversation. The waiter's English was nonexistent, but a translated menu was produced and they ordered the casserole *spécialité* of the house.

For the first time in days Dorcas began to relax completely. The letter lay in its place in the bag beside her chair but she did not want to think about it now. Johnny was watching her and there was approval in his eyes.

"Green and gold become you," he said.

It had been a long time since a man had looked at her as Johnny was looking. It was pleasant to feel that the dead years were slipping away and she might be stirring into life again.

He told her of his efforts to legalize Fernanda's acquisition of the stone catapult ball. The matter was going through channels now. The third official he had talked to had already met Miss Fern Farrar, and Johnny's story had not surprised him. He had ended by deciding that the incident was amusing and had promised to see what might be done. Fernanda, of course, must be kept ignorant of the matter until her story was safely down on paper, unspoiled by tame reality.

The *spécialité* arrived, hot with sizzling cheese on top, and proved to be a mixture of veal and eggplant. Johnny had ordered a bowl of tangy black olives—Greek olives that made the ripe olives at home seem tasteless by comparison. There was a slab of the local white cheese, delicious with dark bread. And he'd ordered *retsina* as well—the resined wine of Greece.

"I won't make you try *ouzo* tonight," he said. "That takes a bit of getting used to."

The wine tasted the way pine resin smelled, Dorcas thought,

and reserved judgment. She ate with greater enjoyment than at any time since she had come to Greece. She refused to think for the moment about the eyes of an owl.

Halfway through the meal Johnny drew something from his pocket and handed it to her. "I found some picture cards for you and Fernanda."

She took the postcard. She saw that it was a photograph of the marble head the museum had been so mysterious about. The photographer had been skillful with his use of light and shadow so that the modeling of the boy's face was brought out in all its wistful perfection. The lips seemed to quiver with life and the poised tear was surely about to roll down one cheek. There was a feeling of rightness about the picture that Dorcas sensed at once. She had not felt the same about the head which had been so reluctantly brought out for their inspection.

"Did anything seem odd to you about the head when we saw it at the museum?" she asked.

"I can't say that it did," Johnny said.

Dorcas studied the card. "At home my father had an especially fine book of Greek photographs. There was a picture of this head in the collection and I always loved to look at it as a child. I made up stories about the little boy and what he was crying about. I'd looked forward to seeing the original. But when they brought it out at the museum something seemed wrong, though I didn't know what. It troubled me."

"I wondered about all that to-do at the museum," Johnny said. "Have you figured it out?"

She was staring at the picture in sudden realization. "I know what it is! Though it hardly seems possible. At the museum the tear was on the wrong cheek—the left cheek. I'm sure of it. It's on the right cheek in this picture. The negative hasn't been reversed. I can tell by that temple lock of curly hair on the same side as the tear."

Johnny's interest heightened. "Come to think of it, I believe you're right."

Something was falling into place in Dorcas's mind. The meaning of certain words. An electrifying meaning.

"I don't believe the head they showed us in the museum was the real one at all. This is the real one." She tapped the card. "The one we saw was a copy. Do you suppose the real head could be missing?"

Johnny took back the card and looked at it. "I don't see how such a mistake could come about. The tear, I mean. It would be too obvious an error. The sculptor making a copy would never make a slip like that."

Johnny's words were reasonable, yet she knew certain things that he did not. She knew that Gino had been trying for a coup of some sort just before his death. And there was something else that drew all the pieces into place and tied them together.

Dorcas picked up the leather bag beside her chair and opened its brass catch. She took out her passport case and slipped a thin envelope beneath the passport.

"This letter from Greece came to our apartment after Gino died. It made no sense to me at the time and I put it aside when I'd read it. A week or two later a man who had known Gino came to ask about his mail. I didn't tell him of this letter. After that the housebreaking began. It happened once before I moved out of Gino's apartment, and again while I was living with Fernanda. Each time the intruder left a queer marking behind him. Two chalked circles—like the eyes of an owl. Although I didn't place the resemblance right away."

"An owl?" Johnny sounded skeptical.

[154]

"Wait—there's more. I thought I'd lost the letter, but Beth had slipped it into a book and it turned up here the first day I was in Rhodes. Read it, Johnny."

He read the words softly aloud. Dorcas threw an uneasy look around the little restaurant, but the German couple was absorbed in paying their bill, and the proprietor and a second waiter were busy seating new arrivals. She listened as he read.

"The bride of Apollo mourns her loss. Done is the fearful deed. Gone the Princess from her Castle. At the hour of devils shadow lies upon the grave. Dolorosa, dolorosa, dolorosa."

His look met hers in frank puzzlement.

"Who else could be meant by the 'bride of Apollo' but the nymph Rhoda?" Dorcas asked. "The very island of Rhodes itself—which has suffered a fearful loss. Johnny, did you know anything about Gino's work?"

"Not much," he said doubtfully. "I gathered that he was scouting around for chances to pick up treasures in the art line. And I found him out on that smuggling deal."

She nodded. "I think he didn't care how he came by the things he got for wealthy buyers."

Johnny regarded her thoughtfully, even a little appraisingly. Now was the moment. She had to make him understand.

"Twice I tried to run away from Gino," she said. "He wouldn't let me go. Sooner or later I would have tried again. He wasn't good for Beth or for me. He wasn't a—a decent person, Johnny."

The words were hard to say and she was afraid to look at him. She did not want to see that chill appraisal in his eyes.

He touched her hand lightly and she went on without meeting his gaze.

"Excuses aren't much good, but for whatever they're worth, I was foolish and very young. I fell in love with an idea I imagined to be Gino. Beth is the one good thing to come out of a marriage that was completely wrong from the start." She could not tell him just how wrong it had been.

"I'll admit that it's been hard to see you as Gino's wife," Johnny said, and the chill was gone from his look. "It has made me wonder."

"I hoped I could start over by coming to Greece," she said ruefully. "But there's been no starting over. I feel as though something is still holding me to the past. Some unfinished business of Gino's. Perhaps something to do with Constantine Katalonos. When I ran away the first time, Gino sent a man to bring me back. When I saw a portrait of Constantine at Madame Katalonos's house, I knew he was the man who came after me that time. His wife told Fernanda that he had gone to America recently to see Gino. So something is up."

Johnny whistled softly. A new thought had come suddenly into her mind, and she went on before he could speak.

"How valuable do you think this marble head of the weeping boy would be?"

"How do you set a price on the priceless?" Johnny asked. "If you mean that it has been stolen to sell, who would dare buy it?"

"Not a legitimate buyer," Dorcas reminded him. "Gino often dealt with wealthy men in various parts of the world. A millionaire with a slight kink in his thinking might like to own such a piece. He might even pay a fortune for it."

"That's possible enough," Johnny agreed. "Art treasures have turned up in strange places before this."

"Constantine Katalonos is a sculptor," she said. "Vanda Petrus knows him. She told me he had done a head of her. So she is in this thing somewhere, too. Do you suppose a sculptor as gifted as this man seems to be could make a convincing copy of a piece like the weeping boy?"

"And place a tear on the wrong cheek?" Johnny asked.

She had to agree that so fantastic a mistake weakened her speculation, but she persisted.

"Look at the symbol at the bottom of that note. It seems to be a little owl with big round eyes. And that ties in, too. The chalk circles I told you about are like an owl's eyes. Fernanda didn't believe in the chalk marks I found on my balcony the first night. Perhaps if I'd seen them before I smudged them with my hands, I'd have found they were circles, too."

"Isn't that stretching things pretty far?" said Johnny.

Dorcas shook her head vehemently. "I think someone here in Rhodes wants this note as much as it was wanted at home. Someone is trying to tell me something, to frighten me into giving it up. Neither you nor Fernanda believed in that man on my balcony. But Johnny, while I was out today someone went into my room at the hotel and marked two soap circles on the glass in the bathroom. I've left them for you to see. Will you believe me now, Johnny?"

She could see that he wanted to believe, that the mood of sympathy was right between them, the current strong. Yet she knew that doubt persisted.

"It's not that these things haven't happened," he said finally. "But you may have put the wrong interpretation on some of this. I'll admit I don't like these marks you've just found on your mirror. But all the same you're leaping over too many gaps."

"The note," she said. "What about the note?"

He read it again. " 'The hour of the devils'—that could be noonday, couldn't it? When evil is abroad in the isles of Greece."

He was trying to humor her, but she caught up his words with new eagerness. "That would be when all shadow goes straight down. So the 'grave' must be at the foot of something."

"What grave?" Johnny asked.

She was impatient with him now. Impatient with the very quality of calm good sense that drew her to him.

"The place where the marble head is buried," she told him earnestly. "What else can it mean than the spot where the real head is hidden? Gino would have known. But Gino is gone. So perhaps the only clue is this letter and someone is desperate to get hold of it."

"So far, so good," Johnny said, still humoring her. "But who is the Princess and why is she gone from her Castle? What's all this 'dolorosa' business?"

"And who is the owl?" Dorcas added. "Johnny, it means something. Something important. Maybe something dangerous to know."

For a moment there was tension in the air between them, touching Johnny Orion as well as Dorcas. For a moment he almost believed. Then he grinned, and the feeling was gone.

"What a story for Fernanda! She'll swallow this letter hook, line, and sinker."

Quietly Dorcas replaced the envelope beneath her passport. He thought she was exaggerating, embroidering. He could smile because he had not felt the terror—at noonday, or otherwise.

"I'm not going to tell Fernanda," she said.

His eyebrows went up a little. "Oh?"

"Fernanda never wanted to see Gino as he was. She won't want to now."

"Maybe you're right, at that," he said.

Their waiter brought bowls of luscious Greek cherries for dessert and small cups of bitter Greek coffee. Dorcas thrust down her growing sense of disappointment. Johnny's skepticism shook her own belief and she could not afford that. To be lulled was too dangerous. She *knew*. But there was nothing more she could offer him by way of proof. Not until they returned to the hotel and she could show him the circles soaped upon a mirror. He would not think now that she had put them there herself. Fernanda might, but not Johnny.

Part of the barrier between them had gone down through the telling of her story and she found herself drawn to him and once more curious.

"That morning when we first went to the old city you gave me a challenge," she said. "You asked me what I was getting out of Greece. I still don't know exactly what you meant. But do you have an answer for yourself? What are you getting out of Rhodes? How are you going to use all this?"

He told her cheerfully. "I'll use it with my kids in school, of course. And for my own satisfaction. I grew up curious, wanting to know about things. It's a sort of disease, I guess."

"What do you mean—use it with your kids? How?"

"To make things I'm trying to teach come to life." He was serious now. "I can talk about history in the abstract till I'm blue in the face and hardly make a dent. But after my last trip to Greece I found I could make them understand these things more clearly. I could make them see a rough mound of earth, not so very high, standing up there, dry and hot in the Peloponnesian sun. There're no marble columns there—only low crumbling stone ruins all over its top—the foundations of a palace where men and women used to live. It's empty country —the plain of Argos, the low hills, deep, rocky chasms dropping to the bed of a river, lending wonderful protection to a good part of the mound. Up there where the earth is brown and dead you can smell the very dust of history. Mycenae! Only a word in a book to those kids, till I made them see it."

He was making Dorcas see it, too, and she waited for what came next.

"I could even make them feel that moment of wonderful astonishment I felt in the museum in Athens when I came upon the gold mask that Schliemann found there and believed was the face of Agamemnon. Telling them, I could make them believe in all those book words. I could make them know with their feelings that such a place existed and what had happened there. I showed them a picture I'd snapped of the Lion Gate—and it was real to them. Once I can get them to feel I can get them to think. Once I've found a springboard into their imaginations I can even get through to them with ideas about places I've never seen myself where history has happened. What went on in Greece says a lot to us today. I want to make these kids listen."

He had warmed to the telling and his eyes were bright.

"Is teaching the thing you want most to do?" Dorcas asked.

"When you like to teach, what more is there?" he said. "I like what I'm doing. I suppose I worry about kids. Not about most of them. Most of them are pretty swell. But about the few that are getting into the kind of trouble I might have got into if it hadn't been for my dad. Maybe I owe it to him to do a good job."

She pounced on his words. "A sentimental pilgrimage?" she reminded him.

He laughed aloud. "I think there's a difference. I'm not trying to be like my father. I'm not trying to see things as he did, or be what he was. There's something in me that needs to be satisfied on its own ground. I suppose it's the old question —what are we here for if we don't do something with what we have? Kids are my job. Maybe there are other jobs that would make me richer, but this is the one I like."

"And I like you, Johnny Orion," she said warmly, and meant it with all her heart.

When they were back in the car, there was a good feeling between them. Before he turned the key in the ignition, he pulled her over in the seat so that her cheek was against his arm as he drove. There was a healing and a comforting in this physical closeness. She watched his hands on the wheel and thought of how different they were from Gino's. Gino's hands had possessed a sinewy strength. They had been long and thin, and as often as not their touch had brought pain.

Neither she nor Johnny spoke on the way back to the hotel, and it was best like that. No challenge lay between them, but only this sense of being together and understanding each other without words. She was sorry when the drive ended and they reached the hotel. Upstairs on a mirror two white circles waited for her and they could not be ignored. Until the answer to the note was found, the answer to this tormenting, she could not relax into a new happy companionship with Johnny.

"I'll come up and have a look at those soap marks," he said as they climbed the steps.

They took the small elevator and she unlocked the door of her room. Everything seemed as it should be. Beth lay asleep and a light burned in Vanda's room through the crack of the open door. Dorcas flicked on the bathroom light and she and Johnny stared at the mirror together. It had been wiped clean of any markings whatsoever.

For an instant doubt of herself assailed her. Had she once more seen what did not exist? But she could not accept that.

"Someone's washed them off!" she cried, and ran to Vanda's door to call her into the room. "Did you wash off the marks on the mirror in my bathroom?" she demanded of the woman.

Vanda shook her head in denial. She had seen no marks. She had come into the bathroom both before and after dinner to wash Beth's face and hands. There had been nothing at all on the mirror. There was scarcely veiled contempt in her eyes, but Dorcas could not tell whether she was lying or not.

"Never mind," Dorcas said. If it was Vanda who had marked the mirror and then washed off the soap, she would never admit the truth.

Johnny waited until the woman had gone back to her room. "Too bad," he said. "I'd like to have seen just what was there."

"Probably one of the maids saw them and washed the mirror," Dorcas said limply.

"Probably," Johnny agreed.

She followed him to the hall door and before he went out he tilted her head with a finger and kissed her on the mouth, lightly, reassuringly. Then he was gone, and she leaned her forehead against the closed door and stood there for a moment. For years a kiss, a touch on the chin, had meant the prelude to fear and pain. But Johnny's kiss had brought only a longing to respond to him openly, freely. Yet something stood between them and she was afraid.

She returned to the bathroom and stared at the bright, clean surface of the mirror. A familiar throbbing had begun again at her temples. She pressed her fingers to the place where it hurt and stared at herself in the glass. Certainty and conviction were fading. The old dreadful question was there in her mind, the vacillating self-doubt. How much was real, how much unreal? Did she really know the difference? She did not dare to turn to Johnny unless she was sure. Had she again seen what did not exist in reality?

When she turned from the mirror and went into the bedroom, she felt depressed and more than a little frightened. Absently she pulled off a gold earring as she moved toward the bed table. Something shiny lay beside the telephone. She picked it up and saw that it was a disk slightly smaller than a fifty-cent piece. It seemed to be a flat, irregularly formed silver coin. A profile had been stamped upon it—the face of a Greek woman in a plumed helmet. Pallas Athena, no doubt. She turned the coin over and stared at the reverse marking. Pressed into the silver was the figure of a small owl with huge round eyes.

Her fingers closed over the coin with a sense of shock. Strangely, there was reassurance in the feeling as well. Here was no soap marking to be easily washed away. Here was tangible proof that someone had come to her room and left this symbol of the owl where she could find it.

With the coin in her hand she went again to Vanda's door and tapped on it sharply. The woman opened it and Dorcas held out her palm, the owl facing up.

"Do you know what this is?"

Vanda looked at the coin without touching it. The black opacity of her eyes betrayed nothing; her face was empty of expression.

"I do not know," she said.

"Tell me where it came from!" Dorcas insisted. "I found it just now on the bed table. Who put it there? Who was in this room while I was gone?"

"No one comes here," Vanda said evenly. "I take the child

to dinner. We go for a short little walk after. The key I take with me. No one comes here."

She would get nothing from Vanda Petrus. Dorcas returned to her own room and went through the shuttered balcony doors. Light from Fernanda's doorway fell in a wide bar across the next section of balcony. She knocked on the partly opened shutters.

Fernanda came at once to let her in. "Hello there. Come on in. Johnny and I are looking over possibilities for a trip to Petaloudes tomorrow. That's the Valley of the Butterflies, you know. Unfortunately, the famous butterflies don't appear until July, but there's a beautiful woodsy ravine and—" The look on Dorcas's face must have reached her, for she stopped abruptly. "What is it now? Is something wrong?"

Dorcas held out her hand. "Look at this, please."

The coin had been recently polished and the silver gleamed in the lamplight. Fernanda picked it up and put on her glasses. "Interesting," she said. "It looks like an old coin."

"I found it just now on the bed table in my room," Dorcas said. "It wasn't there before I left and Vanda says she knows nothing about it."

Johnny left the map and took the coin from Fernanda's hand. "Athena's bird, the owl. With the imprint of an olive twig beside it. All symbols of Athens in its days of power— the 'sterling owl' of Aristophanes." He looked at Dorcas. "This is real enough," he said, and she knew he had sensed her doubting of herself.

"Do you mean," Fernanda demanded, "that some mysterious person came into your room and left an old Greek coin on your bed table?"

"I'm not imagining things now," Dorcas said.

"Of course not, dear," Fernanda assured her soothingly. "In

[164]

fact, I find this quite exciting myself. Undoubtedly we have a little mystery here. I hope the solution won't prove disappointing."

There was no use in talking to Fernanda. Dorcas turned to Johnny, a question in her eyes.

"Show me where you found this," he said. "I'll be back in a minute, Fernanda."

It was an excuse to speak to her alone. As soon as they reached Dorcas's room he put his question.

"The Owl of the note? That's what you think, isn't it?"

"Who else?" Dorcas said. "He has either been here, or sent this through someone else. Vanda, perhaps. As a further warning, I suppose."

"I don't like any of this," Johnny said. "Why not give me that letter to keep? You shouldn't be carrying it around in your handbag, asking for trouble."

"No one knows for sure that I have it," Dorcas said. "I'll keep it where it is for now. It's proof that I'm not imagining these things, just as this coin is proof."

"Stop doubting yourself," he said gently. "There's a perfectly real answer to all this. In the meantime we've got to be more careful. Tomorrow we'll all go to Petaloudes together. No separations. You and Beth—and Vanda, too, if she likes."

He touched her lightly, reassuringly on the shoulder and went back to Fernanda's room.

When she was in bed she lay for a long while thinking over the evening, trying to face and accept her own feelings as they concerned Johnny Orion, yet fearful still of full acceptance. Always her mind returned to the coin and the marks on the mirror.

9

IN THE morning there was an unexpected change of plans. While they were still at breakfast, Madame Katalonos's chauffeur arrived with a note for Dorcas. His mistress wrote that she had discovered the whereabouts of a Mrs. Markos Dimitriou. She would call for Dorcas at ten o'clock and accompany her to this place.

With the desk clerk as interpreter, Dorcas tried to explain to the chauffeur that other plans had been made for the morning. Would it be possible to make this visit in the afternoon?

The man stood beside the lobby desk, foursquare and burly —a large, unlikely figure in his correct uniform. He shook his head, dismissing the suggestion. Madame had given orders, Dorcas gathered, and lesser mortals were expected to accommodate themselves. His words filled the lobby with sound.

"Stavros says he will return at ten o'clock," the clerk translated. "It is better if you are ready."

Dorcas gave in. It was more important to find Mrs. Dimitriou than to visit Petaloudes. She would keep Beth with her today and out of Vanda's hands.

"Tell him I'll be ready," Dorcas said.

Stavros's salute was of the G.I. variety. For a man so large, he trod lightly across the lobby as he returned to his car.

When Dorcas went back to the breakfast table to announce her changed plans and suggest that Beth stay home, she met with double opposition. Beth wailed that she wanted to go to the butterfly place, and Fernanda supported her.

"I can't approve of this delving into the past," she said. "I doubt that Madame Xenia has really found this woman, but if she has, it will only upset you to see her."

"That's for me to decide," Dorcas pointed out.

"I suppose you'll have to go, even if it's a wild-goose chase," said Fernanda. "But let's not spoil Beth's fun. We'll talk about this later."

After breakfast Dorcas confronted Fernanda in her room as she got ready for the trip.

"I want Beth with me today," Dorcas told her. "I can't trust Vanda after what happened yesterday, and—"

"I know," Fernanda broke in, watching herself in a mirror as she wrapped a scarf about her head. "Vanda told me you thought you had seen marks on the bathroom glass and then accused her of washing them off. Not very diplomatic, my dear."

"There were such marks," Dorcas said. "Two white circles like the ones you saw for yourself at home. Circles like the eyes of an owl."

Fernanda regarded her sadly. "Owl's eyes! Dorcas, I wish I knew what to do. I'd counted so much on this trip to iron out these aberrations of yours. But they keep on, and all this is terribly bad for Beth. That little scene at breakfast—"

"There was no scene at breakfast and I'm not having aberrations. I simply want Beth with me today."

[168]

Abruptly Fernanda took her by the shoulders and turned her to face the dressing-table mirror. "Look at yourself, dear—just look!"

Thus forced, Dorcas stared angrily at the girl in the glass. The face she saw was frighteningly familiar. Her reflection had the look of the distraught, frustrated, wildly furious girl whom Gino had given over to the attendants in the nursing home—a girl who had been hysterical. But she wasn't hysterical now, and she had no intention of being made to seem so. She was simply angry, and with every justification.

"Are you looking?" Fernanda asked. "Do you really believe you can give Beth the calm, loving atmosphere she needs about her? Not this morning you can't, my dear."

This at least was true. In this Fernanda was right. She could not deliberately submit Beth to the side effects of her anger, however justified it might be. Beth's welfare came first, although she hated to submit to Fernanda.

"All right," she said. "I'll let Beth go with you this time. But the matter isn't settled. Something is wrong and I'm not going to rest until I find out who is trying to get at me, and why."

Having won her way, Fernanda smiled benignly and Dorcas ran from the room, not trusting herself to further words.

The car trip got off before ten o'clock and Dorcas stood on the terrace, watching them leave. Johnny had tried to reassure her and he had promised to keep an eye on Beth. But he had no knowledge of the words that had been spoken between her and Fernanda, and there was no way to make him understand the true issue.

Anger had left its residue and Dorcas still felt shaken. If only she could meet what happened with a calm, forthright manner, instead of getting furious. Her anger, she knew, grew out of an increasing fear that Fernanda was moving with deliberation to take Beth out of her care. Undoubtedly she fancied herself as the child's foster grandmother and she had, too, an almost fanatical loyalty to her memories of Gino and what she imagined he might want. But she, Dorcas, was not so helpless now as she had been with Gino and she must not let herself be baited and tricked into defeat at Fernanda's hands.

Madame Katalonos was a mere half-hour late, which was not very late in Greece. Dorcas waited in the lobby until Stavros came to fetch her. Madame Xenia greeted her warmly as she got into the car.

"I am pleased if I can arrange this for you," she told Dorcas in response to her thanks. "I think this must be the woman you look for."

Stavros turned the car in the direction of the old city and he and Madame Xenia conversed heatedly in Greek for several blocks. At length her driver raised both hands from the wheel at once in a gesture of defeat. His mistress smiled.

"My friend there thinks this would be a lovely day for a drive to Lindos," she told Dorcas. "He has a passion for driving, that one. It is remarkable that we are still alive. But he is devoted to my interests. He understands that while he may argue with me, I do not have to do as he says. We Greeks are always what you call—individualistic."

For the rest of the drive Madame Xenia chatted about the lovely weather, which of course was to be expected in Rhodes, and asked questions concerning Fernanda's doings. There was no mention of the touchy subject of Constantine's whereabouts.

The car was left not far from the nearest gate of the old

town and Madame Xenia and Dorcas entered on foot and started up the Street of the Knights. Before an open doorway a short distance up the hill Madame paused.

"I think this is the place. We will go inside."

Ancient stones arched the doorway overhead, and they stepped through into a bare courtyard. Here geometric figures in black and white pebbles made a flooring of Turkish design. Worn stone steps rose beneath another arch, curving out of sight overhead. Beyond the stairs sunlight fell upon a patch of garden where a cat lay curled asleep.

Madame Xenia stepped through to the sunny garden and Dorcas followed. Walls studded with windows surrounded them and bougainvillaea dripped brilliant blossoms against the stone. Madame Xenia called out in an imperative voice, and a woman appeared on a stone balcony above and looked down at them.

The exchange was in Greek and it went on with a good deal of fire and excitement, though without producing Mrs. Dimitriou. After listening for a few moments, Dorcas walked across the garden and stood beside the sleeping cat. From a high room with the pattern of a cross in the window symphony music drifted down to her, surprising the silence of ancient stone. Someone up there must have a record player. As she waited for the discussion between the two women to end, she listened to the music and let the thought that was burgeoning come alive in her mind.

At last the woman on the balcony threw up her hands and shook her head vehemently. In apology Madame Xenia turned to Dorcas.

"This I do not understand. She says there is no Mrs. Dimitriou here and that such a person has never been in this place. My servants have asked in the market and in the old city, and this is the place they tell me where Mrs. Dimitriou is living."

She addressed the woman again, and again the response was a vigorous negative.

Dorcas spoke on impulse. "Ask her the name of the cat, will you?"

Though she looked puzzled, Madame Xenia obliged. The woman laughed, rolling out a mouthful of syllables, and her interrogator laughed as well.

"This cat has been given the name of a very famous wise man of old Rhodes," Madame Xenia said. "The name of Cleobulus."

Cleobulus—Cleo, Dorcas thought. Yes, she had been right. And they would not find Markos Dimitriou's wife in this place. She knew that now.

"Never mind," she told her companion. "I'm sorry I've troubled you for nothing."

Madame Xenia shrugged and gave up her inquiries. When they were in the car, she returned to the matter of the work on Constantine's poetry Dorcas had promised to do for her. Would tomorrow be possible, perhaps?

Since her identification of Constantine as the man whom Gino had sent for her that unhappy time three years ago, Dorcas had hoped that Madame Xenia would forget about asking her to come to her house. She found herself reluctant to go. She wanted to let that part of the past be forgotten and do nothing to revive it. But the woman beside her was waiting so anxiously for her assent that Dorcas had not the heart to refuse. After all, what did it matter? Constantine's wife would soon realize that there was nothing to be gotten from her, and it would not be necessary to go again.

"If it is all right with Miss Farrar, tomorrow will be fine for me," she said.

Back at the hotel she waited impatiently for the others to return. Vanda had run off to the old city yesterday with Beth, and Beth had reported petting a cat named Cleo. It appeared likely that Vanda had gone on an errand to Mrs. Dimitriou, who had lived in this place, and had now vanished. There were certain questions she wanted to ask Fernanda as soon as possible.

When the trippers returned shortly before lunchtime Dorcas followed Fernanda to her room.

"I'd like to talk to you, please," she said.

"Must you now, dear?" Fernanda was already shedding shoes, handbag, head scarf, and earrings as she crossed the room. "I do want a tub before we go to lunch."

"Then I'll wait till you're through," said Dorcas, and plumped herself into a chair.

Fernanda gave up and stretched out comfortably on the bed, wriggling her toes in satisfaction. "You sound as though you'd had a bad morning. You didn't find Mrs. Dimitriou, I suppose?"

"You knew I wouldn't find her," Dorcas said evenly. "Perhaps you warned her away."

Fernanda punched a pillow behind her head and crossed her legs. "You'd better begin at the beginning, dear, and explain what you're talking about."

"I don't need to," Dorcas said. "The first time we went to the old city you left us to buy a painting from an artist in one of those courtyards. I think it was the same place to which Madame Katalonos took me today. There was a cat in the garden whose name was Cleobulus. I asked."

Fernanda quirked an eyebrow. "I'm afraid I don't know a single Rhodes cat by name. What on earth are you getting around to?"

[173]

It grew increasingly difficult for Dorcas to keep a rein on her temper. She must not repeat this morning's outburst.

"Yesterday," she went on, "you sent Vanda on an errand to the old city and she took Beth along. Beth said she'd been to see a cat named Cleo. There's too much coincidence for me not to see the truth. How could you want to keep me from seeing Mrs. Dimitriou when you know how much it means to me?"

It was possible to see the changes of emotion chasing one another across Fernanda's innocently open face. She was not dissembling now, but simply trying to make up her mind which direction to take.

Dorcas pressed her advantage. "You might as well tell me the truth."

"You used to be such a gentle girl, Dorcas." Fernanda's sigh was a large one. "Sometimes now you sound almost hard. I'm distressed about you. The whole thing was only a plan for your own protection. You must understand that, dear."

"What whole thing?"

Fernanda sighed again. "When you were ill, Gino and I both knew how terribly upset you'd been by your friend Markos's death. It really threw you a little off balance, you know. In the nursing home you kept talking about seeing Mrs. Dimitriou when you were well. Gino said you must not see her. He said all those upsetting memories must be wiped out of your life."

"Gino said that?"

"Of course, dear. He felt we should do something for Mrs. Dimitriou, since Markos was your father's friend and yours. Gino was capable of a fine, generous gesture more often than you were willing to see. He sent me to Mrs. Dimitriou and I found that all she wanted was to get home to Rhodes. Gino

[174]

furnished the money, with something over as well. She no longer had anyone here, but he had friends in Rhodes and he sent her to them. He wanted you to know nothing about it. He said it was better for your own peace of mind if she just disappeared."

"And safer for him," Dorcas said.

"What do you mean, dear?"

For an instant Dorcas thought of speaking out, of putting into words her belief that Gino had taken a violent hand in Markos's death. But the very look in Fernanda's wide eyes stopped the words on her tongue. What was the use? Fernanda would not believe her. She would not listen, and she would use the accusation as further evidence of Dorcas's own lack of balance.

"So you helped Mrs. Dimitriou out of the country. And you knew where she was staying in Rhodes," she stated.

"I'm afraid that's true, dear."

"Then you've seen her since we came here?"

Fernanda nodded a little guiltily. "Of course I have. For Gino's sake I had to follow the thing up once I was here. That was natural, wasn't it?"

Dorcas walked over to the bed and stood looking down at Fernanda. "I'm glad you've told me the truth. Now you'll be able to take me to her, arrange for me to see her."

Fernanda closed her eyes and moved her head in the negative. "Of course I can't do that. Gino said you were to forget about the Dimitrious. He felt that if you tried to follow this mad notion of yours, whatever it was, you would be thrown back into your illness again. And from the signs you've been showing lately, I'm afraid it's true."

"I'm not ill any more," Dorcas said. "Perhaps I never was as ill as everyone tried to make me believe."

Fernanda reached out gently and touched her hand. "Poor darling. Let's not go over all this again. You can't push me, you know. Not any farther than you have. Gino has left me a trust where you and Beth are concerned. He knew what was best. If only you would believe that."

The impasse was clear. What could one do with a woman like Fernanda? When she chose she could be completely obstinate, and from the most generous reasons in the world. If Dorcas was to track Mrs. Dimitriou down, it would have to be done without Fernanda's help. Finding the woman seemed more important than ever. Only when Fernanda was confronted with the truth about Gino—a truth she could not evade—would she give up her efforts to come between Dorcas and Beth. Until then she would remain a threat and a danger. She had in her hands the weapon of Dorcas's illness and it was frightening to think what she might do if she decided to use it.

Back in her own room Dorcas found Vanda getting Beth ready for lunch. She did not want the woman around. Not now, when all her new worries might be evident. Vanda had been brought here by Fern Farrar. Yesterday she had been sent on an errand to Mrs. Dimitriou. Dorcas was sure of that now. One of her functions must be to watch and report to Fernanda on everything Dorcas said. Or was she really imagining too much? How was she to distinguish, what was she to trust and believe within herself?

"I'll finish Beth's hair," she told the woman curtly.

Vanda nodded and went into her room, closing the door softly behind her.

At least it was quieting to sit on the bed, holding Beth's small, wriggling person between her knees while she combed tangles from fine dark hair. Beth talked about her morning and Dorcas tried to listen. There had been woods and paths and rustic bridges in the butterfly valley. Aunt Fern and Vanda had gone up the hill above a little waterfall, but Beth and Johnny had stayed below to watch the water and drop pebbles and leaves into the stream.

The moment her pony tail was secured with a clasp and a ribbon, Beth whirled away. Pausing in her turn, she stopped beside the bed table and pointed.

"The silver owl, Mommy—it's gone!"

Dorcas spoke carefully. "Did you see it there last night, darling? Do you know who put it there?"

Beth looked surprised. "I put it there. I put it there for you to find, like the lady said."

It was difficult not to pounce and startle all information out of the child. "What lady?" Dorcas asked with forced casualness. "Do you mean Vanda?"

Beth shook her head. "No, it was the lady with the cat. She gave me the silver owl and tied it into my handkerchief. She said you would like to have it and I must give it to you. Only I forgot. So last night after you went to dinner I took it out of the knot and put it there. Did you find it, Mommy?"

"I found it," Dorcas said. "It's all right, darling. I have it."

There was no use in pushing the matter further with Beth. But this was something to tell Johnny.

For the rest of that day, however, there was no chance to talk to him alone. Fernanda kept them both busy. She was her exuberant self again, and if there had been strained moments between herself and Dorcas, no one would have guessed it from her manner. Fernanda had the ability to slough off the unpleasant and turn her back upon it with the utmost aplomb. She believed in Positive Thinking in capital letters and was always full of schemes which would truly improve the lives of other people, providing they would listen and do as she said. That she adopted such plans herself was evident, and they seemed to pay off in a bouncing energy and well-being that those who loved her sometimes found wearing.

In the afternoon Fernanda expounded on the interests of Petaloudes as one of the unique beauty spots of Rhodes, and Dorcas made notes.

"It's a shame we won't be here for the butterflies," she said. "Though of course there are enough accounts so I can write about them anyway. It's amazing how they come out in this one spot and nowhere else in the world. Little striped butterflies that cluster by the hundreds on trunks and branches. I've seen pictures of them."

Before Fernanda was through, she would be as much at home with the butterflies as though she had seen them with her own eyes. She would have made a wonderful fiction writer, Dorcas thought. The catapult ball was still riding around in Beth's tote bag in the back of the car, and every now and then Fernanda added embellishing notes to her story about it. Perhaps fiction was really her forte. Perhaps from the very beginning she had constructed a gigantic fiction about Gino, in which she herself thoroughly believed. Gino would have been well aware of what she was doing and thus able to inject into the picture his own fictions about his wife. He would have known that Fernanda would seize upon them and embroider in the direction he indicated. She was still doing this.

Since no day must be wasted, plans were already afoot for a trip to Camiros. They would go the day after tomorrow, Fernanda announced. Vanda was to have the day off to visit her village, so Dorcas could bring Beth along. Beth had been very good this morning at the butterfly valley—it had been a nice change for her. At Camiros they must have plenty of time to spend among the ruins, so they would pack a lunch and make it a picnic day. Perhaps they might drive into the interior of the island afterward.

No mention was made in this rush of words of Mrs. Dimitriou or any of the subterranean plotting Fernanda must have been engaged in for some time. Dorcas managed along the way to insert the fact that Madame Xenia had asked her to go through Constantine's poems the following morning. Fernanda did not warm to the idea, and if she had not had plans of her own for the morning, Dorcas suspected that she would have put her foot down in opposition. As it was, she gave in reluctantly and Dorcas phoned the Greek woman that she would keep her appointment.

In the evening Johnny went off by himself, so again there was no opportunity for Dorcas to tell him what she had discovered.

At nine o'clock the following morning Madame Xenia sent her chauffeur to drive Dorcas the few blocks to her home. The burly and voluble Stavros was in a cheerful mood. He drove the long way around at high speed, conversing fluently in Greek all the while. It did not seem to matter that she could neither understand nor answer him. He liked to talk, and she listened. Clearly it was enough.

The Greek maid admitted her at the gate, but Madame herself stood at the house door and it was at once evident that today she was playing a different role. Gone were the flowing robes and the air of tragedy. Instead, she wore a white blouse, a hand-woven black skirt with Greek warriors and a Grecian key in silver and blue running around the hem. She greeted her guest as warmly as though they were old friends and was charmingly diffident about Dorcas's opinion as she led her to the sculptor's studio.

"You will know which poems are best, I am sure," she said. "In this folder are the ones my husband translated. There are more in the large envelope on his desk. I have not gone through them all, since I am unable to judge what is best for American publication. You will be comfortable here, yes? There is a bell on the wall if you wish something. I must return now to the kitchen. Today I will make for you a very special lunch."

When her hostess had gone, Dorcas sat in the leather armchair before Constantine's wide desk and stared about her. An American typewriter had been brought in for her to work on, but otherwise the room must have been very much as it was when Constantine himself came here. It was a quiet, bright room, with no sounds penetrating from the rest of the house. Behind the desk windows overlooked the garden. There were plane trees and a distant wall, but no near neighbors to encroach upon the seclusion. She thought of Constantine sitting here idly in the perfection of his prison, or perhaps moving about the room, picking up the tools of his art and laying them down again. Had the genius of some of his earlier work reproached him when he had done so little of late? What resentments had he harbored sitting here, unable to work? Most of all, what was his connection with Gino?

She opened the folder and read through the first of the poems that had been translated into English. It was not concerned with modern Greece, but dealt with the golden past. By the time she had read through the third poem she was beginning to feel that Constantine Katalonos was no Pindar. He did not bring to poetry the gifts he brought to sculpture. Or else he was not very good in his attempt at English translation. Had he sat here turning out such verse on days when marble remained inert and his hands found nothing vital in the clay?

His presence made itself felt too keenly in this place. Like Constantine, she found it difficult to concentrate on work. It was too easy to imagine him watching her from some shadowy corner of the room. Her imagination supplied the narrow, sardonic face of the portrait with a pair of dark glasses and she could almost, almost, catch the sound of his voice. She did not want to hear it. She did not want Constantine Ketalonos to know that she, of all people, was working among his things.

She left the desk restlessly and went to stand beside the shrouded head from whose vicinity Madame Xenia had so firmly led her on that first visit. She guessed what might lie hidden beneath the cloth, but she was curious to see for herself.

As she whisked the covering away, the board the head rested upon swiveled at her touch. The face turned toward her—the face of Vanda Petrus. This was the portrait in the round that Vanda had said he'd done of her, and the reality surprised her. Vanda, in red-brown terra cotta, was warm, earthy, magnificent. In his subject the sculptor had found something worthy of his art. Dorcas studied the head in amazement. She had never glimpsed Vanda in such a light as this. Constantine had caught the woman's somber quality in the clay—the lines of suffering, but of passion as well, and a certain nobility. The face surpassed mere beauty. An inner quality of courage came through. The sculptor must have seen it there, but to see it, he must have known this woman well. Dorcas replaced the cloth and went thoughtfully back to the desk. It was difficult to imagine that sad, rather ominous man of Gino's errand creating something like this.

Perhaps the most surprising thing was that Madame Xenia had not destroyed the head in a fit of jealousy. Perhaps she had never quite dared. She would know that if her husband returned and found it gone she would have to answer for what had happened to it. So she had put it in a corner and shrouded it from view, waiting, perhaps, until it was safe to be rid of it? Vanda had said she would not permit the head to be displayed in an exhibition of Constantine's work held in Athens.

Having uncovered the masterpiece of the head, it was harder than ever for Dorcas to concentrate on the mediocrity of the verse. The rest of the folder revealed little that seemed worth the typing, and she turned at length to the large brown envelope. Among the papers she drew from it were more poems, some written in Greek and untranslated. There was also a sheet of white paper on which the sculptor-poet had been idly doodling. A row of smiling *Korai* looked up at her, and he had drawn the outlines of assorted Greek columns. Here and there among the scribblings was a figure she found repeated many times. Again and again upon this sheet of paper Constantine Katalonos had drawn a small, archaic owl with great round eyes.

Dorcas was staring at the drawings when Constantine's wife came into the room.

10 ᄆᄆᄆᄆᄆᄆᄆᄆᄆᄆᄆᄆᄆᄆᄆᄆᄆᄆᄆᄆᄆᄆᄆᄆᄆᄆᄆᄆᄆᄆᄆᄆᄆᄆ

"HOW ARE you working?" Madame Xenia inquired. "You are finding many suitable poems?"

"Not too many," Dorcas said. "I'm not sure any of them will be right for publication in America. But I'll try to select those I like best and type them for you."

Madame Xenia nodded. "That is good. What do you have in your hand?"

"I'm not sure," Dorcas said, and held out the paper.

"Ah—I see. This he does when his mind is far away. He sits with the pencil and it goes alone making small pictures. It is of no importance."

Dorcas touched one of the owls with a fingertip. "He seems to have repeated this figure a good many times—an owl with big eyes. What do you suppose it means?"

Madame Xenia laughed. "Come, I will show you."

She went to the figure of a marble girl dancing and turned the stand. "Do you see, here in the marble? Give me your hand."

She took Dorcas's fingers and brushed them across a marking cut into the base. Dorcas bent to look at the tiny symbol more closely. Again it was the mark of the round-eyed owl.

"It is his signature. This he puts on all work that is good. He chooses the owl because it is known through all the ancient world as a symbol of the wisdom and wealth and importance of Greece. When Constantine is very young he begins to make his mark like this—for luck, so that one day he will be rich and famous."

"I see." Dorcas laid the sheet aside and returned to her sorting. She was relieved when Madame Xenia tiptoed respectfully away.

So the mark of the owl was the mark of Constantine Katalonos. And if Vanda was right, he might be very much alive—hiding, perhaps in Rhodes itself. The possibility chilled her.

She picked up a new sheet on which he had made several attempts at English lines and read them absently. Then her attention quickened and she read more carefully. The words were no more than phrases, unconnected.

> Done is . . . deed . . .
> . . . Castle of the Princess . . .
> The bride of Apollo mourns. . . .

The Owl had sat at this very desk composing a letter that was to be sent to Gino Nikkaris in America. He had been experimenting on this paper with words that would have meaning to certain persons but not to others. The letter she carried in her passport case must have been the final result. She set the sheet aside and turned to the work of typing the poems. Her eyes dictated the words and her fingers worked automatically on the keys, but her thoughts lost themselves in frightening speculation.

[184]

When Madame Xenia came to summon her for lunch, Dorcas took with her the page on which Constantine had been trying to compose a message.

The meal was as delectable as her hostess had promised— lamb and rice cooked in vine leaves, beans in olive oil. Dorcas ate what was set before her and tasted nothing.

When there was a pause in the desultory conversation, Dorcas gave Madame Xenia the sheet of paper.

"What do you suppose this is? Perhaps the beginning of a new poem?"

She read the words aloud, puzzling over them. "The Castle of the Princess—that must mean Philerimos, where my husband liked so often to go. It is called by this name because in the monastery church there was a very famous ikon of Our Lady of Philerimos—much celebrated in the time of the knights. It is said that when they left the island they took the picture with them. But in the villages they still call the place the Castle of the Princess."

"And the rest?" Dorcas asked, trying to suppress any note of excitement from her voice.

"I do not know," Madame Xenia said. "Perhaps it was to be a poem."

She read the words again and Dorcas, watching her, saw the sudden tightening of her lips. All in an instant comprehension seemed to sweep through the woman and she looked as though she might faint.

"Is something wrong?" Dorcas asked. "You're not feeling well?"

Without answering, Madame Xenia reached for her wine-glass and drank. When she set the glass down, her hand was steady again and color returned to her face in a wave of warmth.

Dorcas gave her no time for recovery. "Perhaps the loss for which the bride of Apollo mourns could be the marble head of a weeping boy at the museum?"

Madame Xenia was still the actress and she controlled herself admirably. "I do not know what you are speaking about."

"When we visited the museum on our first day in Rhodes," Dorcas said quietly, "we had some difficulty in getting to see the famous head of the weeping boy. It had been put out of sight for some reason. When Miss Farrar insisted, it was shown to us, but I felt there was something wrong about the marble head we were allowed to see. I don't believe it was the original. As a patroness of the museum, perhaps you know what has become of the real head?"

The woman drank wine again, her eyes wary. "I do not understand what you say. It is not possible that anything could happen to the treasure of which you speak. I myself have seen it at the museum no later than yesterday."

"And you noted nothing wrong about it?" Dorcas asked.

Diamonds flashed on Madame Xenia's hands as she dismissed such nonsense regally, turning now to her own attack.

"Tell me, please, why are you interested in these unimportant words my husband writes on a sheet of paper? Undoubtedly this is like those small drawings. The words are without meaning."

"I don't think they are without meaning," Dorcas said. "After Gino's death a letter came to our address for him. The letter used some of these same words. There was no name, no return address, but the signature was a drawing of a round-eyed owl."

"If you have such a letter, I wish to see it!" Madame Xenia cried imperiously. "Perhaps it will tell me something of my husband."

[186]

Dorcas had no intention of showing her the letter. She had no reason to trust Constantine's wife. "I'm sorry, but I can't show it to you."

"Then the words of this message—you can repeat them, perhaps?"

"I don't know them by heart, I'm afraid," Dorcas said. "When I found the letter I had no knowledge that it was of any importance."

Madame Xenia released her breath in a long sigh. "You are right. These words are of no consequence. You can understand that to hear of this letter my husband had written—it gave me hope. It was a great shock. Most foolishly so."

"I don't think there was anything in it to help you," Dorcas said.

Madame Xenia went on sadly. "Constantine laughed at Gino Nikkaris and teased him many times. But he feared your husband and was under his spell. He would follow when Gino called. My good Constantine was no match for that man."

"I can't defend some of the things my husband may have done, Madame Katalonos," Dorcas said gently.

It could well have been that they were two of a kind— Gino and the "good Constantine." Partners, perhaps, collaborating in a theft that would shake the art world, once it was known. For the moment the museum officials were sitting on the lid, working secretly perhaps, hoping to discover the culprits and restore the original head to its proper place.

Once more Madame Xenia changed her course. "Please, you will not go to the police with this story? You will not go to the directors of the museum? This you will promise me?"

"But why not?" Dorcas asked. "You tell me the original head is not missing. So I don't understand—"

"Because you will make much scandal for the good name of my husband." She spoke vehemently. "This I do not wish to happen. His name will be very famous in Greece for the work he has done. If you cause a scandal, all will be lost."

"Tell me one thing," Dorcas said. "Do you think your husband could have made a copy of the weeping boy?"

Madame Xenia's response was played to the highest rows of a Greek theater.

"Constantine was the greatest sculptor in Greece today. Perhaps in the world! He would not stoop to make a copy of anything. Never, never!"

As abruptly as she had soared, she left her indignant heights and spoke in a more normal tone.

"I have not asked you here only to read my Constantine's poetry. Perhaps the poems are not important. But I think you must have some information of him. Or perhaps Miss Farrar knows something she does not tell me. This is why I ask you here—so it is possible to speak quietly, like two friends—yes?"

"I wish I could help you," Dorcas said. "But I really don't know anything at all about your husband. Gino never mentioned his name to me. If Miss Farrar has remembered anything, she hasn't told me about it. I have no wish to cause any scandal over this, madame. There's nothing to take to the police. So you needn't worry about that."

Her hostess seemed only partially satisfied with this assurance, but Dorcas agreed to come again, and they parted on a somewhat formal basis. By now, Dorcas suspected, Constantine's wife was glad to see her go. Obviously she had received a shock and was being torn in several directions by her own explosive emotions. Dorcas refused the use of her car back to the hotel and returned on foot.

Johnny had driven Fernanda somewhere and Vanda was out

with Beth, having left a note to say they would visit the aquarium a few blocks away. Dorcas walked in that direction and met them coming back. As the three followed the pleasant, turning streets together, Beth talked excitedly about the fish she had seen in the underwater tanks, but Dorcas's thoughts were elsewhere.

"This morning," she said to Vanda, "I worked for Madame Katalonos, typing her husband's poems. While I was in his studio I saw the head in terra cotta he did of you. It is a fine piece."

Vanda Petrus looked sullen, resembling very little the likeness Constantine had created. Dorcas could see nothing in her face of passion or nobility, but merely the usual careful watchfulness and air of resistance to any friendly overtures.

"At least I found out who it was who called himself the Owl," Dorcas said, alert to Vanda's response.

Vanda, however, did not show by the flutter of an eyelid that she had any understanding of what Dorcas was saying. Her silence seemed indifferent. Perhaps because she knew very well where Constantine was? After all, if he had really gone to America to look for Gino, why would he have mailed a letter to him from Greece? Knowing where the marble head was buried, Constantine might well be lying low in the absence of the partner he had depended upon, waiting for an opportunity to get the treasure out of the country. If a buyer could be reached, a buyer who perhaps waited for it in Turkey, Constantine would find himself a rich man and free of the domination of his wife. In the meantime, might he not fear that the existence of his letter would give the secret away to someone else before he was ready to get the head away?

While this course of speculation intrigued Dorcas, she

[189]

knew that there was too little evidence to rely upon. She was guessing wildly—that was all. And Johnny Orion would say so at once.

She must tell him soon what had happened in the house of Xenia Katalonos and see what he made of it.

For the rest of the day there was no opportunity. Fernanda was full of whims and notions and she kept both Dorcas and Johnny occupied.

In the late afternoon Johnny, hurrying to report to Fernanda, tapped on Dorcas's door and left a book with her.

"Pindar," he said. "I picked this up in a bookstore downtown. Since we're driving to Camiros tomorrow, you might like to have a look at his seventh ode. See you at dinner." He was gone, and there was no chance to talk to him.

Vanda was out with Beth, and Dorcas sat down to leaf through the volume. A long time ago her father had read Pindar loud to her. He had called him the poet of the elite. She found the ode Johnny had mentioned and began to read.

. . . Out of the winding water the island
blossomed, held of the father of searing sun-rays,
master of horses that breathe fire. Rhodes mixed with him
    bore
seven sons that displayed the shrewdest wits of the men of
    old time.
Of these, one sired Kamiros,
Ialysos, eldest born, and Lindos; sundered they held
the land of their patrimony in triple division,
each a city, and these are called by their names.*

* Richmond Lattimore's translation of Pindar's *Odes*. The University of Chicago Press, 1947.

[190]

Dorcas put the book down, thinking of tomorrow when they would see the first of the three ancient cities named for the grandsons of Apollo and the nymph Rhoda. She had begun to look forward to the day. At sometime or other there would be a chance to talk to Johnny, and at least she would be away from the hotel and the strange things that happened here. Vanda would be off to her own village, and Beth would be wholly in her mother's hands.

Restless, and eager for tomorrow to come, she put the book aside and went to stand in the balcony doorway. Palm trees stretched late-afternoon shadows across the pavement below. On the far side of the street a man leaned against a stone wall smoking a cigarette. Something about him arrested her attention. She could not see his face because the collar of his workman's jacket was turned up and his cap visor pulled down. He stood half lost in the shadow of a tree that overhung the wall and his attention seemed focused on the hotel entrance. Dorcas stepped out upon the balcony and the watcher flung away his cigarette and moved briskly down the street.

She was struck by the feeling that she had seen somewhere before a man who walked in that particular manner, and a stab of uneasiness went through her. The smoker had disappeared around the next corner and the street stood empty in the late-afternoon sun.

Dorcas returned to her room trying to thrust back the sudden unease that filled her. She mustn't be up to her old imaginings. There was no reason why a man might not lounge smoking opposite the Olympus. No reason to think he might be watching the hotel, or that she might be the object of such a vigil.

Prompted by a whim, she went to the dressing table and opened a top drawer. In it she kept the zippered satin case that held the few pieces of jewelry she had brought with her. She slid the zipper back and looked inside. Then she dumped the contents upon the bed. For safekeeping she had put the silver owl coin among these things. Although she searched through the trinkets more than once, the coin was not there. Had it been a "loan" then? Something to frighten her with and then take back?

It was Vanda, of course, who had done this. Vanda was the only one who had easy access to her room. True, Beth had brought the coin home originally, but it was Vanda who must have taken it back. Dorcas opened the door between their rooms and stood looking about at Vanda's few possessions The thought of searching through someone else's things was repugnant to her and she made no move. Besides, if she searched and found the owl coin in Vanda's room, what then? She could imagine what might happen if she showed it to Fernanda. It was possible that Fernanda would infer that she had put it among Vanda's things herself. Or else she would find the means to excuse Vanda. Nevertheless, she had to speak to Fernanda about this.

Closing the door, she returned to the balcony and went along it to the next room. Fernanda's doors stood open and her room was empty. As usual, it was in a carefree muddle. Sometimes Dorcas suspected that Fernanda never picked anything up unless she wanted to put it on. Sandals and high-heeled pumps were strewn about under chairs and under the bed—probably where they had been kicked since the maid made up the room that morning. A box of honey-nut candy stood open on her dressing table and Dorcas could count three half-eaten pieces left in various quarters of the room—one in the middle of a pillow on the opened bed. Since Fernanda never smoked, she used ash trays for catchalls and the two in

[192]

sight were heaped with earrings, safety pins, rolls of film . . .

Dorcas stopped her rueful checking and went quickly into the room. An object in one of the ash trays had caught her eye. She slipped a finger beneath a roll of film and pulled out the flat silver coin. She was standing there with it in her hand when Fernanda breezed into the room.

If she was surprised to find Dorcas there, she gave no sign. She'd never had much sense of property or privacy. She borrowed and loaned casually, and seldom closed her doors or paid much attention to the closed doors of others.

"Hi," she said. "Looking for something?"

Dorcas held out her hand. "This. It was missing from my jewel case and I thought Vanda had taken it."

Fernanda came across the room and took the coin almost playfully from her hand. "I do wish you'd get over being suspicious of poor Vanda. We're lucky to have someone so devoted to take care of Beth. As for this—it's mine now. Finders keepers!"

"Do you mean you went into my room and searched through my things deliberately?"

"Oh, dear, you make me sound practically dishonest. I was only doing it for your own sake. I knew that you'd keep taking the coin out and brooding over it. It seemed wiser to borrow it from you for a while. Of course, if you insist on having it back, here you are."

Dorcas did not look at the extended coin. "What were you going to do with it? If it's a genuine coin of old Athens, I suppose it has some value."

"I wasn't going to sell it, if that's what you mean," Fernanda said, laughing without self-consciousness.

"I didn't suppose you were. But you meant to return it to someone, didn't you? Fernanda, what do you know about

[193]

Constantine Katalonos? When you first heard that he had worked for Gino, you thought his name sounded familiar. Have you remembered why?"

The expression on Fernanda's face was suddenly guarded, alert. "What do you mean? Did anything happen at Madame Katalonos's when you went to work for her today?"

"Quite a number of things," Dorcas said. She took the coin from Fernanda and went back to her own room. It would not have surprised her if Fernanda had come after her, demanding to know more. Instead, she heard the soft closing of Fernanda's doors, and then only silence from her room.

Dorcas lay upon her bed and tried to think. It was clear that Fernanda had either remembered something about Constantine, or she had been informed about him. Through Vanda, perhaps, who was quite probably in touch with him. Or even through Constantine himself.

The intruder on her balcony that night had been a man. She was sure of that. It made her shiver to think that it might have been Constantine.

The plan came to her quite suddenly, and she knew it was something she would suggest to Johnny when she managed to catch him alone.

That night she went to bed quietly enough. No slouching watcher with pulled-down cap stood in the street before the hotel. The silver coin remained securely in her jewel case and the letter in her handbag. She fell asleep thinking of her plan. Perhaps Johnny would regard her as wildly foolish, but she had one definite, clear lead now, thanks to Madame Xenia. And she knew it must be followed. Johnny, whatever his reluctance, must be persuaded to help her. She fell asleep still trying to marshall her arguments.

Having a plan had given her a sense of peace and despite the

[194]

happenings of the day, there seemed less likelihood of disturbing dreams that night. Yet some time during the dark hours after midnight the dream enveloped her with all the acute painfulness of reality. She stood in the white halls of a museum, the statue of Apollo before her. She knew it was Apollo, yet she did not at once look up into that calm, familiar face. Therein lay her terror. She knew she must, inevitably, raise her head and gaze into the face of the god. And she knew disaster lay in that moment. Yet in the dream her eyes were open and in spite of herself she raised her head and looked. The face of the statue had the pallor of marble and the eye sockets were blank—yet it was the face, not of Apollo, but of Gino Nikkaris. In the fantasy of her dream she knew that Constantine had somehow imprisoned Gino forever in cold marble, though no prison of stone could contain his evil or suppress it.

Like water stirring, the dream shifted and she knew that in a moment the statue would move. The head would turn to look down upon her, the blank eyes would find her there with tears upon her cheeks. She must have made some struggle to escape, some physical movement that awakened her. Horror was a turbulence that washed through her body in wave after sickening wave, and she lay drenched in her own perspiration.

With a sudden jarring movement she turned to reach for the light. The room seemed quiet and peaceful. She got up to change her nightgown, and thought of going next door to stay for a while in Fernanda's matter-of-fact company. But she knew she must not. She must place no further weapon in Fernanda's hands.

Instead, she sat on the bed with her knees drawn up, her forehead against them. It was only a dream, she told herself.

[195]

It would not return when she went back to sleep. Gino could not touch her. Not any more. Still—there were those whom Gino had left behind, those who watched, those who whispered. Their faces, their very voices, their number—all these were masked, and she feared to see behind the mask. They followed some course that Gino had set for them and it was a course that could eventually destroy her. Where Constantine Katalonos stood in this was the greatest mystery of all. Was he for the watchers, or against them? Was he one of them? Tomorrow, without fail, she must tell Johnny her plan. It must wait no longer lest the faceless enemy move first.

II

THE WAY to Camiros lay inward from the sea. In ancient times, Johnny said, the very road they traveled had been lined with statuary. Now it was edged with trees and wild underbrush. Gently the way rolled uphill and there was no sign anywhere of the place itself. No columns rose on a hillside, no crumbling ruins stood shining in the distance. There were only the woods and the hills hiding the place where Camiros lay dreaming in the sun.

The road turned at length into a sandy open place and a guard came yawning from his hut to greet them. It was clear that they had come at a good hour and would have the place to themselves, free of other sight-seers.

Johnny parked the car and they got out. In Vanda's absence Dorcas felt a certain freedom, but the dream of the night before had left its dregs behind. She had not been able to free herself of fearful brooding. Always the pattern seemed the same. Just when tangible proof was placed in her hands concerning matters far from imaginary something would happen in the old way within herself—something to shatter the

[197]

delicate balance and make her unsure of herself. Like last night's dream.

At breakfast Fernanda had sensed her mood and tried to persuade her to stay home. "Let Beth come with us," she said. "You've got circles under your eyes and you're much too pale. Stay here and rest. I'm sure it will be better for Beth if you do."

Dorcas had dug in her heels and been as obstinate as Fernanda could be. She was quite all right, she insisted, and she meant to make the trip. Johnny had put himself gently on her side, although Dorcas saw concern in his eyes. Fernanda had given in.

When they were on their way, the feeling of an unknown dread had persisted, even though it had no place in a day so brightly blue and gold. At first when they had set out she'd had the jittery suspicion that someone was following them in a car. But after they turned off on the road to Camiros the persistent car had been lost on the coastal road and that particular sense had faded. Now that they were here she felt a little better.

Except for a few rough excavations there was still nothing to be seen of Camiros. The guard showed them the way they must take and then, since he spoke no English, left them to their own devices, posting himself on a high place where he could observe their progress.

Climbing a dirt path up a steeply banked ridge, they came upon the town suddenly, unexpectedly, and stood in silence looking down upon the astonishing display at their feet.

The empty, ancient ruins ran down a gentle slope of hill, from a high point at the back toward the sea they never reached. The two sides were contained and limited by ridges of hill overgrown with pine. Somewhere below the foot of the town the ground pitched off into emptiness and the sea lay distant and beyond.

"It looks so neat," Fernanda said in surprise.

This was true. Where other ruins might lie with tumbled columns all about, patches of restoration incomplete, and the earth rough with scattered rock, none of that was true here. In a sense, the town lay before them intact. Its stone foundations occupied the sloping space solidily from hill to sea, from ridge to ridge. There were no upper walls, no roofs, yet all the rooms were there to be looked down upon. Door spaces opened from one room to the next, partial walls made barriers between the houses. The buildings of Camiros had been built one against the next and there were no openings between except for places where paved streets ran through. A long stone avenue divided the town in half, running up the hill. At its foot were the remains of a market place, a few broken columns, some tombs.

The focus that arrested the eye, however, stood at the highest place above the town—that place to which all Greeks had looked for their gods. Only six columns remained rising against the sky—six slender columns with a narrow stone roofing connecting them, and a stone platform below. The Aegean blue of the sky burned between the shafts and the columns themselves glowed with a soft pinky yellow—the color of a cloud at dawn, the living, breathing color of the sandstone of Rhodes.

"How quiet it is," Fernanda said.

That also was true. Camiros lay sleeping in the golden light, its stone cupping the warmth of ages.

"I think," said Johnny softly, "that this must be the loneliest place in the world. In the end people didn't even die here. They just let the town go and moved away. No one

[199]

knows exactly why the three cities were abandoned, but they all went the same way. Camiros, Ialysos, Lindos, built by the grandsons of Apollo and all forsaken at last for the more recent upstart, Rhodes."

Fernanda started down the dirt path to the level of the town, her expression rapt, absorbed. Dorcas knew that she would make her readers see this, she would make them know what it was like to walk through the streets of this long-dead Rhodian town.

Johnny swung Beth to his shoulder and they followed Fernanda down the path. On the lower level they picked their way across sandy earth where weeds grew between the stones, where pine cones had fallen and sand burrs abounded. The main avenue of the town led upward toward the columns at the top, mounting in the Greek way of long, shallow levels of steps.

"I'm going up there," Fernanda said. "Suppose you look around down here for a while and let me go up alone. I can catch the feeling of it better alone."

They watched her go, sure-footed in her sandals, her new Greek skirt flapping in the wind, making a bright splash of blue and red against the dun-colored stone way. Johnny set Beth down and she ran to explore a roofless stone house whose broken walls came no higher than her head.

This was the moment when she could speak to Johnny, and Dorcas turned to him urgently. "Please—I want to talk to you."

The words seemed to shatter the dreaming quiet and Johnny shook his head at her. "This is no place for worries. Be free of them today."

They found a low wall where Queen Anne's lace grew tall, and as Dorcas sat down upon it a small green lizard darted into a crevice. Johnny stood looking about him. He reached out to a great pile of stone that had been a tomb, bending to examine a faint marking, still unerased by the erosion of time.

"Look," he said.

The calm order of this place, the singing beauty of it, was quieting. The urgency that had welled up in Dorcas lessened a little and something of the tautness went out of her. She bent with him to see the marking. There was only a single word:

Χαῖρε

"Do you know what it means?" Johnny said. "They used it a lot, those old Greeks. 'Be happy.' Just that—'Be happy.' Perhaps it was a farewell to those who were gone, and counsel as well to the living."

Something in her reached toward the meaning, to make it her own. Johnny looked at her and then away, as if he did not want to intrude on what might be a private healing.

"Camiros belongs to the ages before Pericles," he said. "But even then they knew a wisdom that Egypt somehow missed. In Egypt people lived for the hereafter and in constant fear of the gods. They expected nothing but suffering in the present. But while the Greeks honored their gods, they believed in men. They accepted the tragic in life, yet they believed there was something noble in man himself. They were realists in the best possible sense."

So many times Dorcas had heard her father speak of these things.

"Yet the barbarians came from the north and destroyed it all," she said sadly.

"Not all," Johnny said. "Some of the best of all man's thinking was left. Perhaps every breath a civilized man draws had its start here on the Aegean."

He sat beside her on the wall. Beth ran happily through small stone rooms, talking to herself, content in her make-believe. Now that they were a part of this place, small sounds began to make themselves heard through the stillness. On the ridge behind them wind sighed in the tops of tall pine trees, and somewhere cicadas were singing. From underground came the cavernous sound of water running through deep cisterns of the town. The air was fragrant with pine, with the tang of sea air. Beyond the drop off of the lower ground the water near shore was a brilliant, emerald green. Farther out lay the purple-dark Aegean. There was nothing to shut out air and sunlight and the sight of the sea. Camiros had no secrets—all was open and clear in the warm golden honey of the light.

Be happy, the words said in crumbling stone.

Johnny sat near her, and the feeling between them was alive again, as it had been a handful of times.

"You're quiet now," he said. "Tell me what you wanted to talk about."

She found herself free of the terror left by her dream, found herself able to speak without frightened haste. She began to tell him all that had happened to her. Of how Madame Katalonos had shown her Constantine's mark on sculpture he had done—the mark of the Athenian owl.

"Do you see what it means?" she said. "The two circles like the eyes of an owl! Constantine is the owl. Will you believe me now?" She touched his hand lightly in quick, eager pleading.

He turned his fingers and held her own reassuringly. "I believe you," he said.

[202]

She went on to explain how Madame Xenia had identified the Castle of the Princess as Mount Philerimos.

"So that's where Constantine must have hidden the marble head. That's what the note says. If I'm on the right track, then the head is still there, buried in the ground. Johnny, let's go to the mountain and look for it."

"At the hour of devils?" he asked, smiling.

"Of course. If we can get away from Fernanda, let's go there tomorrow. I don't think we ought to wait."

"You don't want to take Fernanda?"

The moments of peace were gone. She reacted almost violently. "No! I don't trust her any more. She came into my room and carried off the silver owl coin. And she's trying to take Beth away from me. Haven't you seen that, Johnny?"

The concern was in his eyes again. He held both her hands tightly, held them until she calmed a little. She spoke more quietly, still trying to make him understand.

"I wouldn't put it past Fernanda to try to finish up some business of Gino's, just because she feels he'd want her to. Take me to Philerimos, Johnny!"

But he would not promise. "We'll see," he told her, and nodded toward the Greek word upon the stone.

She drew her hands away impatiently. "How can I be happy when everything is so wrong? How can I find the way to be happy again?"

"It means more than that," Johnny said. "Do you remember the famous funeral oration Pericles made after Athens had lost so many of her young men in war? He didn't ask those who heard him not to grieve. He didn't tell them they'd made a noble sacrifice and advise them to put grief aside. He expected them to accept what had happened. To accept grief and pain and go on from there with what they had left. To look

[203]

facts in the face and move on. The facts of yesterday aren't always the facts of today."

She sensed something of what he meant—that she was still a frightened prisoner of all that had happened to her. That she must fling off the enveloping memories that stifled her and separate the present from what was done with. But that was already what she wanted for herself, and only she knew how difficult it was to achieve. If those who threatened her were real, then her anxiety was justified and grew from sound cause. If some of this, perhaps a good portion of it, came only from the cobwebby stuff of dreams, then she was, indeed, in a terrifying position from which she must struggle to escape.

Far up the hill from her place between votive columns Fernanda waved to them and called.

Johnny stood up. "She's through meditating. Shall we go up there and join her?"

Dorcas nodded mutely and started up the stone way with Beth's hand in hers. There was nothing more to be said between them for now. If she could find Mrs. Dimitriou, perhaps she could prove what was real out of all this. If she could lead Johnny to where the marble head was hidden, he would have to believe.

They climbed the gentle rise through a town leveled to their knees and open to the sky. Once Dorcas stopped to look at footprints visible in a block of stone. Here a statue had stood —the image of an honored town father, perhaps, or of some celebrated athlete. Now only the imprints of stone feet were left. This, too, was reality.

At the top of the hill a high red bank of earth rose steeply, crowned by the six remaining columns of the temple. They found a way up and mounted the steps to stand beside Fernanda.

There had been restoration here, but tracings of ancient fluting still showed in the stone high over their heads.

Beyond the columns were stone cisterns set deep into the earth, their underground channels running down through the town. From the cisterns one could walk to the edge of a steeply pitched ravine where yellow-flecked bushes grew thick. The hills of Rhodes rolled away, green and alive, unlike the bare, baked hills of the mainland.

As they turned back to the town, windy clouds swept across the sun and the light changed before their eyes. The golden honey hue was swept away and the ancient stones whitened.

"There it is," Dorcas whispered. "Homer's 'silvery Camiros.'"

Somehow her hand was in Johnny's and the current flowed strongly between them. They walked down again into the silvery town and watched as the sun of Greece turned it once more to gold.

"I can feel it all through me," Dorcas said. "The peace, the quiet. It's telling me how to be happy. If I could just hold some of this—carry it away with me!"

She was aware of Johnny smiling even as he shook his head in denial.

"The peace of Camiros belongs only to Camiros. I don't think we can take it with us. I don't think I'd even want to. This is a dead town, Dorcas. The Greeks turned their faces toward life, toward living. I suppose more than anything else peace is an inward thing. Some men know it in the midst of great tragedy or danger. Maybe it comes first of all from belief in ourselves, from liking and trust in ourselves."

She could not accept that. There were too many times when

she did not like or trust herself at all. The peace of Camiros held outward healing in it. She did not want to let it go.

For another hour they wandered among the warming stones. The guard had given up and no longer watched them. No one came to disturb the silence. By the time the sun was high and Beth tired, they were ready for lunch. Back at the car they had their picnic, while Camiros lay hidden beyond its ridges as though they had only imagined it.

When lunch was finished, Fernanda spread a map open on nearby bushes and she and Johnny discussed possible routes. Fernanda wanted to go on through the interior of the island for a few miles and then circle back to the sea. The road from Camiros was good and they would see some beautiful scenery, with several small villages along the way. But Johnny, studying the map, shook his head.

"That's the logical route, I'll agree. But I suggest going off the main road to this nearest village first."

Fernanda peered through her glasses and objected firmly. "That road may not be good and it certainly doesn't go anywhere. A waste of time. No, we'll follow the other route, Johnny."

Johnny cocked his red head on one side in his most exasperating way. "I'm sorry, Miss Farrar, but there is one small matter I've neglected to bring up. It's my fault and I am sorry, but the gas tank is nearly empty and we've got to head for the nearest village."

Fernanda seldom lost her temper, but now she came close to it. She was cross with Johnny and further annoyed when Dorcas tried to back up his choice as the sensible one. She refused flatly to have anything to do with his plan.

"In that case, we'll go back to the coast road," she said. "We'll give up our trip and return to Rhodes."

Again Johnny overruled her. "Look, it's too bad, but this village is close. I think we can make it that far. Not any farther."

For good measure, Johnny queried the guide first, but he apparently lived hereabout and came to his job on foot. He had no supply of gasoline.

Since she had no choice, Fernanda gave in, but she was peeved about the whole thing and would not sit in the front seat beside Johnny. Dorcas and Beth moved up in front and Fernanda sat in the back seat and indulged in a fit of the sulks.

The offshoot of road, while narrow, had been well tended, so the trip was not, after all, difficult. It took them no more than fifteen minutes, traveling uphill beside a dry river bed where pink oleanders bloomed profusely. Now and then as the road climbed they glimpsed the small white village above. Driving through a stand of pine forest, they came into the open where the village clung precariously to a steep hillside. The car bounced along a narrow cobblestone street, took a sharp turn or two, and wound up in the open square of the town on its last few drops of gas.

"We made it," Johnny said with satisfaction. "Now we need to find someone who'll understand what we want. Where's your word book, Fernanda? Though I must say the place looks deserted at the moment."

Dorcas glanced about at whitewashed houses and a small domed church—all seemingly empty of life in the midday sun. But even as she looked, the scene came alive with astonishing speed. Curious faces appeared in doorways and at windows. Children swarmed into the street excitedly and their elders followed. A woman with a baby in her arms and another small child clinging to her skirt came directly to the car window and looked solemnly into Dorcas's face. When

[207]

Dorcas smiled, she smiled back and held the baby closer. The men approached more slowly than the women and children, but they came as well.

"Hello!" said Johnny to the throng in general, and got out of the car. Several children shouted "'allo!" and surrounded him at once.

Fernanda was still peevish. "Do hurry up with it," she called from the back seat.

Johnny did not hurry. He opened the door and took her hand, pulling her from the car. "The least you can do is let them have a good look at you. You, too, Dorcas. I don't imagine Americans come here every day. Play it up. Show them your hair, Fernanda."

Ordinarily, no one had to tell Fernanda to play it up, but today she did not thaw until a little girl offered her a hastily picked handful of wild flowers. Then she, too, came to life and began to make the most of the situation. She lifted Beth and held her for the children to see. In moments she was involved in an English lesson and being parroted by a delighted audience.

With so thorough a focus of women and children around Fernanda, and the men clustered about Johnny—up to his ears in language difficulties, with everyone trying to help—Dorcas found herself free to look about by herself.

The entire town consisted of a handful of houses, a few alleyways, and a main street. Around it the hills rose in a solid mass of green, setting off the white dwellings men had built in this steep place. She found a side street that ran into a bare path winding through a meadow. To reach it she must pass the tiny church, and as she turned in that direction, a woman dressed in black, with a black shawl over her head, came down the few steps. She did not look about her as she hurried up

[208]

the street, but there was a moment when Dorcas saw her full face. The woman was Markos Dimitriou's wife. There was no time to think, to plan. The opportunity was too sudden. It must be grasped at once.

Hurrying, Dorcas walked beside her. She had to speak before the woman was aware of her presence.

"Mrs. Dimitriou, do you remember me? I'm Dorcas Brandt —Mrs. Nikkaris. Your husband's friend. Will you please let me speak with you?"

The woman stopped abruptly and turned to face her, thrusting the shawl back from her head. She no longer looked like an American. She had aged and saddened, Dorcas saw with regret, and she seemed frightened—as though she were ready to dart off through the nearest doorway.

Dorcas touched her arm. "Come, please. Over near that field, where no one will notice us. The village people are all around the car that brought us here."

After a moment of hesitation Mrs. Dimitriou nodded reluctantly and went with Dorcas to a wall where they sat upon sun-warmed stones, while an inquisitive goat trotted over to study them.

A little breathlessly Dorcas explained about the great debt she owed to Markos. Not only the money, but a debt of gratitude she could never repay. The money, at least, she must return. She had it with her in traveler's checks. She would cash these in Rhodes and get the money to his wife.

With a gesture that bespoke dignity the woman stopped her. "There is no debt, Mrs. Nikkaris. Your husband was very kind in my time of trouble. He sent Miss Farrar to see me after Markos died. He could not come himself to see me because he had to be away, but he helped me through Miss Farrar. He helped me to come to Rhodes. Miss Farrar took

[209]

care of everything as Markos would have wished. There is nothing you owe us now."

Dorcas looked into the woman's worn face and her eyes misted. Mrs. Dimitriou saw and responded warmly.

"You must not be sad. It is good that I am here in the hills. In the old city of Rhodes I was not happy. The stone walls crushed me in and I was a stranger. In this village they accept me and I will make my home here."

"Did they tell you I was looking for you?" Dorcas asked.

The woman was silent, glancing around at the goat, as if she could not meet Dorcas's eyes. It was clear that she had been forbidden to speak freely.

"Who is it that doesn't want me to talk to you? Dorcas persisted. "What harm can there be?"

Mrs. Dimitriou spread veined hands in a gesture of pleading. "Please—it is not good to speak of these things that are done. I wish only to live quietly and trouble no one."

"Miss Farrar has been to see you, hasn't she?" Dorcas said. "It was Miss Farrar who sent you here so that I wouldn't find you in the old city?"

Quite suddenly the woman began to cry. She covered her eyes with a corner of her shawl and wept bitterly, silently. Dorcas watched in dismay.

"Markos was the dear friend of my father," Dorcas said. "He was like a father to me after my own father died. You know this is true?"

Mrs. Dimitriou bowed her head in silent assent.

"I would have come to you myself after Markos died if I had not been ill. You know this, too, don't you?"

Again there was the quiet bowing of the head.

"I wanted to come," Dorcas said urgently. "I read in the paper that you reached the hospital before your husband died.

I wanted to ask you about his death. Forgive me if I'm causing you pain, but will you tell me about this now?"

Mrs. Dimitriou managed to dry her tears. She began to speak slowly, painfully. There was little to tell. The police had come to let her know what had happened. She had gone at once to the hospital and a nurse had taken her to Markos's bedside. There was no hope. The miracle was that he still lived for that length of time. He had refused opiates and had called for his wife. Very soon after she came, he died holding her hand.

"Did he say nothing to you about how it happened?" Dorcas asked.

Mrs. Dimitriou shook her head. "He could scarcely speak. He said nothing of the accident. He asked many times for Gino Nikkaris. He said the name over and over, but there was no time to bring Gino Nikkaris there. Later I told Miss Farrar how much he had wanted his friend in that bad time."

Dorcas felt suddenly cold there in the warm sunlight. She had come at last upon the truth she had sought for. It was clear in all its terrible import. Markos had never told his wife how he felt about Gino. He had not been repeating the name of one he thought a friend. He had been saying over and over the name of his murderer. Yet this was not something for Gino's widow to tell the unhappy woman who thought of Gino Nikkaris as her benefactor.

"Thank you for telling me," Dorcas said gently. "I must go back to the others now. It's good fortune that I found you."

Mrs. Dimitriou made no effort to go with her. She stood beside the wall and watched her go. Once Dorcas turned and waved to her, but the woman did not wave back. She followed slowly, and the next time Dorcas turned she saw that Mrs. Dimitriou had stepped into the doorway of a house that faced the square. She was still watching, her shawl drawn over the lower part of her face.

As Dorcas approached the group, Fernanda beckoned to her frantically. "Where on earth have you been? We're waiting for you. We've found enough gas to get us started. So do come along."

Dorcas got into the car and they drove away amid smiles and waving farewells.

As they turned a corner, Dorcas looked back. Not at the waving crowd, but beyond, to the place where a woman in black stood alone in the a doorway. Just as the turning car removed her from sight, a second woman came to stand beside her. Dorcas had no more than a glimpse, but it was enough.

The second woman was Vanda Petrus.

12 〰️

FERNANDA, having recovered from her sulks, once more sat up in front, while Dorcas and Beth rode in the rear. Dorcas held Beth on her lap and waited until they were out on the road, following the route originally intended. For at least twenty minutes she held back her impulse to blurt out everything. When at last she broke in on something Fernanda was saying, she heard the tension in her own voice.

"I saw Mrs. Dimitriou in the village," she said. "That was why you didn't want to go there, wasn't it, Fernanda? You had Vanda take her there, so I would have no opportunity to speak to her."

Beth stirred in her lap and looked anxiously into her mother's face. "Mommy?" she said inquiringly. And again— "Mommy?"—as though she questioned her mother's identity.

"Oh, Dorcas!" Fernanda cried despairingly. "And just when I thought you were improving a little. She reached over the seat and patted Beth's cheek. Don't worry, darling, it is your mommy. She's just upset herself a little."

[213]

Dorcas forced herself to speak more quietly. "I saw Mrs. Dimitriou. I talked to her. When we drove out of the village, I looked back and saw Vanda Petrus standing beside her in a doorway."

"This sort of upset is what I was afraid of," Fernanda said. "I didn't want it to happen in front of Beth. You'll remember, Johnny, that I wanted Dorcas to stay home."

Dorcas hugged Beth so tightly that the little girl cried out that she was being held too close.

It did no good for Dorcas to tell herself that what Fernanda thought and said did not matter. It mattered terribly, and she was afraid. Fernanda was as much under Gino's spell now as she had ever been when he was alive. Unless her mistaken loyalty to him could be turned aside, she might very well succeed in her clear intent toward Beth. What had happened today, even the things Fernanda had just said, made it all the more evident that she would have no scruples about the way in which she achieved her ends. Apparently she was ready to deny the truth and use everything that happened as further proof of instability on the part of Beth's mother.

Because realization of how far Fernanda was willing to go was so frightening, Dorcas tried to put it from her mind for the moment. She forced herself to watch the pine-brushed mountains and deep ravines, the curving road as it spun on ahead of them. She watched the details and tried not to think. Sometimes Johnny slowed for a donkey with a woman sitting sideways on its back, her head and the lower part of her face covered with a scarf, her feet in boots of yellow leather, all in the manner of Rhodes.

On the drive back to Rhodes she turned her thoughts once more upon the quiet memory of Camiros. How lovely the hours there had been. How calming the honey-gold aura of the sleeping town, its silence broken only by the singing of birds and wind in the pine trees, its motionless dreaming disturbed only by lizards that ran among the stones.

"Be happy," she told herself silently. What if she gave in to Fernanda and stopped opposing her? What did it matter if Constantine hid from his wife? Or if Fernanda sent Mrs. Dimitriou away to Vanda's village? What did it matter if a priceless marble head had been stolen from a museum and that Dorcas Brandt might hold the key to where it was hidden? None of these things could help her to find peace. To concern herself with them was not to be happy.

Johnny was wrong. If she let herself die a little and cling only to the peace of Camiros, Fernanda would be pleased. She would let her keep Beth, so long as it was on Fernanda's terms. All the vague threats that hung over her would be lifted. Fernanda was fond of her, really. It was just that she was still devoted to Gino and she put Gino's child ahead of all else. Fernanda herself did not truly know the difference between what was real and unreal.

When they reached the hotel, Dorcas went straight to her room. She stood in the open doors to the balcony, watching a red-gold sun dip toward the sea. In the street below palm trees cast the same long shadows they had cast last evening, reminding her of what she wanted to forget. She would have turned away, but movement caught her eye. The watcher was there in the shadow, slouching, with jacket collar pulled up and visor down. Again she had the feeling that she had seen that slumped, indefinable figure before, that he was here because of her.

Abruptly the safe peace of Camiros evaporated. She ran downstairs and out the hotel door, down the steps and into the street. By the time she reached the sidewalk the shadows were quiet with the serenity of the quick Aegean dusk. She had known they would be empty. It was not yet time for those who watched to let her come near them. When they were ready they would move—and then it would be too late.

She walked among the quiet shadows and strangely there was no terror in her. It was better, she found, to act. Johnny's words were reaching her with a delayed effect. She could not surrender to Fernanda's unreal world. The peace of Camiros was indeed the peace of a place empty of life, and for that she was not yet ready. She had felt herself coming alive through the touch of Johnny's hands and she wanted to stay alive. To "be happy" was sometimes to fight for one's life and one's responsibility to others. Only then could liking for herself evolve. In the growing darkness the scent of jasmine was warmly sweet with a memory of the sun. But the savoring of such sweetness was not all of life.

Why had she thought the finding of Mrs. Dimitriou and the answer the woman had given her meant nothing because Fernanda had turned her back upon the truth? It was for herself—for Dorcas Brandt, first of all, that this reaffirmation of the truth was necessary. She need never have doubted herself. She would not again give in to Fernanda, who wanted to shake her belief in herself because of doubts that were hers, not Dorcas's.

As long as the evil Gino had set in motion lived on she would dream of the statue that looked at her with Gino's eyes and mocked her weeping with Gino's laughter. She could not be free to be happy until the matter was finished. The seventh tear had not yet been shed. Even though Fernanda, and even Johnny, might set themselves against her, she knew herself now and knew that she was ready to fight back.

When she went upstairs, Fernanda was in the hallway with

Vanda Petrus. They must have been talking about her, for they fell suddenly silent when she appeared. Vanda slipped away to the bedroom to stay with Beth.

Fernanda spoke to Dorcas. "Come in here a minute, dear, will you?"

She had nothing to say to Fernanda at this point, but there was no way to refuse.

In her bedroom Fernanda kicked off her shoes and flung herself full length upon the bed.

"Sit down," she said. "I want to talk to you."

Dorcas sat upright in a straight chair, braced for resistance toward whatever was to come.

"What happened today was most unfortunate," Fernanda said. "It was the thing above all else that I wanted to avoid."

"I'm sure that's true," said Dorcas.

"Don't be bitter, dear. What did Mrs. Dimitriou tell you?"

Dorcas did not hesitate. She, too, must use whatever weapon came to hand.

"She told me the last words her husband spoke before he died—the name he kept repeating. Gino's name. Mrs. Dimitriou believed that Markos was speaking of his kind friend."

Fernanda plumped a pillow behind her and sat up against it. "And what did you think?"

"I thought she was misinterpreting," Dorcas said quietly.

"That's exactly what I was afraid of." Fernanda closed her eyes as though she could not bear to see Dorcas's expression. "I think I'd better tell you something, dear. Gino never wanted me to, but there are occasions when I must follow my own judgment. It's time for you to understand what really happened. Dorcas, Gino was driving the car that struck Markos down. He saw the man quite clearly before the impact and he

[217]

knew how hard he had struck. It was one of the few times in his life that Gino ever lost his head. He knew what you would think. He knew the accusation you might make and the danger he was in. So, foolishly, he drove away."

"He told you it was an accident?" Dorcas asked.

"It was more than an accident, dear. It was a dreadful, dangerous, unforseeable coincidence. Gino had to save himself."

"It was not an accident," said Dorcas evenly. "It was deliberate. Gino murdered Markos Dimitriou. He left me in an angry, revengeful mood and he meant to do something violent. It wasn't even a sudden rage by the time it happened. It was intended, premeditated."

Fernanda opened her eyes and there were tears in them. "That's exactly what Gino said you would believe. That's why he told me what really happened. So I would be prepared if you ever tried to make such an accusation. To me, the most tragic thing of all is the way you've turned against Gino, Dorcas. We both hoped so much, Gino and I, that you would come out of your—your illness a new woman. That you would be the loving wife Gino wanted you to be. In fact, it seemed to us that this was going to happen when you first came home. But I knew when he died that he meant nothing to you. For Beth's sake I've been silent, and I've tried to help. But what am I to do if you slip back into your old emotional state? That's why I regret what happened today. Because it has opened old wounds, aroused delusions you should have recovered from."

Dorcas stood up. "Tell me just one thing. What would your position be if you knew without any doubt that Gino had run Markos Dimitriou down deliberately?"

Fernanda's large person seemed to stiffen there on the bed.

"What you are saying isn't true, of course. But if it had been, I would have stood by Gino, no matter what happened. Because if it had been true, then he would have needed me more than ever and I would never have let him down."

What was there to say in the face of a devotion so stubborn and misguided? Dorcas left her and returned to her own room. It did not really matter in the book of Fernanda's devotion whether Gino was guilty or not, or of what crimes he might be guilty. She would oppose any move to throw suspicion upon his name or interfere with what he might have wished to happen. What must be done must be kept from Fernanda lest she take sides, even though innocently, with those who watched.

That evening the three of them went downtown to dinner. It was a strange meal, with Fernanda and Dorcas curiously polite and on guard with each other. Johnny, who did not know what had passed between them, was puzzled by this evidence of a rift, though he asked no questions.

More than once during the meal Dorcas tried to show him in small ways that she had accepted his words, that she had begun to understand. She was no longer seeking for the lifeless happiness of escape. She was ready to build toward something real, with all the risks and dangers being truly alive might imply.

After dinner Fernanda suggested a short walk along Mandraki before they returned to the hotel. The moment they went outside they were aware that something was going on up at the castle. Lights were changing against the walls and recorded voices were shouting down from the castle in Greek.

At once Fernanda's interest stirred. "It's the Sound and Light spectacle they're putting on. This is something I must see. Let's go up there."

Dorcas had done enough sight-seeing and she shook her head. "If you and Johnny want to go I'll stay here outside the walls. There's a bench under the trees where I can wait."

"Go on ahead, Fernanda," Johnny said. "I'll look for you in a little while."

Fernanda was not pleased, but she disappeared through the gate into the castle grounds, and Dorcas and Johnny sat on the bench, heedless of the display above them.

"You're looking better tonight," Johnny said. "You look like a girl who's made up her mind about something."

She turned to him eagerly. "I have! I'm beginning to understand a little of what you tried to tell me today at Camiros. I mustn't let my own belief in myself be shaken so easily. That's part of what you mean, isn't it?"

"So you're no longer an affrighted gazelle?" Johnny said, and there was tenderness in his voice. "I like it better this way."

"This afternoon," she went on, "I found out for certain the thing I needed to learn. Mrs. Dimitriou told me quite innocently that her husband had repeated Gino's name over and over before he died. She thought he was speaking of his friend. But I know better. Markos was trying to tell his wife the name of the man who deliberately ran him down in that car. Fernanda doesn't believe this. She says Gino told her it was an accident. Gino was always able to make her believe anything he wished."

Johnny's arm came about her and once more she knew how very much alive she was. There was belief in his touch. But even if he doubted, she would hold to her own conviction now and let the rebirth of confidence heal her.

"You've had a pretty bad time, but it's over now," Johnny said. He turned her face toward him in the darkness and kissed her mouth. It was not a gentle kiss, and she sensed a comforting anger in him at the things that had been done to her.

"Now that you know the worst of all this, it will fade out if you'll let it," he said. "You've found the answer, you know the truth. Can you set a full stop to the whole thing now?"

He did not wholly understand. How could he? But it did not matter.

"There's more to be done first," she said. "The thing isn't finished. The thing Gino started is still going on. I don't know what it is, but I know it's evil. And there isn't anybody to oppose it but me."

He asked no questions. "We'll go to Philerimos tomorrow," he promised, and she knew he had taken his place beside her, whether he believed or not.

"Thank you, Johnny," she told him. The words were simple but he would understand what lay beneath them.

On the hill above the castle flared into a new combination of light and the clash of a pretended siege grew louder.

"Maybe I'd better go look for Fernanda," he said. "She's a bit peeved with me, I think."

Dorcas nodded. "You go after her. I'll wait for you here, Johnny."

She watched as he walked toward the gate, his figure square-set and strong, silhouetted against flaring lights. "I'll wait for you, Johnny," she repeated softly. Nothing like Johnny Orion had ever happened to her before. A warm happiness released the last tension. Johnny would never hurry, or harass, or crowd her. She would learn courage from him, learn to be alive again as she had not been for so many years.

How long she sat there in alternate shadow and light she did not know. When at length she moved and drew her coat around her, feeling the chill of a breeze from the sea, she saw that she was no longer alone. Others had gathered about this open space beside the wall. There were groups here and there watching the final climax of light and sound. The ramparts glowed an angry red, and the underlying voices beat out the mock danger, the alarm.

In spite of the tumult, the footstep behind her was so near that Dorcas heard it. She would have turned, but there was no time. Out of the darkness a hand reached to touch her. It cupped her chin lightly, quickly, the fingers drawing in a swift caress along the line of her jaw, down the side of her neck. And was gone.

Only one person had ever touched her like that. Only one!

The thing was like one of her dreadful dreams. The cry she tried to utter choked in her throat, frozen there. For an instant terror held her so acutely that she could not move at all. Then she stumbled to her feet and turned about wildly. There were only strangers watching the burning of the castle, strangers whose eyes were not upon her. Yet he had been here, he had touched her. She knew that in the full agony of terror.

13 𐌂𐌂𐌂𐌂𐌂𐌂𐌂𐌂𐌂𐌂𐌂𐌂𐌂𐌂𐌂𐌂𐌂𐌂𐌂𐌂𐌂𐌂𐌂𐌂𐌂𐌂𐌂𐌂𐌂

MINDLESSLY, DORCAS began to run toward the castle gate. High above, red lights faded and a calm golden glow enveloped everything. The music lifted and voices shouted in final triumph. Yet she heard nothing except the cry of desperation in her own mind.

Fernanda and Johnny came through the gate just as she reached it. She ran to him and he put both arms about her to still her trembling with his own steady strength. He said nothing, but held her quietly, while Fernanda tried to ask questions.

Dorcas managed to speak the words at last. "It was Gino! He touched me! He put his hand out and touched me in the darkness. I know it was Gino!"

"I've seen her go into spells like this before," Fernanda said. "We've got to get her to the hotel at once."

Dorcas whirled on her. "Don't talk to me like that! This is what you've been hiding from me. This is what you've known all along—that Gino is alive. He touched me—I know he touched me!"

[223]

"You've gone completely out of your mind," Fernanda said. "If you keep this up, I'll have to call a doctor."

"Let her alone," said Johnny, sharp with Fernanda for the first time in Dorcas's memory. "You can see that something has happened to her."

"I know what's happened to her." Fernanda's hand upon Dorcas's arm permitted no opposition. There was a determination in her that would not be resisted.

Dorcas found herself firmly propelled in the direction of the car. When they reached it, Johnny helped her gently into the front seat, leaving Fernanda to the back.

"Take it easy," he said. "You aren't alone, you know. I'm with you all the way on this. You've had a bad fright, but you mustn't let it destroy the steps ahead you've taken."

For all his concern and kindness she knew by his tone that he did not believe it had really been Gino. There was nothing to do except get herself in hand, lean on herself. She did not doubt for a moment what had happened. What she was dealing with now was real. The misty confusion, the self-doubts were gone. Her fears had been fearfully justified beyond all expectation.

At the hotel Fernanda would not permit her to go alone to her own room. "You must stay with me tonight," she decided. "We can't let you frighten Beth while you're in such a state."

Again she was parroting words Gino had spoken that other time—the warning that Beth must be protected from her mother. This was something Dorcas had experienced before and if she was not careful it would have her once more pounding helplessly against the walls of what amounted to a prison. But Johnny was here now. Johnny would not let that happen, even though he, too, seemed helpless to oppose Fernanda at the moment.

[224]

A second bed was brought to Fernanda's room. Vanda was summoned to fetch Dorcas's night things. Johnny lingered, helping when he could, looking unhappy and not a little alarmed. Dorcas sat in a chair and watched them. The tears had dried on her cheeks and she was quiet now.

Once Fernanda stopped before her and spoke, not unkindly. "Dorcas dear, we're not doubting that something happened to frighten you. It's the way you're interpreting this that's upsetting you so badly. Any flirtatious male might make a gesture toward a pretty girl alone."

"And disappear so quickly afterward?" Dorcas asked.

Fernanda shrugged largely. "Who knows what a Greek will do? But for you to think it was Gino—my dear!"

Dorcas said nothing. No one but Gino could know of a caress that had been his special sign of affection in the early months of their marriage and a frightening mockery of affection later.

From a bottle in her medicine kit Fernanda shook two capsules into her palm. Johnny went for a glass of water.

"A good sleep will help," Fernanda said. "You'll be over this by morning. For Beth's sake you must be."

She did not want the capsules. She wanted to think, to weigh, to understand. But there was no resisting Fernanda. Her strength was waning in sick reaction. As she took the glass of water, she looked at Johnny.

"Philerimos tomorrow?" she said.

He was clearly miserable. "We'll see how you are when tomorrow comes. You may not be up to the trip, Dorcas."

"I'll be up to it," she said. "You promised me."

She felt like a child pleading for a reward: "If I am a good girl you will give me the mountain." There was little logic in her conviction that she must go to Mount Philerimos. She knew only that it was an active step, something to do when no other way of fighting seemed possible.

"What are you talking about?" Fernanda demanded suspiciously.

"I'll tell you later," Johnny said. And to Dorcas, "The promise holds." He put a finger beneath her chin to tilt her head and his touch was not like Gino's. "Have a good sleep tonight. Your friends are close and there's no need to worry."

She closed her eyes, accepting his assurance as far as it went. Johnny still did not believe in the cause of her fright. And he did not understand that Fernanda stood with Gino against her.

When he went away and she was alone with Fernanda, she could only sit staring at her in aversion.

"Come," Fernanda said, "let me undo that back zipper."

She made herself stand docile while Fernanda ran the zipper down and helped her pull the dress over her head. As Fernanda shook it out and reached for a hanger, Dorcas stepped mechanically out of her pumps.

"I hate to say this, dear," Fernanda spoke over her shoulder, "but I'm afraid you're not very good for Johnny Orion. I'm fond of that young man. I'd hate to see—"

"Yes, I know," Dorcas said. "If I have a husband alive, I'm obviously the wrong girl for Johnny Orion."

After that she did not speak to Fernanda again. The fact did not seem to disconcert Miss Fern Farrar. Her assumption that she was dealing with someone emotionally disturbed was clear. Her movements were as efficient as those of a nurse, kindly but impersonal.

When Dorcas was in bed, Fernanda went to bed herself and sat up with the reading lamp turned carefully away from Dorcas's eyes, while she read a paperback mystery novel.

Dorcas lay with her face toward the wall and let the thoughts come as they would. If Gino was alive and hiding here in Rhodes, then she would be faced by the most fearful of all problems before this thing was done. First of all, the problem of Beth. The little girl must not fall into her father's hands. Gino was capable of any unscrupulous action that would give him what he wanted. And if he were alive, he would not let Beth go forever.

Tomorrow on the trip to Philerimos she would talk calmly to Johnny. The panic of first fright would be over by then. She would make him understand and believe, as she had not been able to do tonight. Johnny would help her.

Next there was the problem of Fernanda. If Gino was alive, it was not possible that Fernanda did not know. Under any and all circumstances Gino could trust Fernanda. If she was useful to him, he would use her, and she would allow herself to be used. That was clearer than ever now.

But why would Gino make his presence known to his wife? The gesture he had made was typically cruel and devastating, as only Gino would know it could be. But why, if he was safely hidden for some purpose of his own, would he choose to betray himself to the one person he had most reason to distrust? Had he seen her with Johnny? Had he seen Johnny kiss her?

The chill wash of terror went through her again. Never had Gino relinquished anything that belonged to him. What he possessed, he possessed with an all-enveloping grasp, whether the item had lost value for him or not. He would never have let her go by any choice except his own. What Gino arranged could be permitted. The choice of others did not exist. Perhaps, from the beginning, Fernanda in her role of devoted handmaiden had encouraged his tendency to play the role of a god-like being who could do no wrong and to whom all that he wished must be given. There had been no one like Johnny's father to take hold and do what needed to be done with Gino as a young boy. Or would it have been hopeless anyway?

Gradually the sedative took effect and all feeling deadened. The sense of struggling against walls that closed about her faded and she slept.

In the morning her mouth was dry and she had a headache. She awakened to see that Fernanda was dressed and opening the balcony doors wide to morning air. Dorcas sat up on the edge of her bed, struggling from the fog that had blotted out consciousness all night long. For a moment she did not know why she was in this room.

"Beth?" she said. "Where is Beth?"

"Good morning," Fernanda said cheerily. "Vanda has just taken her down to breakfast. We didn't know how long you would sleep. How are you feeling now, my dear?"

It was all there again, emerging from the fog to engulf her sickly. She stared at Fernanda with a dislike she had never felt before.

"Gino is alive," she said. "You needn't try to fool me any more. He gave himself away last night."

Fernanda came briskly to her side and felt her forehead. "A bit of a temperature, perhaps? Why don't you lie down again, dear? I'll send a tray up for you when I go downstairs."

Dorcas pushed her hand away and got up to walk unsteadily to the bathroom. Under a stinging shower she came slowly to life. She hated this thick-headed feeling. Today Johnny was to take her to Mount Philerimos. She neeeded to think clearly, to be calm and unemotional. She would not pretend with Fernanda that Gino had not touched her last

[228]

night, but she would give her no handhold for treating her like an invalid.

When she came out of the shower, Fernanda had gone downstairs, leaving her a note to come along if she felt like it. Coffee would help, the postscript said. She dressed, fumbling a little, and followed the others downstairs.

Every morning two of the small tables at the dining end of the lobby were put together for them at breakfast—since Vanda and Beth joined them for this meal. They were all there ahead of her—Fernanda looking calm and collected and not at all as though she hid any terrible secrets. Johnny was making Beth laugh, while Vanda watched the child with the same absorption Dorcas had noted in her before and which always made her uncomfortable.

They looked up as she approached the table, Beth with a cry of pleasure, Johnny with a question in his eyes.

"What plans today?" Dorcas asked Fernanda over her first cup of coffee, trying to sound casual.

"I've some appointments," Fernanda said. "And Johnny tells me he has promised you a drive to Philerimos, if I can let you both off. I can't make it up there with you today, but he's probably right that a change of pace will do you good. I won't ask you to make notes, or do any observing for me. I don't think there's much to be seen up there anyway except for the monastery and the view. What time will you leave?"

Johnny smiled at Dorcas. "An hour or so before noon, I'd say." He had remembered about the "hour of devils."

When breakfast was over, Fenanda sent Mrs. Petrus on an errand, and somehow Beth went with her. When Dorcas tried to object and keep the child in her own company, she was quickly overruled.

"You're oozing disquiet," Fernanda told her when they

[229]

were back in her room. "You must know that it isn't good to be with Beth when you're like this. It frightens her. I hope you'll return from your drive fully recovered from your upset of last evening."

In spite of good resolutions, Dorcas lost her temper. In words that spilled out in anger, she repeated her account of what had happened while she waited beneath the castle walls last night. Fernanda listened impassively with the endurance of a nurse who must humor a difficult patient. Before Dorcas was through, she knew fully how hopeless it was. Fernanda had closed a door in her mind and there was no way to get through unless she chose to open it again.

During the morning Dorcas went for a long walk through the streets of the outer city. By the very vigor of physical movement she held herself in check. To accept reality meant to deal with it. There need be no shame in fear so long as she stood up to it.

Standing up to the fact of Gino was desperately hard. All the ramifications were sweeping in now to engulf her. Where yesterday she could move easily at Johnny's side, Gino now stood between—which might well mean danger to Johnny, as well as hurt to herself. She had only to recall what had happened to Markos. Worst of all was the fact that Gino was Beth's father, and the knowledge that he would never willingly give her up. With Fernanda's help it might be rather easy to remove Beth from her mother's hands and give her over to her father, to return Dorcas to the hospital.

She fought back the touch of familiar hysteria that started at the pit of her stomach. This time she would not go to pieces. This time she would fight back with full knowledge of the treachery around her, full confidence in her own sanity.

Johnny had given her that. Johnny did not dream how much he had given her.

That morning she saw no man with a pulled-down cap when she came out of the hotel or when she returned from her walk. But just before she left her room to join Johnny, she looked down from the balcony and he was there again, She called Johnny into her room to show him the watcher. The man must have seen them looking down, for he ground out his cigarette beneath his heel, and went around the corner, stepping lightly and quickly, for all his hunched-over stance. Johnny was unimpressed. Nevertheless, when they got into the car, he drove about the neighborhood to please her. The man she had noted was not to be seen. For the first part of the drive an uneasiness about him remained and she had the same feeling she'd had before—that of being followed.

Again they took the shore road that ran toward Camiros. Johnny talked idly, cheerfully as he drove, and she knew he was trying to distract her from her own fearful thoughts. Only once did she break in on his words.

"You trust Fernanda, don't you?"

"She has never been anything but honest with me," he said readily.

"Even that other time when Gino was along?"

"Even then," he said. "As I told you, I thought he was using her as an innocent cover. I don't believe she had any suspicion of what it was all about."

"This time she would have to know," Dorcas said. "She is helping him deliberately."

"Unless you've made some sort of basic mistake," said Johnny gently.

After that she stared straight ahead through the windshield and did not try again. The old walls were closing to seal her in. Even if she were crushed by them, no one would hear her cries. Not even Johnny. A prisoner falsely accused must feel like this, she thought. Able to get through to no one, to make no one believe. Unless—unless Fernanda and Johnny were right and she was wrong. Unless she was really suffering from a persecution sense, a fear of Gino that made him seem alive and a constant danger to her. But then, surely, she would see him everywhere. She would have believed the watcher at the hotel to be Gino, and this was not true. While she had not seen the man's face, he had been a big man, far larger than Gino.

It was the first time she had wavered into self-doubt since she had come to a reckoning with herself, and she would not allow it. There was no question now that she was dealing with anything but reality.

The shore road ran through little villages. Often the doors of houses they passed were painted a bright particular blue seen often in Rhodes. Drying wreaths hung upon many of the doors—spring wreaths that wouuld later be burned in mid-summer ceremonies on Saint John's Eve.

Their way left the sea and they were again upon the road to the airport. In the distance, across the open plain, could be seen the airport building and the hangars. On the left rose the sheer rocky flank of Mount Philerimos. It was a long bulk of mountain with a flat plateau on top.

"There's a lot of hill up there," Johnny said. "Where shall we start the search?"

"The place must be near the Castle of the Princess," Dorcas said. "That is the church and we can start looking around there. Something will come to us. I'm sure it will."

After the attractive suburban village of Trianda, the road turned directly toward the mountain. Back and forth it zigzagged among the pines, climbing steeply now, until they came out at last on a wide expanse near the top. A tourist bus was there ahead of them and as they got out of the car, a stream of sight-seers came toward them through iron gates that led to the monastery enclosure. Fortunately, the group was leaving, and it appeared that Dorcas and Johnny would have the mountaintop to themselves.

The day had turned gray and intermittently cloudy, with a strong, whipping wind. They stepped through the gates and climbed the steps into the open space before the old monastery. Dust and sand rose with every gust of wind and Dorcas felt the sting of it through her stockings.

"Over there is all that remains of Iyalisos," Johnny said.

In a corner of the grounds lay what few foundations were to be seen of the city that had occupied this height long before the monastery was built. There was little to see, although Dorcas stood for a few moments on the brink of the excavation, looking down upon the handful of broken stones.

"Does anything come to you?" Johnny asked. "The sun is right," he added, glancing up at the sky where a few rays filtered through clouds directly overhead.

Dorcas felt a shiver run through her. The crumbling stones of Iyalisos seemed a place of the dead. Here there was none of the dreaming peace of Camiros. There were no shadows. Everything was gray and lifeless—except the wind.

She turned in relief toward the great medieval buildings of the monastery. Here there was still evidence of life. A huge round bell tower with a deeply arched doorway in its base rose at one end of the building. Narrow stone steps climbed outside the tower. In the courtyard stood an old well, very deep and hollow sounding when Johnny dropped a pebble into it. All about were cypress trees, their tall heads swaying in the wind. No human stirred, and they turned toward low, red-tiled buildings where monks had walked the arcaded passage of a cloister for hundreds of years after the gods of Greece had taken their leave.

This orderly, well-kept place seemed unlikely for their search. There must be caretakers inside, although they were invisible now. The two walked around to the rear of the buildings and found an expanse of field where small daisies and bright red poppies grew wild. Nearby rocky cliffs plunged toward the plain far below. Anywhere—or nowhere—might have been chosen for the "grave."

"How could the person who received that note know where the marble head was buried?" Dorcas said despairingly. "The clues are all given, except the one most important one—*where.*"

"Maybe there's something we're missing completely," Johnny said. "Let's not give up yet."

But searching here seemed pointless and Dorcas turned into the wind and walked toward the iron gates, her skirts blowing against her legs, sand stinging her face.

"There must be a lookout point," she said. "I suppose we ought to see the view, since we're here."

A path opposite the gates ran in a long, straight line toward the place where the light beacon stood. They followed it between cypress trees and discovered that they followed a Way of the Cross. At intervals bronze plaques had been set into stone columns, each representing a Station of the Cross—a scene in relief from Christ's passion and suffering. On the left side of the Way as they passed the fourteen stations lay the steep drop off of the mountain. On the other, beyond guardian cypress trees, lay an open field, flower-sprinkled, and rimmed

[234]

around with a forest of pines. On the cliff side of the path thistles grew thick, their heads in purple bloom.

Dun-colored earth swirled in gusty clouds as they walked toward the end of the mountain. There the path terminated and steps led up to a stone-enclosed circle. As they mounted this higher platform the tremendous view spread out all around.

In the center of the plain below the air strip drew a ruled line toward toy buildings of the airport. Olive trees were polka dots cast across the earth. Beyond, hills rolled away to the interior of the island. Turning from the plain, Dorcas could follow the coast line along a gray, rolling sea clear into Rhodes. The nose of the fish was visible, as if they looked down upon a relief map, and even the distant shores of Turkey could be seen.

They braved the wind for a time because of the splendid view. Here there was no stinging, blinding dust—just a clean, pure wind from the sea.

"I'm glad we came," Dorcas said. "Even if there's nothing to find, I'm glad I'm here. It's so remote from Rhodes and—" She did not speak the name she was thinking. It was no use.

Johnny was watching her, and she sensed his continued concern. She held out her hand as clouds blew away from the sun, and its shadow fell on the stone almost directly below. "This is the time to be afraid. They should be about now—the noonday devils. But how are we to know what they think of us, or whether they are for or against us?"

"With the Stations of the Cross nearby, I expect we're safe enough," Johnny said.

Dorcas turned her back upon the view and crossed the stone circle to where steps led down. The narrow Way stretched from their feet to the Castle of the Princess. She put an arresting hand on Johnny's arm as he came to stand beside her.

"Johnny—the Way of the Cross. Of course, of course! Don't you see—this is a Via Dolorosa."

He whistled softly and repeated the words of the note. "Dolorosa, dolorosa, dolorosa!"

"Yes! There were three of them, Johnny. Now we know where the grave must lie."

They hurried along the Way to find the third Station. Overhead the sun was still clear in the sky and the column that held the plaque cast only the thinnest fringe of shadow at its foot. There was spongy, needle-packed earth beneath the close-growing cypress hedge behind the column. Johnny knelt on the ground and felt of the needles with his fingers.

"We need something to dig with!" Dorcas cried. "This is the place—it must be the place!"

Johnny's red hair was bright in the sun as he knelt and his grin was cocky. He reached into a pocket of his jacket and drew out a gardener's trowel, its handle bright with green paint.

"You'll have to give me credit," he said. "I believed in your notions enough to make this purchase. Would you like to break the earth?"

She knelt beside him, warm with excitement, not feeling the wind as it whipped through the cypress trees. The spongy, cone-strewn earth was easily lifted in the trowel as she scraped it way. Beneath the loose carpet lay earth more solidly packed. Yet this, too, gave way without great resistance to her trowel. She dug only a few inches when the steel edge struck something hard with a sharp click.

"There's a stone in the way," Dorcas said. "A stone or—" Or—marble? She could not say it aloud.

[236]

Johnny took the trowel from her hand and began to dig systematically around the hard shape of whatever had been buried there in the earth. Once, as he worked, Dorcas stood up and looked all around. It seemed for a moment that she had heard some sound. But birds sang in the pine woods and the little meadow behind was empty and quiet. Along the path dark cypress trees stood guard hiding them from view, and all was lonely, secluded, remote. She knelt again and saw the elipse of smooth creamy stone showing in the brown earth.

Neither of them made a sound until Johnny had loosened the packed ground all about. As he dropped the trowel and put both hands into the earth, Dorcas released her breath in a long sigh. Very gently he lifted the head from the grave where Constantine Katalonos must have buried it for safe-keeping. The marble was heavy and he rolled it onto the grass where it lay looking up at them in all its young beauty—this head that must be two thousand years old.

14

HOW SWEETLY the tendrils of hair curled about the young forehead, how terrible was the grief that parted young lips and let fall a single tear upon rounded cheek. One could sense this ancient sorrow as if it were young and fresh.

Dorcas touched one finger lightly to the little marble tear.

"So you were right," Johnny said. "You were right all along. Now we'd better get this back to the museum fast. What are we going to carry it in? I don't fancy bearing it away openly in my hands. And my credibility didn't prompt me to bring along a bag."

Dorcas stood up, brushing pine needles and earth from her knees. "That canvas tote bag Fernanda put the stone ball into—it's the very thing. I'll go fetch it from the car."

"Good girl," he said. "I'll stand watch against the squirrels while you go after it."

She took the long, straight path on flying feet. The wind at her back seemed to carry her buoyantly along. She had been right! She had known. Now Johnny would believe—not only this, but all the other things as well.

The tourist bus was gone and there were no cars but theirs in the open space. She knelt in the back of the car and tumbled the stone ball out onto the floor. With the tote bag in hand, she hurried back. She was out of breath and panting a little by the time she reached the third Station of the Via Dolorosa.

"I've got it, Johnny!" she cried, and went through a gap in the cypress barrier.

For a moment she thought he had stretched out face down upon the grass to sleep. Then she saw the wet red stain upon the collar of his jacket, the matting of the hair above. She dropped to her knees and bent over him in alarm.

"Johnny, Johnny! Can you hear me?"

He stirred as her hand touched his shoulder and moaned faintly.

"Lie still," she said. "Don't try to speak."

She looked all around, but the loneliness prevailed and there was no one in sight. Somewhere down the hill she heard a sound like the starting of a car. The sun was hot and bright now, and the noonday devils must be laughing. She thought of running to the monastery for help, but she couldn't leave Johnny alone and bleeding. She loved him so very much, and she hated with all her heart the one who had done this thing. If Johnny died—

She was praying for strength, for help as she searched her handbag and found a stock of extra handkerchiefs, always carried because of Beth. Only once did she glance toward the empty grave. The head was gone. She had known the moment she saw Johnny that it would be. It did not matter now.

The wound seemed superficial, but scalp wounds could

bleed badly and what injury to the bone there had been she could not tell. She fastened a padding of handkerchiefs to the place with strips of adhesive bandage, and the bleeding seemed to be contained. As she worked he began to recover consciousness. He would not lie still, but rolled over and sat up dizzily, his head in his hands.

"Someone must have been watching us," Dorcas said. "He must have come upon you from behind. You didn't hear anything? Or see anyone?"

He groaned and opened his eyes. "Nothing, no one. I wasn't paying any attention. I didn't expect—"

"I know," Dorcas said. "Everything seemed so peaceful. It's my fault. I shouldn't have believed they'd let us find it. We must have shown them the way. I'm the one who knew about them—I should have been on guard."

Johnny got groggily to his feet and Dorcas put an arm about him, offering her shoulder. This time the distance seemed far greater because he weaved a bit and could not move with any speed. She wanted to stop at the monastery, rout out the caretaker, but Johnny refused.

"I'll be okay. Let's get back to the hotel."

She helped him into the back seat where he could stretch out. She had never been much of a driver in hilly country and the road down to the plain frightened her. But she did what had to be done, swinging the car around the zigzag turns, keeping it under control. It was all right once they were on the level. The road was empty and she could step up their speed.

By the time they reached the shore road, Johnny was sitting up in the back seat, making plans.

"The hotel first," he said. "We'll tell Fernanda, if she's around, and then we'll turn this over to the police. If I'd half

[241]

believed in all this, I'd have gone to them in the first place. Or at least to the museum people. Now all I've done is lose the head for them—perhaps for good."

"Rhodes is an island," Dorcas said. "They can't get it away at once. I heard a car starting up after I found you. We can't be far behind them."

At least he wasn't doubting her now. At least he wasn't regarding her as unbalanced and neurotic. No matter what Fernanda might say, Johnny would be on her side from now on.

When they left the car at the hotel, Johnny refused help and managed to walk in by himself. They went upstairs to Fernanda's room. She had just come back from lunch and she opened her door in amazement.

"Ask the hotel desk to call a doctor—Johnny's been hurt," Dorcas said at once.

Fernanda picked up the telephone without needless questions. "Mr. Orion has had a serious fall," she told the desk clerk. "We wish a doctor to come as quickly as possible."

"Where is Beth?" Dorcas asked as she put down the telephone.

"Vanda has taken her out," Fernanda said. "Lie down on my bed, Johnny, and tell me how it happened."

Johnny seemed glad enough to stretch out on his stomach, one cheek turned to rest gingerly on an arm. "It wasn't a fall," he said. "Tell her, Dorcas."

Dorcas told the story. The whole story this time—of how they had gone searching for the marble head because of the Owl's letter that had been sent to Gino by Constantine Katalonos. Of how they had found the head on the Via Dolorosa—and lost it, with Johnny struck down from behind and left bleeding on the ground.

[242]

As she talked, Dorcas watched Fernanda intently. She saw the flush of color rise in her face, and then recede, leaving a pallor behind. She knew exactly what Fernanda was thinking —that Gino was behind all that had happened. He might not have told her everything.

"What do you propose to do?" Fernanda asked when the story ended.

"We'll see the police," Johnny said. "And we'll call in the museum people, put the job of finding the head in professional hands."

Fernanda walked restlessly to the balcony and pushed open the shutters that shielded the room from the sun. She turned abruptly at his words, her exclamation involuntary.

"Oh, no! Don't do that!"

Johnny lifted his head a little to stare at her, and Dorcas spoke quickly.

"Why not, Fernanda? Why don't you want us to see the police? Is it because you're protecting Gino?"

Fernanda came back to them and it was clear that she had made one of her quick decisions and was once more in full control of herself.

"I was hoping that you'd come home from your drive completely recovered from your hallucinations, Dorcas. I see you haven't, and I'm afraid I'll have to hold to an earlier conclusion I'd come to. I've sent Beth away with Vanda to a safe, comfortable place. She will stay away from you, Dorcas, until you are over this. Beth is Gino's child and I have a duty to her. I will not let her be disturbed and frightened by these notions and this emotional state of yours. I'm sorry to hurt you, but until you recover—because you *are* ill, my dear— she'll have to stay away."

[243]

Dorcas grasped Fernanda by one wrist and was glad to see the older woman wince.

"What have you done with Beth?" she cried. "Where have you sent her?"

Fernanda pulled her hand from Dorcas's grasp and stepped back without answering.

Johnny rose a bit dizzily from the bed and put an arm about Dorcas. "Steady on. We'll get Beth back to you, of course. Fernanda, maybe you didn't understand. I didn't fall —this was a murderous attack. Everything that Dorcas has claimed since we arrived is true. The man on the balcony, the effort to get the information the note contained—I believe in them all now. Today we were undoubtedly followed and because I was a fool and listened to you, instead of to Dorcas, we walked into a trap. There's no need for you to worry about her being unstable or unfit to care for Beth. Dorcas is as well balanced as you are, and maybe more so than I am at this particular moment. If she wants Beth, you'd better bring her back."

Expressions of outrage, indignation, and amazement chased themselves across Fernanda's face, settling into a pattern of obstinacy that Dorcas knew all too well. When the telephone on the bed table rang, Fernanda picked it up and answered without a tremor in her voice, gave instructions, and set down the receiver.

"It's the doctor," she said. "He's coming right up. Johnny, you'll tell him it was a fall and neither of you will say anything else. Neither of you will go to the police, or to the museum people, or to anyone at all. Not for a while, at least."

"You can't stop us!" Dorcas burst out.

"I can stop you," said Fernanda levelly. "Because if you make one move toward the authorities, I can't answer for

Beth. If you want to see her again, you'll say nothing at all."

"You—you wouldn't harm her?" Dorcas faltered.

"Of course I wouldn't harm her. But I'm in a position to keep you from seeing her if that appears advisable. And that's what I'll do if you open this up in any way at all."

Johnny went back to the bed and sat down. "You're crazy, Fernanda. There are laws about kidnaping."

The doctor's rap sounded on the door and Fernanda spoke cheerfully as she went to answer it. "How silly you'd look with a kidnapping story. Especially with Dorcas's history of instability—near insanity. Where do you think you would be if I pooh-poohed this whole notion of an attack?"

"The museum is missing the marble head," Dorcas said quickly.

Fernanda opened the door and the doctor came into a surprisingly silent room. Dorcas looked at Johnny in mute pleading as the doctor walked to the bed. He spoke a little English and when he asked how this had happened, Johnny told him briefly of a fall from a stone wall on Mount Philerimos. The doctor examined the wound and said that the damage did not appear to be serious, though an X ray might be advisable to check against fracture. He arranged a more professional bandaging and suggested that Johnny stay in bed for the rest of the day and take plenty of aspirin.

Dorcas sat in a chair across the room, staring at her hands. She could not bear to look at Fernanda. What had happened was too fantastic to comprehend all in a moment. But she had no doubt at all that Fernanda meant exactly what she said and Johnny knew it, too.

When the doctor had gone, Johnny got up and went to Dorcas without a glance for Fernanda. "How about seeing the invalid to his bed of pain?"

[245]

"Now look here, you two," Fernanda said, a ring of astonishing good will in her voice, "you needn't feel that the sky has fallen. As long as you behave sensibly, all this is sure to turn out right in the end."

"I wouldn't rest easy if I were you," Johnny said. "We're not going to take this lying down, you know. As a start, you can consider that I've resigned from your employment. As of now."

They left Fernanda looking virtuously aghast, and Dorcas followed Johnny to his room.

"I've got to find out where Fernanda has sent Beth," she said the moment the door was closed.

"Of course," he agreed. "We're going downtown to talk to the police as soon as we can."

Dorcas stared at him in alarm. "No, Johnny! We can't do that. Not yet."

"It's the only sensible move," he said. "I hate to involve Fernanda, but I see no other way."

Dorcas shook her head. She knew Gino better than Johnny did. While they were going through the difficulty of making themselves understood by the police, Gino would be off, and Beth with him—if that was where Fernanda had sent her. At the back of Dorcas's mind a plan was beginning to form. But she dared not tell Johnny what she meant to do. In his present state he could not help her and he would be sure to worry. It was necessary to act before Fernanda had a chance to collect herself and take steps of her own.

"You've got to rest, as the doctor said," she insisted. "I'll keep an eye on Fernanda in case she makes any move. She can cause an awful lot of trouble, Johnny. Even though I'm frantic about Beth, I can't afford to make things worse."

Somewhat reluctantly he gave in. He took off his bloodstained jacket and lay down on the bed with a sigh of relief.

"Give me an hour," he said. "I can think better lying down. This nutty stand of Fernanda's will take some circumventing."

She drew the blanket gently over him. What had happened to Johnny was further evidence of the danger of the situation. She wanted no further harm to come to him because of her.

"An hour," she said, and went quietly out of the room.

In the hall she stood listening outside Fernanda's door. There were reassuring sounds from within. She was still there. Apparently she was not flying into immediate action.

Dorcas went swiftly toward the stairs and ran down to the lobby. She walked downtown at a brisk pace and hurried along Mandraki. A crowd of tourists, just off a boat, were streaming toward the city walls. She sidestepped the current and went through the gate at the foot of the Palace of the Grand Master—the castle that had been so brightly lighted in last night's make-believe.

Once inside the walls, she found her way easily to the Street of the Knights. All her moves were assured, and she held both fear and anger in check. If she thought about Beth now it might weaken her. She must be fully braced for the encounter that was to come.

It was easy to see how Vanda had given her the slip that other time. There were back entrances to some of these courtyards. Vanda could have turned up an alleyway with Beth and then slipped back through a second entrance, losing a follower completely. But today Dorcas knew where she was going.

The cat, Cleobulus, dreamed beneath the bougainvillaea vine, but Dorcas did not go into the courtyard. Instead, she mounted worn stone steps and climbed beneath the stone arch to the second level. There she found herself in a passageway above the entry, with doors opening off it here and there. Behind one of the nearby doors music was playing. A record player, perhaps. She had heard it before. It should have spoken to her that other time—he always liked music about him. She went to the door and raised her hand to knock. Then she stood motionless for a moment, fighting back her physical fear of what might lie beyond this door.

When the battle was partially won and her hand steady enough, she rapped sharply upon the wood.

He came at once to open the door and stood looking at her without surprise. "I wondered how long it would take you," he said.

The dark flash she remembered was in his eyes. His smile was the same, giving him that deceptive, disarming look of youth that so charmed Fernanda. And had once charmed Dorcas Brandt.

He stepped back to let her in, and she walked into the small stone room that he had made into his home for reasons known only to himself. There was no sign of Beth, no sign that a child had been here. Faced by reality, she was finding in herself a strength she had not known before. The shock of last night was over. Perhaps all along, from the very beginning at home, this was the thing she had most dreaded and would not face. Now the truth was in the open and nothing mattered except Beth.

She looked about in cool detachment. It was not an unattractive room. Gino Nikkaris had always displayed more sensitivity toward things than toward people. Things could be possessed and held more surely than people. A dark red Turkish carpet of intricate design covered the boards of the floor. A shawl of Greek embroidery hung against the whitewashed wall. There was a stand to hold the record player, and a small bookcase. On the bookcase stood an alabaster vase, simple of line and undoubtedly valuable. Leaning against a nearby wall were several paintings—Gino's efforts to sustain the fiction that he was a working artist. Yes, it was here that Fernanda had come on their first visit to the old city.

He switched off the music and turned toward her with the same disarming smile. "What a temptation you offered me last night, *bellisima*. A young woman alone in the darkness. Alone after the redheaded American went away. I had to let you know that you are not free."

"Wasn't that a risk for you?" she asked. His smile could no longer reach her, terrify her. She saw it as if from a distance.

He shrugged and brought a chair with a rush seat for her to sit on. When she sat down, he took his place on the room's narrow cot and reached for a packet of cigarettes. She watched as the match flared, lighting his dark aquiline face, striking highlights for an instant in his thick dark hair. When the cigarette was lighted, she spoke.

"Where is Beth? Where have you made Fernanda send her?"

His laughter always had a musical sound, even when it set the teeth unpleasantly on edge. "She's in a good enough place, my small daughter. A safe and rather amusing place. All things considered. Fernanda says you are behaving badly again. It's better if you don't see Beth for a time."

She could not remain coolly remote. She clasped her hands in her lap, trying to contain her rising fury. Rage could be as self-destructive as fear. If he could not terrify her, he would like to make her angry.

"You have the marble head," she told him. "You don't need my daughter now. I can see how you've used Fernanda.

But I'm not so foolish as I used to be. If Beth isn't returned to the hotel today, I'll go the police."

He paused with the cigarette halfway to his lips and she saw by the arrested movement that she had startled him.

"I have the what?" he demanded.

"You struck Johnny Orion down on Philerimos today and took the head of the weeping boy. You might have killed Johnny."

Gino was across the room, moving with the lithe speed that had always been his. He caught her wrist in a twisting grip she remembered.

"What are you talking about? I haven't been to Philerimos since I returned to Rhodes. What do you mean about the head? Tell me quickly!" This was no pretense, but genuine consternation.

"I'll tell you nothing," she said.

He dropped her wrist in disgust and went back to the cot to draw furiously on his cigarette.

"What a fool you are! To hold the head in your hands and then let it slip through your fingers. You and the American!"

"Then it must have been Constantine," she said. "It must have been Constantine Katalonos. Someone has been watching the hotel, following me."

His laughter was both angry and derisive. "Again you prove yourself less than brilliant, *bellisima*. Constantine is very dead. I suppose I owe him my life, in a way, since he was on the plane for San Francisco in my place. What a blow it must have been for you to find yourself without warning a widow."

She stared at him. Constantine on the plane? "Then why didn't you come home, if you weren't harmed?"

"I saw a chance for a better plan, a bigger gamble. Things were not going so well at home—and you, *bellisima*, were be-

[250]

Gino nodded. "Instead of me. A great disappointment for you, I'm afraid. I had not yet left the airport when the news went through the place. I went outside and saw the wreckage burning. There was no need after that to share with a partner. This gave me a fine idea. Under cover of my own death I could acquire a new identity and do as I pleased, thus escaping certain sticky matters that were ripening in the States. There was only one thing I needed—that letter from the Owl. And you, *bellisima*, were the one who stood in my way. It was I who searched our apartment the first time. I believed I knew all the places in which to look."

"Then you drew the chalk circles? It was you!"

He looked pleased. "That was no more than a whim the first time—to suggest to you what I searched for, the thing you must surrender. But when Fernanda told me what had happened and of how the chalk marks upset you, I decided to carry them further. Fernanda, to do her justice, did not approve, but she could do nothing. For my sake, she could only conceal and deny."

"It was you on the balcony also—that night here in Rhodes?"

He nodded, his eyes bright. "You did not guess, did you? Yes, it was I who came to your balcony that night and looked at my daughter as she slept. And at her mother. Your head was turned upon the pillow, your throat very white in the darkness. I had no love for you then."

Dorcas pressed her fingers together lest they move involuntarily to her throat.

"I meant to search, but you turned in your sleep and I went back to the balcony and waited. When you left your bed, I made my escape through Fernanda's room."

"The chalk smudges on the balcony rail that first night, the soap marks on the mirror later—you managed those, too, of course. But why? It seems a childish game."

"It was you who were the impressionable, easily frightened child," he said quickly. "So easily swayed in your emotions, so unsure of yourself. I didn't think it would be difficult to push you over the line into madness. You were coming very close."

She sickened, hearing him. It was part of his nature to delight in such tormenting. But thanks to Johnny he could not touch her now.

He watched her with an odd intentness, as if she puzzled him a little. "What has happened to you, *bellisima?*"

She did not reply, but continued her probing for answers he seemed all too ready to give.

"You got Fernanda to send Beth here that day, didn't you? So you could see her again?"

"At least I did not let her see me," Gino said. "It was a nice touch to have my landlady give the child the coin for you. Though I had to part with a treasure to frighten you with that little reminder of the Owl. Fernanda was annoyed with me, I'm afraid. She felt I went too far. And she tried to recover the coin for me."

"You've used her all along, cheating her, deceiving her," Dorcas said.

"I had no choice. I had to bring you here to Rhodes. I had to find out what you knew, whether you held the information. Although I could not tell her about the note, or what it was I searched for. My darling Fernanda has a curious sense of morality at times. In her eyes all my motives are honorable and I prefer to keep it that way. You have yourself helped me to convince her that you are incompetent to care for Beth

—as indeed you are, *bellisima*. With Constantine dead, there was no way to find the head except through you. Now through you it has been found and lost again. There are scores between us to settle."

He came suddenly close to her and for an instant she thought he might strike her across the face in anger, as he had done more than once in the past. She held very still without wincing, and she did not look away.

"I saw Mrs. Dimitriou in the village yesterday," she told him.

Her words stopped him. The flash in his eyes was cold as winter steel. He waited.

"She told me what I wanted to know," Dorcas went on. "She confirmed what I already knew."

He wheeled away from her. "We're wasting time. What does any of this matter?"

"Perhaps the police will think a good deal of it matters," Dorcas said.

"I have never liked to be threatened. You should know that by now. Besides, you are in no position to threaten me."

His anger died in the abrupt way that was possible when he thought of something that pleased him.

"I will find the head, of course. It is out in the open now. And I know where Beth is. So the cards lie in my hands."

She was more alarmed than when he had seemed to threaten her physically. "What do you mean?"

"I'll leave the country, of course, as soon as I have the head. Perhaps I will take them both with me—the marble treasure and my daughter. In that case you will never hear of us again. Of course if you should be so foolish as to go to the police, it is possible that I would let the head wait and take my daughter away first. You are no longer a child, *bellisima*, as you were when I married you. It is necessary that you think of these things."

The old sickness of terror was ready to rise within her and she held herself very still.

"It's true," he went on pleasantly, "that you may be left in a most unfortunate position. It will not be possible to divorce a man who is dead. Yet you will not be able to prove that I am alive. A difficult quandary, I'm afraid. Especially now that you are casting eyes at this American with the red hair. For me, this is amusing."

She could not remain longer in this room. He would not touch her now—not when he could torment her in more subtle ways.

"You won't be able to get away with any of this," she told him, and left her chair. Quite steadily she walked across the Turkish carpet and he sprang to open the door for her with a derisively gallant gesture.

"What a pity," he said. "What a woman you might have been. Tell me—do you still weep for Apollo?"

His fingers moved toward her in the old caress and she struck his hand away and went from him down the steps. She could hear him laughing as she ran through the archway below. Out upon the Street of the Knights pedestrians moved about their everyday affairs and tourists looked endlessly into the finders of their cameras.

She no longer belonged to this pattern of the normal and commonplace. A darker world had drawn her into its being. She hurried to the gate and out into the newer town. There was a cab waiting at the stand and she got into it. When the driver looked about for the address, she hesitated. Not the

[256]

hotel. No help waited for her there. Not with Johnny injured and Fernanda an enemy. There was only one person to whom she could turn in her need—one person who might help her. She gave the driver the name of the street on which Constantine Katalonos had lived.

15

THE THING that happened to her during the brief taxi ride was strange. It was as if in her extremity of despair she began to get a second wind. Perhaps with good reason. She had stood up to Gino. She had not crumpled as she used to do. She had answered him and she had turned her back on him and walked out of the room. Perhaps Johnny Orion had given her a little of his own tough resilience. When there was pressure, you stretched—you didn't snap in two. You kept going as she was doing now. Not hysterically and in terror, but with quiet determination. Johnny would have helped her if he could. But Johnny had been temporarily put out of the picture and she had relied on herself. She had not been beaten and she would not be. Beth and all the future were the stakes for which she played.

The very look of her small daughter was hurtfully in her mind. The way Beth looked when she laughed, the look of her asleep. Her own hands could remember the soft warmth of that small, trusting body, and her loss was an aching within her.

In front of the Katalonos house the cab pulled up behind another car—Fernanda's car. Dorcas had no wish to face Fernanda now, but she braced herself for the meeting.

The Greek maid admitted her and at least she was not unprepared when she walked into the drawing room and found Fernanda standing before the portrait of Constantine Katalonos.

Fernanda looked around with no evidence of rancor. "Well, this is a surprise. I wondered where you'd gone."

"I went to see Gino," Dorcas said bluntly.

Fernanda blinked, but she did not pursue the subject. She went to a corner of the room where a huge Turkish *mangal* stood—a brass brazier of the sort that was used to warm old-fashioned Turkish houses in cold weather. Its brass sides curved upward like the open petals of a lotus, handsomely embossed.

"A fine piece, don't you think?" Fernanda said. "I'd like to find one of those to send home for my living room."

Dorcas watched her in wonderment. Fernanda's talent for detachment was always amazing.

She got heavily down upon her knees and busied herself with a bundle of cloth inside the brazier. "I'm the curious sort. I couldn't resist looking. Do come and see what I've found, Dorcas."

She spread back the soft wrappings and Dorcas looked down upon the face of the marble boy. It was the real head, she saw —the one she and Johnny had found at Philerimos that morning.

"You see?" said Fernanda triumphantly. "I knew it couldn't be Gino behind that attack upon Johnny today. Such a wild story you told, my dear. These goings on won't do, you

[260]

know." She re-covered the head and moved innocently away from the brazier.

"Listen to me," Dorcas said. "Stop mixing up reality and fantasy. Constantine Katalonos was Gino's partner. He stole that head from the museum at Gino's instigation. Gino wants it now. This is criminal action he's involved in. Constantine is dead and Gino is trying to take that head and Beth out of the country. If he succeeds, we'll never see him again. We'll never see Beth again, or the marble head. Get what's happening straight this time, Fernanda. Stop fooling yourself about Gino."

Fernanda regarded her indignantly. "I presume none of these wild notions of yours will come about. Madama Katalonos will return the head to the museum and everything will be settled as far as it is concerned. Beth, after all, is in my hands. Hush, dear, here comes the maid."

Haltingly, the girl gave them Madame's regrets. She was not well and she could see no one at the moment. They would forgive her, please. Another time—

"Well, that's that," Fernanda said. "There was some information I wanted from her, but it will have to wait. Coming, Dorcas? I'll drive you back to the hotel."

"No, thank you," Dorcas said. "I'm going to stay here and see Madame Katalonos, whether she likes it or not."

Fernanda hesitated as though she meant to argue, but something of Dorcas's new determination seemed to make itself felt.

"I don't think I want to force myself on the lady," Fernanda said, and sailed a bit haughtily from the room.

While the maid waited, Dorcas picked up a packet of Greek cigarettes from a nearby table. The flat white under side of the box made a useful pad for notes. She had often seen

[261]

Greeks put the boxes to this purpose. With a pencil from her bag she wrote some words on the packet and gave it to the girl. Then she waited, as Fernanda had done, before the portrait of Constantine. He seemed to return her look with sardonic amuseument, as if he knew very well what a tortuous chain of events his tricks had set into motion. Yet there was a moodiness in the face as well—a touch of the despair she had sensed in him that time when Gino had sent him for her. She no longer needed to be afraid of Constantine.

The maid returned promptly with word that Madame would see Mrs. Brandt. She led the way to the sculptor's studio, where the door stood open and Madame Xenia sat at her husband's desk. Today she wore a flowing gown of light gray that gave her the look of a votive priestess. Only her eyes seemed alive in her white face as Dorcas crossed the room to greet her.

"You have word of my husband?" she said, rising.

"I'm sorry that it must be bad news," Dorcas told her gently. "At least you will know now what happened."

Madame Xenia sat down again. "Continue, please. He is dead?"

Dorcas explained what she had just learned from Gino— that Constantine had been in his place aboard the plane that had crashed. Gino was alive and in Rhodes. He had come here to find the marble head that Constantine had taken from the museum.

A mingling of comprehension, of grief, and of anger, flashed across Madame Xenia's face. She stood up, leaning against the desk, one hand gathering the gray folds of her robe. Although her suffering was undoubtedly real, she could not refrain from making a performance of it.

"It was Gino who sent him to his death!" she cried. "It was Gino who killed Constantine!"

"Not deliberately," Dorcas interposed. "He couldn't have known the plane would crash."

The woman paid no attention. "Those two wicked ones! It was the two of them who destroyed him!"

She walked swiftly to the bust of Vanda Petrus and snatched away the cloth that shrouded it.

"There you see the one who tried to steal my husband's love. That perfidious woman! She is to blame for everything. She and her worthless brother!"

Dorcas repeated the last word warily. "Brother?"

"But of course. That woman is the sister of Gino Nikkaris. And she is his tool, as many women are."

Dorcas stood very still as the truth, the illuminating truth, washed over her. When she spoke, she formed the words slowly, carefully.

"That woman—Mrs. Petrus—is the one Miss Farrar brought in to take care of my daughter Beth. Miss Farrar did not tell me—" She broke off, lost in the alarming ramifications of what she had just learned. How easy it had been to fool her. Gino's pattern of life had always been secretive. He had never talked of the scattered remains of his family. After his parents had died, there had seemed to be no one with whom he was in touch. And of course Fernanda had not told her the truth. This, again, would be something she did for Gino. Now Beth was in the hands of Gino's sister who would do whatever Gino wished. No wonder Gino had been so confident, so sure that he held the winning hand.

Madame Xenia was paying no attention to Dorcas, lost in her own tragic performance. Not for a moment had she stepped down from her private stage. The words she spoke

[263]

came as ringingly as though she played to far more than an audience of one.

"Euripides said it well:

"'What can the face of Modesty
Or Virtue avail,
When what is unholy has power . . .'"

Then she broke off as though she had just heard the last words Dorcas had spoken.

"You say the child is with Vanda Petrus?" she demanded.

"Miss Farrar sent them away together. I don't know where they are. That's why I've come here to you. I thought you might help me."

Madame Xenia swooped down upon her and grasped her by the shoulder. "But of course. This gives us the answer. And I am not helpless. I know where they are. Miss Farrar said you were not well, that the child must be away from you. She asked me to loan her my house in Lindos for the nurse and the child to stay. I agreed, of course. It was of no importance to me. I did not know about the nurse. But now—now it is important. Come, we must hurry."

It was like being swept along by a spring torrent rushing down from the mountains. Dorcas did not resist. If the tide carried her toward Beth, that was all that mattered.

The car was brought from its garage and Madame Xenia absented herself, then reappeared wearing a Paris suit, though she still managed to look like a priestess of Delphi. She took Dorcas with her on the crest of the flood, all but pushing her out to the car. When Dorcas got into the back seat, Madame Xenia sat beside her. The door was left open and they waited.

After a few moments Stavros, the chauffeur, appeared,

[264]

carrying a tenderly nestled bundle in his arms. This he deposited carefully on the seat between Dorcas and his mistress, and without meeting Dorcas's eye. It was the marble head. Stavros got behind the wheel and the car pulled away from the curb. Dorcas stared at his back, while recognition dawned. Out of uniform and in a jacket with a turned-up collar, a cap visor pulled down over his eyes, he would match perfectly the picture in her mind.

"It was you who had us watched at the hotel," Dorcas said to the woman beside her. "You who had us followed this morning?"

Madame Xenia denied nothing. She touched the bundle between them lovingly. "Naturally. When you showed me the words Constantine had written, I began to understand. I had known, of course, long before that he was making a copy of the head. It was I who made it possible for him to make a plaster cast of the original. The cast he was able to copy at his leisure at home. I myself bought him the fine pointing machine that enabled him to make all measurements accurately. What he was doing disturbed me, though the reasons he gave me were innocent. After the theft was discovered, I knew what must have happened."

She stopped and covered her eyes dramatically with both hands. Dorcas said nothing and at length she went on.

"How could I sacrifice all and turn him over to the authorities? It was not possible. And while I struggled with this terrible problem he slipped out of my hands. I knew he would never return. It was better that I think him dead. When you came to work for me and found the words in his papers, I knew what they must mean. But I did not know enough. It was necessary for Stavros to watch you, to follow when you left the hotel in case you went to Philerimos and led the way to the marble head. It was necessary to recover it at all costs."

"Even at the cost of a life?" Dorcas asked indignantly. "Your chauffeur—I suppose it was he—might have killed Johnny Orion."

"Not Stavros," said Madame Xenia with confidence. "He had much practice during the war. He would know how to kill, or how not to kill. The young American—he is not badly hurt?"

"It was no light tap," Dorcas said. "They won't know for sure until there has been an X ray."

Madame Xenia waved her hands. "The X ray will show nothing. I would trust Stavros with my life."

"Our only purpose," Dorcas pointed out, "was to return the head to the museum. If we had brought it home, it would have been safely there by now."

Madame Xenia looked politely disbelieving. "You are Gino's wife. Why should I trust you? Not even when I think Gino is dead, do I trust his wife. The treasure will be returned, of course. But in my own way. It will be done with honor and will in no way reflect upon the good name of my poor Constantine. First, however, I have a use for it. Now that I know Gino lives, we will go to Lindos and wait for him there. You and the child and the weeping boy."

"I'm not going to wait for Gino anywhere," Dorcas said. "As soon as I have Beth, I'll bring her back to Rhodes and take the first plane home I can manage."

The knowledge that she might already be too late and that Vanda and Beth might be gone from Lindos was something she must thrust back in her consciousness. She did not need to face that now.

"Tomorrow, perhaps," Madame Xenia said calmly. "Perhaps tomorrow I will permit you to return. For tonight you are my guest. Gino will come. There will be no change in my plans."

Dorcas studied the regal profile of the woman beside her. She looked as Greek as the head of Athena upon the owl coin. And she looked as regally immovable as Athena might have been. She wished that she had telephoned Johnny before leaving Rhodes. She should have told him where she was going. That, at least. But it was too late to worry about it now. And there was still nothing he could do. Once she had found Beth, she would manage to get away from Lindos.

She was silent for a time, staring at the passing scene. They were now on the side of the island nearest the Turkish coast and the character of the country was different. They traveled inland roads and there were more open valleys, well cultivated, with farms and olive groves. The mountains were higher and more formidable than on the other coast, but for the most part the road mounted no heights, remaining always near sea level. Stavros drove with native aplomb and seemed to head for each new obstacle as if with a fierce desire to demolish it. Miraculously, they missed other cars, scarcely grazed the donkeys, and merely scattered pedestrians.

Dorcas's impatience to reach the end of the journey increased with every passing moment. "Why do you think Gino will come to Lindos?" she asked as the silence grew long.

"Miss Farrar saw the head, did she not?" Madame Xenia said. "Maria watched when she uncovered it to show you. The girl could not understand your words, but she saw. If Gino is like a son to this woman, then she will tell him of the head. Already he must know where his child is held."

Yes, he knew, and he had only to instruct Vanda. As he must have instructed her to make those circles of chalk.

"But why would he come this distance?" Dorcas persisted. "Why shouldn't he wait for you to return to Rhodes?"

"It is a simple thing," Madame Xenia said. "Gino Nikkaris and my husband have in partnership a caïque in which they used to make trips out of the harbor at Lindos. It is kept there. The coast of Turkey is an easy run for a caïque with an engine. Gino has friends in Turkey."

And a buyer for the marble head waiting in Istanbul? Yes, under such circumstances Gino might very well come to Lindos. Which made it all the more imperative for her to find Beth and get her away.

"And if he comes, how will you stop him from taking what he wants?" she asked.

Without warning Madame Xenia burst into tears. "Please —you do not talk to me now. I must mourn for Constantine."

She mourned audibly for several kilometers more, halting Dorcas's questions effectively. Then she dried her eyes, quieted her sobs, and sat up to pay attention to the scene outside the car.

"Nothing in all Greece is so beautiful, so perfect as what you will see at Lindos," she announced. "Soon now we will be there."

It had been a longer drive than the trips Dorcas had made with Johnny, and her own anxiety had made the miles seem endless.

Now the character of the island had changed again and the coastline was intermittently visible, with crescents of sandy beach carved into by rough outcroppings of rock. This was a wilder coast line than she had seen on the other side of the island.

Around a bend of the road the sea disappeared and they seemed to be turning inland. Madame Xenia looked out the window and an excitement seemed to fill her. For this moment which she owed to Greece, to Rhodes, even the thought of Constantine had been put aside.

"Now you will see," she said, and addressed Stavros in Greek.

Dorcas did not care whether she saw or not. She yearned toward the moment when Beth would be in her arms again.

Stavros slowed the car. In the distance could be heard the pounding of surf. The road seemed to dive into a narrow corridor of solid rock—a passage that curved and turned steeply downward, plunging suddenly into the open, still high above the town of Lindos.

This sudden ringing up of a curtain struck Dorcas into awareness. In spite of her preoccupation, she was caught and held by the scene that lay spread below her. An expanse of tightly packed white houses tipped like a tilted saucer toward the small harbor they faced. Across the flat rooftops of the town the eye was drawn to the steep hill of the Acropolis. The hill itself was set between two bays. Its ramparts rode the blue air, seeming to grow from solid rock. Here were no soaring pillars, yet the flat-topped rock ruled the scene with the pride of its own impregnable strength. One looked and was challenged—and could not look away.

"It is the oldest acropolis of all," Madame Xenia said with a ring of pride in her voice. "Men have built there since perhaps twenty-five hundred years before Christ. The fortress of the knights—of which you see only the wall—is comparatively new. You cannot view from here what remains of the temple of Athena Lindia. It is above the sea cliffs on the far side."

The road dropped again, and the car took a tight curve without concern for what might be coming, and arrived in an open square a level above the housetops of the town. The rock was closer now and the castellated walls that crowned it were clearly visible.

On the square an inn offered tables set in the open for dining, and a stone wall rimmed the place where cars could park. The inevitable tourist bus waited there and nearby a group of trippers bargained for donkeys to take them up to the rock.

Though this was clearly not where Madame Xenia had her house, Stavros stopped the car in the center of the square. Dorcas fumed inwardly at the delay, but Madame Xenia did not hurry. She studied the tourists, looked carefully at the parked cars, and shook her head.

"I know none of these," she said, and spoke again to her driver.

He turned the car back to a cutoff on the road and they went down among cypress and olive trees to a white house built in straight geometric lines. It was flat of roof and graced by slender columns across an inset of porch that had been painted a warm bright rose.

The streets of the village were too narrow to permit a car to pass, Madame Xenia explained, so she had built her house on the hillside, with its own roadway and an unrestricted view of the impressive scene.

Dorcas did not wait for her hostess. Calling Beth's name, she got out of the car and ran up the steps to the porch. There was no answer. A plump Greek woman came through the door and stared at her in astonishment. Madame Xenia, mounting the steps more slowly, explained, and the woman stepped aside to allow Dorcas to enter a long, white-walled room that stretched from front to rear of the house.

A doll of Beth's lay upon a chair and Dorcas picked it up. Anxiety had mounted to a pitch she could not hide.

"Ask them about Beth," she urged. "I want to see her right away!"

There was an interchange in Greek between Madame Xenia and the maid.

"The servants do not know where the child is," Madame Xenia said. "The nurse has taken her for a walk. Do not worry. They will return soon."

Dorcas held the doll in both her hands as though she might gain some reassurance because Beth had touched it recently. Was it as she feared? Was she already too late? Gino could have telephoned from Rhodes and Vanda might by now have taken Beth wherever he directed. Yet she could not very well rush out and walk the streets of Lindos, seeking at random for her daughter.

Stavros had followed them into the room with the marble head in his hands. Madame Xenia took it from him and set it gently into the corner of a sofa. Then she picked up a small blanket and wrapped it around the head. Her movements were confident and deliberate and Dorcas felt even more uneasy watching her. The woman seemed so sure of her plan to bring Gino here.

"Can you send someone to look for Beth?" she asked. "Vanda can't have taken her far in this small place."

Madame Xenia seemed unconcerned by Dorcas's worry. "Content yourself," she said. "There is no need to be upset. Come, I will show you your room."

Dorcas had no wish for a room. She had no intention of staying for the night. But her hostess prevailed, and at least there was cool water to soothe flushed cheeks and hot wrists.

When she returned to the living room, the maid was bringing in a silver tea tray. There was nothing to do but sit stiffly in a chair and try to contain her growing alarm a little longer.

Madame Xenia poured tea and passed plates of small sand-wiches and sweet cakes. The tea was hot and reviving and the taste of food reminded Dorcas that she'd had no lunch. She ate for strength, and kept her eyes upon the door.

Once she asked the same question she had asked in the car. "What will you do if Gino does come here?"

"You must not forget Stavros," Madame Xenia said calmly. "Stavros is a very prejudiced man. He does not like one drop of Italian blood."

In a battle it would be well to have Stavros on the same side, Dorcas thought, but while strength and brawn might be a match for the unsuspecting, Gino would come here alert for a trap. His clever, devious turns of mind could be counted on to get him out of any difficulty, to foil and circumvent any plan that might turn against him. He had spent his life devel-oping this talent. And he was never afraid of the daring move that confounded his adversaries. Dorcas doubted that Madame Xenia and Stavros could deflect Gino from anything he meant to do.

When the doorbell rang, she started uncontrollably and would have risen, but Madame Xenia reached across the table to stop her.

"It is Gino," she said. "You will not go to him. You will wait and be silent. Stavros?" she added softly, and the man's doughty figure appeared in a doorway at the rear of the room.

He was no longer in uniform and workman's clothes suited him best. His mustachios looked fiercer than ever and his blue eyes were alight with an eagerness for whatever was to come.

From the vestibule came the sound of a man's voice and Madame Xenia nodded again and raised an eyebrow in warn-ing toward Stavros, who stepped back out of sight. But it was not Gino who pushed past the maid and came without ceremony into the room. It was Johnny Orion.

That he was angry was evident. He stood with his feet braced apart, as if alert for attack, and the bandage about his head contributed to a combative air Dorcas had never seen in him before. He looked wonderful to her. He shouldn't be here, but it was marvelous that he had come.

Madame Xenia recovered from her disappointment and made a hospitable gesture that Johnny ignored. All his attention was for Dorcas.

"Have you found Beth?" he demanded.

Dorcas stood up. "She's not here. Madame Katalonos says she has gone for a walk with Vanda. Johnny, Vanda is Gino's sister!"

"I know," Johnny said. "I made Fernanda tell me what she could and then I headed for the Katalonos house. The maid there said you'd all gone to Lindos. With the marble head. She made quite a point of that."

Madame Xenia tried to break in. "You are the American young man who works for Miss Farrar—" she began, but Johnny went right on speaking to Dorcas.

"You shouldn't have left the hotel alone. You said you'd give me an hour. Anyway, when I found out what had happened, I got Fernanda and brought her along in the car."

"Miss Farrar is here now?" Madame Xenia cried, startled.

Johnny seemed to see her for the first time. "She's out in the car where I left her."

At once Madame Xenia rushed to the door. Whether to make Fernanda welcome or to drive her away was not clear.

Dorcas went to Johnny and he put both hands on her arms. "Steady on," he told her as he had before, and as before she found herself drawing strength from his strength.

[273]

"I think we must go to the police now," she told him urgently. "I shouldn't have kept you from going before."

This time it was Johnny who balked. "The other time I thought we had something to go to them with. Now I know we haven't. Unless you're anxious to have Madame Xenia's chauffeur arrested. Since Madame has the marble head, I suppose it was her man who struck me down. But that's a side road now. It's Gino that matters."

"Madame Xenia says he will come here," Dorcas said.

"She's probably right." Johnny sounded grim. "Apparently orders were left at the Katalonos house to tell anyone who inquired that you and Madame and the marble head were off to Lindos. When Fernanda tipped Gino off—as I know she did by phone—he would have made the same first step I did, and tried the house. So he would know."

"Then he may be here in Lindos already?"

"Probably not. He might have more trouble about transportation than I did. But I think he'll come if he wants the head. So we'll have a little showdown waiting for him."

Madame Xenia returned, bringing Miss Farrar with her. For once Fernanda was not her usual self. She had come out without tying up her hair and she looked blown and untidy and not a little wary. She did not speak to Dorcas, but plumped herself into a chair as though she had been running and was out of breath.

Madame Xenia gave her attention to Johnny. "How is your wound?" she inquired. "It does not hurt too much, I hope?"

"It hurts enough," Johnny said. "Your man didn't do me any good."

"Stavros regrets," Madame Xenia said, and glanced again toward the back of the room.

At the sound of his name Stavros appeared at once. His

[274]

mistress made a sign and he bore down upon Johnny. Astonishingly, a grin stretched his wide mouth, and he held out both hands, speaking earnestly in Greek as he came.

"Stavros wishes no hard feelings," Madame Xenia translated. "He is sorry that what he had to do was necessary."

"I don't agree that it was necessary," Johnny said, but he allowed his hand to be grasped in the two large ones Stavros extended. "At least I'm glad that we're operating on the same side."

At any other time, Dorcas thought, the scene might have been ludicrous. But Stavros somehow managed to give an impression of great and dignified good will, with an underlying quality of grim intent that boded no good for Gino.

When the man had returned to his post at the rear of the room, Madame poured a cup of tea for Fernanda and pressed it upon her. Fernanda took it and drank it as though she needed the strongly steeped brew.

"I know you're all waiting for Gino," she said. "I know you're plotting something against him. But he's not guilty of anything real. That he left the States isn't a crime. Men have slipped out of sight under cover of someone else's death before this. Not one of you understands what it is that Gino wants from life."

Dorcas could find nothing to say, but Madame Xenia leaned forward. "You will tell me, please, Miss Farrar, what it is this man—this Gino Nikkaris—wishes so much to have."

Fernanda answered simply. "He wants his wife and child with him again, of course. I hope that will come about very soon."

Dorcas made a choked sound that was covered by Madame Xenia's quick words. "You are telling me that Gino Nikkaris does not seek to possess the marble head from the museum?"

[275]

She left her chair and went to the sofa, folding back the blanket so that the head was revealed.

Fernanda stared at it uneasily. "He has been interested in the piece, of course," she said. "Why wouldn't he be when his partner took it from the museum? But Gino had nothing to do with that theft. He wants only to see the head returned to the place it was taken from. Why should he want it himself? It would only get him into serious trouble."

All three of them stared at Fernanda, and there was a blank silence. The sound of running feet on the walk outside broke the hush in the room, and a moment later Beth burst through the door. She ran eagerly to her mother and Dorcas caught her up in joyful relief. Over the top of the child's dark head she saw Vanda standing in the doorway. The woman stayed where she was, staring bitterly at Xenia Katalonos.

MADAME XENIA spoke first. "I will not have that woman in my house! No one tells me until today that this is the nurse of Mrs. Brandt's child."

There was a moment's silence, broken only by Beth, whose whole interest was upon her mother.

"Vanda took me to the beach to see Daddy's boat," she announced. "She's going to take me for a ride in it soon."

Johnny and Dorcas exchanged looks and his eyes warned her to be quiet.

Constantine's wife was not through. She rose to her most majestic height and confronted Vanda. "Has your brother told you that my Constantine is dead? That he is dead because Gino sent him aboard a plane in his place—and that plane crashed!"

That the blow went home without warning, without time for protection was clear. Vanda's careful mask was down and naked shock showed in her eyes. But the woman had long schooled herself to the concealment of pain and her guard was back in place almost at once. She answered in a low voice, and only by a faint tremor did she reveal what she must be enduring.

"If this thing is true," she said, "then the death of Constantine Katalonos is of your making, madame, not Gino's." It was a declaration of hatred, a choosing of sides, a further dedication of loyalty to Gino.

In that moment Dorcas found herself admiring and respecting Vanda Petrus. Her loyalty was mistaken, perhaps, but she was a woman who could stand up to a blow with great courage. There were women like this, who seemed doomed through all their lives. Tragedy struck them down not once, but many times. Vanda was such a one, but now she stood up to this further revelation of her fate with outward impassivity.

Fernanda brushed straggling hair from her forehead and made an effort to regain control of a situation that seemed to have escaped her grasp for some time. She picked up her handbag and rose.

"There's just too much emotion flying around here," she said. "I think we all ought to calm ourselves. Vanda, you'd better stay at the inn for tonight, since you're not welcome here. Johnny, if you'll drive us there—"

"He will drive this woman nowhere," Madame Xenia said flatly. "I will not have her in my house, but there is a place in the servants' quarters behind the garden where she will stay with safety. Stavros!"

He advanced upon Vanda, and his intent was clear. He did not touch her, but after a look she went with him, eyes down.

"It will be only for a short time," Madame Xenia said to the others. "We cannot have this woman running to Gino. She would interfere with my plan."

"What is your plan?" Johnny asked.

"We will do nothing," Madame Xenia said. "We will wait.

Gino will come and he will take the marble head. He cannot escape by boat until it is dark. And Stavros will be in the way."

The combative look was alive in Johnny's eyes. He had listened to Madame Xenia with interest and Dorcas saw his faint nod of approval. If Gino were caught with the head, away from this house, Madame Xenia could probably sidestep her own serious involvement.

But Fernanda was incensed. "What nonsense! It's not that hunk of marble Gino will come for. It's Dorcas he wants to see and talk to. Dorcas and Beth."

"All the more reason we need to do something about getting them away from here," Johnny said. "And you, too, Fernanda."

"You needn't think you can lock me up," Fernanda said. "If that—that goon touches me, Madame Katalonos, I'll go straight to the American consul. I'll—"

"Hush a minute," Johnny said. "You're the one who's getting emotional and excited. Nobody's going to lock you up."

Fernanda subsided slightly. "Why don't I just take the car and drive back to Rhodes? Dorcas and Beth can come with me and—"

"And you can meet Gino on the way?" Johnny put in. "You'll have to think of a better scheme than that."

Fernanda rose and walked to the window that opened upon the tremendous view, turning her back on them all. She looked hot and flustered and not at all like herself.

"You understand," said Madame Xenia to Johnny, "this is not a thing we wish to give to the police." She gestured toward the marble head. "It is a very delicate matter, this, and better if we take care of it away from my house. But we cannot invite Miss Farrar to remain and tell Gino what we wish to do."

Fernanda turned around. "What utter piffle! Gino can take care of himself. And he doesn't want that head. After all, I've come to Lindos to go up there—" She waved a dramatic hand at the high rock where Athena had once had her temple. "So that's where I'll go. And Dorcas and Beth can come with me if they like. If Gino comes to Lindos, he won't be doing any sight-seeing."

Dorcas looked hopefully at Johnny. Fernanda's suggestion offered a plan of action at least. Every moment she remained in this house she felt increasingly uneasy. It was time to be up and away—almost anywhere. The top of that high, distant rock offered a likely enough haven. It was the last place Gino would expect them to be at a time like this.

Again Johnny nodded. "It sounds as good an idea as any. So let's get going. I'll take you over and see about the donkeys."

Madame Xenia, too, was in accord this time, and they wasted not a moment more. Johnny drove them to the square and made the arrangements. When Fernanda, Dorcas, and Beth were mounted on the little beasts, and Fernanda had started ahead with a driver leading the way, Johnny held Dorcas's donkey back, his hand on the bridle.

"Here's the car key," he said. "Don't let Fernanda have it. I'll leave the car in the square so you can get back easily, but don't let her know it's there till the time comes. For now there's no way to go but up, and once you're on top you can find ways to keep her there as long as possible. By the time you come down, things should be settled. Take care. And keep your eyes open, in case she gets tricky."

The key was cold in her fingers. Fernanda was not looking

around, and Dorcas slipped it into her purse. Then she bent toward Johnny.

"You're the one who needs to take care. He won't walk into a trap with his eyes open. He'll come expecting trouble."

"Don't worry," Johnny said, his grin reassuring. "I'm in partnership with Stavros now."

He slapped the flank of her donkey and it trotted along to catch up with the others. She sat sideways in the saddle, as Greek women did, and looked back at Johnny. Just before they turned a corner down into village streets he waved, and she saw him walk off in the direction of Madame Xenia's house. She wished she could feel easy about him, but she could not. Gino had seen him kiss her. And where Gino hated there was danger.

The donkeys jogged through cobblestoned streets so narrow that two beasts might pass but never a car. Fernanda headed their line and Beth rode in the middle, happily astride and unafraid. Two-story houses, crowding on every hand, cut off any view of the rock. Turns were sharp and irregular and Dorcas lost all sense of direction. Then, without warning, they were free of the village and out upon a dirt and gravel road that zigzagged upward along a hillside.

Above them the rock of Lindos loomed massively, its sides sheer and seemingly impassable. Close at hand the dark-gray stone seemed stark and forbidding. The soaring grace lent by distance was gone.

Their donkeys were sure of foot and unhurried, setting their own pace. As they turned up the next level of the road, Dorcas could look down upon the white village spread below. Its flat gray roofs were covered with clay as insulation against the sun. Here and there a touch of color showed, but for the most part the scene was black and white until the eye reached the blue harbor. There waves broke in creamy ruffles around a beach of white sand. Several boats were visible, pulled up on the beach. Within wading distance a flat-bottomed caïque was anchored —Gino's boat, perhaps, ready to leave at any moment? Fernanda, too, was looking down at the cove, and Dorcas wondered if she noted the boat and knew its purpose there.

Fernanda glanced back, her good humor apparently restored. "Do try to remember everything you can, Dorcas. I can't make notes jiggling along on a donkey."

She would remember, Dorcas thought. She was unlikely to forget any detail of this day.

The rising zigzag carried them to the foot of the rock and here they were helped to dismount and motioned up the hill. This was as far as the donkeys climbed.

For a long moment Dorcas stood staring up at the high gray mass above. Scattered cypress trees grew where there was earth to hold their roots—black exclamation points against gray rock. In the high, stony places she could see the black mouths of caves. There was a humming of cicadas all around, and behind them a donkey brayed, impatient for the homeward trip. It seemed a desolate and lonely place, but surely the last place to which Gino was likely to come.

With Fernanda leading the way, they climbed over the rough earth of the entryway and stepped into a wide space where pines and cypress grew sparsely. The northern face of the rock wall rose straight ahead and a long flight of stone stairs cut diagonally up beside it.

As they neared the wall, Fernanda stopped. "Look!" she said, pointing.

Dorcas felt the impact of recognition. Cut into living rock was the portion of a ship in relief. Markos had told her of this

[282]

long ago. "A ship so very beautiful!" he had said. "A ship carved into the rock by men of old."

It was a trireme, an ancient galley of Greece, with three banks of oars and a high curving prow like a Viking ship. The outline was still clear, for all the weathering of centuries, and a stone bench had been built where the body of the ship would have been. With the sight came renewal for Dorcas.

As a child Markos had belonged to Lindos. "It is the best of all," he had told her father. "I cannot say it with words—we will go there and I will show you how it is at Lindos."

"We'd better start up," Fernanda said. "We don't want to be coming down those steps in the dark."

Already the sun was sliding down the sky, Dorcas saw. Johnny had said to keep Fernanda up here as long as possible, but the time of day was moving against them. If Gino must come, then she prayed he would do it quickly and be gone before they returned. At least as long as they moved upward they put distance between themselves and Gino, and so had an element of safety.

The narrow stone staircase led steeply upward and at the top was a medieval tower with an arched doorway—a tower whose top was just even with the heights, so that it was invisible from a distance, lost against the gray rock. The steps were without a rail and as they climbed slowly, Dorcas looked up to see a set of still narrower steps running above them at a higher level—ruined steps which these had replaced.

This had been a Byzantine fortress once, guarding the way to Athena's temple. The knights had turned it into a castle and the ramparts, the battlements were clearly visible now, the heraldic symbols still to be seen.

Fernanda counted the steps aloud until Beth distracted her and she lost track. There were more than sixty, she reported.

Sometimes Dorcas carried Beth, and sometimes they rested during the climb.

At the top of the steps they went through the deep archway into bright sunlight. Walls stood all around and further slabs of rock must be clambered over before they reached the summit. They swung Beth between them over the difficult spots, and at last they were out upon the heights.

Dorcas stood looking about, trying to grasp the surprise of all that lay hidden from the ground. From below only the ramparts were to be seen. The top of the rock looked flat and empty. The reality was startling.

They stood at the head of a flight of steps, impressively wide. Fernanda counted again, and announced that there were thirty. In a row across the foot stood seven widely spaced Doric columns.

On every hand reminders of history crowded in. Portions of the knights' castle still stood, and the remains of a Byzantine church. Broken walls and fallen slabs of stone lay all about. Yet it was still Athena Lindia who ruled this place. Lesser structures were dwarfed, earth-borne, by her soaring columns. Here was the winged Athena who belonged to sky and sea. The broken walls, the columns of her temple rose in luminous air that seemed to carry a sparkle of gold in the blue. Rhodes stone burned gold against the eternal backdrop of sea and sky, floating as though it had little relationship to the earth so far below. There was an illusion of security here. It was as if they had reached a place that lived to itself, having no connection with a less peaceful outside world.

Fernanda went down the wide steps into a wind that struck fiercely across the rock. Dorcas followed, clasping Beth by the hand. At the foot of the steps they turned without question toward the temple above the sea cliffs. Here the wind blew more strongly than ever, the sun burned hot, and the bright air danced with gold. Overhead, in the space between two columns of Athena's temple, a great spiderweb had been flung, its strands trembling, shimmering in the wind, yet never breaking. Arachne still wove her gossamer threads, defying Athena through the ages.

Behind the temple a low wall rimmed cliffs that plunged straight to the indigo-dark sea far below. While Fernanda took Beth in hand and wandered across the floor of the temple, Dorcas sat upon the wall. Across the precipice six columns with a broken portion of roof clustered close together—alone upon the black cliff, their beauty heart catching against sea and sky. Only swallows had access to the rocky cliffs and only Aegean waves pounded against their foot. There was no way up or down from this rock, other than the way by which they had come.

Fernanda returned with Beth to stand beside Dorcas and peer down the dizzy fall of rock. She made her pronouncement with the air of a seeress.

"I can just see Gregory Peck struggling up that cliff when they made *The Guns of Navarone*," she murmured raptly.

The gold-and-blue beauty shattered almost visibly around Fernanda's head and Dorcas laughed out loud.

"I doubt that he climbed it at this particular spot," she said.

Fernanda grimaced. "I know—I've done it again. Look—there's the other harbor over there. The little enclosed one where Saint Paul is supposed to have come. You can see the jagged entry rocks they used for the storm scene in the picture."

Dorcas took Beth's hand. "You dream about Gregory Peck while we have a look at the village side."

They left Fernanda and crossed to ramparts where Dorcas

could look down on white houses and the beach with a boat bobbing off shore. The mountains of Anatolia were not so close here as they were in the town of Rhodes, because of the way the island slanted. But the Turkish shore line would be no trip at all, even in a smallish boat.

She tried to make out Madame Xenia's house on the slope beyond the town, but there were too many trees and she could not be sure which small white cube was hers. Had Gino come? What was happening down there at this very moment?

Again Fernanda followed them. If she felt any uneasiness about what might occur in the little town at their feet, she hid it well. She behaved as though this were an ordinary sight-seeing trip. But she continued to watch the sun.

"We'd better leave soon, dear," she said. "It's getting close to sunset."

On this side of the island the sun would not drop into the sea, but would vanish behind the ridge of hill above the village of Lindos. Before too long, Dorcas saw, the edge of the sun would reach the hill. Yet she must keep Fernanda up here awhile longer.

"I don't want to go back yet," she protested. "There's still plenty of light."

She picked Beth up and wandered toward the opposite ramparts. Voices reached her from below, and the sound of laughter. Apparently the donkey drivers had enjoyed a last spate of business before sunset. Dorcas set Beth down and leaned through a notch in the wall so she could look directly down upon the long stone staircase up which they had recently climbed. Several women were coming up the steps, laughing and puffing as they mounted. Behind them, moving in the wake of the brightly caparisoned female group, came a man, alone.

She would have known that head of dark hair anywhere. Swiftly she drew back from the wall lest he look up and see her there. Gino had come. As always, he had done the unexpected. In a few moments he would be on the heights, and she must leave the rock at once, get Beth out of his reach. Yet she could not escape until he was well away from the entrance and she could find a chance to slip out behind his back.

That he would follow her here to this remote spot must mean that time was indeed running out. Only a desperate need for haste would bring him here. Had he not gone to the Katalonos house, after all? Had he circumvented the trap laid for him?

Now that there was need to hurry, Beth hung back. "I'm tired, Mommy. I want to ride on the donkey."

"Soon," Dorcas said. "We're going down very soon now."

A dozen different walls and angles of building offered hiding places and she stood irresolute. Voices warned that the sightseeing group was nearly up. Fernanda had gone to the cliff above the sea and her back was turned. Dorcas picked Beth up once more and ran with her across the space at the foot of wide stone steps. Column shadows lay in black bars across her way as the sun dipped close to the ridge of hill. Shadow must already lie upon the village, creeping toward the rim of beach.

A crumbling stone building stood in her path and she ran toward it. The opening to a sheltering wing offered a space she could step into and be concealed. It offered more, for a slit like an archer's window had been built into the stone, looking out upon steps and columns in the direction of the far cliffs. By standing behind the narrow aperture, she could see without being seen.

"I don't like it here," Beth said. "I want to ride on the donkey."

Dorcas hushed her in quick desperation. "We're playing a game," she whispered to the child. "We're hiding from Aunt Fern. We mustn't make any noise or she'll find us."

Beth accepted the ruse for the moment and slipped into a corner of the wall to hide behind her mother, holding back laughter with a cupped hand. Silently Dorcas prayed for help, for the strength to do whatever must be done. For herself she no longer feared Gino. She could stand against him. For Beth it was a different matter.

It was quiet out of the wind, cool in the shadow of unwarmed stone, and Dorcas shivered. Gino would come out upon the steps and he would see Fernanda near the wall. When he walked toward her, his back would be turned to this hiding place. That would be their only chance to reach the steps, to get to the entrance without being seen. She must take it without fail.

The last of the group had reached the top and women were spilling over the steps, taking off in various directions, exclaiming about everything they saw. Gino was still the one apart. He wore a gray jacket over gray slacks, and his dark head was bare.

Quietly alert, he stood upon the steps, looking about a scene that was undoubtedly familiar. Once more Dorcas sensed his enormous energy—dark, frightening energy held well in check but ready for release at a moment's notice. He saw Fernanda and ran lightly down the steps calling her name.

This should have been the moment, and on the instant it was lost. Fernanda turned and started toward him, shortening the distance. If she had stayed by the wall and Gino had gone to her, there might have been a chance. His back would have been turned long enough. Now Dorcas dared not risk the steps. She must move away from him. If she circled the ram-

[288]

parts, perhaps she could approach the entrance from the far side.

In the brief moments that he and Fernanda moved toward each other Dorcas caught Beth up and whispered that it was still a game. Her eyes sought frantically for a doorway ahead, and she ran across the uneven ground, the child heavy in her arms. She had nearly reached the few steps down to the entryway when Fernanda saw her and called out. Dorcas faltered and almost fell on the slippery stones. Gino would be after her now. There was no choice except continued flight.

She darted through the doorway to a lower level and found herself in a room like a long tunnel—a wide stone tunnel with a rounded ceiling arching overhead. And like a tunnel it opened at the opposite end where the gold and red of sunset had begun to stain the sky. Her instinct was to run for that opening like a rabbit before the hunter, but she forced the urgency down and took quick stock. If she depended upon flight, Gino would catch her. If he trapped her here on this high rock, Beth would be lost to her. She knew that without question.

At her left a small black doorway opened into some sort of cell. She crossed the stone floor swiftly and lifted Beth into the pitchy darkness of the tiny room. It was black and cold and evil-smelling. Beth wriggled in her arms to escape.

"Aunt Fern saw us," Dorcas whispered. "But we can hide here and fool her. Close your eyes tight and put your face against my shoulder."

Beth did as she was told, closing here eyes to suddenly sensed horror as Dorcas crouched well back from the door. Gino went by without a glance for the cell. He would expect her to run, of course. When the echo of his steps died, Dorcas released

Beth, who had begun to whimper, and they crept back to the main room.

Hurrying, they turned toward the door through which they had entered. Dorcas could only pray that Gino would be lost in a search among the buildings at the far end, so they could reach the flight of steps unseen. Although there was still Fernanda to be reckoned with.

"Carry me, Mommy!" Beth wailed, and she picked the child up and stumbled toward the doorway.

A shadow fell across the entrance, blocking the light, and she looked up to see Fernanda standing there. Beth squealed and Dorcas put a finger to her lips, pleading with them both for silence. Fernanda settled herself solidly on the top slab of stone, blocking the exit with her body.

"Pull yourself together," she said crossly. "You've got to let him see the child. He has that right. You can't keep running from him in this ridiculous fashion."

Desperately Dorcas flung a glance over her shoulder toward the opposite opening to the tunnel. It stood empty. Gino was not in sight.

"I'm going through," Dorcas said. "Get out of my way, Fernanda."

Fernanda braced herself and put her hands on her hips. "Don't try anything foolish, Dorcas. He's leaving Greece and he wants to see Beth first just one last time. You've got to grant him that."

Fernanda had sheer weight on her side and Dorcas knew she wouldn't hesitate to use it if need required.

"All right then," Dorcas said. "I'll see him. But not up here. Let me go back to Madame Xenia's—I'll talk to him there."

"Do you think he'd walk stupidly into such a trap?" Fernanda demanded.

"Then I'll see him at the square where there are people around. I'll wait for him there. Please, Fernanda."

Perhaps something of her desperation got through to the other woman, for Fernanda hesitated and stepped back from the doorway. Dorcas was past her in an instant and out in the open. She pushed by an American woman who had started toward the tunnel and ran for the columns at the foot of the steps. The stone flight shone pinky-gold in the sunset as she went up with Beth in her arms. There was a long moment of being dangerously in the open, but she did not hear Fernanda call, nor was there any sound that meant Gino had seen her.

It seemed an age going down, before they reached the place where the donkeys had brought them. Dorcas had no time for transportation that was slow and picturesque. She waved the waiting drivers aside and jumped down the high step to the dirt road.

Now she found a physical strength she had not known she possessed. She quieted Beth's protests and, partly carrying her, partly pulling her along, started down the zigzagging road that led to the village. Behind her she heard voices and looked around to see the donkey men beckoning her and pointing. Perhaps they meant that there was a better way down on foot than the rough road she had chosen. But she had no time or wish to turn back. The road beneath her feet led away from Gino and she asked for nothing more.

Once, when she was forced to stop for breath, she looked up toward the rock towering above. In the reflection of a sunset sky the sheer cliffs shone like rosy glass. Below in the village streets were already eaten by shadow. Nothing stirred along

[291]

the walls, no sound of voices reached her—nothing. The illusion of emptiness up there was again complete.

The village received them, and its narrow streets, its crowding houses hid them from view. The graying dusk swallowed them in protective shadow. It was only a little way to the square. There she would not be alone. The car waited and perhaps she could get away in time and reach Madame Xenia's and Johnny.

17

ONCE MORE the narrow streets were bewildering, hiding everything except the tightly packed white houses. She took two turns and then a third. At the third corner a man stepped from the shadow of an arched doorway with a suddenness that terrified. It was Gino.

He snatched Beth up in his arms, frightening her so that she cried out in alarm.

"Be quiet!" he said. "It is I—your father," and he did not set her down for all that she fought him with both her small fists. The contagion of terror had touched her, and this man was a stranger. His roughness frightened her.

"How foolish to run away," Gino said to Dorcas. "It was simple to take the foot walk and cut you off."

She stood in the cobblestoned street with the blind eyes of the houses unseeing about her and no help anywhere. Even if someone came, she could not ask for help in Greek and Gino could tell any passerby what he pleased.

"So now we bargain," he said. Excitement lay upon him

like a patina of uneasy light. Dorcas knew well this dangerous, reckless mood.

The noise of hoofs around a corner reached them and Dorcas whirled toward the sound. If only someone who spoke English would come along. But it was only Fernanda riding a donkey. When she saw them, she dismounted and sent her driver away with the beast.

Dorcas wasted no more than a glance at her. She could expect no help from Fernanda. All her attention was for Gino.

"What bargain? What do you mean?"

"If you want Beth, you'll do exactly as I say. You'll go back to Xenia's house and you will get the marble head. Bring it to the beach at once. When it's in my hands, I'll return Beth to your keeping. If you try any other course, it will be the worse for you—and any who try to stop me." He patted his jacket pocket and she saw the bulge of a revolver.

Fernanda spoke blankly. "But why should you want that head? Gino, it will only mean trouble and—"

"You'd better help her get it," he told Fernanda, and his tone was curt. Without waiting for an answer he went around the next corner, with Beth sobbing bitterly against his shoulder.

Fernanda was visibly shaken. She stared after him helplessly. "We'd better do as he says, dear. I don't understand, but its the only way now."

Dorcas turned her back and started toward the square, walking fast. She heard Fernanda following and spoke over her shoulder.

"How did Gino find us up there? How did he know where we were?"

"Vanda told him," Fernanda said, hurrying to catch up. "Vanda got out of that room they locked her in and waited

[294]

for him at the square. She saw the car and talked to the donkey drivers, so she knew we'd gone up the rock with Beth. Gino says she's down at the boat now waiting to help him. There's not a chance to get Beth back, unless we do as he says."

"I thought you didn't want me to have Beth," Dorcas said scornfully.

Fernanda did not answer. She made a futile effort to push back her wind-blown hair. This day seemed to have shocked her out of the imaginary world in which she existed—a world where only Gino was right. But she did not know how to conduct herself on other terms, and Dorcas knew she would be useless now. It did not matter what side she was on.

All that mattered was to reach Madame Xenia's and get the marble head. The risk of any other way was too great. She did not know what she would do if the others opposed her. She would fight even Johnny for Beth's safe return.

When they were in the car and Dorcas had turned over the key, Fernanda drove almost as furiously as Stavros. They reached Madame Xenia's and Dorcas ran up the steps, with Fernanda at her heels. The door stood open and there was no one in sight. Dorcas stepped into the living room and saw the marble head still in its place on the sofa.

"Take it down to the beach," Fernanda said brusquely. "I'll stay here and deal with Madame if it's necessary."

Dorcas had no reason to trust Fernanda, but there was nothing else to do. Neither Johnny nor Stavros was about. The plan had been to wait for Gino. But where? Perhaps they had gone down to the beach. Perhaps they would stop him there. If only they saw him before he could use his gun. Fear for Johnny mingled with her fear for Beth. The marble head was a hostage for their safety and she did not hesitate.

A maid came into the room and watched open-mouthed as

Dorcas picked up the marble head, padding the blanket around it for concealment, and left the house unopposed. She could count on nothing now except herself.

She dared not follow the road back to the square. It would take too long on foot. Instead, she cut straight downhill through sparsely set olive trees and spiky stands of cypress. There were few houses to be seen—the village was farther to her right, with the black rock of Lindos riding above it in the darkening sky. Dusk came swiftly now, but there was still enough light so that she could pick her way, following the sound of waves in a downward course to the beach.

With the sun gone, the wind had a cold bite to it. It blew with forceful intent across the inlet, stinging her with sand. In her arms the marble head seemed a dead weight—unlike the lively weight of a little girl. Underfoot the earth was sandy, pebbly, and more than once she slipped and slid in her plunging descent. Once, when she paused for breath, it seemed that she heard someone coming behind her on the hill, and that spurred her on again. At last she was free of the trees and upon a narrow path that led to the beach.

As she ran onto the sand, she saw the dark, bobbing shape of the caïque a little way out upon the water. Near the edge of the surf a shadow moved and came toward her up the beach. She knew it was Gino. There was no one else—no Johnny or Stavros.

"Where is Beth?" Dorcas cried.

How well she remembered the way Gino could laugh. He was laughing as he took the blanket from her arms and opened it. The little white head shone in the darkness, the features of the child just visible in the dying light. Gino ran his fingers almost reverently over the marble cheek.

"It is the right one," he said.

[296]

He would have turned away, but she flung herself upon him and caught him by the arm. "You shan't take the head until I have Beth!"

He pushed her away carelessly and she fell upon her knees in stony sand.

"There are a few more tears for you to weep," he said, and turned toward the water. But before he had taken three steps there was a crashing in the brush above them and the sound of stones rolling beneath running feet. Gino paused, ready to run or to fight, as the need demanded. But it was only Fernanda rushing toward him across the sand.

"Where is Beth?" she cried, as Dorcas had done. But she did not wait for an answer. She saw the blanket in Gino's arms and guessed what he was about.

"Put that down!" she ordered. "Put it down there on the sand and get the child first! You can't be such an idiot as to take Beth with you."

It was to be expected that he would laugh at Fernanda, but strangely he did not. He stood where he was for an undecided moment and she went to him and took the head firmly from his hands and set it upon the sand.

"Go and fetch Beth," she told him.

Gino turned and went down the beach without argument. Dorcas ran after him, and as they neared the water's edge she saw a small shadow crouching on the sand, mutely terrified by the events that had caught her up.

Dorcas called out to her and ran to pick the little girl up in her arms. She felt Beth's cold cheek, wet against her own, and swollen from crying, and she held her fiercely close. Out on the water a lantern bobbed in the stern of the flat-bottomed caïque and she knew Vanda was there. Now it did not matter.

[297]

Let Gino take the head. After a moment she set the little girl down and they started up the beach hand in hand.

He had seen her reach the child and had turned back to Fernanda at once. As Dorcas came up the beach, he met her with the head in its blanket safely under one arm. He began to run as he neared Dorcas, and before she saw what he was about, he had snatched Beth up like a rag doll beneath his free arm and was gone down the beach, splashing out into the water.

Dorcas cried out once and not again. She hurled herself in pursuit, but he was already beside the boat, handing Beth up to Vanda, and the head after her. She heard the chugging of the engine now and saw Gino pull himself over the boatside and disappear.

If she tried to follow and he saw her, he would not hesitate to thrust her back into the water. Already the boat had begun to move upon the dark surface. Dorcas ran through the surf, into deeper water on the opposite side of the boat, knowing only that she must reach Beth. That if Beth was to be taken away, then she must go with her. The water was warm from the sun and salt drops struck her face as she ran. Under water there were stones and the bottom slid away steeply at this place. She was swimming before her hands touched the wooden side of the boat.

She reached up and caught the rail, clinging to it, unable to get the leverage to pull herself aboard. She was being towed helplessly into deeper water. Then hands reached for her, grabbing at her dress, her arms, pulling her up and over the side. She tumbled into the bottom of the caïque and found that it was Johnny Orion who had hauled her on board. He held her against the boards with one hand, whispering to her to stay down.

Darkness and the noise of the engine had hidden what had happened. A black shadow that was Vanda stood at the tiller, with Gino beside her. If Beth was crying, the sound was hidden by the engine. Dorcas lay with her cheek against a coil of rope, her wet dress cold upon her body in the raw wind. The smell of salt and wood, engine fuel and sea water engulfed her sickeningly.

Johnny rose to a crouch and she whispered to him. "Be careful—he has a gun."

Beside her the shadow that was Johnny rose quietly, steadied itself with a roll of the boat, and stood braced and ready.

There was a sudden shout from Gino, but he had not turned toward Johnny. Dorcas rose to her hands and knees, the better to act when the moment came, and now she saw what had made Gino cry out. In the prow of the boat a great figure had risen and was coming step by careful step toward Gino. It was Stavros, monstrous seeming on the small deck.

A shot crashed as the gun in Gino's hand flamed briefly. But Stavros was not there. The bullet spat harmlessly into the water beyond. Johnny moved softly, creeping toward the child. Stavros came up with a curiously familiar movement that made Dorcas think incongruously of a basketball player with a ball in his hands. The gun fired again, and there was the unmistakable sound of a bullet striking stone and ricocheting away. The marble head glowed white in Stavros's hands as he hurled it with deadly intent. For the third time the revolver fired, but the gun's aim went awry as the heavy head struck its target. Gino fell backward over the side of the boat without a cry, and the marble head went with him. The splash was tremendous as Vanda cut the engine.

Johnny had drawn Beth from the line of fire and she came scrambling over the rough deck to her mother. Vanda left the tiller and would have gone overboard to seek her brother, but Stavros pulled her back and held her, shouting angrily in Greek. She struggled and fought him, but he bound her with his great arms and it was Johnny who went over the side, diving into the black water of the harbor. Vanda bit the arm that held her, and when Stavros let her go, she snatched up a rope coil and hurled it toward the swimmer.

Light from the lantern sent a shimmer across the dark rippling. An arm shattered the pattern, and bright drops leaped upward. Johnny shouted unintelligibly and dived beneath the surface again. Dorcas stood at the rail, with Beth's arms about her neck, Beth's face hidden against her shoulder. The moment of waiting was agonizing, endless. The path of light had closed over whatever lay below, its surface movement unbroken. Then the wet white oval of Johnny's face was turned toward them and there was a dark head beside his own.

Stavros caught the end of the rope from Vanda's hands. He pulled in the length and flung it again, so that it spat into the water within Johnny's reach. There was a splashing struggle of movement while the swimmer secured the rope beneath Gino's armpits. Then Stavros was hauling them both in. First Gino, still unconscious, was pulled over the side, and after him Johnny, with a helping hand from Stavros.

Vanda wasted no time. She attended the engine at once, turning the boat about, heading for the sand. For the first time Dorcas looked toward shore. Lanterns moved upon the beach. The men of Lindos were there. Vanda drove the boat hard in, grounding its prow.

Men splashed into the water. Ready hands helped Dorcas and Beth ashore. Someone flung a jacket about her wet shoulders. Strangely, it was Stavros who had picked Gino up in his arms and jumped into shallow water to carry him up the beach. Men moved in the lantern light and shouted to one another. Stavros dumped his burden face down on the sand. He stood back and Johnny knelt above the prone body and began to work rhythmically, silently. Beside him Vanda knelt, her face drawn and tight in the yellow lantern rays.

Beyond the circle of light someone moved. Men whispered and stood aside, and Dorcas saw Fernanda. She did not come through at once, but stayed where she was, stricken and alone. And for once silent. Beth saw her and rushed across the sand to someone who spelled safety in the midst of nightmare. Fernanda held out her hands to the child.

Dorcas stepped closer to the center of the chiarascuro that had formed upon this ledge of beach. Gino's head was turned and there was a mark upon his forehead where the marble had struck. If there had been blood, the water had washed it away. Black hair dripped wetness into the sand, and no light of excitement stirred him now. His eyes were closed and his face held less of life than the face of the marble boy.

That which was unholy had lost all power, Dorcas thought, and felt tears stinging her eyes. For the last time she would weep for the dark Apollo. Weep, not in fear, but for the waste and the loss and the squandering.

Stavros said something in Greek, and Johnny looked up from his motion. "He's not conscious, but he's breathing. Can we take him somewhere?"

The men on the beach looked at one another and Vanda gave quick directions. Before Gino could be carried to the village, however, there was a further stir at the edge of the semicircle of watchers. Lanterns parted, and Xenia Katalonos came across the sand.

She stopped beside Johnny and looked upon the mute face of Gino Nikkaris. "He is dead?" she asked.

[301]

Johnny shook his head. "He's still alive. But I don't know how badly he's injured. Stavros knocked him overboard with the marble head."

Xenia gave a small cry. Her concern was not for Gino. "Where is the head? The head of the weeping boy?"

Johnny gestured toward the harbor. "Somewhere out there on the bottom. It saved Stavros's life. It took a bullet meant for him."

Xenia cried out despairingly and covered her face with her hands.

Two of the men picked up Gino. Someone had flung a blanket over his wet body. As they moved with him, Fernanda came to life. She let Beth go and moved across the sand. She walked beside the men who carried Gino and pain lined her face as never before. Once she reached out a hand to touch him in despair, and bent to speak to him as they walked along.

"It was my fault," she said. "Forgive me, Gino."

Unexpectedly he opened his eyes and looked up at her as though, out of all the sounds about him, her voice alone could reach through the deepening mists.

"Not—your fault," he said in a sigh so soft that Dorcas, moving beside Fernanda, barely caught the words.

They carried him away and Fernanda followed no farther than the place where the path began.

So now, Dorcas thought, Gino would go out of their lives forever. Out of Fernanda's and out of her own. And there were no tears left to weep.

Fernanda walked alone up the beach and bent over something in the sand. When she straightened she carried a burden in her hands. She brought it to the place where Xenia Katalonos stood with Johnny, looking out at the dark water.

Fernanda did not speak, but held out the thing in her hands.

By lantern light it sprang to life—unshattered, unmarred, as perfect as when it had first been created eternities ago—the marble head of a weeping boy.

For once Madame Xenia was without words. It was Johnny who exclaimed.

"But, Stavros—I saw him with the head in his hands! He threw it—"

"You saw what you expected to see," Fernanda said. "What Gino took out to the boat with him was the stone catapult ball. I brought it from the car and left it near the edge of the sand when I followed Dorcas. Then I took the marble head from Gino and sent him down the beach for Beth. Before he came back, I'd wrapped the stone ball in the blanket and he picked it up without knowing. I couldn't let him take the marble piece out of the country, it would have brought him nothing but trouble."

"But of course!" Xenia cried, life coming back into her voice. "Stavros would have known what he was throwing. He would never have sacrificed the marble head."

Fernanda agreed. "That's what I mean—that it was my fault. Trying to save Gino, I put the weapon into Stavros's hands."

There had been more fault in Fernanda than that, Dorcas thought sadly. She had long ago set into motion the events that had culminated with a stone ball in Stavros's hands.

Madame Xenia, however, had no time for such notions. She clasped the marble piece to her breast ecstatically and faced the three of them—Fernanda, Dorcas, Johnny—dominant again and in authority.

"It was Gino Nikkaris who took the head. You understand

[303]

this? He would have escaped with it to Turkey if we had not stopped him. No one else was involved. You have helped Greece today. You have saved one of her finest treasures."

No one contradicted her. It did not matter. They would let the story stand. Even Fernanda would do nothing now. Constantine need never be brought into the picture and his wife's plans for his posthumous fame would suffer no defeat. The true guilt, in any event, lay with Gino.

"You will come to my house, please," Madame Xenia said in a voice rich with hospitality. "I will find for you dry clothes. A hot dinner will be waiting."

Fernanda turned from her without speaking and went alone toward the village. Johnny picked up Beth, and she clung to him with both arms. Ahead of them another woman moved alone, following the lanterns. It was Vanda Petrus, moving with all the dignity of deep sorrow—a woman grieving, the symbol of ancient tragedy.

The beach emptied about them, and Dorcas stood beside Johnny. She remembered the warm stones of Camiros and the meaning they had held for her—not empty peace, but a grasping of life and belief in herself.

"It takes courage to be happy," Johnny said, and she knew how well he understood.

Beth had gone sound asleep against his shoulder. She did not waken as Johnny put an arm about Dorcas and they moved together up the sandy ledge.

Overhead the deep blue of the sky was pierced with stars. The rock of Lindos soared against the heavens as it had done for thousands of years. Gods and men—the rock had seen them come and go. Apollo was gone from his firmament and Athena from her temple. Yet as she looked, it seemed to

[304]

Dorcas that something trembled in the starlit air like a vast, silent laughter. She walked close to Johnny, wondering if the old gods might still amuse themselves on their Olympic heights.

Claire of the Sea Light

T he morning Claire Limyè Lanmè Faustin turned seven, a freak wave, measuring between ten and twelve feet high, was seen in the ocean outside of Ville Rose. Claire's father, Nozias, a fisherman, was one of many who saw it in the distance as he walked toward his sloop. He first heard a low rumbling, like that of distant thunder, then saw a wall of water rise from the depths of the ocean, a giant blue-green tongue, trying, it seemed, to lick a pink sky.

Just as quickly as it had swelled, the wave cracked. Its barrel collapsed, pummeling a cutter called *Fifine*, sinking it and Caleb, the sole fisherman onboard.

Nozias ran to the edge of the water, wading in to where the tide reached his knees. Lost now was a good friend, whom Nozias had greeted for years as they walked past each other, before dawn, on their way out to sea.

A dozen or so other fishermen were already standing next to Nozias. He looked down the beach at Caleb's shack, where Caleb's wife, Fifine—Josephine—had probably returned to bed after seeing him off. Nozias knew from his experience, and could sense it in his bones, that both Caleb and the boat were gone. They might

wash up in a day or two, or more likely they never would.

It was a sweltering Saturday morning in the first week of May. Nozias had slept in longer than usual, contemplating the impossible decision he'd always known that he would one day have to make: to whom, finally, to give his daughter.

"Woke up earlier and I would have been there," he ran back home and tearfully told his little girl.

Claire was still lying on a cot in their single-room shack. The back of her thin nightdress was soaked with sweat. She wrapped her long, molasses-colored arms around Nozias's neck, just as she had when she was even littler, pressing her nose against his cheek. Some years before, Nozias had told her what had happened on her first day on earth, that giving birth to her, her mother had died. So her birthday was also a day of death, and the freak wave and the dead fisherman proved that it had never ceased to be.

The day Claire Limyè Lanmè turned six was also the day Ville Rose's undertaker, Albert Vincent, was inaugurated as the new mayor. He kept both positions, leading to all kinds of jokes about the town eventually becoming a cemetery so he could get more clients. Albert was a man of unmatched elegance, even though he had shaky hands. He wore a beige two-piece suit every day, just as he did on the day of his inauguration. His

eyes, people said, had not always been the lavender color that they were now. Their clouding, sad but gorgeous, was owing to the sun and early-onset cataracts. On the day of his swearing-in, Albert, shaking hands and all, recited from memory a speech about the town's history. He did this from the top step of the town hall, a white nineteenth-century gingerbread that overlooked a flamboyant-filled piazza, where hundreds of residents stood elbow to elbow in the afternoon sun.

Ville Rose was home to about eleven thousand people, five percent of them wealthy or comfortable. The rest were poor, some dirt-poor. Many were out of work, but some were farmers or fishermen (some both) or seasonal sugarcane workers. Twenty miles south of the capital and crammed between a stretch of the most unpredictable waters of the Caribbean Sea and an eroded Haitian mountain range, the town had a flower-shaped perimeter that, from the mountains, looked like the unfurling petals of a massive tropical rose, so the major road connecting the town to the sea became the stem and was called Avenue Pied Rose or Stem Rose Avenue, with its many alleys and capillaries being called épines, or thorns.

Albert Vincent's victory rally was held at the town's center—the ovule of the rose—across from Sainte Rose de Lima Cathedral, which had

15

been repainted a deeper lilac for the inauguration. Albert offered his inaugural address while covering his hands with a black fedora that few had ever seen on his head. On the edge of the crowd, perched on Nozias's shoulder, Claire Limyè Lanmè was wearing her pink muslin birthday dress, her plaited hair covered with tiny bow-shaped barrettes. At some point, Claire noticed that she and her father were standing next to a plump woman with a cherubic face framed with a long, straight hairpiece. The woman was wearing black pants and a black blouse and had a white hibiscus pinned behind her ear. She owned Ville Rose's only fabric shop.

"Thank you for putting your trust in me," Albert Vincent now boomed into the crowd. The speech was at last winding down nearly a half hour after he'd begun speaking.

Nozias cupped his hands over his mouth as he whispered something in the fabric vendor's ear. It was obvious to Claire that her father had not really come to hear the mayor, but to see the fabric vendor.

Later that same evening, the fabric vendor appeared at the shack near the end of Pied Rose Avenue. Claire was expecting to be sent to a neighbor while the fabric vendor stayed alone with her father, but Nozias had insisted that Claire pat her hair down with an old bristle brush and that she straighten out the creases on the

16

ruffled dress that she'd kept on all day despite the heat and sun.

Standing between Nozias's and Claire's cots in the middle of the shack, the fabric vendor asked Claire to twirl by the light of the kerosene lamp, which was in its usual place on the small table where Claire and Nozias sometimes ate their meals. The walls of the shack were covered with flaking, yellowed copies of *La Rosette*, the town's newspaper, which had been glued to the wood long ago with manioc paste by Claire's mother. From where she was standing, Claire could see her own stretched-out shadow moving along with the others over the fading words. While twirling for the lady, Claire heard her father say, "I am for correcting children, but I am not for whipping." He looked down at Claire and paused. His voice cracked, and he jabbed his thumb into the middle of his palm as he continued. "I am for keeping her clean, as you can see. She should of course continue with her schooling, be brought as soon as possible to a doctor when she is sick." Still jabbing at his palm, after having now switched palms, he added, "In turn, she would help with some cleaning both at home and at the shop." Only then did Claire realize who this "her" was that they were talking about, and that her father was trying to give her away.

Her legs suddenly felt like lead, and she

stopped twirling, and as soon as she stopped, the fabric vendor turned to her father, her fake hair blocking half of her face. Nozias's eyes dropped from the fabric vendor's fancy hairpiece to her pricey open-toed sandals and red toenails.

"Not tonight," the fabric vendor said, as she headed for the narrow doorway.

Nozias seemed stunned, drawing a long breath and letting it out slowly before following the fabric vendor to the door. They thought they were whispering, but Claire could hear them clearly from across the room.

"I'm going away," Nozias said. "Pou chèche lavi, to look for a better life."

"Ohmm." The fabric vendor groaned a warning, like an impossible word, a word she had no idea how to say. "Why would you want your child to be my servant, a restavèk?"

"I know she would never be that with you," Nozias said. "But this is what would happen anyway, with less kind people than you if I die. I don't have any more family here in town."

Nozias put an end to the fabric vendor's questioning by making a joke about the undertaker's mayoral victory and how many meaningless speeches he would be forced to endure if he remained in Ville Rose. This made the fabric vendor's jingly laugh sound as though it were coming out of her nose. The good news, Claire thought, was that her father did not try to give her

18

away every day. Most of the time, he acted as though he would always keep her. During the week, Claire went to the École Ardin, where she received a charity scholarship from the schoolmaster himself, Msye Ardin. And at night, Claire would sit by the kerosene lamp at the small table in the middle of the shack and recite the new words she was learning. Nozias enjoyed the singsong and her hard work and missed it during her holidays from school. The rest of the time, he went out to sea at the crack of dawn and always came back with some cornmeal or eggs, which he'd bartered part of his early-morning catch for. He talked about going to work in construction or the fishing trade in the neighboring Dominican Republic, but he would always make it sound as though it were something he and Claire could do together, not something he'd have to abandon her to do. But as soon as her birthday came, he would begin talking about it again—chèche lavi: going away to make a better life.

Lapèch, fishing, was no longer as profitable as it had once been, she would hear him tell anyone who would listen. It was no longer like in the old days, when he and his friends would put a net in the water for an hour or so, then pull it out full of big, mature fish. Now they had to leave nets in for half a day or longer, and they would pull fish out of the sea that were so small that in the old days they would have been thrown back. But now you

had to do with what you got; even if you knew deep in your gut that it was wrong, for example, to keep baby conch shells or lobsters full of eggs, you had no choice but to do it. You could no longer afford to fish in season, to let the sea replenish itself. You had to go out nearly every day, even on Fridays, and even as the seabed was disappearing, and the sea grass that used to nourish the fish was buried under silt and trash.

But he was not talking to the fabric vendor about fishing that night. They were talking about Claire. His relatives and his dead wife's relatives, who lived in the villages in the surrounding mountains where he was born, were even poorer than he was, he was saying. If he died, sure they would take Claire, but only because they had no choice, because that's what families do, because no matter what, fòk nou voye je youn sou lòt. We must all look after one another. But he was being careful, he said. He didn't want to leave something as crucial as his daughter's future to chance.

After the fabric vendor left, colorful sparks rose up from the hills and filled the night sky over the homes near the lighthouse, in the Anthère (anther) section of town. Beyond the lighthouse, the hills turned into a mountain, wild and green, and mostly unexplored because the ferns there bore no fruit. The wood was too wet for charcoal

and too unsteady for construction. People called this mountain Mòn Initil, or Useless Mountain, because there was little there that they wanted. It was also believed to be haunted.

The fireworks illuminated the mushroom-shaped tops of the ferns of Mòn Initil as well as the gated two-story mansions of Anthère Hill. They also illuminated the clapboard shacks by the sea and their thatched and tin roofs.

Once the fabric vendor was gone, Claire and her father rushed out to see the lights exploding in the sky. The alleys between the shacks were jam-packed with their neighbors. With cannon-like explosions, Albert Vincent, the undertaker turned mayor, was celebrating his victory. But as her neighbors clapped in celebration, Claire couldn't help but feel like she was the one who'd won. The fabric vendor had said no and she would get to stay with her father another year.

The day Claire Limyè Lanmè turned five was a Wednesday, Market Day, so her father woke her up at daybreak. They walked past a sandy pool that had formed near their shack, where a group of children whose parents could not afford schooling for them spent their mornings helping the fishermen or splashing inside the ring of brackish water, then plunging into the sea to rinse themselves. Claire wore the same pink muslin dress that Nozias had ordered from a seamstress

21

in town but in a slightly larger size than the year before. The cloth came from the fabric vendor's shop.

Dressed in a crisp white shirt buttoned to the Adam's apple, Nozias felt the sticky air tickle his skin as though he were trapped in one of the many humid air pockets where the sea breeze met the stifling heat of the town. Even before they turned their backs to the sea, Claire knew that, just as they'd done the year before, they'd be visiting her mother's grave that morning.

Pied Rose Avenue was already crowded with pedestrians either dodging or hailing motto taxis and tap taps. Nozias held his nose up and sniffed the air, breathing in the scent of morning coffee on streets lined with houses, whose pitched roofs were bordered with intricately carved wood that looked like his wife's favorite lace. Nozias walked at a steady clip, as if daring Claire to keep up. They passed a Vodou temple whose outside walls were covered with images of Catholic saints doubling as lwas, and Nozias pointed out, just as he had many times before, the glowing face of a pale Mater Dolorosa with a sword aimed at her heart.

"The goddess of love," he said, "Ezili Freda. Your mother liked her."

Claire had never seen a picture of her mother. There were none. And if not for the class portrait hanging in the preschool wing of the École Ardin,

a portrait that her father could not afford to purchase, there would be no pictures of her either.

They bypassed the center of town by getting off the main road and entering one of the épines, cutting through a narrow dirt track with wooden houses enclosed by cactus fences. Claire trailed behind her father as he followed the smell of burnt sugar in the air. A rubber-booted man returning from the cane fields with a cane-burdened mule called out to them, "Paying a visit to the dead, Msye Nozias and Manzè Claire?"

Nozias nodded.

The cemetery was enclosed by a wall of pale sea rock. Inside, under the bright-orange weeping willows, near the cemetery gate, were the earliest tombstones, most washed out and bleached by the sun. The marble headstones dated back to the early 1800s and belonged to the most prominent families in town, including the Ardins, Boncys, Cadets, Lavauds, Marignans, Moulins, Vincents, among others. Soon, in the newer part of the cemetery, they found the house-shaped pastel-hued mausoleums and the plain cement crosses, which rose out of the terra-cotta earth. Claire forgot at first which cross was her mother's, but Nozias took her hand and walked her over to it. He bent down and, using the end of his shirt, wiped the light coat of red mud off the hollowed letters that had been carved on the cross. Claire could only this year read the letters of her

mother's name. Her mother's name had also been Claire, Claire Narcis. Her father had named her Claire Limyè Lanmè, Claire of the Sea Light, after her mother died.

Nozias's most remarkable physical attribute was that, aside from eyebrows, eyelashes, and nose hairs, he was basically hairless. For reasons he'd never fully explored, he had never grown any hair on the rest of his body. A bald man, with sun- and sea-air-battered ebony skin, Nozias squatted with one knee lodged in the moist earth and spat on the end of his shirt, but couldn't wet it enough to clean all the red dirt from his wife's name.

Not far from Claire's mother's cross, on the indigo-colored Lavaud mausoleum, was a pink metal wreath with a gold name sash across the middle. Next to the wreath was a small bouquet of white roses. This was one of many times that Claire wished she knew how to read and write more than her own name. Her father didn't even know that much, so she couldn't ask him to read the name for her, to tell her who the child was who had been left such a pretty child's wreath and white flowers.

The entire front of Nozias's shirt was coated in red earth. He had cleaned his wife's headstone as best as he could. Sitting down on the cement slab beneath the cross, he seemed at home among the dead. But when he looked up, he spotted the

fabric vendor, who was heading toward them, wearing a white lace dress, a polka-dot scarf wrapped around her head.

"I knew she would come today," Nozias said, standing up. He looked down at his soiled shirt and seemed ashamed. He grabbed Claire Limyè Lanmè's hand, gently placing her in the woman's path.

"Do you remember my daughter?" Nozias asked while nervously patting Claire's shoulder.

"Please," the woman said, "let me remember mine."

The day Claire Limyè Lanmè Faustin turned four, the fabric vendor's seven-year-old daughter, Rose—one of hundreds of girls who were the town's tokays, or namesakes—was riding in the back of a motto taxi with her teenage caretaker when a car rear-ended them and sent Rose flying into the air. She landed headfirst on the ground.

Rose was plump and honey-skinned like her mother, and her hair was always perfectly coiffed. Her mother did it herself in playful and colorful designs, carving simple flower or geometrical shapes into the girl's scalp. Those like Nozias who witnessed the accident swore that when Rose's body ascended from the rear of the motorcycle, she seemed to actually be flying out of her primary-school uniform, an angel in a navy-blue pleated skirt and white blouse, raising

both her hands and flapping them like wings, before she hit the ground.

It was not the first time Nozias had seen an accident like this. This was, he felt, a small and unlucky town, and the narrow, mostly unpaved Pied Rose Avenue was too crowded with motorcycles, public transportation vans, and private cars. But none of the previous accidents had been as shocking. Nozias had expected little Rose to scream—just as the mothers and other spectators had as they rushed up to the spot—but the girl had not made even one sound. The motto taxi had nearly reached the mother's fabric shop when the accident happened, so it didn't take long for word to reach the fabric vendor, who, even before she was told the details, was bent over and retching as she made her way through the stalled traffic to where her child was lying, bloody and still, in the dust. Nozias had not seen such despair since the public high school in town had collapsed some years back, killing 112 of the 216 pupils enrolled there. The day of the motto taxi accident, though, the fabric vendor was the sole owner of that tragedy. The driver of the car, the motorcycle driver, and Rose's caretaker were miraculously fine, like those students and teachers who had crawled out of the rubble of the collapsed high-school building. Nozias was grateful that Claire, after having visited her mother's grave that morning, was safe with a neighbor, away from

cars and motorcycles. Still, in that moment he missed his little girl more than he had at any other time since she was born. He missed her so badly that he even felt jealous of the way the fabric vendor was holding her daughter. At least she'd been able to look after her own child during the girl's entire short life, he thought. But he was a man. What did he know about raising a little girl? Maybe if she were a boy, he could try to do it. But with a girl, there were so many things that could go wrong, so many hopeless mistakes you could make. He would always need caretakers he couldn't afford, neighbors from whom he'd have to beg favors, and women he could either pay or sleep with so they would mother his child. And even those most motherly acts, like bathing and dressing and plaiting hair, did not include embraces like those the fabric vendor was lavishing on a blood-soaked corpse. It took watching another child die in her mother's arms to remind him once again how much he'd miss Claire if he gave her away for good.

The day Claire Limyè Lanmè turned three, she was returned to Nozias from the mountain village where she had been living with her mother's relatives since she was two days old. His wife's death had been so abrupt that seeing the child's tiny face had not only saddened but terrified Nozias. To most people, Claire Limyè Lanmè was

a revenan, a child who had entered the world just as her mother was leaving it. And if these types of children are not closely watched, they can easily follow their mothers into the other world. The only way to save them is to immediately sever them from the place where they were born, even for a short while. Otherwise they will spend too much time chasing a shadow they can never reach. Children dying during or shortly after birth were common enough. Children and mothers both dying was also not unusual. But when the mother died and the child survived and the mother had shown no sign of sickness before, people assumed that a battle had taken place and the one with the stronger will had won. Nozias liked to think of it, though, as a kind of loving surrender. Only one of them was meant to survive, and the mother had surrendered her place.

Still, as soon as his wife's body was removed from the shack, there was the next most pressing problem—of feeding the baby. The midwife had dressed baby Claire in a yellow embroidered jumper from the extensive layette Nozias's wife had spent months sewing. Nozias had picked up the baby, wrapped her in the matching yellow blanket his wife had made. After feeding the baby some sugared water from a bottle his wife had also bought for the layette, the midwife had left the baby with him and rushed into town, looking

for formula or a wet nurse. Even from those very first hours, Claire was an easy and quiet child. It was as though she already knew that she could not afford to be picky or make demands.

During that first evening with baby Claire, Nozias had visions for which he detested himself, fantasies about letting her starve to death. He'd even imagined dropping her in the sea. But these were things he was thinking of doing to her because he couldn't do them to himself. He could not poison himself, as he so desperately wanted, couldn't leave her completely parentless and have her end up in a brothel or on the streets. Already he was worried that mosquitoes and sand flies might bite her, that she might get malaria or dengue fever. He feared for himself too. He feared being lost at sea or getting hit by a car, or being struck with a terrible disease that would separate them forever.

An hour passed since his wife's body had been removed, then another hour passed, and when the midwife did not return, he wrapped the yellow blanket more tightly around baby Claire and took her into town.

Evening had fallen quickly, and as he walked through the town, he felt as though he were seeing it anew. It was cloudy and the sky was grumbling, though there seemed to be no sign of rain. The sea had risen a few feet and was

becoming agitated, pushing larger waves toward the shore. A few of the townspeople were cautiously lurching about, most with their backs to the wind, as they made their way home from work or the fields. Others were grabbing rocking chairs and planters from their filigree porches, moving anything that could be lifted and carried inside. The wind slowed his steps as he picked flying twigs off the baby's blanket. He felt the baby squirm against his chest, and to avoid thinking about how hungry she must be, he thought instead of his wife, who, even on days when she didn't have to go to work washing and dressing the dead at Albert Vincent's funeral parlor, or have to go buy food, would walk through town sometimes, not to do anything in particular, but to look at people and faces and browse through the open markets and fancy shops and pick up things that both she and the vendors knew she would only put down again.

He and his wife had met when she'd come to buy fish for one of the food vendors in the covered market in town. She made her rounds three days a week, inspecting everyone's catch before filling a small basket with snapper and cod. Soon he began saving his best and biggest fish for her. On days when he was expecting her and couldn't go out to sea, or days when he had a bad catch, he was doubly sad.

He called her "wife," my wife, madanm mwen,

when it should be really "woman," except he didn't like the words "fanm mwen." "My woman" sounded illicit to him, like a mistress. They were never officially married. Still, it wasn't hard to convince her to come live with him. She was sleeping in one of the sheds in the market while every day she'd go to the funeral home to ask if she could help there—work, just as she had been doing in the mountains before she moved to town, washing and dressing the dead. Whenever he told the story of their meeting to his fishermen friends, he often added that he was the only man she liked who wasn't dead. So one day he asked her to come live with him and she said yes.

The day before she moved in, he cleaned up a bit, touching up the shack's walls, replacing some rotting wood panels and plugging a few small holes in the tin roof. He even bought a brand-new foam mattress and cot. He changed the name of his boat from that of an old love's to hers. From then on, all his fishing boats were named Claire.

Things were going all right, until they began trying to have a baby.

Nozias felt baby Claire stir again as he hurried past the white corner building that housed the town hospital, L'hôpital Sainte Thérèse. For months after she came to live with him, Claire Narcis, the daughter of mountain undertakers and

professional mourners, drank rum-soaked herbs and leaves that were supposed to make her pregnant. Instead they made her drunk, which increased the frequency of sex, but led to no immediate results. For a year, he kept wishing he had known before she'd moved in with him how much having a baby meant to her. He would have at least told her about his near-operation.

Fearful of being bound to a handful of children he couldn't feed, he had always carried around his desire not to have them like an awful secret, something that made him feel like less of a man. That is until one day, he was walking by L'hôpital Sainte Thérèse, as he just had, and rather than the usual early-morning crowd of sick and dying people, he saw a long line of young healthy men waiting. Curious, he approached them and was told there was a simple way to prevent him from having children, something that would require him to still take precautions so he wouldn't get sick from sex, but would keep him from being a father.

After a lengthy presentation in the hospital's courtyard, and a short movie filled with the testimonials of grateful men, a white doctor who also appeared to be in his twenties told the men to go home and think about it. Of all of them, Nozias was the only one who'd said he wanted the operation that same day.

The doctor had wanted to do blood tests, but

Nozias, through a translating Haitian nurse, had refused. He simply wanted the operation, he said, and nothing else. The doctor relented.

He was told that he would be awake the whole time. A sheet was placed mid-waist so he couldn't see what the doctor was doing to him. But when he felt the pinch of a needle on one of his testicles, he let out a loud screech and yelled that he had changed his mind. Nozias leaped from the table, put on his pants, and ran out of the hospital, feeling certain then that he would like to be a father one day.

He wished he could be as certain now as he hurried past the town cathedral with the infant Claire pressed against his chest. The bells began ringing the seven o'clock hour as if in alarm, while people rushed inside the church for the evening Mass and to seek shelter from the wind. Through a crack in the massive wooden doors, he glimpsed the crucified Christ, the stained glass and candle flames. Given the way that she was born and given what some people thought about children like her, he wondered if he should stop and have Claire blessed. But remembering how long she'd gone without being fed, he decided against stopping. Just at that moment, as he was rushing by, a white-haired priest held the church door open for him. It was Pè Marignan, Sainte Rose de Lima's head cleric. The priest raised his hand and hastily blessed them from a distance.

Nozias gave the priest a nod of gratitude and continued past the church toward Chez Lavaud, the town fabric shop. There, he saw the fabric vendor standing by her burly, armed, and uniformed night watchman as he chained and padlocked the shop's metal gates. Next to her, her three-year-old daughter was tugging at her skirt. Claire began to cry, and the fabric vendor turned to see where the cry was coming from.

"Madame," Nozias said, walking toward her.

He could already see on the fabric vendor's face that she knew what had happened. How could she not have? Nowhere does news spread faster than Ville Rose. Most of the women in town had probably heard how his wife's heart had suddenly stopped toward the end of her labor, yet, fearful of the mother's spirit returning to claim the child, no one but the midwife, who was used to such things, had yet rushed to his and the child's aid.

For his part, Nozias had heard that the fabric vendor was still nursing her pudgy three-year-old girl. The fact that she had not yet weaned such a big child, whose name he knew was Rose, was so unusual for a woman of her stature that everyone knew about it. Proving herself kinder and braver than he thought, the fabric vendor asked her night watchman to reopen the front gate, and motioned for the watchman to wait for her outside and for Nozias to follow her inside. She pushed open another door, then flipped a light switch, turning

on some lightbulbs dangling over the fabric-filled shelves and towering spools of cloth. Nozias, the fabric vendor, and her sleepy-looking daughter all sat down on a long wooden bench in the waiting area. The fabric vendor unbuttoned a silk blouse, making no effort to shield her large breasts, which were a few shades lighter than her face.

Claire latched on quickly and, first right, then left, emptied both the fabric vendor's breasts while Rose looked on awestruck and broken-hearted, as though she had not been aware until that moment that this was something her mother could do for anyone but her.

Nozias thought he might bring Claire to the fabric vendor every day, but after smiling and cooing at the baby, the woman tightened her face and handed his daughter back to him, giving him the scowl one might imagine she reserved for her credit-seeking customers. Pointing to the sleepy three-year-old sitting next to her, the fabric vendor said, "She needs my milk."

He did not say it, but he was thinking that his child and hers were now milk sisters. The fabric vendor had offered baby Claire her breasts. Couldn't he ask her to be his child's godmother? She certainly had the means. She also had a long history in the town. One grandfather had been an engineer. He had built the Anthère Hill lighthouse and had helped rebuild parts of the town several times after hurricanes. Another grandfather had

been a pharmacist and lay medicine man. One grandmother ran her own sugarcane business. Another had been a schoolteacher at the lycée. Her father had been the town magistrate and her mother, a potter, made clay vases for sale, which she was now selling in her own shop in Port-au-Prince.

The only thing Nozias didn't like about the fabric vendor was her reputed loose ways, her rumored desperation for male companionship. Nozias knew that his wife had come to the fabric shop often to barter her hand-embroidered baby blankets. He now wondered if the two women had ever spoken at length. Did they ever talk as more than just client and customer? As potential young mothers?

While he stood there, near the shop's front door, rocking the warm, contented baby in his arms, he thought that if he waited long enough the fabric vendor might change her mind. Would she find his daughter so pretty or pitiful that she would let her come again to nurse? Instead, she reached into her skirt pocket and fished out a few bills and pushed them toward him.

"Do you have any other family?" she asked, stroking her own daughter's perfect hair. "A sister?" Before he could answer, she added, "If you don't have a sister, you should send her to your woman's people.

"Do you have a place to bury your woman's

body?" she continued. "You can, if you like, make use of part of the plot we have in the cemetery."

The wind had subsided. He thanked her and hurried home with the child asleep in his arms. The midwife was waiting for him on his doorstep.

"You took this child out after dusk?" she chided.

The midwife had bottles and powder and treated water and was frantic to feed them to the sleeping baby. Those bottles and powder, that water, along with the funeral expenses, would wipe out most of the money he and his wife had been saving for another place away from the sea.

The next day, the fabric vendor had one of her employees bring a package for baby Claire. It was the size of a small pillow and was wrapped in the brown paper and bound with the beige sisal rope the fabric vendor used to tie bundles of cloth from her shop. Inside was an embroidered green blanket bordered with white lace and some hand-embroidered baby jumpers. They were the type of baby layette items that his wife liked to sew and had made plenty of for her own child.

When Nozias's wife's sister arrived for the funeral, he gave her the two-day-old baby, along with the layette his wife had made and the fabric vendor's package and the little money he had left.

He was relieved not to have to worry about

baby Claire for a while, yet he didn't leave Ville Rose. He kept his boat and shack. He worked harder and spent more time at sea so that he'd have enough money to send for her care. Yet he didn't visit, nor did he ask for her to be brought to him.

Sometimes, in the months that followed, during his long hours at sea, he would wonder who and what she looked like. Would she be cross-eyed or bow-legged, fat or skinny? Was she serene or dezòd, an insolent child? Would she even know that she'd had a mother who was dead?

As her third birthday approached, he felt he was ready to see her again. So he sent word to his sister-in-law to bring her back to him on her birthday. And when he saw her, she was loose-jointed and gangly, heartbreakingly, a smaller version of her mother. He had a dress sewn for the occasion, one that he would have replicated by the same seamstress in a larger size, but the same style, year after year. His wife had made one just like it, imagining that their daughter would wear it for her first birthday. He'd kept that very first dress when he had sent her away. Often he'd lay it across his chest at night, as he might have done with the child if she were with him.

Midday on Claire Limyè Lanmè Faustin's seventh birthday, Nozias rushed her to the cemetery for their annual visit to her mother's grave. The sky

had cleared and turned aquamarine, and if not for Caleb's disappearance, that morning's rogue wave might have already become a distant memory.

Claire was wearing her largest version yet of the pink birthday dress, and as Nozias watched her pull at it, tugging the fabric away from her skin, he told himself that this would be the last year he would get this dress made. Next year, for her eighth birthday, if she were still with him, he would let her choose what to wear. He might even take her to a vendor in town and have her pick out a ready-made dress for herself.

Guiding the girl past the large planter of red azaleas in front of the Lavaud mausoleum, past the bouquet of white roses that seemed a little bigger each year, he stood with her before the cement cross that was her mother's grave. The girl shielded her face with her hands, squinting to keep the sun out of her eyes. Even though he visited the gravesite regularly, Nozias always felt the same rush of pain, almost like being punched in the heart, each time he was there. He asked himself if his daughter felt the same way.

His daughter let go of his hand and lingered a few steps behind. She too seemed lost in her thoughts. Nozias feared that she was no longer interested in these visits to her mother's grave. The girl paced back and forth, while still tugging at the hem of her dress. She raised her face

toward his, removing her fingers from her eyes and allowing the sun to strike them.

It is time to leave, her eyes seemed to be saying. Now that it was clear to him that she wanted to go, he too became eager to return to the sea. A relay search party was being launched for Caleb, and he wanted to be part of the second group.

That afternoon, he and a few other fishermen put a fleet of canoes and dinghies and sloops on the water, with his boat and its colorful sail made from old advertising banners in the lead. He liked a festive sail and, over the years, once he had modified his rowboat, had collected from Msye Pierre, the editor of the town newspaper and also a party promoter, old banners for music groups. His sail was now a patchwork of band names and long-past dates for shows at the seaside speakeasies or the plaza in the middle of town. The other fishermen had tame, grasshopper-shaped, unicolored sails, but Nozias's sails were like rare butterflies. If Caleb had been around, his would have been the lead boat, as he was the oldest of all the fishermen and his cutter, *Fifine*, had always been the biggest and strongest on the water.

The sea was windless that afternoon. From his boat out on the water Nozias saw Claire Limyè Lanmè standing next to a group of boys hanging a throw net to dry in front of one of the shacks.

The boys were too involved in their work to notice her and she was too busy watching the water, trying not to lose sight of him, to pay attention to them. In the end, he spent more time looking at her than he did looking for Caleb, whom he already knew the sea would not surrender.

Claire walked back to their shack after a while, her gait sluggish in the afternoon sun. Now he could no longer see her. Even this far out at sea, he realized that he should never have told her that had he woken up earlier that morning, he too might be dead.

When he and the other fishermen returned from the water at dusk, dejected that their search had not yielded Caleb, although there was a full and dazzling moon on the horizon, some of the fishermen made a bonfire. Every once in a while one of the fishermen would throw a handful of rock salt in the fire to make sparks, hoping to draw Caleb's spirit out of the sea. As Josephine, Caleb's wife, silently wept, Nozias and the other fishermen sat on the warm sand next to her, drank kleren, and played cards, just as they would at an official wake.

In the distance, Nozias saw his daughter holding hands in a circle with five other girls, spinning one another in a dizzying game called the wonn. One of his neighbors had probably brought her a plate of food, or had invited her in

to eat, just as someone always did whenever he was at sea. As he watched her, sensing his daughter avoiding him, dozens of townspeople came by, bringing, as was the custom, small sums of money to Caleb's wife.

Pè Marignan, who was often called on to bless nets and baptize new boats, came to offer a blessing. One of the town's many Protestant ministers, Pastè Etienne, also came. He was accompanied by a group of elderly women who were dressed in white from head to toe. Caleb's wife, Josephine, was a member of Pastè Etienne's charismatic evangelical congregation. Before joining their hands together to lay on Josephine's head, Pastè Etienne and the women helped Josephine drop to her knees. When they were done and had helped her back up, the mayor/undertaker, Albert Vincent, came by. During the few minutes Albert Vincent was chatting with Josephine, one of the fishermen around the bonfire said loudly enough for everyone to hear that the mayor part of him was investigating a disaster, but the undertaker side was trolling for corpses. In fact, Albert Vincent was looking around him, as if searching not just for a corpse, but a ghost.

Nozias got up and shook Albert Vincent's unsteady hand. Even after all these years, he was grateful that Albert Vincent had given his wife a job at his funeral home when she was still new in

town, a job that had meant everything to her. Albert Vincent was also the one who'd sought out a scholarship for his daughter at his friend Max Ardin's school, in honor of Claire's mother's memory.

"How is Ti Claire?" Albert Vincent asked. He often referred to Nozias's daughter as Ti Claire, Little Claire.

Nozias nodded, indicating that his daughter was fine. Despite his gratitude, he always found it hard to be in Albert Vincent's presence and not feel a groundswell of grief, especially on a day like this. Even in the sea air, Albert Vincent smelled like his wife had smelled when she'd been working for him. His smell, like hers, was the smell of death, covered by fragrances intended to mask it.

Nozias also felt ill at ease with unsolicited kindness. He was ashamed that his need for charity was so obvious, especially to someone he could never repay, except with a fish here and there or with his humblest, meekest, most self-effacing expression of gratitude every time their paths crossed.

"I don't know how to thank you again, Msye Albert, for all you've done for the girl," he said, shortly after his hello.

"Then stop thanking me," Albert Vincent said, patting him on the shoulder. "The girl's mother was a part of our Pax Vincent family."

On that particular night, Nozias felt that Albert Vincent was stretching the meaning of family so far that Albert Vincent, perhaps without meaning to, was debasing his. She was *my* family, he wanted to say. Not yours. Or the funeral home's. Instead, he said, "Wi, Msye Albert. Mèsi anpil. Thank you very much."

Walking away from Albert Vincent, Nozias realized that he'd lost sight of Claire. The kleren that had been passed around the bonfire had fogged his head a bit. Then there was the throat-tightening experience of speaking with Albert Vincent, after which he was unable to even string together the words to properly ask the people he stumbled into whether they'd seen his daughter.

He wasn't even sure now how much time had lapsed since he'd last seen her. But while approaching his shack, he spotted her. She was sitting next to a woman. It was a woman he knew, except he had never seen her like this. Her hair was wrapped in a black net, above some giant pink sponge rollers, and she was wearing a long silver-looking evening gown. It was the fabric vendor, and she was in deep conversation with his daughter.

He was afraid to walk up to them and would have been happy to stand where he was and just keep watching them, except the fabric vendor noticed him and he thought he saw her wave.

She and Claire were each sitting on a boulder.

He crouched down and sat between them on the sand.

Why was life still able to surprise him like this? he asked himself. Maybe it was this day. This most impossible of days, this day of both life and death.

But wasn't this what he had been waiting for, hoping for, some interest in his daughter from a woman of means, a woman who had been the first and only person to have nursed her? Suddenly the full moon seemed to have drifted directly above their three heads. He felt as though everyone were watching them, waiting to see what the fabric vendor would do, what the fabric vendor would say.

"Wi," the fabric vendor blurted out, as though she and he were at the end of a very long conversation. "Yes. I will take her. Tonight."

Claire kept her eyes on the sand, but Nozias could see a tear slide down the side of her face. He wanted to reach for her, bury his nose in her cheek just the same way she liked to needle hers into his when he was sad.

"Why now? Why tonight?" he managed to say.

"It's now or never." The fabric vendor reached down to wipe Claire's face, but the girl pulled away. "I need another way to remember this day." The fabric vendor brought her hands together in a fold in her long thin satin gown, between her knees. "Now or never," she said again. She then

moved her hands to the girl's back and attempted to stroke it.

Claire's body was shaking as she watched a second pile of driftwood being placed in her father's friends' spluttering bonfire.

"Claire Limyè Lanmè," Nozias called out to her. Claire did not turn her face. He wished he could tell her a few things before she was no longer his, but most important this.

One evening after he'd learned that his wife was pregnant, they went out to sea together for some night fishing. That night, the wind seemed to be circling them, and he found himself going around and around the same small area before his sloop stalled as if it had reached a wall. He was afraid that they might be stuck on a reef, but he managed to push back. He had not yet switched on the lantern he had borrowed from his friend Caleb, when suddenly his wife removed her sundress and was sitting there in only her panties, arching her body so that it could be aimed at him like an arrow.

He took note of her slightly larger belly and breasts and realized that she was trying to get him used to it. But before he could say anything, she slipped both her legs over the stern, nearly toppling the boat as she slid into the sea. Her body parted the moonlit surface of the sea, pulling her forward as she sunk her head in, then raised it up and out again. She was now gliding

away from him, her long plaited hair floating on the surface as if separate from her face. He rowed faster, trying to catch up.

"Claire, reken, reef sharks," he shouted. "There could be reef sharks!"

She pulled her head out of the water and let out a deep, breathless laugh.

"There will be if you keep calling them," she said. "Come and look here."

As he rowed toward her, his face relaxed, and he saw what she had swum out to observe. Surrounding her was a dazzling glow. It was as though her patch of the sea were being lit from below. From her perfectly round breasts down, she was in the middle of a school of tiny silver fish, which were ignoring her and feeding on gleaming specks of algae floating on the water's surface.

He stopped rowing and rested his arms as he pondered her new body and what—who—might emerge from it, just a few short months later. The sea was calm but for the gentle lapping, as she circled her arms and legs to stay afloat. He turned his gaze away from her, keeping it instead on the water. But soon his panic returned and he shouted her name again. "Claire, come back now, Claire!"

She backed away from the fish, splitting the shimmering school in half as she splashed and paddled toward the boat. And in that moment she was his Lasirèn, his long-haired, long-bodied

brown goddess of the sea. With an angelic face like a bronzed Lady of Charity, Lasirèn was, it was believed, the last thing most fishermen saw before they died at sea, her arms the first thing they slipped into, even before their bodies hit the water. Like most fishermen he knew, Nozias, in his boat, next to his trap, net, hook, line, and tin can full of bait, kept a burlap sack in which he had a mirror, a comb, and conch shell, an amulet to attract Lasirèn's protection.

Even the regular hum of the sea seemed menacing until his wife, swimming faster now, reached the boat. He leaned over and offered her his hand, and she took it and climbed back in, even as the twinkling fish and algae vanished, as though they had been only a mirage, returning the sea surface to an uninterrupted gray.

In his sloop, the water streaming down her body, his wife craned her neck to look up at Anthère Hill and its many large houses, their lights glowing in clusters in the distance. Above those houses, before Mòn Initil, was the Anthère lighthouse. Its stone tower was usually abandoned, but every once in a while, some young people, on a quest for adventure, would make their way to the steel door at its base, climb up the tower's winding staircase, and shine flashlights from its gallery, as if to duplicate its broken lamp. Tonight, it seemed, was one of those nights. Wiping the salt water from her face, Claire

watched the flickering lights from the Anthère lighthouse, and then leaned toward Nozias.

"If it's a girl," she said, "Limyè Lanmè. Limyè Lanmè." Sea Light. She cleared her throat and in a louder voice added, "Claire like me. Then Limyè Lanmè. Claire of the Sea Light."

"What if it's a boy?" he asked.

"Then Nozias, like you. Then Limyè Lanmè. Nozias of the Sea Light."

He laughed at the ridiculous possibility of that name for a boy, but the girl name he liked a lot.

Now, on Claire's seventh birthday, up in the hills, in the gallery of the old lighthouse, there were once again lights. Some were flashlights. Some were hurricane lamps. But all of them were being lit, he knew, by young fishermen, as a tribute to Caleb, his friend.

Turning his eyes away from the lights, Nozias heard himself say to the fabric vendor, "You will not change her name?"

The fabric vendor shook her head no.

"You will not let her ride motto taxis?"

"Non." Both the woman's hands immediately rose to her chest, as though she had been struck there. "I would never do that again," she said.

Even after all these years of wooing the fabric vendor for Claire, he had never expected this to actually happen. But there was no turning back: from now on his Claire would be the fabric vendor's daughter.

"Before you leave Ville Rose," the fabric vendor was saying, "there are papers you must sign."

"I had a letter written for her," Nozias said. "You can give it to her when she's older."

"All right," agreed the fabric vendor.

"Thank you," he added, feeling the same unrelenting ache he sometimes felt standing at his wife's grave.

Nozias would later try to figure out where Claire got the courage to raise her skinny arms at that moment. He had underestimated her attachment to her few belongings and had assumed that she wouldn't want them in her new life. But at that moment, she raised her hand and pointed to the shack.

"Bagay yo," she said, "the things." Not *her* things, but *the* things, as though she knew that nothing in the world was truly hers.

Nozias and the fabric vendor watched Claire make her way to the shack, weaving in and out of different groups of children, including the girls she had been playing with, and ignoring their attempts to catch her attention. From the time she had been returned to him at age three, Nozias had always been able to see her mother in her. Their lithe and limber bodies moved in the same way, their arms glued to their sides as they walked, their legs moving too slowly, languid from one step to the next. Nozias saw the girl pull open the wobbly door of the shack, then he turned away.

50

Claire did not have that many things, Nozias thought, only two navy-blue skirts and two white blouses for school, the pink birthday dress she was wearing and the one he'd had made before it, her nightdress, her notebook and reading primers, and the foam mattress and patchwork blanket with which she covered her cot, the one that had belonged to her mother. She wouldn't be able to carry everything by herself. The fabric vendor might not even want those things in her house. Gaëlle. The fabric vendor's name was Gaëlle. Now he could think it again. Now he could even say it. He could at least call her Madame Gaëlle. Madame Gaëlle Cadet Lavaud. His daughter was now Madame Gaëlle's daughter.

Madame Gaëlle was shifting the weight of her round frame from one fuzzy slippered foot to another. She looked over at the two wooden steps one had to climb to enter the shack, then turned toward the dimming bonfire, where Caleb's wife, Josephine, was sitting, surrounded by her church friends.

Judging from the pattern of the stars in the sky, it was close to midnight. The lights from the hills had faded and the crowd was thinning out. The townspeople were drifting away, heading home. He felt sad that he had nothing more to say to this woman who was offering Claire a new life, this woman who from now on his daughter would call mother.

"How much is she bringing with her?" Madame Gaëlle now asked.

"I'll find her," he said.

He felt her possibly judgmental stare on his back as he headed for the shack. He was doing his best not to keel over, but each time his feet became lodged in the sand, he was certain he would. But even before Nozias entered the shack, he sensed that Claire wasn't there. He pulled open the door; he was right. Her cot was covered with its usual blanket, untouched since she had tucked the corners under that morning. Hanging from a wire hanger on the wall were her school uniforms. On her pillow in a neat stack were her notebook and school primers.

His feet sure beneath him now, Nozias ran toward the water and called Claire's name. He then turned around and walked the dark trails between the shacks all the way to the entrance of the alley of coco de mer palms leading up to Anthère Hill.

Madame Gaëlle trailed behind him, joining him in the shouting of Claire's name. Others did too, walking off in different directions. Msye Sylvain and some of his children and grandchildren left the flaming clay oven of their bakery to also look for Claire. Msye Xavier, the boat builder, dropped his tools and followed the crowd. Madame Wilda, the net weaver, joined the search too. She, along with a group of others, walked to

the edge of the water, looking for any sign of unusual movement.

When after some time Claire did not surface, many of Nozias's neighbors walked over to him and took turns telling him some variation of the idea that she had probably fallen asleep somewhere and would surely be home soon.

Caleb's wife, Josephine, came to embrace him. Her face was swollen from her many hours of crying, and the mourning scarf around her coarse black hair slid toward the back of her neck. Josephine was mute and suffered from elephantiasis in her right leg, which was double the size of her left leg. So Josephine moved slowly and spoke with her hands in a way that over the years Nozias and a few others who were close to Caleb had grown to understand. She touched her lips and mimed, "Mèsi, thank you." For what he wasn't sure. For spreading news of her husband's death among their neighbors? For witnessing the death itself?

Pounding both hands against her chest, she signaled "kouraj, courage," perhaps wishing it both for herself and for him.

As Josephine limped away from him, dragging the weight of her leg behind her, Nozias begged those heading to town to keep an eye out for his daughter. But inside of him was a new calm. He was certain that Claire would return, and he wanted to be there when she did.

Madame Gaëlle offered her white Mercedes. They could drive around town, looking for Claire, she said. But he was convinced that Claire hadn't gone too far, and he wanted his to be the first face she saw when she came back.

"I can't leave." Madame Gaëlle reached over and squeezed his shoulder. "She left because of me."

She was probably right. Claire had never done anything like this before. Yes, she would sometimes go off walking, wandering around town, as her mother used to. But someone—if not him, then one of the women who kept an eye out for her—always knew in which direction she was headed, where she was going, and when she'd be back. But he felt it wouldn't be right to let Madame Gaëlle spend whatever time it would take Claire to return standing out on the beach. She also sensed his unease and suggested she wait in his shack.

"Don't worry, Nozias," she said. "Haven't I been here before?"

Madame Gaëlle's pearly gown now seemed as bright as the shiny side of the moon. She smelled like gardenias, like the gardenia-scented pomade the fishermen's wives who combed Claire's hair sometimes used to grease Claire's scalp. Madame Gaëlle walked in, just as she had the year before, when she'd come to see them. But this time she sat down on his cot. Her eyes were like two

vacant pits, and in them he recognized a void that he could easily identify but could never soothe, not even in himself. She was there but not really. At one moment, her mouth opened and closed but nothing came out. She seemed to be recalling things she could not put into words.

He, though, was concentrating on his modest surroundings, on the way his cot caved in slightly under her weight. On the way the lamp was fluttering between shadow and light. Was it too hot in there? he wondered. Too cool? Too bright? Too dark? Her insistence on staying made him ashamed of his lack of comforts, of the smallness and feeble nature of his world.

"She will return, Madame," he said. "Excuse me."

He backed out of the door, as though to show her his behind would be the height of disrespect. Then he left her alone in the shack and walked over to wait next to the rocks where the two of them had been sitting with Claire before Claire had disappeared.

The Frogs

Ten years before the night she showed up to take Nozias Faustin's child, Gaëlle Cadet Lavaud was expecting her own child. It was so hot in Ville Rose that year that dozens of frogs exploded. These frogs frightened not just the children who chased them into the rivers and creeks at dusk, or the parents who hastily pried the slimy carcasses from their young ones' fingers, but also twenty-five-year-old Gaëlle, who was more than six months pregnant and feared that, should the temperature continue to rise, she too might burst. The frogs had been dying for a few weeks, but Gaëlle hadn't noticed at first. They'd been dying so quietly that for each one that had expired, another had taken its place along the gulch near her house, each one looking exactly the same and fooling her, among others, into thinking that a normal cycle was occurring, that young was replacing old, and life replacing death, sometimes slowly and sometimes quickly. Just as it was for everything else.

After one sleepless night during which she'd been haunted by visions of frog carcasses slithering into her mouth and down her throat, Gaëlle had lingered under the mosquito net

draped over their mahogany four-poster bed, as her husband, Laurent, slipped out of the room.

It was only after she heard the jingle of silverware in the dining room and her husband's effusive compliments to Inès, the housekeeper, about Inès's fried eggs and herring, that Gaëlle opened her eyes. But she didn't leave the bed until the engine of her husband's old Peugeot Cabriolet had been started, signaling that he was leaving for the fabric shop.

Soon after he was gone, she got up. Without changing out of her nightgown, she grabbed the ceramic chamber pot, which she kept by her bed. With the ever-vigilant Inès out of sight, Gaëlle walked out of the house and followed the almond grove that veered into a field of wild vetiver grass, then into a brook.

The sun had not been up for long, but it was already blazing in the middle of the sky. Still, the rocks and pebbles around the brook felt icy under Gaëlle's bare feet. She walked on them as she would a bed of dirt or grass, following the water's flow downstream until she spotted her first frogs. Just a few inches from the nearest lily pad, she noticed a green-horned frog that looked like a leaf with horns. Its legs were like a chicken's and it seemed to be almost frowning. Soon after, she found a brown dwarf jungle frog, which had the more ordinary look of a frog, except for what seemed like a long middle finger on its hind legs.

The third was a tiny scarlet koki, whose melodious staccato song was believed to lull babies to sleep.

Gaëlle looked more closely. All three frogs, she saw, were dead, though of a more natural-seeming death than the frayed remains she'd seen in recent days. The three dead frogs were in crouching positions, as though frozen mid-jump or -crawl.

Rubbing her belly, she crouched down to pick up the frogs, then dropped them in the chamber pot. As she walked toward the base of a particular almond tree, where every day in the last week she'd performed a wordless burial for a handful of frog skins, she cradled the pot against her stomach. Most mornings when she'd reached the brook, she'd hoped to find at least one live frog, but carrying the dead frogs away made her feel useful, as though she were performing a crucial service that no one else would or could do. At times, it also felt like an extension of some of the childhood play she and her husband had relished as kids: the lizard burials in matchboxes, the butterfly and firefly trappings in glass jars. Though she vowed that each morning's brief hunt would be her last, she couldn't stop, so much had she convinced herself that the frogs needed her and she them.

She dug into the dew-softened dirt with her fingers, making a hole large enough to bury the

frogs under the almond tree, then went back into the house and spent the day in bed. Some days, she felt so free that she hardly remembered the baby in her body at all. But on other days, days like today, she felt as though she were carrying a nest of snakes in her stomach. Inès brought her meals to her in bed on those days, but she barely ate anything: the breakfast of boiled plantains and fried eggs, the lunch of rice and beans, and the baby-fattening fried fish and stewed meats all looking to her even less appetizing than the dead frogs she'd planted in the ground.

"This heat and all this trouble with the frogs is surely a sign that something more terrible is going to happen," Laurent told her when he came home that evening from town. He bent over to kiss her cheek, his face soaking with sweat.

Laurent Lavaud—Lolo to intimates, Lòl to his wife—was a small man, thinner and shorter than Gaëlle in her bare feet. He had a head of thick peppercorn hair and a wide grin that he seemed unable to restrain even when he was angry. He was from a family of tailors and textile shop owners, and because of the abundance of fabric at his own shop in town, dressed very well, lately favoring airy custom-made guayaberas and loose cotton pants.

While sliding into one of the two rocking chairs on the porch, Laurent told Gaëlle how when

leaving Ville Rose's only radio station, WZOR, Radio Zòrèy or Ear Radio, where he sponsored programs and sometimes sat in the studio to listen to some broadcasts, he'd seen a group of young thugs hanging around the station entrance. Rubbing her belly with one hand, as had become a habit now, while fanning herself with a straw hat with the other, Gaëlle was only pretending to be listening when she said, "Don't think about it, Lòl. It will ruin your appetite."

He nodded, and then went back to talking about the frogs. "In all my life, I've never heard of creatures dying like this."

As an adolescent, Laurent had been a frequent hand-rolled-tobacco-leaf smoker. At times, when he made some pronouncement—for he had one of those voices that sounded as though it were always making pronouncements—he sounded a bit out of breath.

With their house in the middle of a notorious floodplain, near a tributary that joined several brooks, creeks, and rivers, Gaëlle thought that hundreds of rotting frogs might be an obvious catastrophe. But each morning, she made it a point to sniff the morning air and found no smell of dead frogs at all. As soon as their burnished skins and tiny organs were exposed to the sun, she realized, most of the frogs dried up, dissolving beneath the lily pads or into the riverbeds.

That there was no putrid odor was a lucky

thing. At this stage of her pregnancy most things still sent Gaëlle retching. And yet two smells bothered her not at all: the clammy odor of dead frogs and the inky fragrance of brand-new cloth, which she enjoyed so much that at times her husband suspected her of secretly nibbling away at their merchandise whenever she was at their fabric shop.

A few weeks after they first began to die, the frogs and their cadavers disappeared altogether. The early-summer rains flooded the town's creeks and rivers, drowning the remaining frog population and depositing a tall layer of sandy loam near Gaëlle and Laurent's house. The waters had been strong enough to unearth the lengthy roots of the young vetiver grass that grew wild near their home. Some years they'd actually made a profit from their wild vetiver, which was not only good for the soil but also much sought after by two perfume company suppliers in the nearby southern city of Les Cayes. Those years when the vetiver flourished, Laurent and Gaëlle would use the extra money to plant a few more rows of almond trees near the outer sections of their property. Gaëlle especially loved the almond trees, and before she was pregnant and developed an aversion to them, would crush their fibrous fruits with river stones to dig out the kernels.

One evening, noticing that Laurent had returned

late from the shop yet again, Inès, the bold and barrel-chested woman who'd been their house-keeper since they'd gotten married, greeted him with a silver tray and a glass of lemonade.

"Will Msye be eating tonight?" Inès asked in a scolding voice as deep as Laurent's.

Laurent shook his head no. He didn't like to eat at night and often arrived home late, after his wife had had her supper.

It had crossed Gaëlle's mind—as maybe it had Inès's—that since Gaëlle had known her husband since she was a girl and had become pregnant only a month into their marriage, he might have already taken up with another woman in town. Gaëlle also knew of his interest in the radio—his eagerness to watch the program hosts and hostesses work from the control booth was as strong as his erotic desires—and she believed him when he said that this was what he was doing in town after he closed the shop.

The next evening, Laurent came home early, carrying a handful of red azaleas for Gaëlle. Over the past few months, Gaëlle had learned that she could tolerate her husband's errors and obsessions, as long as they ended with red azaleas. There was comfort in that.

To escape the heat, they got in his Cabriolet and Laurent lowered the top and drove into the oldest part of town, past the vine-covered lookout tower

of a castle that had been started in the years when Haiti was still a French colony, as a gift for Napoleon Bonaparte's sister Pauline. The castle, one of the town's most remarkable relics, had been left unfinished in 1802, when Pauline Bonaparte's husband died from yellow fever and she sailed with his body back to France. Some of its stone walls remained, although no one had seen fit to make any type of official monument out of them. Tubers were planted where Pauline's drawing rooms and boudoir should have stood. Cows and goats grazed around them. Children played afternoon soccer games in what would have been the zoological park meant to house Pauline's large menagerie of wild native animals.

Once they passed the ruins of the castle, which was called Abitasyon Pauline, Laurent drove over the old tracks behind the sugarcane fields and the umbrella-shaped roof of the kleren plant emerged. The smell of raw liquor filled the entire street; it was said that if you stood long enough on that street you could get drunk just from the air. Laurent and Gaëlle had tried it many times and it hadn't worked. They tried again that night to inhale some hazy happiness and forced light-headedness, but it still didn't work. They then continued to the public lycée on the corner. The first floor was made of concrete and the second story was made of wood. Most of the structures in that part of town were built like this; construction

materials were randomly mixed, creating a piecemeal that the people called achitekti pèpè.

Those drives, to her, were also journeys into their past. When they were students at this school, so few people had cars that dreaming about having one of your own was like wishing you had an airplane in your front yard. When Lòl was seventeen and his father bought him the black Peugeot Cabriolet they were still driving, he became the leader of their pack, the prince of their crowd. And she, being his intended, was the one scheduling the car, organizing trips, deciding who could or could not be a part of their inner circle. During the feast day of Sainte Rose de Lima, because roses were too expensive and she didn't like lilacs, they would cover the front of the car with red azaleas and she would sit next to him in the passenger seat as he drove in the religious procession with the car's top down.

They now drove farther uphill toward the old Anthère lighthouse, near where Gaëlle had spent her childhood. They parked in front of the bougainvillea-covered gates of her grandparents' house, which had been empty since her mother and father had moved to Port-au-Prince. Looking down at the dark horizon over the beach, her husband reached for the flashlight on the dashboard and turned it on before they got out of the car. They followed a long and narrow footpath through the alley of palms that led down to the

water. Hand in hand, they walked between the canoes and sailboats, most of which were named after saints, mothers, lovers, or wives. The flaps of many of the fishermen's windows were open, even at this late hour. Every few feet offered a glimpse of some private act by the light of a kerosene or hurricane lamp: a child being nursed or smacked, a husband and wife arguing, another pair undressing, a late supper of bread and tea being savored.

The fishermen's wives called out greetings to her and Laurent as they walked by. This was both the blessing and the curse of a town like theirs, a kind of village, really, to which Gaëlle and Laurent and their families had always belonged.

"Sea air's good for the baby," many of the women called behind her.

The baby? What did they all know about the baby? Soon enough they would know everything, but for now the baby's story was only hers, Laurent's and hers.

Gaëlle hadn't wanted to do it. But because he claimed the fetus was developing too slowly, the gynecologist at Sainte Thérèse had insisted on a sonogram. The baby, determined by the images to be a girl, was shown to have a cyst growing in her chest and down her entire spine. If she lived long enough to be born, the doctor said, she would probably die soon after. Both the doctor and Laurent had thought Gaëlle should abort before

66

she was too far along. But Gaëlle wanted to carry full term, to see the whole thing through.

The next day Laurent had some other business in town and asked Gaëlle if she could spend a few hours at the fabric shop in his place. Gaëlle welcomed the idea. She relished the thought of standing behind the counter and greeting customers, who'd offer her an excuse to roll out the massive spools of muslin, kaliko, organza, and gabardine that lined the shop's crowded shelves. All of this, she hoped, would also keep her mind off the baby.

Gaëlle's first customer that morning was Claire Narcis, a pretty young woman whose long, tightly cornrowed hair sometimes made her look like a child.

After Gaëlle had become pregnant, Claire Narcis, like almost everyone else, brought her a few small presents now and then when she came into the shop. Most of the time it was food, often fresh snapper, which Claire Narcis's man had caught and which she would show Gaëlle in the shop and then carry to Inès so it would be cooked fresh. Other times it was mangoes, avocadoes, or yams. But every once in a while, Claire Narcis would bring her something for the baby, blankets or jumpers, neither pink nor blue, but yellow or green, almost as a way of quietly inquiring about the sex of the child. This time, Claire Narcis

brought an embroidered green blanket bordered in a delicate bridal lace that Gaëlle had sold her a week earlier without knowing its true purpose. That morning, with her pregnancy-sharpened sense of smell, Gaëlle could even detect on her the dead that Claire Narcis washed and dressed at Albert Vincent's funeral home most days. She caught a whiff of the embalming fluids and lemon-scented disinfectant and tried to ignore them as she untied her own shop's beige rope, unwrapped her own brown paper, to behold Claire Narcis's offering.

"I know it's bad luck to offer such a thing before the baby is here," Claire Narcis began, lowering her gaze as people of a lesser station in life were expected to.

Gaëlle reached over the counter and raised Claire Narcis's face, rocking it gently in her palm. There was no time to say or do anything else. Other customers were walking through the gate, and although Gaëlle had two salespeople helping her, she was the only one Laurent trusted to collect payment.

"Thank you for everything you've given me," Gaëlle told Claire Narcis, looking into her eyes. "But no more."

A gentle sheet of rain began to fall outside. As the sun dimmed and the air darkened and the sound of the rain grew louder and louder on the shop's tin roof, a group of soaked passersby

entered the shop's front gallery and stood, packed next to one another, in the space between the counter and the door. They were quiet, strangely so, as the rain grew in intensity, pounding the dust into mud.

Gaëlle couldn't help but worry that the rivers near her house might swell again, bringing mudslides down from the hills. Hers and Laurent's was now the only house so close to the rivers. The other houses, newer yet shabbier, had been dragged downstream year after year in flash floods, many with entire families inside. Soon after they'd gotten engaged, Laurent had chosen the land and location as a surprise. He'd sketched the plans for the house himself and had spent his nights after work at the shop updating and revising each detail as the house was built from the ground up. He had driven to the capital to purchase the gables and louvers himself. (He had refused to get married until the house was done.) So now, after all that, he wasn't going to just pick up and move.

Many of the peasants living in the villages surrounding Ville Rose were just as stubborn. Laurent often held meetings in the shop with the peasants who lived up- and downriver from them, warning them that the rivers were swelling in response to the lack of trees, the land erosion, the dying topsoil.

"What do you want us to do, Msye Lavaud?"

they'd ask him in return. "Help us find something to replace the wood we need for charcoal and we will stop."

Sometimes, in Laurent's attempts to get the villagers to stop cutting down trees, he'd reach for the basest of metaphors, the most melodramatic pleas.

"It's like killing a child," he'd say.

"If I have to kill a tree child to save my child," they'd reply, "I'll do it, sou de chèz."

And now, because of the town's and villagers' needs, her husband's dream house might soon be underwater. She and Laurent might wake up one night floating in their bed, might have to climb on top of their roof to wait for the current to die down. Silently pondering all this, Gaëlle put her hands on the back of her widening hips. Might she even have to give birth in a tree?

"It's terrible," Claire Narcis declared in a now thunderous voice so that she'd be heard above all the others and above the pounding rain. "With all the heat and rain this year, we'll either melt or be washed away," she added, as though interpreting each layer of worry on Gaëlle's face.

Gaëlle continued to measure Claire's order, adding a few more yards as degi, in gratitude, and leaving it to the others taking shelter in the shop to continue the discussion.

"These frogs dying earlier this year weren't a good sign either." Suzanne Boncy, the octogenarian

florist and a Miss Haiti during the Second World War, was the only one participating in the discussion in French rather than Creole. All the voices now came booming out, almost deafening in the shop's small space, competing with hers.

"Not all bad the frogs died," Elie, the town's best car mechanic butted in. "Knew a crazy woman once. Would catch small frogs by the river, throw them in her mouth. Smaller and more colorful they are, more poison frogs have in them. Woman died from this, everyone said so. Better for the children and for crazy people the frogs are not around."

Madame Boncy reached into the side pocket of her billowing pink dress and pulled out a folded copy of the town's one-page weekly newspaper. She pointed to a story about the dead frogs and, for those who couldn't read, explained erpétologie, or the study of reptiles and amphibians, including frogs. The article in the paper had been written by a herpetologist who had come all the way from Paris to uncover the reasons for the frogs' dying. According to Madame Boncy, the herpetologist had stated that, given his studies of the condition of the frog carcasses and the dirt and water samples he'd taken of their environment, and given the climate and blistering temperatures in Ville Rose that summer, the frogs had probably died from a fungal disease caused by the hotter-than-usual weather.

The rain was winding down, and soon it was sunny outside again. The people who'd come into the fabric shop to seek shelter were now making their way back into the street. The bells of Sainte Rose de Lima chimed the noon hour and the camions and other public transportation vehicles began circulating again, splashing muddy water everywhere.

"Mèsi, Claire," Gaëlle said as she handed her the package.

Claire's eyes were once again lowered, her shoulders slouched. "Fòk nou voye je youn sou lòt," she said before walking out. "We must look after each other,"

The next few mornings were dazzling, filled with splinters of daylight that, all over the house, crisscrossed the mahogany floors. These were the types of mornings—quiet, sun-soaked—that evaporated all of Gaëlle's fears about the outcome for the baby, even about living in the path of dangerous waters.

One of those mornings, a few weeks later, Gaëlle was planning to work with Laurent in the shop for the day and he was waiting for her in the car. She detested wearing muumuus, but at this point she had no choice.

The passenger seat had grown small for her as her belly had expanded. Though Laurent was already inside the car, looking pensively down the stone pathway leading toward the road, the

passenger side door was locked. Before she was pregnant, she might have hopped over the open top, but no more.

He unlocked the door, then held out his hand and helped her squeeze her body into the seat. He reached back and placed his hand on her lap, tapping it gently, as was his habit, as though following a beat.

Before he could put the key in the ignition, she said, "I want the baby to be named Rose."

"For Sò Rose?" he asked.

She nodded.

Sò Rose, a direct ancestor of Gaëlle's, was the free colored woman, the wealthy affranchie, who'd founded the town after Pauline Bonaparte had left. Sò Rose herself had been named by her slave mother and French father after Sainte Rose de Lima, the patroness of the southern region.

Gaëlle wanted to tell her husband that, whether their child was dead or alive, maimed or perfect, she would always love her. She loved that this child would connect them through time and that she would be born during their very first year of marriage. She wanted him to know that she couldn't bear the thought of being separated from this Rose sooner than she had to. Instead she said, "It's a good name. Rose is a good name."

"Common, though," he said. "She'll share it with so many. And then there's history."

"A saint, a heroine, and a town. There's no

shame in a name like that," she said. "She will carry it fine. It's a good name."

Under normal circumstances, choosing a name—especially the name of their first child—would have been a glorious task, an occasion for those pleasant types of arguments that families discussed for years. He wanted this name, you often hear mothers say, and I wanted another. I won, or we compromised. But her husband wanted no name in this case. Whatever she'd proposed would have been okay with him, because he was convinced, just as the doctor was, that the child would not live even an hour, much less a day.

"Don't stay out too long tonight," she said, covering his hands with hers on her lap.

"You're not coming to the shop?" he asked.

"Non," she said.

She had been feeling some cramping in her lower back and down her legs, which had intensified since she'd sat down in the car. The baby was using her head to pound against Gaëlle's lungs and spine, and it didn't seem as though she'd stop anytime soon. At least she was still moving, Gaëlle thought.

"Should we call the doctor?" he asked.

"Not yet," she said.

"Certain?"

"It's not so bad," she said, and he seemed to believe her.

"Are you going to the radio station after closing?" she asked.

"Tomorrow is payroll," he said. "They're expecting me."

"Why don't you have someone bring them the money?" she asked.

"I won't stay long," he said, then kissed the side of her neck. It had thickened and grown darker as her due date approached, and part of her was eager to see it return to normal again: long and thin with a slight dusting of talcum powder.

She pressed her head against his so that his face could remain buried in her neck awhile longer.

"I have to go now if I'm coming home early," he said, and turned away.

She opened the door and stepped out of the car. He got out and rushed to the other side, helping her to land on her feet, as the baby weight pulled her forward. She was grateful to remain upright as, after she repeatedly turned down his offer to walk her back into the house, she watched her husband get in the car and drive away. Standing there, watching him disappear behind the almond trees, she felt the muscles in her back tighten. She took slow, careful steps toward the house, then crawled into bed. She fell into a deep, exhausted sleep that was not even disrupted by Inès's occasional rumbling forays into the room to make sure she was all right.

• • •

When Gaëlle woke up, it was midafternoon and the pain in her body was gone, so she decided to go for a walk. A mound of stones had been brought down by a recent mudslide, turning the brook a deep brown. Some of the almond trees had prematurely shed their fruits and in many places her path was blocked by large branches.

Gaëlle stood on the edge of the brook and tried to imagine it filled, as it had been in better days, with crystalline water, rippling over the rocks. She imagined her husband and herself as teenagers, jumping in for summer-afternoon swims with their friends, splashing one another and muddying the flow in some spots. Then one of the regular afternoon drizzles would start, a sun shower, or ghost rain, as her husband and his friends—a year or two older and thus considerably wiser—liked to call it. The devil was beating his wife and marrying his daughter, they said. The drizzle was both the wife's and daughter's tears. The sun was God drying their tears.

Another sun shower was also starting that afternoon when Gaëlle saw a tiny red koki lodged between two rocks. It was a baby frog, smaller than the size of her pinky finger, and it was lying on its side covered in ants, its four tiny legs stiff and up in the air, as though it had made some effort to crawl away from the ants and had failed.

Squatting down, she picked it up, slapping the ants away. They scattered madly, while others crawled up and down her arms, stinging her. The ants must have not been there for long, because the koki was still whole, its interior organs, which she could spy through its sheer skin, intact. Without thinking, she wiped a warm mist from her face and stuffed the koki into her mouth.

The frog stank of mold and decay and was slippery as it landed on her tongue. And though the koki was dead, she imagined it struggling as she pushed back her head and allowed it to reach her throat. Among the many dreadful, difficult things about her pregnancy, after the doctor's dire verdict, was that she had grown to hate the smell of her own body. Most days she thought she smelled like a latrine. The very air that floated around her disgusted her. And sometimes, even though she had decided to keep it, the child growing inside of her repulsed her too.

Her body tried to resist the koki in her throat, her gullet forcing it back upward, nearly making her vomit. She took another vigorous gulp and forced it down farther until she could almost feel it land, somewhere deep inside of her.

Here they were, she thought, drawing the thought out in her mind. Two types of animals were now inside of her, in peril: her daughter, Rose, and now this frog. Let them fight it out and see who will win.

The sun shower ended and the sun peeked out brighter than before as she walked back to the house. She stopped walking now and then to fight the stirring in her belly, swallowing hard to dilute the bitter taste in her mouth. When she returned home, she was smiling more than she had for days.

"I was just going to come after you," Laurent said, rushing to greet her at their front door. "Inès told me you weren't feeling well. Did she prescribe rain?"

He was smiling his crooked smile. She was happy that he was smiling, but she was also happy that he had listened. He had come home early just as she'd requested. When he asked where she had been, she said, "Avec les grenouilles. Par le ruisseau. La douche solaire."

With the frogs, by the stream, when the sun shower began, had been a good enough explanation for him. She needed to walk to help the baby drop, to make easier the labor that lay ahead, possibly in a few short days, she said. That's why she walked to the brook every morning and sometimes in the afternoons too. He now understood that.

"But no more in the rain," he said.

"It was not rain. It was a sun shower," she said. But he no longer seemed to think there was a difference.

Her stomach now settled, she changed muumuus

and that evening ate more of her cornmeal porridge supper than she had of anything else in weeks. She'd marveled at her own peaks of joy followed by self-pity, over the full course of her pregnancy. These dark moods, almost like strange premonitions, were normal, given the circumstances, the doctor had told her when she'd found it hard to trust that she and Laurent wouldn't also die along with the baby.

"After we survive this, no matter what happens to the baby, our obituaries in *La Rosette* will say that we died after a valiant battle with a long illness," Laurent would try to comfort her by saying. "We have many babies in us still."

The following evening, the evening Gaëlle and Laurent's daughter, Rose, was born, was a clear and bright night with a full moon and a cloudless sky, crammed with stars. On one side of Gaëlle's room was a giant mirror and a lamp, both powered by the loud hum of the house generator. Seeing her half-naked body in the mirror at the foot of the bed made Gaëlle think of a jellyfish whose hood was billowing onto itself. Having the mirror there was originally her idea. She wanted to see her daughter as soon as she emerged from her body. She did not want to miss a second of looking into her child's face. But in the end, she changed her mind right before she began pushing, and she motioned for Inès to place a sheet over

the mirror, just as one would after a death. She also refused to have either her husband or the doctor called.

"They are going to take her away from me," she kept saying. Folding her body in two to push the baby out, Gaëlle felt flattened and weak one second and invincible the next. Soon after Inès reached down between her legs and pulled out her daughter, Gaëlle cut the umbilical cord herself with a pair of brand-new scissors from the shop.

Both Gaëlle and Inès wept at the child's swift arrival, but most of all at her unexpected flawlessness, at how magnificently whole she looked. She was plump and gorgeous, a swirl of tiny curls covering her perfectly round head. She let out a long wail when her bottom was slapped. Her arms flailed in the air with gusto. There were no cysts on her back, or anywhere else on her body.

She was perfect, a perfect little Rose, who nonetheless looked like her father. It was obvious that she would not grow up to be a tall or stately woman, but soon after her umbilical cord was clamped, her dark eyes were already open, and when her mother held her up to her breasts, she immediately opened her still blood-tinted little mouth and started nursing.

On that perfectly starry night, Laurent Lavaud did not make it home in time to meet his daughter, Rose. There had been a shooting at

Radio Zòrèy, where, not knowing that his wife had begun her labor, he'd stopped for a minute to drop off more sponsorship money. The shots had rung out as Laurent was leaving the station, and he was struck by three bullets to the heart and died on the spot. Even before his body was cold and the pool of blood under it had been covered with limestone powder, people immediately began to declare that his shooting was related to a new, urgent plague in Ville Rose, one that was even deadlier than the frogs: gangs.

Ghosts

Bernard Dorien was living in Cité Pendue, a destitute and treacherous extension of Ville Rose. Some people called it the region's first circle of hell.

In spite of its stark reputation, Cité Pendue—twenty-eight miles from Port-au-Prince and eight miles from the center of Ville Rose—was actually only a midlevel slum. After all, it had a few Protestant churches, many Vodou temples, some restaurants and bakeries, and even a couple of dry cleaners.

For a while, there were no gang wars, just one gang, whose headquarters was a former food-storage warehouse that the dozen or so young male inhabitants called Baz Benin. (The men of Baz Benin gave themselves the monikers of Nubian royalty, which also happened to suggest menacing acts in Creole—Piye, for example, meaning "to pillage," Tiye, meaning "to kill.")

Bernard's parents were restaurateurs in Cité Pendue. They had a slightly larger yard on their pebbled street than most of their neighbors, so they'd closed it off with corrugated metal, and there they served at least thirty customers per night, more if the turnover was fast. At the center of their business were four long wooden tables

spread out beneath a string of generator-fueled lightbulbs. They sold rice and beans, plantains, and cornmeal, but their specialty was barbecued pigeon meat.

The place was called Bè, Bernard's parents' nickname for him. Bè also meant "butter," and Bernard's mother liked to say when everyone asked her how she was doing that she was churning butter from water—m ap bat dlo pou m fè bè—which meant that she was always attempting the impossible, trying to make something worthwhile out of little or nothing.

Bernard's parents had moved to Cité Pendue from a village in the surrounding mountains at a time when Cité Pendue was being used by most people as a temporary perch while their peasant children finished primary school. But as the trees in theirs and other provinces vanished into charcoal and the mountains crumbled and gave way, washing much-needed topsoil into the sea, the Doriens stayed in Cité Pendue, much as their neighbors had to, and raised their son—and hundreds of pigeons that over the years they sold both alive and dead for breeding or for food.

Most of their customers at one point had been nervous young men who wanted to perform a Cité Pendue ritual before their first sexual encounter. They'd slit a squab's throat, then let it bleed into a mixture of Carnation condensed milk and a carbonated malt beverage called Malta.

Sometimes their fathers would come with them and, after the sons had held their noses and forced down the drink, the fathers would laugh and say, as the pigeon's headless body gyrated on the ground, "I pity that girl."

It was a ritual Bernard's parents didn't approve of. But for each bird that was killed this way they were paid enough to breed more. They mourned the days when people had come to buy pigeons for racing, or to train as carriers, or as pets for their small children. Then they began missing the days of the fathers and sons, because suddenly their customers were beefy young men who'd gathered themselves into what were at first called "popular organizations," then gangs.

The gang members were also called chimè, chimeras or ghosts, and were, for the most part, street children who couldn't remember ever having lived in a house, boys whose parents had been murdered or had fallen to some deadly disease, leaving them alone in the world. Later, these young men were joined by older neighborhood men. These older men were "connected"— that is, ambitious business owners as well as local politicians used them to swell the ranks of political demonstrations, gave them guns to shoot when a crisis was needed, and withdrew them when calm was required.

Sometimes, before one of these demonstrations, so many men came for the milk-Malta-pigeon-

blood mix that Bernard's parents were tempted to close the pigeon-killing business for good. And finally they did.

Still, with the money they'd made from the pigeons, the Doriens were able to add to the menu. They bought the house next door to them, the one attached to the Baz Benin warehouse, and added a few more tables to serve their growing clientele. Bernard's father also bought a small camion that he drove back and forth between Cité Pendue and Ville Rose daily, packed with people and sometimes livestock. He was always at the restaurant for their busiest time, though, between nine in the evening and one in the morning, when the gang members, many of whom had brought the drug trade with them from the capital, would take over most of the establishment. Watching these boys drift from being mere sellers to casual users of what they liked to call the poud blan, the white man's powder, watching these boys grow unrecognizable to anyone but one another, Bernard's parents were repulsed and afraid. But they still kept the place open, because the same blight that was destroying Cité Pendue was allowing them to prosper, to send their son to school with the heirs and heiresses of Ville Rose's tiny middle class, to make contacts that one day might help him get a good job or find a decent match for marriage.

To stay out of the gangs, Bernard had joined the

regular national police force (not the Special Forces). Although he was just twenty years old, scrawny, and had the distinctive family trait of a disproportionately large head that gained him the nickname Tèt Veritab, Breadfruit Head, the police academy in Port-au-Prince had accepted him. But Bernard had found that, even though his training was in the capital, he couldn't be a police rookie and have his parents survive in Cité Pendue. Every time a gang member was arrested in Cité Pendue, Bernard was blamed for it, putting his parents' lives in danger. More than this, his parents were heartbroken that he had left. His mother told him every time they spoke on the phone how she wished he'd return home. It was his first nearly fatal asthma attack in some time—he'd suffered from them since childhood—that forced the police academy to let him go during a particularly taxing training session. But while he'd been in Port-au-Prince, spending endless hours in traffic, in tap taps, communal buses, and taxis, he'd fallen in love with the radio, especially the news and commentary, call-in, and interview programs, which seemed to blast from every house, car, street-corner business, or shop. So now Bernard spent all the time he wasn't helping out at his parents' restaurant working as a modestly paid newswriter at Ville Rose's only radio station, Radio Zòrèy.

Having grown up in Cité Pendue, and having

seen many of the changes there firsthand, Bernard imagined himself becoming the kind of radio journalist who'd talk about what he preferred to call the "geto," from the inside. An idea came to him one night while he was walking from his parents' small concrete-block kitchen, which they had built close to the street to tempt passersby with appetizing smells, to the table where Tiye, a one-armed gang leader, was nursing a beer and a massive cigar. Tiye was wearing his plastic-steel-combination artificial arm under a long-sleeved peacock-blue shirt and was expertly raising and lowering the beer to his mouth with the prosthetic's shiny metal hooks. Surrounded by three eager "lieutenants," Tiye was laughing so hard about the way he'd once slapped a man, when he had both his arms—sandwiching the man's head between his palms and pounding both his ears—that he had to dab tears from his own cheeks. Bernard, eaves-dropping, wished he'd had a video camera, or at least a tape recorder. He wanted the rest of Cité Pendue, the rest of Ville Rose, the rest of the country, to know what made men who were the same age as he, men who lived in the same place he did, men like Tiye, cry.

We can't move forward as a neighborhood, as a town, or as a country—he'd thought as he brought Tiye and his friends another round of beers—unless we know what makes these men cry. They

cannot remain chimè, chimeras, phantoms, or ghosts to us forever. His commentary segment at Radio Zòrèy, if he were ever given one, would be called *Chimè*, or *Ghosts*.

His only viable competition at the station would be a popular weekly program called *Di Mwen*, or *Tell Me*, a weekly interview/gossip show, hosted by a raspy-voiced woman named Louise George. Just as *Di Mwen* had been at first, *Ghosts* would be controversial, but soon people all over Ville Rose would tune in to it—Bernard was certain of it. A kind of sick voyeurism would keep them listening, weekly, monthly, however often he was on. People would rearrange their schedules around it. They wouldn't be able to stop themselves from discussing it. What are the men and women in the geto up to now? listeners would ask themselves. They'd be encouraged to figure out ways to alleviate the gang problem. Also featured on the program would be psychologists, human-behavior experts, and neighborhood planners.

Max Ardin, Jr., who was Bernard's friend and the host of a rap music program at the station, liked Bernard's pitch. But he was also skeptical. Though he was only nineteen and had gotten the job through his father's connections, Max Junior still knew a lot about the radio business. Besides, Bernard trusted him.

"I'm feeling everything you're saying, but the management won't buy it," Max Junior said

while keeping Bernard company one afternoon as Bernard typed away on an old electric typewriter at the far end of a long desk in the newsroom. "Who'll sponsor a program like that?"

"The government should sponsor it," Bernard said, as he retyped that day's news from the wires into conversational Creole for the announcer to read on the air. "We'd be offering a public service."

"You should pitch it to our boss," Max Junior said. "But I bet he'll be too scared to take it on."

Just as his friend predicted, Bernard's program was not picked up, at least not with his involvement. But a few weeks later, while typing that afternoon's news script, Bernard heard a taping for a program called *Homme à Homme*, or *Man to Man*. The program, announced the host, a former army colonel, would consist of in-studio conversations between gang members and Cité Pendue and Ville Rose business leaders.

"They'll hash out their differences," he heard the colonel say, "with the help of a trained arbitrator."

The first program did just that, pairing an ice factory owner, who'd had his place broken into at least once a month for over a year, with another gang leader from Cité Pendue, a nemesis of Tiye's, who was believed to have vandalized the ice factory.

"What do you expect?" the gang member told

the ice vendor. "You're chilling in all this ice while we're here boiling in hell."

The arbitrator, a female psychologist, who'd called in to the station from Port-au-Prince, then suggested the obvious, that the businessman find some way to share his ice, sell it at a lower price to the people who lived near his factory, and that the gang leader respect the property of others.

What's worse, Bernard was forced to hear the entire show again on the radio his mother sometimes had on in the restaurant, as he was serving drinks to Tiye and his crew, among others. Tiye and his friends had known about Bernard's pitch for the show—he had approached them as possible guests—and, as he served them their beers, they teased him. "Hey, man, they stole your idea!"

A few of them tried to grab Bernard as he put the bottles on the table—as if to squeeze out the anger they knew was bubbling inside him. The more they laughed, the angrier he got. Tiye was still laughing when he said, "Bernard, bro, that show is kaka. I should find them all and kick their ass."

"That's right," Piye, Tiye's second lieutenant, chimed in.

"Bernard," someone else said. "You should kick the ass of the guy who stole your show."

Just then Bernard's mother called him over to the kitchen, to pick up more beers, he thought.

But on top of the old refrigerator in which they kept the drinks was his mother's most lavish personal acquisition, an old rotary phone. His friend Max Junior was on the line.

He thought Max Junior would be calling about the show, but instead his friend said, "I'm calling to say good-bye, man. My fucking father is sending me to Miami."

"Really?" Bernard said, both incredulous and sad. "When are you coming back?"

"I don't know," his friend replied.

"Who's doing your show while you're gone?" Bernard asked.

"I'm not sure," Max Junior said.

"Maybe I can fill in for you," Bernard said.

"Maybe," Max Junior said, then added, "Man, they stole your idea."

"Truth is, *Homme à Homme* is not the show I wanted to do," Bernard said, trying to contain his sadness over both his departing friend and his show. "I wanted something closer to the skin. Something more personal."

Tiye and his guys were chanting from their tables, "Kraze bouda yo! Kraze bouda yo! Kick their asses! Kick their asses!" Their voices were so loud that Bernard could barely hear Max Junior anymore.

"I'll call you from Miami," Max Junior said.

After he hung up, Bernard stood with his head pressed against the concrete wall and waited for

Tiye and his crew to leave before returning to the tables. His mother and the neighborhood girls she'd hired came in soon after to wash the dirty dishes. His mother's stern expression never changed. It was as if the heat of the kitchen had melted and sealed it. He thought, miserably, that even if she didn't work again for the rest of her life, whatever beauty she'd had when she was young and wasn't cooking for dozens of people every day would never come back.

He convinced his mother to go to sleep a little earlier than usual, before going to bed himself. In his room, whose walls and ceiling he'd painted bright red when he was a teenager, he felt both Max Junior's sudden good-bye and the loss of the show deep in his gut. Now it would be much harder to pitch his idea to another radio station in the capital or somewhere else. The programmers could always say, "But *Homme à Homme* is already airing. We don't want to give these gangsters too much of a platform." He fell asleep thinking he'd have to redefine his idea, sharpen it, add music. When he came back from Miami, Max Junior could help him with that. They could play reggae-influenced hip-hop like Max Junior played on his show, while in between songs Bernard would let his neighbors speak.

Bernard was still asleep the next morning when a dozen Special Forces policemen dressed all in

black and with balaclava-covered faces knocked down the front gate of his parents' house, climbed up to his room, and dragged him out of bed. He was shoved into the back of a pickup even as his mother wailed uncontrollably and his father shouted that a great injustice was taking place.

When they reached the nearest commissariat, a small crowd of print, TV, and radio journalists, including his boss, were waiting for him. The night before, Ville Rose's police spokesperson, a shrill-voiced woman, explained, there had been a shooting at Radio Zòrèy. Four men with M16s and machine guns had been seen jumping out of an SUV. They had shot at the front gates of the two-story building, killing Laurent "Lolo" Lavaud, a fabric shop owner and very generous Radio Zòrèy sponsor. The police had arrested Tiye, the notorious head of Baz Benin. Tiye had named Bernard as the auteur intellectuel, the mastermind, of the crime, the person who had sent him and his men to do the job. Bernard was not allowed to speak. He was only meant to stand there, like a menacing prop, surrounded by the hooded police team with his wrists handcuffed behind his back, while the same flashbulbs kept erupting and a video camera light pierced his eyes and questions were shouted at his accusers.

The box of a room where Bernard was then taken to be questioned was narrow and hot, with the

stench of fresh vomit wafting in the air. In addition to the creaking metal chair, on which he was placed with his hands still cuffed behind him, the room had a cement floor and a ceiling light box whose flickering beams streamed past the black cloth that one of the policemen had placed over Bernard's eyes.

During his questioning by the police, Bernard was repeatedly punched on the back of his head. This reminded him of Tiye's description of the two-handed slaps given to the men who'd once been hit by Tiye's lost arm.

"You know Tiye?" Because of the blindfold, which also covered his ears, many of the voices sounded distant and distorted, until some of the officers moved their mouths close to his ears and began shouting so loud that he thought his eardrums would pop. One of them blew smoke into his face. In his brief police training, Bernard had not yet gotten to the classes on suspect interrogation methods. Were these the methods they would have covered? he wondered bitterly.

"Wi," Bernard replied, coughing. "I know Tiye." His lungs felt as though they were closing in a new way, as though they would never open again. The constriction forced out chunks of last night's dinner onto the front of his pajama top, and when he was allowed to bend his neck, down on his lap.

"How you know Tiye?" The questions continued,

sometimes from two or three mouths yelling in a deafening chorus in each of his ears.

"Lives in my neighborhood . . . He comes . . . He eats at my parents' restaurant," he stammered.

"You're a big man, uh? Your parents have a restaurant in the slums. I'm hungry now. Feed me. Feed me," one of the officers shouted.

The others were laughing even as Bernard hiccupped. To his now burning ear, there was no difference between their laughter, their taunting, and that of Tiye and his crew. They could all have switched places and no one would have noticed.

"How much did you pay the crew from Baz Benin to shoot at the station?" another officer yelled.

"Nothing . . . I . . ."

"So they did it for free?"

"Non . . ."

"You paid?"

"Non . . ."

"Which is it?"

"No involvement . . ."

"You trained with the police for a while, didn't you, so you could become a big-shot criminal?"

They threw some ice water on his face and laughed some more. Panicked, he tried to rise from the chair, but someone shoved him back down. With the smoke and the vomit and the cold water, he felt as though he were drowning.

After the questioning, Bernard was left alone in the dank cell, still blindfolded and shackled. That afternoon, his mother and father came to see him. They were allowed to remove the strip over his eyes before kneeling down on the floor to get closer to him. His mother was quietly weeping over his body, which was curled up in a fetal position.

"Bè, could you have done such a thing?" his father asked. Bernard's father sounded at once worried and stern, and even more distraught about scolding his son. An old facial tic, the quick batting of his eyes and involuntary twitching of his mouth, had returned to Bernard's father's face. Bernard had not seen it in such a long time that he'd almost forgotten it.

Bernard shook his head no.

"I did nothing, Papa," he said, his throat aching as he tasted the chunks of vomit still lingering in his mouth. His father, he knew, needed a denial from him in order to proceed full-force with his fight.

His mother reached into her bra and handed him an inhaler. "Bè," his mother said breathlessly, as though she were having an attack herself, "we had to pay extra to bring this in to you."

"They're not beating me too bad," he mumbled. "Not yet anyway. You see I have no blood on me."

The mother raised his filthy pajama top,

covered with vomit and sweat, to look for cuts, wounds.

"The lawyer we got for you," his father said, "her cousin is a magistrate. She says she's going to try to move things quickly, in your favor." Somehow his father's mouth now remained a controlled line. "You might have to go to the pénitencier in Port-au-Prince, until we get you out."

They'd talked to Tiye's second lieutenant, Piye, a few hours before, his father told him. His father had told Piye that Bernard would have never asked Tiye to kill anyone. Piye had told his parents to stay calm. The case was a lamayòt, a vapor, he said. Nothing was going to stick. Give it a few more hours. Let it cool off.

With his father's help, Bernard pulled himself up. Had they called his radio colleague and friend Max Junior? he asked. Max Junior was supposed to leave for Miami, but might still be in town. He too might have some helpful contacts.

He'd tried to see Max Junior at his home, his father said, but was told by Max's father that his son had left the country.

Bernard raised both his hands to his face and began sobbing. Neither of his parents could remember seeing him cry like this before, not as a grown man. His body was shaking, the hopelessness sinking in. In spite of having his parents' arms around him, he felt deserted and alone.

• • •

But it turned out that, in fact, he was actually on a fast track. An hour or so after his parents left, a black-robed magistrate came into Bernard's cell—an exception to his having to go before a judge weeks and months or even years after being put in jail—and informed him of the charges against him. He was not only considered the mastermind of the radio station shooting, but was said to be a turncoat police rookie. Bernard feared that he'd rot in an overcrowded jail cell at the pénitencier in the capital or be disappeared before he even got there. He began plotting ways to get his story out. He would write something for the radio, for Radio Zòrèy. But would the people who ran Radio Zòrèy and the people who listened to it even want to hear his side of the story?

That same evening, in the interrogation cell, having slept through the dinner hour, as Bernard lay there with his face pressed against a particularly cool and hollow groove on the floor, he saw a line of black shiny boots march toward him. He was blindfolded once again, then thrown into what felt like the backseat of a car. He was shoved out on the street in front of his parents' restaurant, still blindfolded, at around 10 p.m.

After his own arrest, Tiye had made a deal. As head of Baz Benin, Tiye had collected drug-related dirt on everyone, from the lowest policeman in Cité Pendue to a few of the area's judges.

And now he'd talked to the police and exchanged his slew of records, including records of bank deposits for bribes, for both his and Bernard's freedom.

Later that evening, bathed and clean, Bernard was lying on his bed in his red room, staring at the crimson ceiling. He had called Max Junior's home and asked for him, and after he said his name, Max Junior's father—Max Senior—had slammed down the phone on him. That's when he began writing.

Yes, he'd write something for the radio, a report that would contain all the details of the experience he had just been through. He would make it clipped and fast, like a story told out of breath, but since he would no longer have his own radio program, or even sit in for Max Junior, he would have someone else narrate it for him. He would, if he could convince her, get Louise George, the hostess of *Di Mwen*, to read his story on the air. He could imagine her not interviewing anyone else the week she'd read it. His story, read in her signature down-tempo, yet passionately hoarse voice, would, along with the many sponsor spots and commercial announcements that only she was able to get, fill the entire hour of her show. Her boss, the owner of the station, would probably not want her to do it, but, ballsy as ever, she would threaten to quit if he stopped

her, and since hers was the most popular show on Radio Zòrèy, she would prevail. She would begin her program in the usual way that evening, as though he were actually sitting across from her inside the studio, at the radio station, from which he was now surely banned.

"Tell me, Bernard Dorien," she would say to the empty studio chair. "We need to hear your story." And then she would read his story and explain why he wouldn't be there to talk to them directly about his experience.

But soon his parents interrupted his writing and fantasizing. They hovered over him, leaning over his bed as his mother handed him a hot cup of verbena tea to further calm his nerves.

Even though his mother hadn't cooked, so as to discourage her regular customers from coming, people had still stopped by for drinks, and to express their relief and offer their congratulations about his release. His parents were also here to tell him that Msye Tiye was downstairs and wanted to see him.

Bernard handed the teacup, still full, back to his mother, then raised the edge of his mattress and placed his notebook under it, on the metal spring.

"Down soon," he said.

"Don't be tardy," his mother said, as though he were about to be late for school.

His parents filed out dutifully, one after the other, their bodies tense with a new level of worry.

． ． ．

In the yard, Tiye and the lieutenants were already settled at a table with drinks.

"No need to pay tonight," Bernard's father said, before joining his mother in the kitchen.

Tiye had a few more guys with him now for extra protection. These men listened with rapt attention as Tiye described some of what he'd just been through. "I thought they were going to jack me up real bad," he was saying. "Real bad."

Bernard could hear Tiye's slow and severe voice grow louder, drumming like the policemen's voices, deep inside his head, as he walked over to Tiye's table.

Tiye said: "You know how they take some of the guys to Port-au-Prince and you don't never hear from them again. Or how they just beat the shit out of you. Then yeah, I thought I was done, fini."

He said all this casually, almost matter-of-factly, with a kind of amused air, which indicated that, if this had happened, it wouldn't have been a big deal. This was how Tiye and his guys faced the inevitable, Bernard thought.

Crossing the yard on shaky legs, Bernard realized that this was all a game to Tiye. He had turned Bernard in, then rescued him, and now he was having a few laughs and some beers. It was all in a day's work. Still, Bernard couldn't shake the feeling that one day they would all be shot.

Like the fabric shop owner Laurent Lavaud and like almost every young man living in the slums. One day it might occur to someone, someone angry and powerful, and maniacal—a police chief or a gang leader, or a leader of the nation—that they, and all those who lived near or like them, would be better off dead.

Bernard walked over to Tiye's table and held out a hand to him. Pounding his fist on his chest, near his heart, in greeting, Tiye said, "No hard feelings?" Then Bernard noticed that Tiye's gums were as red as the walls of his room, as though he had a perpetual infection or had been eating raw meat.

"Did they jack you up?" Tiye asked Bernard.

"Wasn't so bad," Bernard said.

Tiye wasn't wearing his prosthetic arm and the sleeve of his shirt sagged. With his good hand, Tiye motioned for the guy who was sitting next to him to get up so Bernard could sit down.

Bernard looked more closely at the space where Tiye's missing arm would have been. He thought he saw something white, as though a polished piece of bone were protruding from under thinly scarred skin. He tilted his head to see it better, while trying not to seem obvious. For a flash of a moment, Bernard looked over his own body to see if anything of his was gone.

The restaurant was unusually full for the hour. Above the din of voices requesting drinks,

Bernard could hear people asking his parents whether it was true that he had been released, then walking by the table where he was sitting with Tiye to see for themselves. Some even shook his hand, a few women kissing him on the cheek.

He was now a kind of everyman hero, someone who had seen the bowels of hell and returned.

He now imagined beginning his own radio program with a segment on lost limbs. Not just Tiye's, but other people's as well. He would open *Chimè* with a discussion of how many people in Cité Pendue had lost arms, legs, or hands. He would go from limbs to souls—to the number of people who had lost siblings, parents, children, and friends. These were the real ghosts, he would say, the phantom limbs, phantom minds, phantom loves that haunted them because they were used, then abandoned, because they were out of choices, because they were poor.

It was nearing closing time. His mother brought the final beers to the table. She avoided their eyes as she lifted the bottles from her tray and put them down. Bernard waited for her to return to the kitchen before raising his drink toward Tiye and clinking the top of his bottle with his. Tiye's bottle struck his with force. Bernard saw a brief spark, and the top of his bottle broke apart, leaving a jagged gap in the glass. A shard landed on the table with a splash of beer; another fell to the clay floor.

Tiye laughed, a loud, haunting laugh that reminded Bernard of the officers at the prison, a laugh that flashed his crimson gums as he pointed his beer bottle in Bernard's direction. "If you're doing a little piece on the radio," he said, "can't be some homo masisi bullshit like that *Homme à Homme*. Needs to be real."

Tiye stopped laughing, then filled his mouth with beer, swishing it around loudly, as if he were gargling.

"Don't worry," he said to Bernard, but also, it seemed, to himself. "As long as I'm here, nothing will happen to us tonight."

The next morning, Bernard Dorien was found dead in the bed of his red bedroom. He had been murdered in the same way that Laurent Lavaud, the owner of the fabric shop, had, with three bullets expertly, and, in Bernard's case, silently, administered to his heart.

The restaurant had already opened for breakfast when his parents found him, so the neighborhood girls continued to serve the food they'd cooked, as a Cité Pendue magistrate and an anti-gang prosecutor came and wrote up their reports.

"An eye for an eye. Another bandit has been erased from the face of this earth," began Radio Zòrèy's morning newsflash. It was a piece that, were he still alive and working there, Bernard Dorien might have been assigned to write.

Home

Max Ardin, Jr.'s girlfriend was missing. Crowding his father's vast ring-shaped living room were the hundred or so guests who'd come to greet him on the first night of his first visit home in ten years.

On the phone from Miami, Max Junior had told his father, Max Senior, that he was coming home with a girl.

"What kind of girl is she?" Max Senior had asked.

"Just a girl," Max Junior had said.

"What family?" Max Senior insisted, hoping his son would rattle off the cognomen of one from their milieu, from Miami or the capital or some other respectable town. But instead Max Junior had replied in jest, "The human family," causing his father to confess that he was worried Max Junior was bringing home a poor foreigner.

"She's Haitian and she knows where Ville Rose is," Max Junior said, in an attempt to console his father.

"Mon Dieu." Max Senior feigned a gasp, then laughed. "A poor blan who's also Haitian and knows where Ville Rose is."

From the lowest step of the old rosewood staircase, which had been buffed and shined back

to life for the special evening, Max Junior now scanned his father's book-lined living room for familiar faces. He spotted two of his father's oldest friends, Suzanne Boncy, ageless beauty queen, and Albert Vincent, the town's funeral director and now also its mayor. Around Suzanne Boncy were a slew of other aging beauties, most of whom had too much rouge streaked across their cheeks, and the one or two representatives from the other group of his father's friends that Max now found most bearable, the children of these women and their Ville Rose men, the Canadian-, French-, Mexican-, or U.S.-educated sons and daughters, who preferred the capital, but made the occasional quick trip to Ville Rose to check on their parents.

Before he'd left Ville Rose ten years ago, Max Junior had spent countless afternoons and evenings in the company of leaner, more attractive versions of these people. He had attended birthdays, weddings, and funerals, watched soccer matches, and played epic games of cards and dominoes after countless Sunday dinners. Aside from the children in his school and the occasional girlfriends he was rumored to have, these were the only kinds of people whose company his father enjoyed.

Things had been different when Max Junior was younger. Before his mother had divorced his father and moved to Miami, Max Senior had

taken the time to attend conferences and lectures with Max Junior and his mother at the Alliance Française or the foreign embassies in Port-au-Prince. By the time he was nineteen, and his mother had left, Max Junior had already completed his primary- and secondary-school studies and had also gotten a U.S. mail-order bachelor's degree in education. He had attended École Ardin for primaire; once he was too old for the school, his father had become his sole instructor.

It had always been Max Senior's dream to have his son help him run his school. But at nineteen years old, Max Junior wanted to be a radio deejay. So Max Senior used his connections to help, arranging for his son to host his own program on Radio Zòrèy. Max Senior had also encouraged his son to continue his studies in Miami. He'd never lost the hope that one day Max Junior would return and take over École Ardin. But instead Max Junior chose to stay in Florida, to manage the sandwich shop his mother had opened in Miami's Little Haiti neighborhood.

Max Junior had met Jessamine at the sandwich shop, where she'd come to interview for a part-time job. He was even heavier at that time, bulky, a sloppy nineteen-year-old with a neglected Afro, but she still seemed to like him. He'd done the entire interview with her in Creole, which had won her over. Jessamine, a college senior, was looking for a way to support herself while

continuing her studies in nursing. She was lively and confident, but what struck him most about her were the two gold studs she wore on either side of her cheeks. Until she finished her schooling and started working full-time as a pediatric nurse, she was his best hire, his mother's favorite employee. And she was still his best friend.

But where was Jessamine now? he wondered, as he mingled and exchanged pleasantries with his father's friends. Could she be lost? In the bottleneck traffic that snaked through potholed Route Nationale Numéro 2? Had she been robbed? Kidnapped on the way out of Port-au-Prince?

They had parted ways before his father could see her at the airport. She told him that she had to go see her aunt, after which the cousin who'd picked her up at the airport would see that she got to his father's house in time for the party. He hadn't taken the cousin's phone number. He had been dialing the number at her aunt's house all afternoon, but no one had answered. Maybe her aunt's phone wasn't working. Could the cell phone that Jessamine had brought with her from Miami not be working either?

Max Senior's firm hand was pressing down on his son's shoulder as Max Junior attempted absent-minded small talk with Albert, his father's closest friend. These two men were so close, in

fact, that sometimes it seemed as if they were living the same life, following, if not the same career, the same emotional path.

"You've been gone too long," Albert told Max Junior, his hands shaking, as they always had, even when Max Junior was a boy. The fedora that Oncle Albert—as Max Junior still liked to think of him—always carried with him was meant to shield his shaky hand, but it only brought more attention to it, especially when it fell and he had to bend down and pick it up.

Rumor had it that the shaking was the reason Albert's wife was living near their fifteen-year-old twin son and daughter's boarding school in Massachusetts, while he was running a funeral parlor that had been in their family now for four generations.

"Where's your girl?" Max Senior asked his son.

"My girlfriend?" Albert interrupted, laughing. "She and my wife don't get along so I didn't bring her."

Max Junior remained quiet, feeling out of step now with the two men's long-standing comic banter.

Albert's tall and elegant wife, younger by two decades, was indeed in town. She was standing in the back of the living room, by the bookshelves, chatting with a small group of expatriate wives, as his father liked to call them, women who lived in different countries than their husbands did, and

when they returned for visits, were never quite at ease or appropriately dressed, wearing leather boots in May, or shorts in December, or any other time of the year. Katya Vincent looked like she had gained only a few pounds since Max Junior had seen her more than ten years ago, but he recalled his father saying of the so-called expatriate wives that they came back each time fatter and reeking of citronella, every mosquito and salad and untreated glass of water suddenly their mortal enemy.

Max Junior remembered being the ring bearer at Katya and Albert Vincent's wedding. His parents had hosted one of the engagement parties. His father had been the best man. It was a time in his life that he sometimes wished he could have back. But as he later came to realize, his mother—and perhaps Katya Vincent too—had never been happy here. His mother, particularly, had always considered her life elsewhere, in the countries that the foreign embassies and cultural alliance organizations represented, and, unlike Katya Vincent, his mother couldn't both escape Ville Rose and hang on to her husband at the same time.

"How is running the town?" Max Junior asked Albert.

"I'm told that some executioners cross themselves before they shoot their victims," Albert said. He had a gentle, melodious voice, almost

soothing to Max Junior's ear. Max Junior had always liked his voice. Unlike his father, who sounded like he was fighting back a stutter, Albert spoke like a singer, a singer of seductive boleros or love songs, which would be great, Max Junior thought, for his new political career. "I wish I had seen all the voters cross themselves before they cast their ballots for me," Albert said. "When something goes right, the national government takes credit. When something goes wrong, I get the blame."

"That's politics, isn't it?" Max Junior said.

"That's life," his father added.

"In the end, I see them all, though," Albert said, "both victim and executioner."

"Does that give you the right to insert this type of death talk into every conversation?" asked Max Senior.

"I wanted to talk about wives and girlfriends, but you wouldn't let me," Albert said, once again laughing his generous, melodious laugh.

"Do you have bodyguards now?" Max Junior asked Albert. "Security?"

"Why would I?" Albert said. "If someone wants to kill me, they'll just shoot the bodyguards first, then me. I'm saving the town money and the criminals bullets."

Albert then started across the room, heading for his wife. Max Junior watched his father's friend place his arms around a woman who many

believed had married him only for his money. She had even taken his children away from him, his father liked to say, locking them up in that boarding school, where they must spend their time mostly hating their country. Indeed, the twins didn't like to return to Ville Rose, choosing winter excursions with their friends and summer camps in France over visiting their father, whose obligation it was always to visit them. One day they would return, Max Junior was certain, when it was time for them to cash in the funeral parlor or take it over.

"Why didn't you send the chauffeur for your girl?" Max Senior now asked his son.

"I don't know about chauffeurs and girl-friends," Max Junior cracked. He imagined the punch line coming out of Oncle Albert's mouth. "I've lost many good ones that way. Many good chauffeurs, that is."

Later in the evening, Max Junior was moved when his father stood at the top of the stairs in front of a room full of his friends and delivered a brief welcome.

"I'm glad my son is back," his father said while raising his Champagne glass clear above his head. "I don't know how I have survived here so long without him."

He had run a school most of his life, but public speaking was not the old man's forte, which made

his gesture that much more meaningful to Max Junior. When it was his own turn to speak, he followed his father's example and kept it brief. Standing stiffly at the old man's side, he said, "It's good to be home, if only for a while."

"Only awhile?" his father shouted, feigning surprise, as a room full of Champagne glasses clinked once more.

But between all the talk and casual chatter with his father and his guests, all Max Junior could think of was the reason he'd had to leave Ville Rose and Haiti in the first place and whether or not he would ever see Jessamine again.

That night, after everyone had left and his father had gone to bed, Max Junior kept calling Jessamine's Miami cell phone, only to get a busy signal. No matter how late it was, he would have gone to look for her, except he had no idea where her aunt lived in Port-au-Prince. How stupid of him not to have asked her in advance!

He'd been too nervous about this trip to think all the details through. But could his carelessness mean that he would not need Jessamine here as much as he'd thought? In Miami she was the only person to whom he could speak openly about everything. Too damaged herself to be judgmental, she listened to all his confessions with a blank face. She was the only girl he'd told, for example, that he'd fathered a child ten years

ago, a child whose name he didn't even know, a child whom he had never met.

As he lay on his back in the same room he'd slept in since he was a boy, Max Junior hit the redial button for Jessamine's cell phone number again and again. His bedroom felt unbearably hot, so he got up and opened the shuttered terrace door that overlooked the peanut-shaped pool and screened gazebo and the maid's quarters for both his father's house and the house next door. Looking up at the sky, he took in the glow of a cluster of stars, something he was never able to see in Miami.

He should be driving all over Port-au-Prince looking for Jessamine, he thought. Isn't that what he should be doing, instead of dialing her number every five minutes while watching the sky? He should be looking for her. Just as he should have been looking for Bernard Dorien a decade before. He should have at least come home for Bernard's funeral. Bernard's parents had probably taken his body to the mountains and buried him there. He felt burdened by the thought of Bernard being suspended somewhere in a hillside grave. To fight so much to live in town, then return to a mountainside grave? What was the use of sacrificing so much to leave a place, only to end up exactly where you'd started? But wasn't he doing the same thing now, in returning home, looking back when he should be moving forward?

He thought of going for a late-night swim to calm himself, then nixed the idea. Instead, he went back to bed and called Jessamine's number, only to get the same busy signal. The generator had already been shut down for the night. The ration of electricity allowed for their part of town had expired. So he had no choice but to lie in the dark, in his swimming trunks, his eyes seared open.

When he woke up midmorning the next day and got the first busy signal from Jessamine's phone, he thought of borrowing his father's Jeep and heading out to Port-au-Prince. But then he heard a knock on his bedroom door.

Before he had a chance to collect himself, his father walked in, wearing the gunmetal-gray sweat suit in which he practiced his judo, alone, against a star fruit tree in his garden every morning.

"You have a visitor," his father said.

"Jessamine?" he asked, grabbing a pair of khakis from the back of a nearby chair and throwing them on.

"Who did you say?" his father asked, moving closer to help him into his pants.

"Is it Jessamine?"

"The one who didn't come last night?"

"Is she down there?"

Max Junior then threw on a red T-shirt that Jessamine had given him long ago, as a gift for

hiring her at the Little Haiti sandwich shop. He had promised her that he would wear the shirt when he returned to Haiti since it was half the color of the Haitian flag.

Both the khakis and T-shirt were a bit wrinkled, but he didn't care. He was about to run out the door when his father grabbed him by an elbow and held him back. Though the old man's salt-and-pepper hair had grown grayer and he had become thicker and slower with each visit to see his son in Miami, and though the old man occasionally complained about his achy shoulders and back, he was still pretty strong. If they ever got into a tussle, Max Junior thought his father could easily throw him.

"Listen to me," his father said. "Hold still. Calm. Are you supposed to be in love with this one, what's her name, this Dessalines woman?"

"Jessamine."

"Anyway, are you in love with her?"

"Papa," he said, both plea and protest. "What are you asking me?"

"You liked Flore too, didn't you?" the old man asked.

His father's grip tightened on his biceps. He would have to shove the old man aside to get past him and out the door. He was not of the proper mind-set to think this through in any kind of detail. "Papa, this is no time," he said, trying hard not to raise his voice.

"Yes, actually it is a good time," his father said, "because Flore is down there right now. And she's with your son."

"Flore?"

"In the flesh," the old man said, releasing him. "En chair et en os, with your son."

Max didn't remember climbing down the stairs. He simply felt his feet skipping over them two at a time until he was at the bottom. From where he was standing, on the other side of the room, he could first see the back of a woman in an off-the-shoulder mango-colored dress. The woman's hair was short but meticulously curled, as though each strand had been separately attended to. When she finally turned around, he saw that she was wearing lipstick that made her lips look as red as cherries.

It was Flore, but not really Flore. It was Flore, but no longer a skinny teenage girl who wore the same beige maid's uniform that was sometimes stained from food and dirt she picked up in the kitchens and bathrooms of his father's house. It was Flore, but not really Flore, who was now a fierce, older-looking sienna-brown woman. The whole series of incidents—his having had sex with her, her having gotten pregnant—were all in this woman who was standing a few feet from him now.

"Flore?" he asked, more as a request for confirmation than a greeting.

She bobbed her head in his direction but said nothing.

"How have you been?" he asked her, his eyes still taking in all that she had become. "What are you doing here?"

He didn't mean it to sound like a rebuke. He was genuinely curious, interested in how she had gotten there, back into his father's house, in his father's living room, in the middle of the day.

"Flore has a beauty shop in Port-au-Prince," his father answered instead. "I asked her to come see us."

Max Junior was trying to think of a way to ask about his son when he heard a child's voice call out from behind the divan, where Flore had walked over to sit.

"Kounye ya? Now?" asked a boy's voice.

"Wi," said Flore.

Shy, as Flore had been before she'd so drastically changed in face and in body—but also in attitude, it seemed, for Flore's eyes never wavered from his, her face never softened—the child kept his eyes on Max Junior as he pulled a massive grape-colored lollipop in and out of his mouth. The boy was wearing a plain white T-shirt and jeans, and though he was obviously aware that he was the focus of everyone's attention, he took time to survey the room, examining the giant bamboo planters behind the ancient leather couches and the massive abstract paintings on the

walls. The boy grimaced at the paintings, large fluorescent blots, which made no sense to Max Junior either. He looked stocky and strong, but Max Junior didn't know many children his age, so he wasn't sure. Neither he nor his father was a lean man. They were men of average height, paunchy and round, like this boy might one day be, when he grew up. As a matter of fact, the boy looked exactly like them, like he might fall perfectly in line with all the generations of men in his family.

"And what do you do with him for school in Port-au-Prince?" Max Senior asked from behind the banister, where he was now sitting. "Is he getting some good schooling? You know very well, Flore, that we have a school here, a good one."

Shifting a small, woven straw purse from one shoulder to the other, Flore gazed around the room as though searching for an anchor for herself. "He's well, as you can see," she said.

Max Junior was now standing right in front of his son and his son was looking up at him and he was looking down at his son. He kneeled so that his face was at the level of his son's and said, "Alo."

"Alo," the boy echoed, with the lollipop still lodged in one of his cheeks.

For a moment Max Junior worried that the child might leap at him and tackle him to the ground as

his own father watched from behind the banister. "My name is Maxime Ardin, Jr.," he said.

Max Junior thought the boy a handsome child, a stoop-shouldered little boy with an open face and generous smile. Max Junior himself had been a boy like that. He waited for the child to say his name. Thought for a moment that he might not. The boy looked over at his mother for some clue as to what he should do. She tilted her head and seemed as eager to hear what would come out of the boy's mouth as Max Junior was.

"My name is Pamaxime Voltaire," the child said.

Because Max Junior had not legally recognized the boy, the child had been given Flore's family name, Voltaire. But with "Pa," a Creole prefix meaning both "his" and "not his," the child's first name could either mean "Maxime's" or "Not Maxime's." Only the mother could know for sure.

"Pamaxime," Max repeated, copying the child's hesitant voice.

It surprised him that Flore had named the child this way.

"If he were a girl, we could at least call him Pam," Max Senior said, drawing a stern, hateful look from Flore.

Looking back at Flore, who gave Pamaxime a small nod of approval for the perfect enunciation of his name, the child, still with the lollipop in his mouth and with a coy voice that sounded a bit

122

rehearsed, asked, "Ou se papa m? Are you my papa?"

"Wi," Max Junior said. He was amazed how quickly the word came out of his mouth. Though he had not offered Pamaxime the family name, now looking at his child's face, he was even more certain that this boy was his, in spite of or because of the negation or affirmation of his own name.

Kneeling there next to his son, Max Junior remembered a story Jessamine had told him when he'd confessed to her that he was thinking of coming home for a visit. Jessamine's parents had met in Miami while working at a hotel where her mother and father were both part of the cleaning staff. Soon after they got married, her father decided to return to Haiti to live. Her mother stayed behind in Miami, promising to join him in a few weeks. During that time, her mother discovered that she was pregnant with Jessamine and, no longer wanting to move to Haiti, filed for divorce. Her father didn't know about Jessamine until she was in her first year of high school and he, sick and dying from something or other, returned to Miami for treatment. In the meantime, Jessamine had been told by her mother that her father had abandoned her. Jessamine hadn't seen her father live and wasn't sure she wanted to see him die. She went with her mother to visit him in the hospital anyway. Right before they got there,

he took his last breath. They were allowed to stay in the room with the body for only a few minutes before her father was wheeled out under a white sheet and taken down to the morgue.

Ever since Jessamine had told him about her own father, Max Junior had replayed that scene in the hospital over and over in his mind, casting his son in Jessamine's role and himself as the dead father on the gurney being rolled out. The worst possible case of unrequited love, Jessamine had told him, was feeling abandoned by a parent.

Both he and his son were in a mild trance now, their eyes locked on each other's, which he became aware of only when Flore snapped her fingers and whistled, motioning for the boy to walk to her. The Flore he knew before would have never made such crude gestures.

Pamaxime was still standing in front of him. He wanted to reach over and take his son in his arms now, but he was afraid of overwhelming the child. In her continued attempt to capture the boy's attention, Flore clapped and clapped again, yet the child did not move. Looking back and forth between him and Flore, he seemed torn. The boy looked at Max Senior, his grandfather, who motioned with his index finger for Pamaxime to go to Flore.

"Why such a hurry?" Max Senior then said. "Let the child stay here a day or two. Let's see

more of him. He can play, have a swim with us in the pool."

The child turned to Max Senior, who was now standing with both his hands in the air as though pleading to the heavens for a special favor.

"He will not stay here," Flore said, as though she were speaking from behind a grille locked inside her mouth.

And with those words, Flore rushed forward and grabbed Pamaxime's hand, but he did not move. Max Junior tried to reach for the boy's other hand, the one farther from Flore, not to stroke or kiss, but just to touch him to say a tactile good-bye. But before he could, the boy was led away by his mother. Reaching down, Flore motioned for the boy to hand her the remainder of the lollipop, then dropped it in her purse.

Max Junior was still kneeling there as his son walked off. The child did not turn around. He remained on his knees, hoping that the boy might run back, to hug or kiss him, to tell him his first good-bye after his first hello. But what had he done to deserve it?

He heard some voices coming from the next room, by the front door. It was Flore talking to an older woman, who, though she'd been working for his father now many years, he could only think of as the new maid. It seemed that Pamaxime had something he wanted to give him, and Flore was asking the new maid to take it, so the child

wouldn't have to come back. Max Junior thought of running out to collect it, but stopped himself. Flore had every right to make all the decisions.

He heard the front door slam shut.

"From the child." The new maid handed him a folded piece of white paper.

He could feel his father watching him. Back when he had his music show at Radio Zòrèy, he had gotten notes dropped off for him at the station and at home all the time. Many of the girls had handed the perfume-scented missives to Flore at his front door.

He opened the sheet of paper his son had brought for him. On it was the word "papa" in small slanted letters along with a sketch of a man with a blank *O* for a face. He yearned for an explanation that he knew he might never get. He folded the paper and placed it in his pants pocket, then he rose from the floor and rushed out the door. His father followed, as though both he and the old man had come to the same conclusion at once.

A tiled driveway parted the lush tropical garden that led from Max Senior's porch to his front gate.

"Tann," Max Junior called out after Flore. "Wait."

Flore spun around and the child did the same, mimicking his mother. Max Junior caught up

with them near where his father's car was parked, by the low iron gates.

"Let me take you wherever you're going," Max Junior said.

He imagined they were going back to Flore's mother's house in Cité Pendue. While stroking his son's closely cropped hair, he added, "Mwen la kounye a. I'm here now."

The boy squirmed and craned his neck so he could see both his father and his mother at the same time. Max Junior felt as though he were in a public square as his father watched from a wooden bench on his front porch. But none of it mattered. He was no longer a nineteen-year-old boy. He was an adult now, a man who shared a child with this woman.

His father walked over from the bench and placed himself at the boy's side.

"Can I borrow your car to take them home?" Max Junior asked his father.

Flore raised her eyebrows in surprise.

"Would you know the way?" Max Senior asked his son.

Max Junior nodded.

Max Senior walked back into the house and returned with the keys to his tèt bèf, everyone's cow-horn nickname for this kind of Toyota Jeep. He handed the keys to his son, then walked to the front gates, sliding them open, for the car to pass through. He walked back to his front porch and,

before he went into his house, called out, "Bye!" to his grandson. But the boy didn't even glance at him; he was too busy paying attention to his own father to hear.

First Max Junior helped the boy into the car. This gave him another opportunity to touch his son as he held the child's hands, guiding him to settle in the backseat. He tried to pull the seat belt across the boy's chest. The straps rose to the child's neck, so he decided to forgo it. He shut the door, opened the passenger side for Flore, then finally climbed into the driver's seat. The hem of Flore's dress rose high above her knees as she settled into her seat and quickly she pulled it down. She could have sat in the back with the child, making him feel like their chauffeur, but she didn't.

He had never been deep inside Cité Pendue. He had only driven with his parents, on their way farther south, by the main road that circled it, the road by the sea. Still he felt as though he had already been there. He'd been there in the way his friend Bernard Dorien had described his parents' restaurant, which was, according to Bernard, practically attached to the Rue des Saints warehouse, once occupied by the men of Baz Benin. He'd been there through the music that the Baz Benin men had produced and recorded and brought to him on CDs and even cassettes, to play on his radio program, their

praise of and laments about precarious life and certain death in the geto.

"What's a good way?" he asked Flore as he turned the Jeep toward a line of calabash trees in front of his father's gate. Ten years before, it would have been best to use the road by the sea, but he wasn't sure anymore and wanted to confirm this with her. And she agreed with a reluctant nod.

Even after ten years, the road along the sea was still tarred and mostly paved. There were more cars now, and the traffic crept along the two wide lanes going in opposite directions. Several young men and women tapped on the car window, offering to sell him fried foods and meats, plantain chips, and bottled water. Others followed, hawking cell phone chargers and batteries.

In the cars and camions in front and on the other side of him, he saw that many of his fellow drivers and their passengers passed the time by talking on cell phones, something which, a decade before, when he'd left the country, you wouldn't have seen. On the opposite side, a funeral procession was stuck in the gridlock with a hearse leading a small caravan of cars that motto taxis snaked through.

When the traffic did move along, it reminded him how pretty Ville Rose still was. On one side of

them were the same moss-blanketed marshes he remembered from years ago and in the distance some funnel-shaped mountains.

Soon, though, they passed a new line of low-grade brothels, where women sold sex in individual bungalows. A loud bell sounded in Flore's purse and she pulled out a cell phone, then switched off the ringer. She turned around and handed the phone to the boy, and occasionally when Max Junior looked in the rearview mirror, he would see the boy tapping the keys hard and fast while playing some kind of game. He realized that he had forgotten his own cell phone in his room at his father's house.

Glancing now and then at Flore's profile, which she kept nearly frozen, almost like a statue, he found it difficult to remember most of what they'd once talked about. It was never consequential, nothing ever too deep. Aside from the usual things about what he wanted her to cook on a particular day, he would try to make her laugh with him at the love-stricken girls who wrote him letters, for example, but she never did. He would make fun of some friend of his father's who had come to dinner with his wife and met his mistress there—a dinner she had served them. She would never join in his teasing and criticism.

Back then, she'd seemed interested in magazines, especially the beauty magazines left behind by his father's female friends. He would

sometimes catch her staring at the women in those pages, her mouth open, her eyes widened in awe. He would try to bring home more of those magazines from the radio station, as many as he could, and he would leave them lying around the house for her to pick up and look through when he was out. She often straightened her own hair with a box of relaxer she'd buy from a vendor of hair extensions at the open market, but they never discussed any of that. They never even discussed how she had come to his father's house when she was barely sixteen, why she had been made to leave school to replace an aunt who'd worked there for years until the aunt was too old to work.

The child was still lost in the cell phone game, pounding the keys even harder now, as though there were something dire at stake.

"Why did you name him that?" he asked her quietly.

"What?" she snapped, without turning her face.

"Why did you give him such a name?" He did not even want to say it so as not to bring the child's attention to their conversation.

"Because I wanted to," Flore said.

But what he meant to ask her was which way she'd intended the name. Not his? Or his? But he couldn't think of a way to ask without the child understanding exactly what they were talking about. He looked back in the rearview mirror, and

the boy now had the phone closed on his lap and his thumb wedged in his mouth.

"Aren't you too old for that?" he asked the boy.

The child pulled his finger out of his mouth and placed his hands on the seat, under his thighs.

"I've tried so many things," Flore said, more to the boy than to him. "Even rubbed a hot pepper on it."

"A hot pepper?" Max Junior grimaced. "Terrible."

When it grew quiet in the car again, Max Junior turned on the radio. A newscaster was droning on about demonstrations against high food prices in Port-au-Prince. Could Jessamine have been caught up in that? Could that have kept her from making it to Ville Rose either last night or this morning? It already felt like weeks since he had seen her, although it had been only twenty-four hours.

"Are there any children's programs on Radio Zòrèy the way there used to be?" he asked, trying to think of some other way to entertain the child.

Flore shrugged. She either didn't know or didn't care.

When Max Junior looked back in the rearview mirror, he saw the boy was now asleep, lying across the backseat with both his legs fully bent. He was indeed a beautiful boy, Max Junior thought, not just handsome, but beautiful. It was a kind of beauty that he thought everyone could

admire. No one could look at this child sleeping, his eyes tightly closed, his chest rising up and falling down, his face so relaxed that he looked defenseless, no one could look at that child, he thought, and not find him free of blame and shame.

It had taken nearly ninety minutes to drive eight miles, but they were finally entering Cité Pendue. He could tell by the way the sea on the side of the road had turned from green-blue to brown to ashen black. The streets narrowed, rising in a line of sloped hills packed with cement and cinder-block homes, tin shacks, and open markets filled with exhausted-looking women and wilted food.

"The house isn't too far in." Flore was guiding him. "My mother wanted something not far from the street."

He turned a narrow corner that seemed like it was never made for a car to pass through, then down a crisscrossed trail, where he finally found the house.

It was different from what he'd expected, prettier. Box-shaped with pink grille metalwork covering the front. He tried to park the car as close to the front as possible and leave room in the narrow alley for people to walk by.

The boy was still asleep in the back. Max Junior picked him up, cradling him in his arms. This is what it must have felt like to hold him as a baby,

he thought. A very heavy baby. The child was breathing deeply, and when he pushed the boy's body into his chest, the child wriggled, twisting himself back in place.

"Where should I put him?" Max Junior asked once Flore opened the front door.

Inside, the house smelled overpoweringly of vanilla essence, the liquid type you might add to lemonade and cakes. The living room was sparse, with four plastic-covered chairs facing one another across a narrow table pushed against a back corner. A lightbulb dangled on a cable from the ceiling and on the walls were beauty-queen calendars, advertising beer and skin-bleaching soaps and creams.

A bamboo curtain hid a bedroom with a large bed that took up most of the room, along with two large stuffed-looking suitcases. As he placed Pamaxime on the bed, Flore turned on a standing fan and aimed it in the sleeping child's direction. Flore seemed surprised that the fan came on, that there was any electricity at all.

"Where's your mother?" he asked when they stepped back into the front room.

"In the market," she said.

His nose full of the vanilla essence—his eyes nearly watering from it—he was filled with regret, but did not know how to tell her. In the end, in spite of these surroundings, she seemed to have somehow triumphed. She had now proved,

by letting him meet his son, for one thing, that she was no longer afraid of him. And what had he done? He'd brought into the world a child whom he had ignored. He'd left his home and his country for years. And he'd kept secrets.

"I'm sorry, Flore. I'm sorry for what was done," he said, pacing now, across a cement floor that was as uneven as the ceiling.

"What was done? You mean for what you did." She seemed to have been waiting for him to bring up the subject—or dreading that he would. Her arms began shaking as she tried to dust one of the plastic-covered chairs with her bare palms. She rubbed her hands together, then balled both her fists as though she were getting ready to punch him. He could tell that her anger had been simmering not just today, but for the last ten years, and now that she was in her own neighborhood, in her mother's house, she could release it.

"I went there today," she said, "because your father found us in Port-au-Prince and asked me to come. But now? No, no, I don't want to see you again."

Looking around the room, which was a fifth the size of his room at his father's house, he thought that it could use a window. A window might take away some of this awful vanilla-essence fragrance. It might let in more light. It might allow the boy to see the sky when he woke

up from his sleep. A window might make the entire house feel bigger, make them feel freer. A window and some plants, like some of the plants in his father's garden, were what this little house needed, he thought. But the spot in the wall where the window might be was needed for the neighbor's wall, and a window might make them less safe here. A window might make it easier for someone else to come in and hurt them.

"What about the boy?" he asked, because everything was now centered on the boy. The boy was everything. "He drew me," he said. How could the boy have known what he would look like? What would he have drawn if he'd been asked to sketch the boy? "He drew me without a face. Just a circle, a blank circle."

"Did you want your face to look like an ass?" she asked, a triumphant smirk flashing across her mouth. She tried to suppress it, but it remained there, like her own personal victory.

A decade ago, he'd tried to convince himself that he might love her, that he might want to make a life with her. He tried to make himself believe that this would be best. But this was one of many false dreams he held close to his heart, like the one of finally making love to a woman who could fully satisfy him, whom he would long for and miss every morning when he woke up.

"I'd like to contribute," he said, now raising his head to examine the slab-sided pink ceiling above

their heads. "I'd like to contribute to a good school in Port-au-Prince. A school like Papa's school."

"Your father gave me some money," she said. "Your mother sent me some too. You must know that."

Actually he did not know that. He found it easier to believe that his mother would wire her money from Miami, but not that his father would hand Flore some. Or that this was something his parents would do together.

Flore walked to the door, grabbed the wobbly metal handle to open it, then motioned with an abrupt movement of her head for him to leave. He reached into his pocket for his wallet nevertheless, but he'd left his father's house in too much haste and, along with his cell phone, had also left behind his wallet. He made a gesture toward her, but, pushing his empty hands away, she said, "Ale tanpri. Please go."

She followed him out. He muttered hello to some of her neighbors, who were sitting out on their cement porches as he climbed into the Jeep.

"Where can I find Rue des Saints?" he asked once he'd slouched down behind the wheel.

Flore looked up at the closest neighbors, two women, one old, one young, and a teenage boy who seemed to be the older woman's grandson. A curious look passed between her and her

137

neighbors. Had Flore told them, told everyone, about what he'd done?

"Rue des Saints is no longer Rue des Saints, I know," he said to the young man. "I just want to find out how to get there."

He'd heard about it in Miami. The morning he'd left Ville Rose, Bernard Dorien had been arrested. The next day he was found dead. Then someone had set fire to Baz Benin, a fire that not only had destroyed Baz Benin but, as it spread, had razed Bè, Bernard's parents' restaurant. He didn't know where Bernard's parents were spending the rest of their lives. (Had they returned to the mountains? Did they start another restaurant elsewhere?) In the Haitian newpapers he'd read in Miami, only Tiye and his lieutenant, Piye, had been listed as having died in the fire.

This cascading news had shattered him, but there was nothing he could do from Miami. Or was there? Even if he'd returned to Haiti, Bernard would still be gone and his parents' business too. There was nothing he could have done.

"Can I still get to Rue des Saints?" Max Junior asked.

The young man used the life lines in Max Junior's palms as coordinates on an imaginary map. Max Junior followed his directions, driving nearly a half hour between tin shacks on dirt roads before he reached Rue des Saints.

The street that was once Rue des Saints was

now mostly a row of wooden shacks next to a reeking landfill smoldering on the edge of an oil-streaked storm drain. Max Junior stopped the car. On both sides of him were mountains of trash, tires, and thousands of tiny plastic juice bottles and foam food containers. A few people stopped to stare at him before continuing on their way: two old women returning from the market, a group of sweaty boys taking turns clutching a ball on their way home from a soccer game. If not for those people, it would have been impossible for him to imagine that this had ever been the kind of place where people lived, where his friend Bernard had lived.

Sitting in the car, he thought of the last time he'd seen Bernard. Bernard had been typing a news script at the radio station and had taken a moment to look up and invite him for a meal at his parents' restaurant. Max had been too embarrassed to tell Bernard he was afraid to go there.

The windows were closed now. Still the fetid smell of decomposing trash penetrated the car and was nearly choking him. Max Junior started the engine and kept driving until he found the sea once again. He followed the sea out of Cité Pendue until it turned a robin's egg blue, the Ville Rose color he had longed for most when he was in Miami.

He rolled down the windows, and with a hot

gust of air blasting his face, spent all afternoon going home. He allowed himself to linger in the bottleneck traffic, then he realized that it had been some time now since he'd thought about Jessamine. He looked in the tight wedge between the driver's seat cushion and backrest and found the white envelope with the five-hundred-gourde note his father always kept there for emergencies. He stopped at a street corner for fried plantains, goat, and pork, which he ate from a dented metal plate in front of the vendor's pot of sizzling oil, then washed it all down with a bottle of imported fluorescent juice. Leaving the food vendor's, he drove slowly, purposely taking the wrong turns, stopping to sit on the side of smaller streets and out-of-the-way trails before returning to the busy main thoroughfare by the sea.

It was nearly dark when he pulled up in front of his father's house and saw Jessamine sitting with his father on the brightly lit front porch. She was wearing dark leggings and a plain white tunic top, yet still looked elegant, as though she were heading out to a ball. Both Jessamine and his father saw the Jeep through the open gate. He lowered his head, pretending he had some task to complete in the car before he could come out. A radio program was blaring from one of the neighboring houses and he could have sworn he heard Flore's voice on it. But that couldn't be

right. He had left Flore in Cité Pendue not that long ago.

A bouncy commercial jingle cut off the Flore-like voice. It was followed by a loud pitchman touting health shakes, cigarettes, and beer in the same breathless voice. He stopped paying attention. He was contemplating instead the fact that Jessamine didn't call out his name or run to him.

Watching her and his father sip something or other, he imagined his father learning that Jessamine was a nurse and asking her for medical advice about his old judo injuries. He imagined them talking about his father's paintings, his garden and flowers. But he could imagine Jessamine having also told his father how she was not really his girlfriend and how she had agreed to come with him just so his father would think he had a girlfriend, and how they had even debated whether he should buy her a ring and call her his fiancée. Maybe she was telling his father how she had agreed to come with him, as a good and loyal friend, only so that he would come and meet his son.

His father got up and waved. Though he didn't move from behind the wheel, he waved back, indicating he was coming. It was obvious that Jessamine had already conquered his father, most likely with compliments about the town, the house. Or maybe his father was overly impressed

that though she was born in Miami, she could still speak Creole, even with an accent. Jessamine was glad, he knew, to see the place that had, in part, made him.

The commercial jingles continued on his father's neighbor's radio. A scripted dialogue between two popular comedians about two competing cell phone companies was playing now. Max Junior wondered whether if he were still living in this town—not in his father's house, but in a house of his own—he might feel obligated to drive by every afternoon to see if his father was all right. Might he also sit outside, in a car, feeling grateful that he'd escaped this house and its rueful memories? He pretended that he was actually inside this moment that would never be, and the second both Jessamine and his father turned their faces away from him and toward each other, he started the car and drove away. He sped forward, heading down Pied Rose Avenue toward the beach.

One way he had delayed accepting Bernard's invitation to his parents' restaurant in Cité Pendue was to invite Bernard to the beach. They would go to the lagoons, then dive in and out of the reefs. Every once in a while they'd spot a large flying fish or a sea turtle, which were as mythic as ghost crabs because they were so rare. At night, they would walk up to the Anthère lighthouse, climb the winding staircase, and lie

on the gallery floor in the dark to better see the stars.

He had left Ville Rose the day before Bernard was killed. Flore had told his father that she was pregnant with his child, and his father had sent him to his mother in Miami. He was nineteen, banished from his home for creating a life just at the moment when his friend lay dying. The irony of this was still weighing on him.

When Max Junior arrived at the beach that evening, he saw a crowd gathered around a large-legged woman who was speaking to everyone with her hands. She was wearing a dark scarf around her head, which nearly swallowed her face.

Next to her, a fisherman, a man the people were calling Nozias, leaned in. He was interpreting the movements of the woman's hands. She held both hands toward the crowd, one palm facing the dimming light of the early-evening sky and the other facing the sand, then she reversed them, the sand palm now fixed at the sky and the sky palm aimed at the sand.

"Mouri," the man next to her said. "Dead. She thinks he's dead."

Dead. This single word seemed the proper conclusion to Max Junior's day.

He spent the rest of the evening under a dense grove of palms that had grown in a curve, their

intricate roots spilling over the sand. He bought a bottle of Prestige beer, which he drank before dozing off at the foot of the crescent palms.

When he woke up, a bonfire had been started and the dead fisherman's wife was sitting in its glow, in a low sisal chair, receiving well-wishers. Too large for her long white skirt to fully cover, her heavier leg looked like a piece of driftwood waiting to be placed in the fire.

Watching the dead fisherman's wife reminded him of a Grimm's fairy tale his father had told him when he was a boy. The way he remembered it, one day a fisherman pulled a talking flounder out of the sea. Claiming to be an enchanted prince, the flounder begged to be returned to the sea and the fisherman released him. When the fisherman went home, he told his wife what had happened, and she scolded him for asking nothing of the enchanted flounder in return for his release. The fisherman's wife convinced her husband to return to the sea, find the flounder, and ask him for a cottage to replace the shack in which they were living. The flounder granted the wife's wish and soon they had a cottage. This was not enough for the wife, who made her husband return several times to ask the flounder for a castle, then to make her an emperor, then a pope, then a god.

The part that Max Junior remembered best—because it was the part of the story that his father

seemed to disapprove of the most—was of the wife wanting the power to make the sun rise.

What is wrong with wanting that? Max Junior had always thought. Who wouldn't want the power to make the sun rise at will?

He now found himself in the somewhat familiar predicament of being a so-called rich boy who was out of money. His head ached. He was hungry again. Where was his enchanted flounder? he wondered.

He thought of returning home, but how would he explain his having left so abruptly? His father would be angry with him. Jessamine would probably be angry too. Still, they had not come looking for him. They both should have known where he might be.

Max Junior got up and walked through the small crowd of people still gathered on the beach. Then, just as the fisherman's wake was drawing to a close, a father began crying out his daughter's name, and people joined in looking for her. The father of the missing daughter was the fisherman Nozias, the one who had been interpreting the fisherman's wife's movements for the others.

Max drifted in and out of different sections of the crowd, and he did as they did, hollering, "Claire!" the missing girl's name.

The name was as buoyant as it sounded. It was the kind of name that you said with love, that you whispered in your woman's ears the night before

your child was born. It was the kind of name you could easily carry in your dreams, in your mouth, the kind of name that made you clasp your hands against your chest when you heard it being shouted out of so many mouths. It was the kind of name you might find in poems or love letters, or songs. It was a love name and not a revenge name. It was the kind of name that you could call out with hope. It was the kind of name that had the power to make the sun rise.

But soon everyone stopped calling the girl's name and began to drift away. And when he looked up at the hills, he saw that even the people who had been flashing lights from the lighthouse gallery were also gone.

When it came to the town's mores, he was now at a disadvantage, after being away so long. He was no longer aware of who was sleeping with whom, or who was allowed to sleep with whom, without causing a scandal. And yet just then he thought he saw his parents' old friend Gaëlle Lavaud go into one of the fishermen's shacks. He had some vague recollection of his father telling him that they were to have dinner at her house one night before he returned to Miami. Was that really her? Was she now his father's lover or the fisherman Nozias's lover? Or both?

In any case, it seemed that Gaëlle Lavaud and the fisherman Nozias would be sleeping apart. For soon after they went in together, the

fisherman left the shack and lay down on the sand between two boulders, confident, it seemed, that his daughter would return. Just as his father might also be certain that he too would soon be home.

Part Two

Starfish

Louise George, hostess of the radio program *Di Mwen*, had been coughing up blood during her periods ever since she began menstruating at age thirteen. Over the years she had seen many specialists and had many tests, but no doctor could satisfactorily explain how blood from her uterus also showed up in her lungs, then in her mouth. What's worse, no one could tell her why, at fifty-five, she had still not gone through menopause, making it seem as though this could possibly go on forever. And since in Ville Rose all things unexplained were attributed to the spirit world, Louise tried to keep as much to herself as possible when she wasn't taping her radio program.

This was not hard to do because the few people who had seen her bloodstained teeth or handkerchiefs had worried that she might be pwatrinè, or have tuberculosis, and so had stayed away. That is all except Max Ardin, Sr., who not only occasionally slept with her, but would now and then invite her to read to the students at his school.

Max Senior had known Louise long enough to be aware that her condition was rare, but that a certain type of lung surgery or hormone therapy

151

might treat it, though the hormones were extremely expensive and were not yet available in Haiti and the surgery potentially fatal. So Louise got used to tasting her own blood, agonizing about it only on those three or four days a month when she had to completely withdraw from everything and everyone.

During those days when she was home alone, Louise wrote. She wrote about the people in Ville Rose, tidbits she picked up from the gossip mill, or teledyòl, or what she'd gathered over the years from the interviews on her radio show. Her book had begun as an extension of the show, but had grown into a type of choral piece. She called it to herself a collage à clef.

A few nights after she'd gone to read to one of his younger classes, Max Senior called to ask her if she would do him the extra favor of teaching one of the school's adult literacy classes, after he came up with the idea of helping some of the students by teaching their illiterate parents to read. Most of the children who could afford the high tuition at École Ardin had professional parents—public functionaries, business owners— or sponsoring relatives abroad. But there were a few bright students whose parents were indigent, or nearly so. Max Senior had given them scholarships to make their way.

Louise was still dreading her first moments with these scholarship parents when the time

came. Unlike the children, the parents wouldn't simply look up at her with glee as she read them some of her favorite stories and poems. But teaching these adults was an opportunity for her not only to use the training she'd gotten as a young woman at the Faculté d'Education in Port-au-Prince, but also to gather potential subjects for her radio show.

The show had begun six months before one of Radio Zòrèy's biggest sponsors, Laurent Lavaud, had been shot right outside the station gates. She didn't know him very well, but she had been one of the last people to see him alive. He'd rushed into the control room to drop off an envelope for the station manager, and she had seen him through the glass during a commercial break.

The next day, a young newswriter at her station had been arrested for Laurent Lavaud's murder, then, soon after, had been murdered himself. She had closely followed the investigation (or lack of it). It was like all police investigations in Haiti. At first it was all everyone was talking about, then it went cold, and then for years, whenever it came up, everyone from the chief of police to journalism students would say "L'enquête se poursuit. The investigation continues." Even though it had not.

After those deaths and others, she had considered changing the format of the show from one that allowed people to air personal grievances to

one that pursued justice. She'd thought of renaming the show *Seriatim*, the Latin word for "series." She'd also considered *Verbatim* or *Word for Word*, or the legal term that combined both, but she didn't want the station's core audience of plain and regular people to be put off. Hearing Latin once or twice a week at Mass was probably all they could bear. So now she found herself doing only confessional, but sometimes accusatory, interviews. The show's very large audience favored gossipy subjects over true crime, unless there were elements of gossip in the crime. She liked to start the hour by welcoming her guests with the words "Di mwen." "Tell me," she would say. "We are ready to hear your story."

Before the charity parents showed up at Max Senior's school that night, Louise suddenly got cold feet. Over the years, her gaunt body had grown even tinier, making her look, in the different shades of purple dresses she always wore, more like a nun than a popular radio personality. She was such a mystery to most people in town that once, while attending Mass in the town cathedral, she heard a man who was sitting behind her say that it was rumored ke li manje chat, that she ate cats, which implied that she was also an alcoholic, a lonely lush who somehow kept herself under control only to tape her show.

The first parent who arrived for the literacy class was Nozias Faustin, a bald young fisherman. He was dressed in a church-worthy secondhand brown suit with an open-necked white shirt. He was father to Claire Limyè Lanmè Faustin, an attentive little girl from one of the primary-school classes at École Ardin. Claire Limyè Lanmè Faustin's hair was always braided in what seemed to be a hundred yarnlike plaits, each individually fastened with a different colored bow-shaped plastic barrette. Aside from the barrettes, which thankfully had not been in vogue when Louise was a girl, Claire was the one child in the classes she read to who reminded her much of herself when she was young. The girl was so quiet that Louise worried that there might be some other frightful things about Claire that would link them. Had she, also like Louise, been born with absolutely nothing, from people who had absolutely nothing? Was she the surviving twin who had lost a sibling at her birth? Had she been born with a sixth finger on each hand, which had been forced to atrophy by having strings tied tightly around them? Did she have a spider-shaped birthmark on her belly?

The other parent, Odile Désir, was a strapping, scowling woman who, when she showed up, was still wearing her ocher uniform and apron from her job as a server in a restaurant in town. Louise had seen that scowl before and not just on Odile's

face. She saw it whenever she was around certain adults. Was it a scowl of fear or pity? Why did it matter in the end? Why should she even care? But this type of self-questioning made her realize even more that she did care. She cared because, just like the people she interviewed every week, she was floating through her life, looking for some notion of who she was, and in those scowls and rumors she often caught a glimpse, even if a distorted one, of what that might be. But that evening at the literacy class for three, it was very clear what she was to Odile Désir: her sworn enemy.

Odile's son, Henri, was by far the worst-behaved student in any class that she had ever read to at Max Senior's school. Even the shy and quiet Claire was not spared Henri's taunts and hair pulling. A restless, rambunctious boy, he had, early in the school year, lost two front milk teeth, which still showed no signs of being replaced by adult ones, a gap he often used to spit at the other children.

"Why me?" Louise had asked Max Senior when he'd first suggested she teach the evening class. "Surely one of your full-time teachers can do this."

"Don't you want the satisfaction of being a miracle worker, of making the blind see?" he'd asked, smiling, his face softening in a way that even after all these years still enchanted her.

Ever since they had met at the Faculté—where she was a scholarship student—Louise recalled that Max Senior was always researching educational methods that demanded a lot of those around him. Sometimes she was thrilled by those experiments, like his asking her to tell or read her favorite stories to the children. And other times they annoyed her, like the evening literacy class, which she now wished she'd declined. Sometimes, with all his pedagogical lecturing, framed by his sweet-faced smile, she even wanted to hit Max Ardin. Not hard and not often, just one quick slap. But there were also many times when she found herself feeling grateful to him, because even as he was orchestrating his pedagogical schemes, building his career, getting married and divorced, he never forgot her.

The two parents had only nodded at each other when they arrived that evening. Both looked equally exhausted after long days at physically taxing jobs.

"Why do you want to learn to read?" Louise asked each one in turn.

Henri's mother, Odile, shrugged. "I don't want people to take me for an imbecile," she replied, her face a tight mask.

"For Claire," Claire's father, Nozias, said simply, "so I can help her with her lessons."

"Those are both very good reasons," Louise

157

said, leaning back into the same rocking chair she had demanded that Max Senior provide for her to read to the children, in part to connect her reading to them with the porch-style storytelling sessions of their parents' childhoods.

"I don't want either of you to feel ashamed," she added. "You didn't have the opportunities that your children now have."

Louise had prepared that little speech beforehand, before she'd even known who'd be there. She had also prepared to tell these parents about ancient civilizations whose indigenous populations never knew how to read or write but used hieroglyphs with which it was easy to recognize water as wavy lines, and a man or a bird as a drawing of such. And she reminded them both of the well-known saying "Analfabèt pa bèt," or "Illiterates are not stupid." But then she got tired of the whole thing and of herself and told them to go home.

On their way out, the two parents stopped by Max Senior's office together to complain, each adding that they had, at Max Senior's request, gone through a great deal of trouble to get there and that Madame Louise had not properly addressed them.

"Tant pis," Louise told Max Senior when he recounted their complaints to her in bed later that night. "Too bad."

Louise and Max Senior had been sleeping together on and off since the Faculté. They had stopped while he was married and had picked up again after his divorce. Louise was not in love with him; she did not think herself capable of being in love with anyone. Being alone was simpler, the intermingling of lives too confusing and too messy, a fact confirmed for her on her radio show each week.

That night in bed, at her house across from Sainte Rose de Lima Cathedral, Max Senior held one of Louise's hands under the sheets. She dangled the other over the side of the bed and, after a sudden rush of blood to her fingertips, felt them go numb. Lying there, she wished that she'd agreed, as he had suggested to her one night, to paint her bedroom ceiling in a glow-in-the-dark shade of fluorescent green. Max Senior had once confided to her how when he was a boy he had been deathly afraid of nights without lights, starless and moonless nights without any electricity, nights that he'd called "Ki moun sa a?" nights, or "Who are you?" nights, because it was hard to recognize anyone. It was so dark that when you opened your eyes, you saw the same inky gloom as when your eyes were closed, he said. At that time, she'd laughed and said no, she didn't want her bedroom to look like the walls of a kindergarten classroom. But now she thought she might reconsider the glow-in-the-dark paint. If

159

she had a bit of luminescence to stare up at on nights like this, might it be easier to pretend that she was somewhere outside, with blades of grass tickling her cheeks?

"Je voudrais . . ." His words interrupted her thoughts. "I would like to talk to you about something," he was saying.

He released her fingers to run his hand across her abdomen, tracing, in the dark, the baby spider birthmark that grew into a full-blown black widow when her stomach swelled during those days she was menstruating.

"What is it?" she asked.

"The school," he said, moving his face closer to hers in the dark. She wanted to turn away, but instead she pressed her eyelids together so tightly that they made another kind of sky, a sky full of fireflies and tiny torches.

"You slapped one of my students the other day when you came to read," he said. "One of the children of the parents who came to the class tonight."

It was just like him to set her up by bringing those parents there and then try to make a lesson out of the whole thing. He had been that way since the Faculté, always eager to teach someone a lesson in a totally roundabout way.

"The children at our school are never hit on our premises" was often the theme of their school-related pillow talk. That and his insistence that

she was a great teacher in a country with so few and that she should have been teaching for decades, and even now could still be teaching. And that she was wasting her time on that show. It was useless for her to keep telling him that she thought she was "teaching" on her show.

His was one of a few schools in the region with a no-hitting philosophy, which some of the parents welcomed and others detested. Most other schools carried out some type of corporal punishment, from ruler taps on the hand to cowhide straps on the legs and flat-board taps on the bottom. But Max Senior felt that corporal punishment was archaic, even barbaric, and he kept close watch on everyone, especially any teachers accused of abusive practices, to make sure they didn't take place at his school.

"Henri's mother wants to meet with you and me tomorrow afternoon after school." His voice was tight, distant. And without saying anything more, he turned his back to her so that they were now facing opposite sides of her room.

"Must I go?" she asked, knowing, in spite of having one of the most listened-to voices in town, that she now sounded like a child who was being sent to the headmaster's office. "I'm not even a teacher at the school."

"This must be resolved," he said. "And I hope you will grant me and this boy and his mother that courtesy."

• • •

It wasn't meant to be a slap, just the flutter of her hand, like a conductor guiding members of an orchestra, each with the same goal in mind, but different instruments in hand. Mazora Henri, or Toothless Henri, as even the other children with missing teeth called him, had long legs, which he constantly knocked together, and a loud, jumpy laugh.

Of all the children she had ever read to, he interrupted the most, both with his clamorous laugh and by reaching over, whenever her back was turned, to grab, pinch, or shove the other children. Whenever she tried to keep him still, by making him stand alone in the back of the room, he mumbled a long list of audible curse words under his breath. She should have discussed the situation with Max Senior from the beginning, but she had thought herself capable of handling him.

The particular morning of the slap, she was reading out loud to the class a poem called "Le Soleil et les Grenouilles," "The Sun and the Frogs," by the French fabulist Jean de La Fontaine. Given that the town, like many other coastal towns, no longer had any frogs—something that the French herpetologists had linked to the increased possibility of seismic activity and freak waves—and since the children were already familiar with their parents' or older siblings' accounts of the summer a decade ago

when the frogs had disappeared, Louise thought it might be instructive to share the poem, one of her favorites, with them.

As she read aloud, she became completely enthralled, as she did on the radio, with the sound of her own gravelly voice. Rising from the rocking chair, she walked back and forth between the evenly spaced benches, stopping now and then to accentuate a certain part of the poem for a particular row or child.

> . . . Aussitôt on ouït d'une commune voix
> Se plaindre de leur destinée
> Les Citoyennes des Etangs.
> . . . Abruptly, a cry
> From all the frogs in the land
> Who could no longer bear their fate.
> What will we do if the Sun has children?
> We can barely survive one Sun.
> If half a dozen come
> Then the sea will dry up, with all that is
>   in it.
> Farewell, marshes, swamplands: our kind
>   has been destroyed . . .

For a while, she ignored Henri, who was mimicking her facial expressions and lip movements and grimacing to distract the others. But the more Henri was ignored, the more animated his impersonation became, until most of

163

the children stopped listening to laugh at him. Or really to laugh at her.

She couldn't tell when it started, but at some point while she had her back turned, Henri had yanked a ribbon from one girl's hair, then had walked (or jumped) to the next row and pulled a handful of barrettes from Claire Faustin's hair. The sight of Claire's stoic face and the barrettes, spread out now like so many dead aphids on the floor at her feet, enraged Louise, who put the book down and slowly walked toward Henri.

As she approached him, he straightened his body and looked ahead. Even as she was standing beside him, she had not yet decided what to do. Should she send him to the back of the room? Send him home?

She had meant only to accentuate whatever command she gave him by pounding on the notebook in front of him with her open palm. But as she stood before him, a toothless smirk came across his face. She wanted to erase it, the way one might erase words and numbers from a blackboard.

She realized that she'd hit him only when she heard the other children gasp. Henri rubbed the side of his face. There were no finger marks that she could see, no blood streaming past his lips. He didn't cry. Instead, he went on smiling, his toothless gap growing wider, until Louise walked back to her desk and continued reading.

• • •

That night, Max Senior left her house without saying a word. It was likely that he wouldn't even speak to her again unless she attended the meeting with the boy's mother and all of this was resolved.

Louise spent the next morning in bed, writing. She had been wrong to hit the boy, she knew, but it wasn't the end of the world. He needed it. In fact he deserved it. This is what she planned to tell his mother. Or maybe she wouldn't. This, she knew, was what was worrying Max Senior the most: that she might not show any remorse.

He was finally letting her go. She sensed this, though he'd not said it out loud. Now she would no longer have the children to read to, including that devil of a boy Henri. And that luminous child Claire. Now she would not even have Max Senior. She had long felt him slipping away, the intrigue of her biblical affliction waning as she moved deeper into middle age.

In the beginning, he had liked the taste of blood in her mouth. He would describe it to her in great detail as though his tongue were not inside *her* mouth.

"It is salty," he would say. Then he would add, "It is sweet." He was convinced that the taste was based on her moods, and she would let him go on and on about it, expressing the same thoughts with different words. And she would daydream of

other things as he spoke and she would daydream of how free she would feel without this affliction and she would marvel at how some things could destroy a person's life, like being housebound for a few days when you were bleeding out of your mouth and you had trouble remembering when you had not. And all of a sudden, the past was your haven and the time you felt freest was when you least understood your body, when you were like Henri Désir's favorite victims, when you were a little girl. And this is one of the reasons that Henri Désir had to be stopped. Because boys like him became anguish-causing men, men who felt like they could freely ravage and maim, and they had to be stopped. This is why she would never regret slapping him. She would even slap him again, even more purposefully this time, if she had the chance.

Odile and her son were in Max Senior's office that afternoon, just as he said they would be. Sometimes when Louise walked into a place like that, a place bursting with old things—dusty ledgers and educational manuals, creaky desks and chairs, things that could easily be fixed or changed or discarded but were kept as if out of a nostalgic reverence for the past—she felt as though she too were a relic. Everything was old in that room except the boy, Henri.

Max Senior was sitting behind his cracked

desk. He seemed relieved to see her, letting out a loud sigh when she came in. Again Odile was wearing her uniform and apron. It was as though she wanted to show the entire town that she had a job. She and her son were sitting across from Max Senior in a pair of tall wicker chairs, one of the boy's feet hanging off the edge. An extra chair had been brought in for Louise and had been placed halfway between them.

Max Senior appeared torn between his roles, his eyes swerving back and forth to look at each of them. Louise could see that he was choosing his words carefully. Finally he simply said, "Allons. Let's begin."

Odile sprang up and massaged her buttocks, where the chair had left a damp sweat crease. Louise also rose up from her chair and then Max Senior did too.

Everyone was standing now except Henri, who gripped the sides of his chair with clenched fists while tapping his sneakers against one of the footholds without making any noise.

"Madame?" Odile took a few hesitant steps toward Louise. "They say you slapped my son?"

Odile kept moving closer, until Louise could feel and smell Odile's warm breath on her face, could almost describe, if pressed, what she had eaten for lunch.

Odile reached toward Henri's chair and, without taking her eyes off Louise, grabbed him

by the shoulders and plopped him between herself and Louise. He was, she observed with a cool disinterest, uncharacteristically obedient, flaccid; his arms hung limply at his sides.

"My son has always told me," Odile said, "what a good person you are. He told me you are like none of the teachers here, that even if we are poor, you treat him like all the other children and that you have read many wonderful things to him. I said to myself, 'My son has much to learn from this woman, this big, famous woman.' Am I telling a lie, son?" Odile grabbed her son's chin and pushed his face forward, toward them. Henri shook his head no. His mouth was closed, but his lips trembled, and it seemed to Louise that, for the first time since she'd been around him, he might start to cry.

"Let's all sit down now," Max Senior said, his fingers drumming his desk.

"You see, Msye." Odile turned her attention now to Max Senior. "I know your school does not strike children. I was told this the first day you accepted him here. I am a poor woman. Still you accepted him. I thank you for that. But I can't thank you for the rest. If my son did something wrong, I would give you permission. I would put my cross on a paper, if I have to, to let you punish him the proper way. But I would never let anyone slap my son on his face, like he was some type of chimè, some brigan, or some

168

criminal. Non, non. That is not correction. It is humiliation."

Odile now gently took Henri's hand and moved him aside. Freed, he buried his face behind one of the chairs. Stepping back, Odile took a deep breath, then aimed for Louise.

The slap landed on Louise's cheek before she could see it coming. Her head swung so fast that each of her ears tapped against each of her shoulders for a moment. Her cheek throbbed. It felt hot, then warm, then deadened, so that if Odile slapped her again, she probably wouldn't feel a thing. Yet the most painful thing about it was that it felt as though the slap had come from Max Senior. It was as if he had hit her.

"Finished now," Odile said to both her and Max Senior. "No more hitting talk. Just teach my child. And remember, correction, not humiliation."

Odile grabbed Henri's hand and yanked him toward the door. On his way out, with the contented look of the vindicated, Henri turned to face Louise, opened his mouth, and flashed her the gap between his front teeth: his version of a celebratory smile.

Louise heard herself breathing loudly as she tried to massage some sensation back into her cheekbone. The old office door squeaked behind Odile and Henri as they moved into the yard.

Max Senior slipped back into the ancient chair behind his desk and motioned for Louise to also

sit down. His gaze was fixed on her as though, she imagined, he was thinking of the two of them alone in one of those dark rooms of his childhood on those "Ki moun sa a?" nights, those "Who are you?" nights, and was trying to figure out who she really was.

She was Louise George. That's who she was. She had always done her best to protect herself from insults and injuries like this. Only for him had she let her guard down with these children, and look where it had led her, into a pitch-black moment of her own.

A droning sound was ringing in her ears, but she thought she heard him ask, "T'es bien? Are you okay?"

"Why did you let her do that?" She pressed her palm against her cheek and massaged it in a gentle circular motion.

"After so many years of friendship," he said, "you think I would tell her to do that to you?" Still, he seemed neither shocked nor outraged, and he did not get up from his chair and walk over to console her.

No matter what he said, she found it hard to believe that he did not approve of that woman slapping her. Odile must have sensed it too. Otherwise she would have never taken the chance. She would have never risked her child getting kicked out of the school, or worse.

Louise was feeling a bit dizzy now. The sound

of Max Senior's creaking chair echoed inside her head, his voice drifting in and out of her ears. Why didn't he slap her himself? she wondered.

He no longer wanted her in his life or at the school. She had felt it for some time, but she hadn't been absolutely certain of it. He now turned to look at one of his old wooden cabinets, bursting with years of student dossiers and records. "The school is my whole life now," he said, "and it has to be done right."

She had heard him go on about all of this before. Here, at the school, he could still nurse and guide childhoods without taking full responsibility for their outcomes. The children were not his children. He could not fully blame himself for their lack of self-possession, their selfishness and failures, their willingness to ruin their lives and the lives of others. But he could at least shield them while they were still young and in his care.

"Even though this is my school," he said, "my son, when he was this boy Henri's age, was often misunderstood by the teachers here. And though they never slapped him physically, they often slapped him with words. This is why I would never allow something like you've done here."

"We are not talking about your son!" she shouted.

"There is such a thing as a social contract then," he said.

"I did not deserve to be slapped," she said.

"Neither did that boy." He pushed his chair forward in her direction, increasing the screeching noise coming from it.

"You didn't even explain to his mother," she said. "You didn't even try to help her see my side."

"You have no side here," he said. "Besides, you were not there every moment I was with her."

"So why was the other man there last night, that man Faustin?"

"Because," he said, "as I heard it from the other children, Henri struck his daughter. I was hoping you would be brave enough to reassure both of those people that their children were still safe with us."

"Then you should have had the whole class there last night," she said, "because that boy has hit every one of those children."

"That may be," he said. "But—"

"So this was a konplo," she said, cutting him off. "A plot to humiliate *me?*"

"Don't be dramatic, Louise," he said. "We are not on your show here." And the way he twisted his mouth and curled his lips reminded her how much he hated her show.

This might just be an elaborate send-off, she thought. She herself might have chosen a simpler way to say good-bye. But this was Maxime Ardin we were talking about here. Maxime Ardin père, le premier, senior. The son was fils, deux, junior.

Maxime Ardin, Sr., did not know of any simple ways to say good-bye. And when he couldn't divorce or banish you, unless you were one of his students, he apparently had you smacked.

"If I did what you did," he said, while looking so on edge that his teeth were nibbling on his bottom lip, "I would remove myself from my position. I couldn't continue here."

He got up, sat down, got up, then sat down again, but did not make an approach toward her. That dreaded feeling of loneliness she felt so often returned.

"Now you can have more time for your show," he said. Again she noticed his scowl of disdain, for the show and now also for her. He had told her many times that she could have been a great teacher and that the show had kept her from it. But now he knew that she could never be that kind of teacher, and there was no longer much to admire.

"You can also keep writing your book," he was saying. The slap he'd assigned to another woman was also meant to propel her toward this other redeemable talent, the writing of her book.

One of his favorite things to say to her was that she was like a starfish, that she constantly needed to have a piece of her break off and walk away in order for her to become something new. Of course this had always been truer of him than of her.

As she turned around to leave his office, she saw what he thought he was trying to slap back to life, a stronger and freer woman, one he could both salvage and admire. This slap, she knew, he perversely considered a gift to her, a convoluted act of kindness.

Anniversary

The night Gaëlle Lavaud's husband died, she thought that everyone should die. After Laurent's murder outside Radio Zòrèy, she'd sold their house in town and moved into her grandparents' house on Anthère Hill. She had turned the fabric shop over to her employees, then had lain in bed for months, also waiting to die. Although everyone said that her milk would be tainted by her sadness and would fill her daughter, Rose, with sadness, Inès, her housekeeper, insisted that Gaëlle nurse her daughter as a way of saving both the child and herself. Gaëlle got out of her bed only when she could no longer keep her daughter in it, when the child began to crawl. And when her daughter started to walk, Gaëlle walked again. And when Rose began to talk, Gaëlle talked again.

She was tempted to close the fabric shop, but she returned to it, because it had meant so much to her husband and, unlike the house, was in a part of town that was less prone to floods, mudslides, and other potential disasters. Business had slowed anyway. People were buying less fabric and more ready-made used clothes, pèpè, from abroad. She was now mostly selling fabric for school uniforms and even that was dwindling.

Besides, during her time of mourning, many of her friendships had dissolved. She no longer attended baptisms, communions, or wedding receptions in the best houses in town. She even refused to listen to broadcasts from the radio station, where her husband had spent so much of his time.

Her husband's murder was never going to be solved. That she knew. There would never be a proper trial. Bribes and corruption would keep anyone from being brought to justice. So she accepted the offer of two Special Forces policemen—childhood friends of both hers and her husband's—to seek another type of justice. And when they had returned from their missions, they'd provided even more details than she had sought. They had walked into a young man's red bedroom, crossed themselves, then shot him dead as he lay in his bed, a young man who used to work at the radio station where her husband had been killed. Later they had returned and set fire to the warehouse the neighborhood gang called home, by spreading gasoline at the entrance, and killed their leader, Tiye, and his second in command. The blaze had spread through the warehouse, then the restaurant next door.

She had not felt the kind of relief she'd expected when she'd heard all this. She hadn't thought that the deaths would bring her husband back, but she'd expected a hole to feel plugged

that never was. She likened it to making prints. No matter how long you soaked the cloth in the dye, as long as the fabric was waxed, the color wouldn't change. Little had changed for her. Nothing had been returned to her. A few high-level friendships had made her judge, jury, and executioner. Yet she still felt powerless, incapacitated, cursed.

For a long time, she hadn't ever allowed herself to think about all this, that is, until the day her daughter died. Perhaps it had been no accident, but some terrible cosmic design engulfing everyone involved. Maybe she was not worthy of growing old with the man she had loved most of her life. Or of seeing her daughter grow up. Could it be that there was a puppet master somewhere who despised her and had decided that she was to be made an example of? Had she doomed herself further when she'd turned her rage over to her Special Forces friends? Maybe that's when it was also decided that her daughter's obituary in *La Rosette* would not say that she died after a valiant battle with a long illness.

The driver whose car had struck the motorcycle her daughter was traveling on, sending her only child hurtling into the air to her death, was someone she knew, a young hotelier from a prominent family in town. He was a Moulin.

She had not wanted her daughter to grow up like the Moulins or those other rich kids, who

177

seemed even richer because they lived in a poor town. But she blamed herself every day for not picking Rose up from school that afternoon in her own car.

After Rose died, she would often think back to the first time she had to leave her for a few hours. It was to attend her husband's funeral. Do you know that feeling when you are about to leave your child and she cries like she will never see you again and you fear that her intense sadness might be some terrible omen? She wished she had never stopped feeling that. She wished she'd seen every simple good-bye as a curse for what she'd done. She wished she'd never let her daughter, not even for one minute, out of her sight.

A few months after Rose died, Inès's eyesight began failing. There were younger people to do the job that she was not doing, Inès had told her, and Inès wanted to spend her last days in her ancestral village in the mountains. Although Inès had been gone for years now, Gaëlle sometimes still craved her company so much that she would wake up in the morning and wait for Inès to come and serve her breakfast, just as she would sometimes wait for her daughter to skip through the doorway and bounce into her bed. At night, after a whole day of watching little girls stream in and out of the fabric shop with their mothers, Gaëlle would imagine Rose as an eight-, then a nine-, now a ten-year-old girl. Her baby teeth

would be gone, her baby fat yielding to early prepubescent brawn. Her voice would be more defined, more confident. She would be dressing herself too, picking out her own clothes and combing her own hair. She would be riding a bicycle, swimming in the sea. Her childhood passion for pressing wildflowers into her notebooks would most likely continue. Next to them she might now be pasting cutout magazine photos of film and music stars. Rose would still be getting excellent grades in school—Gaëlle would have seen to that—but would she still want to play with the dozen or so cloth dolls that, ignoring her fancier toys, the two of them had made together? Would she still want to climb up the lighthouse steps and look down at the sea? Would she still want to dance, along with her friends, in their school's maypole dance at Carnival time, or wear the same feathered hat with her Taino costume for the children's parade? Would she still want to fly kites on Saturday afternoons, then go down and watch the fishermen's children launch their miniature boats on the water and run along the beach behind them, chasing the plastic bucket covers they used as Frisbees? Would she still want to know what heaven was and what her father was doing there? Would she still push her head back now and then and shout "Papa!" to the clouds, then ask if everyone was in heaven, why there was any need

for cemeteries? Why didn't the dead just float up and drift away like balloons?

Gaëlle had filled some of the years since her daughter's death with these types of unanswered questions and with the company of men who were interested in either money or sex or both. Couldn't they tell, she often wondered, that she was a shell, a zombie, just as she had been when she was pregnant with her daughter and was sure that her daughter would be born damaged or dead, just as she had been too during those early days after her husband had died? Couldn't they tell that wherever her husband's and daughter's spirits were was where she longed to be? Only Max Senior had understood this, because he had listened intently to her story about hiring the Special Forces avengers, while holding her hand.

The night of the vigil for the lost fisherman, Caleb, Gaëlle had been expecting Max Senior and his son for dinner. She had skipped Max Junior's welcome-home party the night before and had chosen instead to invite the younger Ardin, through his father, to her home. But earlier that evening Max Senior had called to cancel, offering no explanation.

Before heading to the fisherman's vigil, Gaëlle's young housemaid, Zette, had left her a plate of fried pork and plantains, which Max Senior had requested as part of his dinner. Gaëlle wolfed

down the food while lying in bed, wearing a long silver satin evening gown, which she had intended to wear for dinner with the Ardins, father and son. Her hair, though, was still wrapped in rollers when Max Senior had called. With the wide-paned jalousies of her bedroom windows open, she could see some of the houses lit up on the hill, many of which were occupied only part of the year because their owners lived in the capital or abroad. She could also see the Anthère lighthouse, around which her entire neighborhood had been built.

The lighthouse gallery was filled with young boys, some of whom were fighting with the wind to light hurricane lamps, while others twirled flashlights. Gaëlle's grandfather, her mother's father—a mason and engineer—had built that lighthouse with help from a group of fishermen. Some of those fishermen were still alive, but most were living elsewhere or had died. When a fancy neighborhood—Anthère, named after the anther of a rose—sprang up on the hill, there was little need for the lighthouse, the lights from the homes becoming beacons themselves. The mayor and other town officials had shown no interest in spending to maintain the lighthouse. But it had been constructed so well—with a fifty-foot tower and an equally high focal plane—that it refused to rot.

In the old days, when the lighthouse was

functioning, it was painted all white and had a red lamp and a windbreak on top. Her grandfather and the other volunteer light keepers would ensure that the kerosene lamps that fueled the lantern were lit every night at dusk, producing ten flashes per minute. All this she had learned from her grandfather. He would guide her by the hand, up the spiral staircase toward the lighthouse gallery. The air was always damp and stale in the inside chamber, the spaces under the stairs covered with intricate spiderwebs.

Reaching the lighthouse gallery, though, was always her favorite moment. From there, she could see the land, the mountains, and the sea bathed in sun, mist, or fog, depending on the season, or the time of day. Her grandfather would let her pull the lever that would sound the lighthouse foghorn, and she'd scream over the blast, unable to hear her own voice. Every now and then, if she was lucky, they'd see a rainbow. Her grandfather could spot even the faintest band of light in the clouds or distant fog banks.

But now the lighthouse was placed in rescue mode only when someone was missing, or in remembrance mode when someone was dead. The paint on the outside had long since faded, leaving the cement and rocks exposed. The lantern too was long gone. Battered by wayward birds, it had been crashed into so many times that it had collapsed. Before that the lamp had been infested

by bats. The foghorn had also disappeared, removed, she suspected, by someone or a group of someones who'd found a better use for it. She'd not been inside for so long that she didn't know what shape the staircase was in, but the fact that so many people were always in there meant it must be holding up well.

As she watched the lights flicker from the gallery she'd loved so much, she told herself that she should fix the lighthouse. She should have it repaired and equipped with modern gadgets, a solar panel or something that would make it operate on its own. Placing her empty plate on the nightstand by her bed, she decided that she would offer a lighthouse, restored, to the town as a gift and would officially reopen it with a massive celebration.

She rose from her bed and walked to another room in the house, one that was furnished like all the others, with a canopy bed, an armoire, and a woven rug the same color as the drapes. From there she could see dozens of people pacing from one end of the beach to the other, as though hoping that they would be the ones to find the lost fisherman.

Watching the bonfire from yet another room, the room she'd imagined would be her daughter's one day, when her daughter stopped sleeping with her, Gaëlle stepped out on the wide terrace that made that room the second-best one in the house.

She first felt a chill and wrapped her arms around her body, but soon she forgot about it, concentrating instead on the voices swirling around her in an uninterrupted murmur, some coming from the lighthouse and some from the beach.

Already she was trying to forget her vow to repair the lighthouse. How do you even choose what to mend when so much has already been destroyed? How could she think, she asked herself, that she could revive or save anything?

Her thoughts returned to Max Senior and his son not coming to dinner. She'd been counting on it so much, as a way of filling up a few more hours in this awful day, as a way of making it mean something else, if only for a short while. It helped, after visiting her husband's and daughter's graves, to take part in these normal types of activities on this day, to pretend for a few short hours that she was no longer hurting as much as the year before.

Her daughter had been a student at École Ardin, Max Senior's school. Last year, on the anniversary of her daughter's death, after attending their friend Albert's mayoral inauguration, and after a meeting with the fisherman Nozias about his daughter and deciding not to take her, and after Max Senior had grown tired of the Anthère Hill fireworks celebration party, they had spotted each other at Pauline's, a popular bar with an upstairs brothel on the outskirts of town. The dim, smoke-

clouded speakeasy was run by another old friend of theirs, a cross-eyed Canadian bartender in his late fifties. She'd been wearing a white hibiscus behind her left ear. The flower had caressed Max Senior's cheek when she kissed him hello. The kiss lingered awhile, which seemed to surprise him, and he asked if she was alone. She said yes and he said he was now too, but was only there to have a drink.

When it was time for her to leave, she reached up again to kiss him, this time on the lips. After their lips parted, he raised his hand to the spot and traced her mouth's outline on top of his. They became linked by that kiss, and soon he started visiting her at her house.

He was an inconsistent lover, and she even thought he might be sleeping with someone else. She would see him once or twice a week, but never more than that.

"I know today is an infinitely difficult day for you," he'd said earlier on the phone, just as he had that night a year ago, at the bar.

"Every day is an infinitely difficult day for me," she'd replied.

That first night after they'd made love, she'd told him that she was going to find a man to marry, that she'd convince that man to take her away, to Port-au-Prince, or even to another country. There were too many memories in this

town to bind her and make her want to flee at the same time.

"No one will ever love you more than you love your pain," he had replied, his words ringing even louder in the dark.

She had not understood what he meant at first, but eventually it occurred to her that he might be right. Her pain, her losses: these were what was keeping her in this town. His grasping this, his understanding of it, made him seem even more appealing, more powerful. This momentary ability to comfort her made them all seem powerful: the Special Forces policemen, the bartenders, the Max Seniors, these men who seemed able to fully exist in the world, something that she wished she could extract from them.

Looking down at a row of bougainvilleas beneath her terrace, Gaëlle ran her fingers across her lips just as, at the beginning of their affair, Max Senior had so often done. This house, with all its creaking wood and empty spaces, often drove her to desperate gestures. Whenever Zette or the yardman was away, she felt the full weight of being alone. The only children of only children often end up with no kin. This had always been her husband's argument for the three other children they had intended to have.

Gaëlle stepped into her slippers, then walked out of the house, with every intention of walking down to the beach. But then she saw next to her

husband's rusting old Cabriolet the new, boxy white Mercedes that she had bought, wishing that they'd had something like it when he was alive. With Elie, the genius town mechanic, keeping it going, she had driven the Cabriolet until a year ago, when it, like everything else, had died.

Running back to her room, she grabbed her keys from her purse. She thought of changing out of the evening gown, of removing the rollers from her hair, of exchanging the slippers for shoes, but decided against it.

Pauline's was nearly empty, except for a few men who'd come to see the girls who were upstairs in the brothel section of the place. Her bartender friend was at his station, and rather than sit in the restaurant with the waiting men, she sat on one of the wooden stools across from him. He reached over the bar and wrapped her shoulders in a tight alcohol-scented embrace. Someone was watching them from one of the tables on the other side of the empty dance floor, a muscular, olive-skinned man with a full beard. He looked young and sophisticated in spite of his beard, while his expensive shirt, the type with the designer's name emblazoned in sequined writing on the back, proclaimed that he had money. He was the kind of man the girls would fight over in a place like this, the kind they would assume could detect that they weren't all common, that some had even been

educated, to whatever extent possible, by their families. Some of them had gone as far as university, but for financial reasons had not been able to either finish or find any other type of work.

On her regular visits to the bar at Pauline's, Gaëlle had seen very pretty girls present themselves in pairs, trios, and quartets to men like this. In her fancy body-hugging evening gown and rollers, she might have been mistaken by the young man for one of the older house girls, or even their madam, on a break.

"Who's that?" she asked the bartender.

"That's Yves Moulin," he said, quickly placing a glass of red wine in front of her and sharing her apparent agony at hearing the name. "With that beard and all the weight he's been lifting," he added, "it's like he's got a bag over his head."

Yves Moulin was the young man whose car had hit the motorcycle her daughter had been riding on. His family owned a popular hotel between Ville Rose and Cité Pendue. Before the accident, Yves Moulin had been a star in the youth soccer league in Ville Rose and everyone thought that he'd be recruited by a team in Europe. But after the accident he gave up playing altogether and stayed mostly in the private residence at the hotel. People said he was unable to get the image of her daughter out of his mind, of her daughter's body taking off from the back of the motorcycle and

seeming to fly. They speculated that he couldn't separate this image from that of kicking a soccer ball. The ball too was flying. And it was his foot that was refusing to let it rest on the ground.

The way the town gossip mill was able to make his private nightmares public made her wonder what kinds of stories they told about her. What kinds of words had they placed on her lips? No matter what he'd lost, or how much regret he'd shown, no matter that every year on the anniversary of the accident Yves Moulin placed a small bouquet of white roses at her daughter's gravesite, each rose for one year of the age that her daughter would have been, had she lived, no matter that he had tried to show that he too remembered her daughter, still, she could not forgive him.

Her eyes met his across the empty dance floor. He looked at her, then his eyes wandered toward the front entrance, as though he were searching for an escape.

She hadn't seen or heard from him since he'd come to her house the day after her daughter's death to offer to pay the funeral expenses. Her parents, who'd come from Port-au-Prince for the services, had turned him away at the door, and he kindly had not returned. He had done a good job of making himself scarce, until now. Or it could be that she had seen him and not recognized him. Sometimes she would think she saw him, in a

crowd or from a distance, but the next second he would disappear, making her wonder if thinking she saw him was like those times when she thought she saw her daughter too.

"Looks like he wants to say hello to you," the bartender murmured.

And before Gaëlle could climb down from the stool and flee, Yves Moulin was standing right in front of her, less than an arm's length away.

"Bonsoir," he said. His body was large, imposing, his voice deeper.

When she did not answer, he turned around and walked back to the table where he'd been sitting. He downed his half-finished drink in one swift move and left.

Soon after, a few of the girls came downstairs to say good-bye to one customer and greet another. The bartender offered Gaëlle a more potent drink than wine. Mixing portions from the contents of several containers, he slid a tall, colorful concoction toward her. The drink numbed her the way she'd hoped it would, enough to give her enough courage to get back into her car and head to the beach.

Driving the shortcuts and back roads, the épines, as she watched the cloud of insects the car's headlights were attracting, she couldn't help but think that had the bartender not told her who Yves Moulin was, she might have possibly walked over to his table and offered herself to

him. On this night, like so many others, he might have ended up being just one more kind face, one more comforting voice, one more set of arms to be wrapped around her body. He wouldn't have had to say much. What he did say, "Bonsoir," might have been enough. The sad thing was that she was foolishly thinking it might still be possible. She wondered whether their coming together in this way—to love rather than kill—might resolve everything at last. Might her looking down at his sorrowful face, and his being in her sorrowful bed, help them both take back that moment on the road? She would also judge for herself if what everyone said was true, that he was as wounded as she was.

When she finally made it to the beach, she spotted a group of little girls. They were holding one another's hands and moving clockwise in a circle, a singing circle, a wonn. She was too far away to hear what they were singing, but she could hear their laughter, each girl, it seemed, trying to outdo the next. They seemed to be the happiest people in Ville Rose, six little brown and black angels skipping around fallen sea hearts and sand dollars.

She moved slowly, not wanting the pleasure of her approach to end. She had played the wonn as a child, during recess, and at night in her parents'

191

yard, with visiting friends. What she remembered most about it, though, was how less lonely she felt holding someone else's hand.

It would have sounded odd—people have been accused of sorcery for less—if she told someone how much she wanted to take all those little girls home, set them up in the many empty rooms of her house, and, whenever she was sad, ask them to play with her. There were many days when she wanted to grab a little girl and hold her in her arms, just to inhale her smell, the smell that these men lacked. Their smells were musty: they smelled of roads and dust and cologne that never quite covered their musk. They smelled of work, of sweat, of other women. But little girls smelled of roses and wet leaves, of talcum powder, and the dew.

In spite of what Inès and nearly everyone else had told her after her daughter died, longings like this had never subsided. And her losses had not made her stronger; they had made her weak. They had given others control and power over her. She didn't want to continue being weak, but she didn't want to die either. She was too eager to see what would come next, what her husband and daughter had missed. She was both hungry for life and terrified of it. Her evenings with these men let the rage and confusion disappear for a while and allowed her to make it through her days. They allowed her to sell thread and cloth

and remain close to the graves of the people she really loved.

There were times, as she'd told Max Senior, that she wanted to take off, leave Ville Rose, leave the country, and never come back. But she'd heard too much about the difficulties of starting a new life in another land to want to try. She'd heard about people who had been infantilized while learning a new language, people who'd ended up cleaning houses or wiping the asses of other people's children. She saw these people return to Ville Rose at Christmas or in the summertime, with extravagant hairstyles and expensive-looking clothes, but their eyes always betrayed them. All the humiliation they had endured could be detected there. Their skins betrayed them too, the burns from the dry cleaner's steamer or the car wash or the restaurant kitchens, as visible as brands on animals. Non, none of that was for her. Her ancestors on both sides were buried at the town cemetery, among the town's oldest families. She could not be dyaspora. She liked her ghosts nearby. She could never live in a foreign land, then return only a few times a year. She could not ever risk dying and being buried in a cold place. She would always be here, she thought, like the boulder that stopped her feet when at last she reached the little girls.

One of the girls, Claire, realized that she was being watched and occasionally glanced her way.

Like her mother, Claire was beautiful. She moved more gracefully, more purposefully, than the rest of the girls, even the ones who were older. Gaëlle walked over to the girls, and immediately her presence stopped the game.

"Do you remember my daughter?" the girl's father, Nozias, often asked Gaëlle when they saw each other.

How could Gaëlle forget a child whom she had nursed as a baby on the very night that she was born, a child who was so gentle, so docile, even on that first day, and had grown so lovely, so radiant, with each passing year?

"Is your papa here?" Gaëlle asked Claire.

The girl nodded; she was looking down at her hands, then at her sand-coated feet. Impatient, the other girls lost interest and drifted away.

Gaëlle motioned for the girl to follow her. Claire sat down next to her and from behind one of the boulders pulled out a pair of rubber sandals. Gaëlle waited for her to finish placing the sandals on her feet, then said, "I knew your mother."

Claire's eyes seemed to light up the way children's eyes do when they're hungry for stories.

"I knew her longer than you've been alive," Gaëlle said. "Your mother was my friend."

It was not altogether a lie.

The girl's head was arched toward her, her

mouth wide open, as though to inhale Gaëlle's words, which came out so fast that Gaëlle could barely stop. Gaëlle was not sure what she was thinking and what she was saying out loud. "When your mother was pregnant with you, your mother gave up washing and dressing the dead. Then she had all the time to do nothing but go out on the water with your father and sew. She waited so long to have you, your mother. I wouldn't even say wait. She tried. She tried. She tried to pull you out of the sky, pry you out of God's hands. Yes, God's hands, I'd say. I don't go to church every Sunday. I don't go to church at all, but she wanted you so bad. I know she pulled you out of God's hands. That's the only way I can put it. She was well the whole time you were inside her body. Never even seemed tired when she came into the shop, except the last week, when she didn't come. Then the midwife was sent for. No one knows what happened while you were being born. I hear the midwife thought all was going well. You should not blame yourself. That revenan talk is superstition. Nobody *returns*. That is not real. You're gone. You're gone. Back in God's hands, and no one can pull you back. Not you. Not you, Claire. I hope you understand. Not you back in God's hands, but your mother and my Lòl and my Rosie and your mother too and everyone else who has died who didn't deserve to die. Though who deserves to die? Too many

people die here, and why do the rest of us get to live?

"Happy birthday, Claire," Gaëlle said, both her thoughts and her voice now slowing down.

There was still so much more she wanted to tell the girl, though. She wanted to tell her about seeing her mother at her husband's gravesite service, but this part might be impossible for the girl to grasp. Claire's mother might have even been at the cathedral for her husband's funeral Mass—the whole town, it seemed, was there— but Gaëlle hadn't noticed if she was. But she remembered well seeing Claire's mother at the burial ground, standing near the cemetery gate.

In the normal course of life as a new mother, Gaëlle, according to custom, shouldn't have been outside in the open air at all, for fear that her nouris body—weakened by childbirth—might be too frail. But against everyone's advice, the morning of her husband's funeral Mass and burial service she'd left her infant daughter at home with Inès and attended both. During the gravesite prayers, her breasts ached and swelled, wetting the front of her white dress. She looked beyond the deep hole in the ground, beyond the bronzed coffin, beyond Pè Marignan and the large crowd of townspeople around her, toward the cemetery gate, eager to be at home with her baby. This was when she saw Claire Narcis standing alone under a flame-colored weeping willow by the cemetery

gate. Claire Narcis was wearing the same plain black dress she wore to the funerals of all the townspeople whose bodies she had washed and dressed for burial.

That morning, it seemed that Claire Narcis and the weeping willow had become one. Claire's body seemed indistinguishable from the small part of the willow's trunk that was not covered by its drooping branches. Claire's head was topped by the willow's golden crown. Claire Narcis had seemed that morning to be a dazzling mirage, a veil between the dirt being piled on her husband's coffin and the wailing baby waiting at home. And Claire's presence at the cemetery gate, and the surprising way it had both jolted and comforted her, was one of the reasons she'd agreed to nurse Claire's daughter when she was newly born, and one of the many reasons she could honestly call the girl's mother her friend.

Nozias was now standing over Gaëlle and the girl. He plopped himself down next to them, nearly falling over his daughter.

Fòk nou voye je youn sou lòt, Claire Narcis had often told her. Gaëlle put her hands on the girl's back and felt the child's body shaking. She had finally made up her mind. Yes, she would take her.

"Tonight," she said.

Immediately she began to worry. Maybe she

had said too much. Maybe she had upset the child with all that talk. Maybe things were moving too fast.

"Now?" her father asked. "Tonight?"

He immediately shifted his total attention to Claire, almost as if Gaëlle were no longer there. This surprised her. Hadn't he been trying to give the girl to her for years?

He mentioned something about not changing her name and his having a letter for her, then Claire raised her arms. "Bagay mwen yo," she said.

What about her things? Gaëlle wondered.

But the girl did not wait for them to give her permission; she simply turned and started toward their place.

Gaëlle wasn't sure how long it had been, but people were slipping away and heading home, and the girl had not returned.

"I'll get her," Nozias said.

Gaëlle watched him head for the shack. He was doing his best to stay upright under the weight of his sadness about seeing his daughter go. He too disappeared inside the shack. Then he walked out, shouting the girl's name.

Gaëlle rushed to his side. She followed him through the alleys between the shacks, then down toward the water, all the while calling the girl's name along with him and his neighbors.

"We should take my car and look for her in

town," she finally said, when it seemed to her that Claire might have left the beach.

"Non," he replied firmly, as if to put himself back in control. "She's just hiding. She will come back." She understood his need to remain in control. Even though he had just given her to him, she was still his child.

"You keep looking," she said. "And I will wait at your place for her."

She followed him to his doorstep. He rushed ahead of her and lit up the small shack, which was the size of one of her terraces. It did not smell like the sea, like it had the last time she was there. It smelled like the long matchstick he had just pounded against the side of the matchbox and the kerosene wick on the hourglass lamp he had just lit. Part of the room was now filled with a flaxen glow, the rest full of shadows. He reached above his cot and unclasped, then pushed open, the flaps of a small window, letting some air in and some smoke out. Then he closed the flaps just as quickly. He seemed nervous, scared even, but was doing his best not to let her see it.

Gaëlle tried very hard to not, once again, confuse her heartache with desire. Still, she thought she'd give him a hint of her temptation by sitting on his cot.

He walked out.

He left anyway.

Di Mwen, Tell Me

Tell me, Flore Voltaire," Louise George was saying, her gaunt body erect, her spine ruler straight, behind the studio microphone. "We are ready to hear your story."

"There was a hailstorm . . . ," Flore began, closing her eyes to avoid looking directly at Louise's bony face.

There was a hailstorm the night Max Ardin, Jr., came to Flore Voltaire's bed. The ice balls, tiny at first, were pounding the roof of the first-floor room attached to the kitchen. It was a narrow room, the smallest one in Max Senior's house, perhaps built for someone who was spending the night but not staying for long, as Flore and her aunt, the previous maid, had.

Exhausted from a long day of cleaning and preparing dinner, Flore was flipping through a beauty magazine that she'd found lying around in the living room when the thumping on the roof grew louder. The sequined dresses, long legs and necks, and high-heeled shoes she was idly studying made her beige polyester night slip feel even flimsier, older, and uglier, but she kept flipping the pages anyway.

She had been in hailstorms before, in Cité Pendue. Sometimes during these storms, a house

not as sturdy as this one would be pummeled so badly that it would be blown over by the winds that followed.

The lights were out all over Max Senior's house, and Max Junior seemed to be just wandering around with a flashlight when he came into her room. At first she thought he'd come for the magazine, so she quickly handed it to him, ashamed of her stargazing at long hair and made-up faces. He took the magazine from her without saying a word—not even hello—and he left. She pulled the door closed behind her, turning the small lock. It was not the first time he'd been in her room. It was his father's house, after all. Those times, he would come to ask her where something was, or to put something together, a sandwich or some tea, for him or his father. But that night, she sensed, was different. He seemed lost.

She walked back to her bed and lay down on her side, raising the blanket over her body, all the way up to her neck, as she'd slept most of her life. She could then hear the footsteps approaching. He was returning. The lock was no use. The door, it seemed, was made to be opened easily. He walked over and sat on the edge of her bed. The sound of the hail seemed to grow more and more distant until it stopped entirely, giving way to the patter of rain and the occasional sparks of thunder and lightning.

He said nothing. She closed her eyes and tried to pretend he wasn't there. Then she opened her eyes again and looked around, her gaze settling on the flashlight illuminating his blank, vacant face. Underneath his shave coat, he was naked.

At first she thought he was asleep, sleep-walking, dreaming on his feet. Or that she was. She was too frightened to speak. The lightning and thunder did not seem to trouble him, and he moved his face toward hers until her body was pinned beneath his on the bed. He was heavy, twice the size of most nineteen-year-olds. She thought this had something to do with his having done his secondary and university schooling locked up in his father's office at École Ardin, getting lessons from his old man. He had never, as her mother liked to say, even been sprinkled by the rain.

As he pulled her night slip up toward her chest, she thought she saw a few drops of rain in a corner of the room, sliding down the walls from the ceiling. Maybe the roof had been damaged in the hailstorm. And if the roof were damaged, then she was no safer inside than she would be outside.

When he left the room—was it some minutes or hours or days later?—the rain was still falling, though not as heavily as before. She walked out into the courtyard rose garden, next to the pool, raising her face to the sky. The wind rattled her, her body soaked.

When she went back to the room, she saw that he'd left his flashlight behind. It was still on. She aimed the light at her drenched face, in her confusion thinking somehow that it might have the same effect as a mirror, allowing her to see her eyes. She left the flashlight on and laid it on the floor outside her door in case he should return for it. There was no point in locking the door—she knew that now.

The rain kept on falling with a persistence that made it seem it would last forever. Slipping back under her blanket, she felt the torment of the fabric scraping her skin. She could still feel the danger brewing both inside and outside the house, the scorched smell of lightning cracking open the surrounding palms and the echoes of swelling waves meeting the seashore. She imagined water pouring underneath the door, after rising over the flashlight, quenching its light, and carrying it away. It would be warm water, filled with leaves. She imagined seeing, as she had in other floods, fire-red ants floating in fist-size balls on the water's surface. The house would then dislodge from the earth, and she would open the door and peek outside and the water would be like a black sheet all around her and she would not see land for miles.

She felt a stabbing pain in places where he had pummeled his body against hers. She had used all her weight to try to push him off of her,

but could not. She had tried to slap his hands off of her, as though they were cloying animals, leeches or a jellyfish. He still had not spoken, was not making any sounds. He had been swimming earlier that evening and still smelled like the sea.

The house had rocked as his entire body covered hers, but the house had shaken before, during other storms. What was new was the water coming up so fast, with fire ants, which meant that it was coming down from deep inside the mountains and the hills, and not the sea. She smelled rum on his breath. She gasped for her own breath.

The next morning the sun seemed to rise even earlier than usual, as if in defiance of all that had taken place the night before. Flore looked through a crack in the door and saw him and his father emerge from the orchid nursery by the gazebo in the middle of the garden. A humming-bird flew over the pummeled rosebushes, and Max Junior raised his fingers, as if to grab the minute wings. Both men looked solemn and stone-faced, their eyes focused on the hail-crushed flowers, as they inspected the storm damage.

While they were in the garden, Flore walked out of the house and took a taxi to Cité Pendue. The traffic, detoured from flooded areas, crawled, her bones throbbing with every lurch and sway of the car.

When she got to her mother's house, her mother was not there.

She opened the door and waited inside. She was feeling too dirty to sit on her mother's plastic-covered chairs. Instead she sat on the cool cement floor.

Her mother was a short but robust woman. When she finally walked in, she was carrying on top of her head a large wicker basket filled with aluminum bowls and cups that she used to sell breakfast foods at the market. As she approached Flore, her mother's lips were rounded as though she were whistling.

When her mother got close enough, Flore helped her mother lower the basket from her head and place it on the floor. Before Flore could say anything, her mother made her stoop down again and, looking at Flore's tear-swollen face, she traced her fingers over Flore's cheek.

"If you're home for good," her mother said, "I don't know how we'll get by."

Flore pulled herself up, reached into her dress pocket, and handed her mother the month's salary that she'd hoped to use for her escape. Then she returned to the Ardins that afternoon, in time to cook their supper.

"You mean to tell me you went back there, back to the Ardins?" Louise finally interrupted Flore now as they taped her show.

Louise was dressed that morning in one of her

signature A-line mauve dresses, her hair pulled back tightly, her chin pointed, her eyes narrowed, focused. She was determined to extract the entire story from Flore, along with every detail that she considered necessary. "Di mwen," she said. "Tell me, tell everyone why you went back to the Ardins that afternoon. But first, a commercial break."

There were no commercials played during the actual taping. They waited just a few minutes as Louise took a sip of water from one of the two glasses in front of them, then said to Flore, "Relax—you're doing well."

Flore raised her eyes from her intertwined fingers and looked around the studio, a square room not unlike the one she had slept in at Max Senior's. On the triangular table were two microphones and the water glasses, Louise's now only half full. Louise had bypassed the headphones, offering the ones she usually used to Flore's son.

Pamaxime was sitting underneath the table at his mother's feet, taking turns doodling with a pencil and pad Louise had given him and quietly playing a game on Flore's cell phone. Flore's eyes traveled between her son's headphone-covered ears and the man sitting at the large control board on the other side of the glass, but she made every effort to avoid looking at Louise George, the fierce but tiny hostess of the program.

Flore now picked up the glass of water that was meant for her and took a sip from it. She had called the station and asked for Louise George as soon as she'd learned from Max Senior that his son was coming home and that he wanted to meet the boy.

This was the premise of these personal interviews, Louise had explained to her—you are talking about one moment that changed your life. A moment that made everything that had come before it seem meaningless. A moment that had transformed you inside and out. That night in the maid's room with Max Junior on top of her had been that moment for Flore. Beyond that, Louise had explained, you had to name names, and in this particular case the names had to be repeated as often as possible. Those whose names were mentioned on the program, those who were accused, could always come on her show the following week to defend themselves.

Flore initially had no trouble with the naming, but she was now finding it difficult to go on with the rest of her story. Even though Louise had allowed her to record the show early in the morning—to be aired later that evening and a few more times during the following week—Flore could not forget that her son was right there, sitting at both their feet, under the table, and although he was wearing headphones, Pamaxime might still be able to hear.

"These commercial breaks take up a big chunk of the hour," Louise said as she prepared to start again. "And they are long. But what can you do?"

The man at the control board on the other side of the glass signaled to them to continue.

"Go on, tell me." Louise moved even closer now, their cheeks almost touching. "Tell me what happened next," she urged.

"I became pregnant with his baby," Flore continued in a steely voice that had long replaced the girlish voice she'd once had, the sound of which she could no longer remember.

This interview was good preparation for what was coming, Flore thought, for seeing Max Junior later that same morning. She wanted her son to see him too, if only this one time. Flore was curious to experience for herself how she would hold up in front of Max Junior. There would be no more tears, though. If anything, she would now do everything possible to drive him and his father to tears, with this show. Thankfully, she and Louise seemed to have similar goals.

"By his baby, you mean Maxime Ardin, Jr.'s baby?" Louise pressed her.

Flore nodded.

"This is not television," Louise said. "You have to speak."

These little remarks in the middle of a painful story always made people in the listening audience laugh. Sometimes, while sitting in her

house writing, on those nights that her show aired, Louise could hear laughter erupt from an entire row of houses. She never even had to turn on her own radio. She could hear the show blasting simultaneously from dozens of houses, and during those moments she felt she was the most powerful person in town. Her only regret was that due to the station's limited capacities, the show aired only in Ville Rose and a few surrounding towns, not all over the country.

"Yes," Flore continued, as if having paused for the expected laughter from the television remark.

Louise turned dead serious again. "I still don't understand why you went back. Why would you go back there after something like this had been done to you?"

The words had not come out as clearly as Flore had hoped. She wanted to explain how her mind had been all mixed up that night after he had appeared in her room, how she hadn't been quite sure whether or not she was dreaming.

"Why would you go back?" Louise insisted.

"I could not lose my job" was all that came out now.

"Are those the only choices you had?" Louise asked her. "Couldn't you have gone to the commissariat and filed a complaint?"

Somewhere in the audience, Louise knew, someone would chuckle. Probably many would. What good would it have done to have filed a

police complaint against Max Senior's son? A few dollars to some low- or high-level police official would get Max Junior off. Case in point, one of Max Senior's best friends was the current mayor.

The audience would be aware that Louise was playing devil's advocate, and when Louise played devil's advocate the listeners enjoyed the show even more.

Flore answered the question anyway. "Tell me, how many people in my situation get justice?"

Louise scratched her gaunt chin and paused to ponder this. She moaned so that the audience might hear and take part in her contemplation.

"Couldn't you have found another job?"

"I am—was—paying," Flore said, "the rent for my mother's house."

"I'm sure your mother understood that you were in a bad situation and would have liked for you to get out," Louise countered.

Flore's feet jerked so fast that the sound of her knees hitting the table could be heard when the show aired. "If that is the way you want to see it," she said.

Just then her son's hands brushed against her calf. When she looked down, she saw the back of his neck and his hands as he placed his pencil to the pad Louise had given him to start his drawing.

"When did you realize that you had become pregnant?" Louise continued.

"I realized I was pregnant a few weeks later, when I started vomiting," Flore said. She looked down and made sure the headphones were tightly wrapped around her son's ears, then added, "The vomiting was so bad that I sometimes vomited in the food I was preparing for them."

Louise would be able to feel that question pulse through her listeners' minds later on. She anticipated the collective gasp that would rise all over town. Has my servant been vomiting in my dinners? some would ask themselves.

They paused for another commercial break. Louise was smiling, the dark lines between her teeth showing. Flore looked down to check on her son, who seemed actively engaged in both doodling on Louise's pad and tapping the keys on the cell phone very softly, as he had been admonished not to do. Flore couldn't see what her son had drawn on the page because the phone and his hands were covering it.

When they started again, Louise asked, "Who did you first tell that you were pregnant?"

"I told the father first," Flore continued.

"You mean not your son's father. You mean Maxime Ardin, Sr.?" Louise asked.

"Yes," Flore answered.

"The owner and headmaster of École Ardin?"

"Li menm."

"You told him first?"

"Wi."

"And tell me, what did Maxime Ardin, Sr., say when you told him?"

"He said he couldn't know that this was his son's child. Then he gave me two thousand dollars American from him and his wife, to disappear, to go away."

"Two thousand dollars U.S., which converts into sixteen thousand dollars Haitian or eighty thousand gourdes, from the father who's here and the mother who's in Miami, to disappear. Is that the going rate?" Louise let out a purposefully forceful laugh to make her point.

So much for Max Senior's righteous indignation. It was just like him to make up his own rules for everything. She should have slapped him back after he'd made that woman slap her.

Louise imagined heads nodding all over town when her audience heard about the two thousand American dollars. That wasn't so bad, some might mutter. Another family might have just thrown her out and not given her anything at all.

"I took that money and I did leave," Flore went on. "I went to Port-au-Prince to live with one of my mother's cousins, and while waiting for my son to be born, I started a business."

Beauty had always fascinated Flore. She found it as resilient as wozo, the colorful weeds and wildflowers that grew, despite being regularly trampled, in the muck beside rivers and back roads. She liked to see women perfectly coiffed

213

and garbed in elegant-looking, even if cheap, dresses. She believed that even the poorest and unhappiest of women could fight heartache with beauty, with bright or muted kerchiefs, head wraps, or hats, relaxed or braided hair, wigs, and talcum-powdered necks. Even while sitting across from Louise, Flore thought that Louise could look prettier if she did more than pull back her hair, which made her face look so severe. She thought that Louise could use some lipstick in a pale shade and a black dot from an eyeliner pencil as a beauty mark.

"What kind of business did you start?" Louise asked.

"A beauty parlor," Flore said.

Louise imagined cheers erupting all over town. "Even in their misery," Louise purred into the microphone, "our women try to be beautiful."

This was Louise's favorite part of the show, the part where the horrible story began to take a positive turn. It was the equivalent of a first goal during an impossible soccer match, the moment where everything changes, if only for one side. This is why she was glad that this story had been plucked from the town rumor mill and landed on her lap, why she was thrilled, overjoyed, that this young woman had sought her out. That and to return Max Senior's slap to him. No, she was not a turn-the-other-cheek kind of gal, and in that moment in his office, Max Senior had forced her

to be. She believed in an eye for an eye, and though she had never used the show for revenge in the past, she was not above doing it.

"The beauty parlor grew fast." Flore was catching her stride now, stammering and hesitating less. "We made a lot of women beautiful," she said.

"And you?" Louise asked. "How were you changed?"

This is what had kept *Di Mwen* on the air all these years. This is why people loved the show. She always looked for the pot of gold at the end of her guests' rainbows.

"Well, I'm still here," Flore said, relieved that the program seemed to be drawing to a close. "Nou la."

Finally, the closing question, which Louise asked of every guest, in part to cover herself, to show that these people had sought her out and not the other way around. The question showed, or at least made it appear, that all she did was offer them a platform, to tell their stories themselves, that there was no ill intent on her part, nothing in it for her.

"Why did you come on *Di Mwen*?" she asked Flore. "Why did you want to get this off your chest?"

"With all their money, even after the way he came to be, they could take my son away from me," Flore said in her most defiant voice yet. "As if they could say I am not worthy of him."

"The Ardins. Father and son, you mean?"

"Yes, them."

"They want to take your child from you?"

"I won't let them."

"So what do you do now?" Louise asked.

"I am going far away," Flore said, pausing to further consider the possibility.

"I suppose you can't tell me where."

"Non."

"You told me that Maxime Ardin, Sr., and his wife had given you money for the child."

"Wi."

"And you have put that money into your beauty business?"

"Yes."

"Will it be hard to live without that money?"

"It will be harder to live without my son."

"So, just to be clear, you are taking your son with you?"

"My mother and my son are coming with me, yes," Flore said. "They will never see us again. I am here to tell them to never look for us again, because they will never find us. Even when I am dead and my son is a grown man, I will be sure they never find him. He will have a different name. He will be a different kind of man—"

This seemed a good place for Louise to close, without forcing her guest to compromise her plans and offer hints as to where she would end up. They had only a few seconds left anyway, so

Louise had to interrupt her to have the final word.

"Thank you, Flore Voltaire, for sharing your story with us," she said. Then, in a dramatically grave voice, she added, "I hope you achieve your goal and find the right place for you and your child."

Soon after the recorder was turned off, Flore removed the headphones from her son's ears, but it turned out that the boy had been—as nearly everyone in town would later be—glued to every word. He looked up at her and smiled a toothy smile of both confusion and pride at what he'd understood: that he was now going to meet his father, before going someplace far away.

Louise took the headphones from Flore, then held out her hand for the child to return the pad he'd been drawing on.

"Let's see." Louise looked at the stick figure on the pad. It was obviously meant to be a person, possibly a man, since the boy had not drawn hair or a skirt. The man had no eyes, nose, or mouth, the outline of his face a simple *O*. Searching for some hint of what the boy meant by his drawing, Louise smiled at him and guessed out loud. "A goat?" she asked, teasing the boy.

He laughed, covering his mouth with his hands, then answered, "Non."

"A cow?"

"Non."

"Me?" Louise ventured.

"Papa mwen," the boy said. "My father."

"Write 'Papa,'" Louise recommended.

The boy wrote the word *papa,* the tiny letters spread wide apart. Louise took the pad and tore out the page and handed the drawing back to the boy along with a large grape lollipop that seemed to appear in her hands like magic.

Turning to Flore, she said, "The child's father should see this picture."

Max Senior was sitting on his wooden bench on his front gallery with Jessamine when his cell phone began to ring and ring again.

"You won't believe who's on *Di Mwen,*" he kept hearing from each person who was calling him.

But he refused to turn on the radio. He didn't want to hear it. Besides, he had never cared for that mawkish program, even when he and Louise had been on speaking terms. Out of spite—or would it be to humiliate him?—the maid in the house next door turned her radio to the loudest possible volume so that the entire neighborhood could hear.

It was hard to pretend to the lovely young woman sitting next to him that the program did not concern them, since his name was being called out nearly as often as his son's. The girl mercifully said nothing, following him into the house as he showed her his bookshelves and the

abstract paintings on his living room walls, the rose garden and the swimming pool, the gazebo (the one, he realized with chagrin, that was just now being mentioned on the program). At least his cook and his gardener were not listening, he thought. Or they could be listening, like he was, catching the juicy snippets from the radio next door.

His son's friend seemed strangely unaffected. She already knew everything, he realized. Otherwise how could she not be incensed, outraged?

She was a stunning girl with an African mask of a face, all high forehead and high cheekbones, giant loop earrings, and one gold stud on either side of her cheeks. She was obviously one of those modern girls, the kind of girl whom frankly he didn't think he would be able to welcome with open arms into this family, with her cheek studs and hippie tunic and the word *POP* tattooed in red-ink calligraphy across the insides of both her wrists.

He escorted her to the kitchen, and they divided a half pitcher of lemonade between two glasses. Surprisingly, he thought, unlike a lot of returning dyasporas, she was skinny and wasn't reeking of bug spray. He asked her why she hadn't come to the party the night before, and she said that her cousin's car had broken down and she was unable to find a ride in time. Why hadn't she called his son? he asked. She said her phone wasn't

working. Couldn't she have borrowed someone else's phone? he asked. Then she confessed that she thought it was better for his son to see everyone for the first time on his own.

He wasn't sure why her explanations mattered so much to him, yet they did. He offered her some leftover codfish patties from the party. She declined. His cook was nowhere to be found and he was afraid to call out for her. He could accept neither pity nor further scorn from his employees.

He decided he wouldn't stay inside the house and hide. He would eventually have to face all of this head-on, at the school, and in any number of places in town. The girl followed him back to the porch. If the whole town wanted to parade by his open gate and condemn him, they could. He and his ex-wife had done what most parents he knew would have done. They'd tried to protect their son. And by providing the money for what had become the beauty parlor, they'd tried to protect Flore's child the best way they knew how. Should they have demanded a shotgun marriage? Should he have sent Flore off to Miami with their son? It was clear that something other than love had been made in that room that night. And perhaps that night was not the only time it had happened either. But what do you do when your misguided child, in some stupid effort to distract you from who he really is, commits a horrible act? Do you have the police come over and arrest him?

Do you have him paraded on the street and humiliated on the radio? Your child. This boy. This man, who had once been a good, simple, and innocent boy. Just like this boy he had violently made. So if Flore wanted to keep this boy for herself, let her. She might have a better chance of turning him into a decent man. Good luck to her, though. He hoped she would succeed. Let her try to raise a boy and help him become a man. Let her teach him how to tie his shoes, to shake hands properly. Let her show him how to swim, how to fly a kite. Let her show him how to sharpen a blade, to shave or otherwise, how to defend himself when attacked. Let her teach him to read and write and tell him all kinds of stories, the true meaning of which he never seemed to understand. Let her feel proud, then ashamed of him, then proud again. Let her long for him when he is gone and despise him when he's in her presence. Let her wish for him to be another kind of son and for her to be another kind of mother. Let her see what it's like to protect him from even his worst desires, to keep them from tainting his life forever. Let her try to show him the difference between right and wrong. Let her guide him to adulthood unscathed in a society where people are always looking for the next person to tear down. Let her school him on legacy, how one should honor and respect it and defend it at all cost. Let her learn one day

how to forgive him and eventually to forgive herself.

Flore's own mother had certainly tried to do her best for her. It must have felt like success when her daughter had landed in his house. A particular detail in Flore's story wounded him even more than the rest. The morning after the hailstorm, he had picked up his son's wet flashlight outside Flore's door and had handed it back to him.

"I forgot it there," Junior had said. He had not questioned him further.

He had even seen Flore leave the house while he and his son were in the garden.

He had known none of the details until now, hearing what she was telling the world through the radio. He regretted not hearing anything but the storm that night. In the end, he was Max Junior's father and not hers. If he had to choose between anyone and his son, his son would always come first.

Better Louise's kind of talk, he'd thought, than others. Better that kind of shame than an even worse kind. Sleeping with the house servant was not an uncommon rite of passage for young men in houses like his. "Droit du seigneur," his own father had called it. Though Max Senior himself had never taken part. But wasn't even the girl expecting it? The faultiness of his logic seemed obvious now in being exposed. Could he go on

Louise's show next week and use that dreadful explanation to absolve his son?

Jessamine was still respectfully silent, watching the calabash trees on the street along with him until his son pulled up in front of the house in the car he had lent him to take Flore and the boy home. When had Flore found the time to record this monstrosity of an hour? Max Senior wondered. But now his attention was on his son. His son, his brilliant scholar son, who was now cowering inside his car, hiding from him and this girl. His son, the lover of stories as a boy. Quick, he wanted to think of a story to tell him now, a story of dangerous mistakes made by both fathers and sons. Jessamine was looking at the Jeep, at his son, her eyes dancing between them and Max Senior's face. He was now seeing her in full, carving out of her dark face another impossible grandchild for himself. Even though he was with a school full of children all day long, what did he even know of young people these days? At the school and elsewhere in town, he had seen several groups go from matènèl, prekindergarten, to close to his son's age. Not many lived out their early promise. Some of this you could blame, as his ex-wife often did, on the town, its lack of opportunities, its rigid social hierarchies. But his son, with all his opportunities and contacts, had done no better.

There was something tragic about a generation

223

whose hopes had been raised, then dashed over and over again. Had they been poisoned by disappointment? Their leaders and elders—including himself—had made them so many promises that they'd been, for whatever reason, unable to keep. Idealists had been killed to make room for gangsters. Life had become so cheap that you could give anyone a few dollars to snuff it out. When had they entered, he wondered, what Rimbaud, in his time, had called "le temps des assassins," the age of assassins? Maybe his generation was the problem. They'd built a society that was useless to their children. Still, these children seemed to lack the will to sacrifice and build their own. He had been willing to at least try to make this right. He had been looking forward to turning his school over to his son, to the next generation, to see if he—they—could or would do any better. But now he might never get the chance.

He was surprised that Jessamine did not rush into his son's arms when she saw him. His son, in turn, was looking down the road, then looking back at them. Maybe the radio was on in the car and his son too was listening to the program or he was overhearing snippets from the street. Maybe he didn't even realize the program was on. Being a subject of Louise's so-called show was like getting a scarlet letter. One that at times was only temporary. You were hounded by murmurs and

whispers, but only until the following week, when it was someone else's turn.

Max Senior wanted to rush to explain that to his son, to reassure him, but he hoped that Jessamine would make a move before him. Jessamine did not. Was she shell-shocked? He didn't know, but he could see in his son's face that he felt he had no choice but to quickly drive away.

Where would he go but to the beach? Aside from the lighthouse, it was his favorite place. Weighted down by more important concerns, the people at the beach might not even be listening to the show.

"Shouldn't we go after him?" the girl was asking him now. And it seemed the kind of simple question that might be asked by someone who did not fully understand that there was nothing simple about a situation.

"Yes, we could go after him," he replied. "But I suspect if he wanted to be with us, he would have stayed."

"Then what are we supposed to do?" she asked. Both of them were staring out at the front gate, at the calabash trees on the road, their branches stagnant in the heat.

"We wait," Max Senior said, which was the usual course when it came to his son. He was always waiting for him: waiting for him to come to his senses, waiting for him to understand his duties, waiting for him to take up his

responsibilities, waiting for him to return home.

"Do you think he'll come back?" asked the girl.

"He will," Max Senior said, fully certain of this, if nothing else. "He always does." The girl shook her studded face and grimaced, now allowing her frustration to show. She pulled a cell phone out of her purse and dialed it. She was trying to call his son, Max Senior assumed. But hadn't she just told him that her phone wasn't working? He wanted to remind her of this, but said nothing. She held the phone up to her ear for a while and when there was no answer, she threw it back in her purse. She kept watching the front gate, the road, leaning forward as if to better see each passerby. She remained sitting there next to him, long after the show ended and the station switched to a music program, and the neighbor's maid finally lowered the volume.

"We're not going to take it sitting down," Max Senior said, then he realized how ridiculous that sounded because they were actually sitting down.

"I'll find Flore and Pamaxime again," he continued, "and I will go to the radio station myself and denounce Louise on her own airwaves." He was rambling now, he realized. "Nothing will change, not with the school, not with my son. All of this will be forgotten." But what about Pamaxime? he wondered. What would become of Pamaxime?

"Byen. Okay," the girl said.

He thought of her few words, in her heavy English accent, as banalities of the kind people say when they are feeling the opposite. He had been young once and might have said something like this, but never to one of his friends' parents. But this girl was saying this to him now, because in some way she considered herself equal to him. She might even consider herself wiser than him, her apparent lack of condemnation, her friendship with his son a sign—or so she probably thought—that she possessed a kind of compassion that surpassed everyone else's, that even surpassed his.

Just then, thankfully, his friend Albert walked through the front gate and on the path toward them. Jessamine jumped up as if she thought it was his son returning, or maybe she was just grateful to have someone else there.

"I'm not dead, am I?" Max Senior shouted to his friend.

Albert laughed, then walked faster, shifting his hat from one hand to the other when he reached them. Albert bowed his head in Jessamine's direction while tapping his hat against his thigh. Jessamine looked up at him and returned his greeting with a nod. Then, as if she could restrain herself no longer, she reached into her bag and pulled out a lighter and a cigarette. Walking to the end of the gallery, she sat on the edge of the railing and lit it. Max Senior was curious to see if

smoke would come out of the side of her face through the studs in her dimples. (It didn't.) He was also horrified to see her dropping her cigarette ashes, then the cigarette butt itself, on the African violets around the porch. Some of the flowers were already withering from the increasingly hot temperatures. He had planted them around the front gallery in corners where there was neither too much light nor too much shade. He had made sure that there was the right balance of perlite and soil, and now she was using his flowers as an ashtray. He wanted to shout at her to move away from them, but before he could say anything, she started walking back toward him and his friend. She walked, he realized, as though she were doing an upright backstroke, rotating her arms with every step.

Albert was watching her too, as he had sat in her place on the bench, leaving her with no choice but either to squeeze in next to them or to remain standing. She chose to remain standing.

Had she not been there, Max Senior would have gone inside and picked up his dominoes and card table, and he and Albert would have talked nonsense and played a long game late into the night. But she was standing there looking at them, and they could not ignore her.

Max Senior could see that his friend was doing his best to take a break now and then from staring at her face. Because of his work as an undertaker,

Albert was naturally intrigued by body modifications, amputations as well as embellishments, especially rare markings or piercings. His friend had probably never seen piercings like the ones on the girl's cheeks. What would one call them, Max Senior wondered, earrings, but not on ears, zanno machwa, cheek rings? His friend, he was certain, was probably imagining his own son and daughter in the United States with these cheek rings, or worse.

"Are you here because of that program?" Max Senior asked Albert, in part to divert his friend's attention from the young lady.

"Am I only allowed to come here when you have parties?" he asked.

"You can also come when we have tragedies," Max Senior said.

"I can't stay long," Albert said, his eyes returning to Jessamine. She wrapped her arms around one of the porch's pillars while looking at the trees on the road.

Max Senior could imagine how much his friend would taunt him at the next marathon domino game about having a girl like this—striking, as slender as a dancer, studded, tattooed—as his daughter-in-law.

"Where is your wife?" Max Senior asked his friend.

"She's already left," he said.

Max Senior thought how sad it had been that

his friend's wife and children had not even come home for his swearing-in as mayor, because the twins were in some kind of swimming tournament. That day Max Senior had been grateful for his own divorce. How can some people not fully understand their ability to shatter hearts?

Jessamine walked back over to the far end of the porch and stared down at the same African violets she'd doubtless singed with her cigarette.

"What are these flowers?" she called out.

"Violets," he told her.

"They grow here?" she asked.

They are growing, aren't they? he wanted to say. At least they were trying to, before your cigarette.

"Everything can grow here," he replied instead.

Max Senior then wished that his friend had not come so soon, that it was still just him and the girl talking in this new way about things, about his son being okay and about African violets. Max Senior then realized that he hadn't properly introduced her to his friend.

"Albert, this is Jessamine," he said. "Remember, we were waiting for her last night. Jessamine, this is Albert Vincent, an old friend."

"Old only in the length of my friendship with Max," Albert said.

"I see." The girl did smile this time.

"And where is Junior now?" Albert asked.

230

Max Senior shrugged. "Most likely at the beach. Or at the lighthouse," he added.

"Let him be," Albert advised. "He'll come back when he's ready. Let's just let him be."

"That's what I told Jessamine here," Max Senior said.

It was getting dark, and Max Senior's hope that his son would return grew stronger. Otherwise, it would be up to him to decide where to put the girl for the night. She had somehow reached his house on a camion that her relatives had put her in from the capital. The driver had been kind enough to drop her off at the gate, but she had no sure way of going back to Port-au-Prince, at least not tonight.

"I suppose you heard the program," Max Senior said, keeping his eyes on the few people walking by on the road, looking, he thought, with new interest at his house.

"Part of it," Albert said, resting his head on the wall behind him. "I heard it after meeting with the mother of a young man who got a machete in his gut from a land dispute, so I had some perspective."

Jessamine raised an eyebrow, looking curious in a way that seemed to flatter his friend.

"You're Oncle Albert," she said. "Maxime told me about you."

"Did he?" Albert said. "I thought he had forgotten about all of us."

"Seems like no one here forgot him, though," the girl said.

"Did he want us to forget him?" Max Senior asked, ashamed when he heard how forlorn his own voice sounded.

"Of course, as Louise constantly reminds us, there are things we should never forget," Albert said, as though lecturing his friend.

"Kolangèt manman Louise, screw her!" Max Senior shouted, finally allowing himself to blurt out the full extent of his anger: at himself, at his son, at Flore, but most especially at Louise George.

Jessamine shrank back a little, hugging the porch pillar tighter, as if to give him room. Looking at her face, her high brow, her tattoo, and her pierced cheeks, Max could sense some deeper story there, some story he would probably never know. Albert said nothing, letting his friend stew for a moment. Instead he placed his hat on his lap, allowing his hands to shake openly for her to see.

It was growing even darker now, so dark that on Max Senior's street one could already see lights through the windows of a few houses. The silence among the three of them now bothered Max Senior so much that he did not feel as timid as he might have asking what he did next.

"Are you and my son in love?" he asked. "Nou renmen?"

Once the words crossed his lips, he realized that they sounded more like a plea than a question. Please, please, love my son was really what he was saying. And for once he was grateful that Albert restrained himself from jumping in and facetiously asking, for example, "Who, me? Am I in love with your son?" Instead it was the girl who asked, "Me?" and Max Senior said, "Since we're neither on the radio nor on television, I'm going to both nod and say yes."

Max Senior nodded and Jessamine frowned her disapproval at his poking fun at the show and at Flore.

"Your son is my friend," she said, her eyes following the fireflies lighting up, then disappearing around them. "He is my very terrible and imperfect and dear friend."

Max Senior thought this an accurate description, one of many he might have used himself.

"I fell in love with your son when I met him and knew nothing about him," she continued.

"And he?" Max Senior interrupted her to ask. "Did he fall in love with you?"

"What do you think?" she asked brazenly.

"Obviously he doesn't know what to think," Albert interjected. "That's why he's asking you."

"As lovable as I am," she said, now waving her hands as though to reach for the fireflies, "he is not capable of being in love with me."

"How's that?" asked Max Senior.

"I thought you would already know this," the girl said to Max Senior as plainly as she had said everything else. "Your son has been in love only once in his life, and the person he was in love with is dead."

Max Junior was lying on his back, under the palms that inclined as though to touch the sea. He tucked his hands under his head and stared up at the dark clouds, which were blocking, then fleeing the moon. That everyone could and should despise him, there was no question, and they had good reason. Flore most of all.

He remembered the hailstorm that seemed like it might pummel the world to pieces. He remembered her flailing arms. He had foolishly wanted to prove something to his father that night, that he could be with Flore. He wanted his father to hear her screams.

To this day, he had never been with any man but Bernard. He and Bernard would come to the beach on nights like this and would remove their shirts, then plunge into the water. Initially, Bernard had been afraid of the sea. He was a strong swimmer, but was always worried that he would be caught in a current and towed away. That he would disappear forever.

Now, as he walked fully clothed to the water, Max Junior thought of his father's version of a

Cornish folktale, one the old man had told him when he was little.

A boy is lured into the woods by music. The deeper the boy walks into the woods, the denser the woods become and the more beautiful the music. The boy follows this music until he gets so lost that he no longer knows where he is. He becomes so scared that he wants to return home, but he also wants to follow the music to see where it leads. After he walks so far that the woods become impassable, he begins to cry for help. And that's when a spirit emerges and makes a path for him. The path leads to the sea, where suddenly the music stops and the boy is now so tired that he lies down and falls asleep. When he wakes up, the boy finds himself back home, safely in his own bed, with his head full of music and mermaids and crystal palaces under the sea. The spirit in the woods saved this boy, his father said, because the spirit wanted the boy to remain innocent and good and that innocence and goodness was as precious as the dreams she'd placed in his head. And because of that innocence and goodness, she would watch over him forever.

Max Junior now slipped into the water, feeling the cool waves rise and fall around him as the water ballooned his red shirt, the one Jessamine had given him for his return trip home. In the sea, he thought of music, the rap-filled kind he had

once played on his radio show, the kind Bernard had liked. He also thought of flowers and birds. He thought of the birdhouses he and his father had built together, after hours of schoolwork and judo practice, when he was a boy. He thought of the somber plumage of some petrels and storm-signaling seagulls. He thought of the pigeons, alive and dead, in Bernard's stories. He thought of the orchids and roses in his father's garden, the dragonflies that buzzed around after a heavy rain and the fireflies that bombarded them at night. He thought of how the roses had been pummeled the night of the hailstorm but had still had enough nectar to attract a hummingbird the next morning. He thought of yellow jasmine, his mother's favorite flowers. She would tie a bouquet to the bell on the front of her bicycle, then the two of them would ride next to each other through town. They would ride to the kleren factory and his mother, sniffing the air, would become giddy from the raw liquor smell. He thought of his mother's history lessons about the ruins of Abitasyon Pauline. He remembered the talk they'd had in the middle of the ruins shortly before she left town. You are who you love, she'd told him. You try to mend what you've torn. But remember that love is like kerosene. The more you have, the more you burn.

He liked his mother's blunt aphorisms. He also liked how she tried to explain the rogue waves.

Lasirèn, she said, made her presence known by swelling a wave several feet, whenever she craved human company.

One night ten years ago, after he'd learned that Flore was pregnant, he was sitting alone on the gallery of the old Anthère lighthouse when he thought he saw a supernova exploding above the sea. It was so dazzling that he could make out the uneven edges and emission line, even after closing his eyes. That's when he also thought he saw the night sea swirl into a massive funnel, as if a mid-ocean whirlpool had come near the shore. Then the same waters quietly retreated—a tsunami in reverse—the waves turning into liquid mountains. He stood up, pressing his ribs into the lighthouse railing until he saw what he believed was part of the seafloor, a mountain-size ridge with reefs and sandbanks stripped bare for miles. Then just as quickly, the waves buckled and the water collapsed, hastily covering the ocean floor, as if nothing had taken place.

He had wondered then whether he was in shock, or overtired, or hallucinating. But now he believed that he had neither dreamed nor imagined all this, that it had actually happened.

He was remembering this, he knew, as a way of avoiding thinking about his son. He imagined the O face drawing melting, coming apart, even now in his pants pocket. A drawing made by his son,

237

whom he'd just met, his son, whom he might never see again. Would meeting him today have meant anything at all to his son? How long would it take the boy to forget him? Would his son grow up calling another man "Papa"? And if he did, would there ever be some hesitation, a hint of doubt in the back of the boy's mind, something that would ring false in the sound of his voice? The worst possible case of unrequited love, Jessamine had told him, was feeling rejected by a parent. Was the second worst being rejected by your child? He knew quite a bit about unrequited love, unreciprocated love. Until he'd met his son, he'd felt as if every other love were a phantom version, a shadow of the one he'd once had.

People like to say of the sea that lanmè pa kenbe kras, the sea does not hide dirt. It does not keep secrets. The sea was both hostile and docile, the ultimate trickster. It was as large as it was small, as long as you could claim a portion of it for yourself. You could scatter both ashes and flowers in it. You could take as much as you wanted from it. But it too could take back. You could make love in it and you could surrender to it, and oddly enough, surrendering at sea felt somewhat like surrendering on land, taking a deep breath and simply letting go. You could just as easily lie down in the sea as you might in the woods, and simply fall asleep.

• • •

Nozias's eyes had been closed for only a few minutes when he was awakened by a strange sound in the water, echoes of a person crying. Or was it laughter?

He felt a chill, shuddering as he made his way to the edge of the water. A few of his friends, the other fishermen who'd left their own shacks to surround him in support, were still fast asleep, their bodies strewn in fetal positions around him on the sand. Others, he knew, were in town or up by the lighthouse, looking for his daughter.

Was it Claire Limyè Lanmè he had just heard in this water, though? he wondered. Was that what had awakened him, the draft of her spirit drifting past, the gust of her final breaths? He'd felt something similar the day his wife died. It was hard to explain, but in his wife's case, it was a momentary stillness, as though the entire world had grown completely silent.

He was feeling this now, but not as strongly. Could it be Claire sinking in? Or Caleb settling at the bottom of the sea?

He peered out into the water, and the seaweed mixed with the reflection of the night sky made it seem as though there were stardust on its surface. He squeezed his arms around his body as if to hold himself in one piece while he waited for the girl's voice to surface from the waves.

"Papa, se ou?"

239

Some mornings when he would walk into their shack from the sea, Claire would ask in a half-sleeping voice, "Papa, is that you?"

"Ki yès ankò?" he would ask. "Who else would it be?"

Now, he hurried back to the shack, remembering midstep that he'd left Madame Gaëlle there. And when he walked in, the lamp was still burning.

Madame Gaëlle and her shiny dress hadn't moved from the edge of his bed. She was watching the lamp wick's shadows flicker across the newspaper-covered walls when he cried out, "Daughter, was that you?"

The midwife had told him that his wife's last words before she died had been to Claire's crowning head and shoulders. Though feeble and weak, she had still managed to say, "Vini." Come. But she was gone before Claire came.

He closed the door and pressed his back against it, again not knowing what to say.

"Did you find her?" Madame Gaëlle asked.

He shook his head no.

The day before Claire Limyè Lanmè's seventh birthday, he had gone to his friend Caleb to request a special favor. Caleb was one of a handful of his fisherman friends who could read and write, so Caleb acted as his and some of the other fishermen's document checker and letter writer. The fact that Caleb's wife was a deaf

240

mute—she was always present during his letter writing—also guaranteed that the words dictated in her presence would not spread through the town's teledyòl gossip mill.

Nozias had gone to Caleb to have him look over the documents that would be required should Madame Gaëlle adopt Claire. There was Claire's birth certificate and school report cards, which showed her to be excelling at everything, including good behavior. But sitting in Caleb's shack, which was twice as big as his, he decided at the very last minute to dictate a letter to Claire.

At sixty-nine, Caleb was older than most of the men who were still going out on the water. Unlike most of the fishermen, whose hands looked as though they had been sliced many times over and patched back together, Caleb's hands were the smoothest, and the smallest, that Nozias had ever seen on a grown man. The way Caleb copied the words that spilled out of his mouth seemed magical to him. Nozias was astonished when Caleb read his words back to him. The phrases, as few and as banal as they were, seemed gentler, neater, as if Caleb had entered his head and reorganized everything.

Madame Gaëlle now watched as he walked to his cot and raised the pillow where his head usually lay. They were close enough that she could reach over and touch the back of his smooth, bald head with her hands. He pulled out

241

the black plastic bag in which Claire Limyè Lanmè's papers and his letter were carefully wrapped. He untied the bag, taking special care not to tear any holes in it. He pulled out the letter and handed it to her.

Madame Gaëlle squinted as though she were having trouble seeing the words, then she slid down to be closer to the lamp, leaving even less space between them.

She began reading the letter to herself, then raised her voice:

Claire Limyè Lanmè,
I thank God for the ability to use my voice to dictate this letter to you. Claire, please remember these things I am about to tell you. No matter what you might hear later in your life, I am not doing this for money. I did not sell you. I am giving you a better life. Please be nice to Madame and do everything she tells you. Continue to do well in school and you will grow up to be a smart and important woman. Also remember to not sleep on your back, so you won't have bad dreams. And don't ever forget your papa because I will never forget you. That is all I wish to say for now. Thank you for taking the time to read these words.

Nozias Faustin, Your Father

Madame Gaëlle refolded the letter and returned it to the bag. She pressed her lips against the back of his neck, letting them linger there in a kiss.

He hadn't been kissed by a woman in that way since his wife died, a kiss so pure that it felt like it was polishing him. He felt as though his body had turned to gold. A stream of light was coursing through him, and when he reached up to touch her face, he felt both their bodies expand beyond the size of his room.

"What will we do when Claire returns?" she asked, removing her lips from the back of his neck, sliding, slipping away from his side of the cot, away from him. Yet she had said "nou," we, and he was glad that she had said it.

What will *we* do when Claire returns?

This is what he wanted more than anything for his daughter: a lack of cruelty, a feeling of safety, but also love. Benevolence and sympathy too, but mostly love.

He wasn't sure what he would do when Claire returned. He didn't know. Maybe he would still have Claire go live with her. Or maybe he would postpone again for another year. Then another. Then another. And soon he would see for himself whether what people said about children growing up so fast was true for more than seven years. Avan w bat zye w. In the flicker of an eyelid. Before you know it, they're living their own lives. Maybe Claire would be old enough by then

243

to be the one leaving him behind. Or maybe something terrible would happen to him before she was grown. Or maybe, like Caleb, he would be lost at sea and Madame Gaëlle would remember that tonight a promise had been extracted from her. She had said yes. She had said "nou." She had agreed to take Claire. But first Claire had to come back. And when she did, would she come back to live with him? Would they have another year together, on the beach? This is what he hoped his wife might have said, if she'd found herself in his position, giving their child away: better a child cry for a parent now than for everything later on. But would she, could she—she his wife, she his daughter, and she Madame Gaëlle—could they even see it like that?

Madame Gaëlle got up and moved to Claire's cot so that she was now across from him, facing him.

"I want to ask you again," she said, "why you want to give her away. And to me."

"I am not the first," he said, trying to remain calm, to stay composed, "nor am I the only one to ever give up a child."

"I used to see you," she said, "walking by the fabric store, on your way to visit her at the funeral parlor. You loved that woman, her mother, so much . . ."

And with those words still in the air, Nozias abruptly got up and walked out of the shack once

244

again, hoping to avoid this part of the exchange, to avoid thinking how much even the idea of giving away their daughter would have devastated his wife. And what if both Claires were now gone for good? What if he never saw his daughter again?

After he'd stepped outside, Gaëlle thought she heard him scream. She grabbed the kerosene lamp and rushed out the door, and to the sea, to the edge of the water, where he was standing with the waves lapping at his feet.

Nozias Faustin had indeed loved his wife. And one way he liked to show it was by visiting her at the funeral parlor where she worked, whenever he wasn't out at sea. One afternoon when he got to the funeral parlor, she was scrubbing the waist-high cement table where she washed and dressed the dead. The table was attached to the floor and was wide enough for two or three people to be laid out comfortably. But only his wife was there when he arrived.

During his visits, he would often find her in the middle of her work, her small frame swimming in her sand-colored plastic work coat, her long, gloved fingers wiping beads of water off a naked corpse. Sometimes it was someone he recognized and he would wonder how she could touch so intimately in death someone she had spoken to in life. Sometimes, if they had drowned, the bodies

would be bloated, unrecognizable. On those occasions, she would hand him a cloth mouth-and-nose cover, just like hers, and would then seem to forget that he was there. She would talk to the dead instead. Moving her masked face close to their ears, she would recount everything that had happened in town since they had died.

Most of the time, she would, he knew, have other company than him. Family members would come and help wash and dress. She would tell him later that she had watched them for hints of tenderness that she'd then apply to those whose family members preferred not to come. Sometimes she would apply special perfumes, sneak in a pair of socks or stockings of her own choosing, though the dead were never to have shoes. Shoes could only weigh a person down in the afterlife.

She would sew some of the clothes for the dead, especially the babies, for whom it was too heartbreaking to buy burial clothes, but whenever necessary, she would adjust the clothes that were brought in, which were often either too large or too small. She would also tell him about families who would bury the dead in a secret place, ahead of the cement-filled closed coffin at the funeral service, for fear that their dead might be snatched from the cemetery and turned into zombies. She often marveled how so many of the photographs brought in for the funeral programs were from

decades ago; a centenarian's funeral program cover photo was usually a wedding portrait or a special-occasion likeness from when the person was barely out of adolescence.

Every now and then, she would be asked by the family to extract gold crowns from the dead's mouth, but that she would never dare to do herself. She would ask Msye Albert to do that.

She was glad, she sometimes told Nozias, that she never had to go into the walk-in freezer to take a corpse off the shelf by herself, not even a baby corpse, which she could have easily lifted and carried. Whenever she had to wash and dress the bodies, she would find them already on the table waiting.

Nozias was there once when she was putting a final dab of powder on a young man's face, and both the man's eyes abruptly popped open. Nozias had jumped back, terrified, but she hadn't even flinched.

"I just have to tell Msye Albert to sele, or set, the eyes again," she said as she went on with her work.

Setting the eyes, he learned that day, did not mean placing one's fingers over the eyelids and sliding them downward, as he had seen laypeople do. Rather, it meant putting thumbprint-size pieces of rubber under the eyelids, then gluing them to the insides of the eyes so they would remain closed.

Some of the corpses would break wind as if they were alive, except it was a fouler, stinkier wind. But there was no such smell that day, just the lingering fragrance of the lemon-scented disinfectant she scrubbed the cement table with after she washed each body.

As he walked toward her in the washroom that afternoon, she did not rush to greet him. The plastic coat she was wearing was weighing her down, he thought, or maybe it was something else.

He could hear above him, around him, the creaking and echoes coming from other parts of the house, the loud footsteps and muffled conversations from the offices upstairs. Next to the room they were in was the showroom, with the sample coffins lined against the wall. Next to that was the chapel with a stained-glass window of the Last Supper, made locally, with brown faces, by a Ville Rose artist.

His wife removed her work coat, letting it fall at her feet. Underneath she was wearing her favorite dress, a bell-shaped parrot-green dress that she had sewn herself. Her hair was neatly brushed, the cornrows lined up like roads on a map to some mysterious land. Her hands were folded over her breasts and she closed her eyes, looking as though she were sleeping on her feet. He wondered if this was what she'd been doing

before he'd come in, listening with her eyes closed to everything around her.

"We are no longer two. Now we are three," she said. He opened his eyes wide. Her childlike face, her usually serene childlike face, was tied in an inexplicable knot as though she were fighting back tears.

"How do you tell someone you're pregnant in a funeral parlor?" he asked when she was done speaking. He was too delighted not to laugh. He rushed over and grabbed her, then stepped back for fear of crushing her. She was laughing too when he threw his arms around her. Then he was a bit sad, and his sadness, mingled with intense joy, made him hold her tight again. How does life itself, as much as you must want it in your body, not feel futile when you have seen so many dead?

She'd told him about pregnant mothers that she'd dressed for their burial with the babies still inside them. How could this not have been on her mind that afternoon?

"I told Msye Albert," she said, "that I won't be washing and dressing the dead anymore."

He had grown used to the dead being part of her life. Because she had touched so many corpses, some of their friends and neighbors wouldn't even allow her to shake their hands or wouldn't eat the food she cooked. But he was happy to live with all of that, if it meant living with her.

Sometimes he could even smell the dead on her, in the embalming fluids and disinfectant. The hands that stroked the faces of the dead stroked his. He ate from those hands. He kissed them. He loved them. He loved their constellations of scars from all the sewing she did without thimbles. He loved how rough her fingertips could feel, how like a tiny grater, even when she was gentle. And he knew that her sympathy for the dead, her compassion for everyone, would make her a good mother, a great mother.

That afternoon in the funeral parlor, it was as if life had sprung up to embrace him, even in this place of death. He raised her dress to her waist, bent down and pressed his ear against her still-flat stomach and held it there, listening for some faint new sounds.

"I told the baby not to tell you anything yet," she joked.

After she died, he would remember seeing her body laid out on the cot where they had slept together since she had come to live with him. He was shocked to see that, in death, though the baby was no longer in it, her stomach was still round like a frigate bird's bill.

The midwife had put that same parrot-green dress on his wife and it looked small, too tight on her body. Her dead hands were folded over her chest in a way that had reminded him of how she'd been standing against the wall in the funeral

parlor the afternoon he'd learned that she was pregnant. When he bent over and pressed his ear against her belly in the wash-and-dress room, she kept muttering, "Sa se pa nou. Se pa nou. This is ours. Ours. Ours. Ours."

Claire de Lune

Sometimes Claire Limyè Lanmè Faustin would dream about the day she was born. In her dream, it was a gray morning and the sky too was pregnant, with rain. On one side of the room was a brand-new sisal broom, which, as in many home births, a midwife would brush across her mother's bare stomach to help "sweep" her out. On the other side of the room would be a chair with a yellow baby sheet draped over it. A breeze would flow under the sheet, making it rise and fall along with her mother's breath. The echo of the heart that had been thumping so loudly above her head would stop as two hands would free her shoulders, then yank her out.

"A revenan," she would hear the midwife saying. "She is a revenan."

This would mean, of course, that her mother had died.

Soon after she was born, the midwife would wash her body, plunging her into a pot of blood-warm water, then the midwife would use the same water to wash her mother. In the dream, Claire would glimpse her mother as the midwife raised her out of the water. Her mother is bony and long and laid out on her father's cot in a leaf-colored dress. Her mother's face is turned

sideways, showing the highest peak of a cheekbone. Over her mother appears her father's face and the furrows of concern carved into it, like miniatures graves.

Then she would dream of breasts, full, cushiony, pillowlike breasts, whose tips would turn from flesh to rubber, and she would dream of her feet becoming dusty when she walked on the ground, and of rivers becoming muddy when she stepped into them, and she would wake up wishing that she could stay asleep forever, just so that she could see more of these things in her dreams and fully understand them. And finally she might understand why in her real, waking life she had to wash herself in buckets beside the latrines behind the shacks when there was water everywhere, although it was seawater and if you bathed in seawater, you would get a layer of salt on your skin that looked like ash and dust and when you put your tongue on your arm you would taste salt like you tasted salt when you secretly ran your tongue over your father's gutted and salted fish and your tongue would bleed from rubbing against the salted scales and the salt would sting where you had cut your tongue, making the salt even more delicious.

Salt was life, she would often hear the adults say. Some of the fishermen's wives would throw a pinch of crushed salt in the air for good luck, before their men left for the sea. (Some would

also refuse to eat, or wash, or comb their hair until their men came back.) When zombies ate salt, it brought them back to life. Or so she'd always heard. Maybe if she ate enough salt, she would finally understand why her father wouldn't let her wander, flannen. She would always try, though. Sometimes while her father was at sea, she would walk through the open market and pretend that she was one of those children sent to buy provisions to bring home to a mother. And she would pick up things at the market and put them down, raising, then crushing the hopes of the vendors, who would mumble under their breath as she walked away.

Every now and again one of the vendors would shout, "Just like her mother!" and she would ask herself what else she might do to make them say even more often that she was just like her mother. Besides dying, that is.

Aside from hearing the vendors say that she was just like her mother, she liked walking through the market because everything there was mixed in, the braying goats, the cackling chickens, the vegetables in season, her favorite of which was breadfruit, because people called breadfruit lam veritab, veritable souls. She would have liked to have flannen into the seaside eating places and hotels too, the ones where the women were said to spend days and nights in their bras and panties and the men walked in the

doors quickly as if they were too frightened of being seen. But these places were not for children, and she'd heard her father say, when he'd been told that she'd wandered too far off course and had approached one of those places, that a girl who went into a place like that might not come out the same. She might enter a girl and someone might put a hand over her mouth and she might come out bleeding between her legs and people would start calling her Madame, because she would no longer be considered a girl. If she went anywhere near those places, her father had told her, people would whisper behind her back that she was the Madame of many men. There had been a girl in school like that, who'd had someone put his hands over her mouth, someone who had made her bleed between her legs. The girl had to leave school after that. People in town talked about the schoolmaster's son like that too. They called him a Madame, another kind of Madame, they said. They also said that he had stolen (vòlè) or he had violated (vyole) a girl who had (vole) flown away. Vòlè vyole w, ou vole. The girl who had vole, flown away, wasn't a girl anymore but a woman, a woman who later had a child by the school-master's son. It was like one of those stories Madame Louise George used to read to the preschool matènèl classes when Madame Louise was still coming to the school. In Madame

Louise's stories, everything was organized a certain way; everything was neat. Things would start out well, but would end up being bad, then would be well again. Claire didn't believe stories like that, even when she felt like they were aimed at her, even when they were meant to defend her or teach her some kind of lesson. She disliked people too sometimes. She felt them moving around her, exchanging places. Sometimes she wished people, especially adults, were trees. If only trees could move. With trees, you'd have to be the one who moved around them. But trees didn't cry. They didn't complain.

People liked to complain. Even her father, who was usually so quiet. Yet most people thought they were smarter than trees because they could talk. But talking wasn't everything. Who cared if you could talk, if you decided to get up and leave? That was why the smartest person she knew was Madame Josephine.

Madame Josephine had no voice, so she made up a new language with her hands. It was a more direct language than the one the other adults spoke. Her father knew this hand language, and people could understand Madame Josephine because of him. It was as if her father and Madame Josephine could have been twins, born at the same hour on the same day. She wondered what people would have said if she and her mother had died on the same day. For a while

they were twinned, when she was inside her mother's body. But she never dreamed of being inside her mother's body, except in that last moment when she had to come out and that last moment always made her think of water.

Sometimes when she was lying on her back in the sea, her toes pointed, her hands facing down, her ears half submerged, while she was listening to both the world above and beneath the water, she yearned for the warm salty water to be her mother's body, the waves her mother's heartbeat, the sunlight the tunnel that guided her out the day her mother died. From the sea, even while lying on her back, she could see her home on the beach and above it the houses on the hill and the Anthère lighthouse and above that all the densely packed ferns of Mòn Initil. At night, it was impossible to see Mòn Initil. Even when a full moon was parked right above it and it attracted dozens of shooting stars, Mòn Initil still looked like a blank spot at the foot of the sky. This was just as well, because people were afraid of Mòn Initil.

One story that Madame Louise had read to the class when Claire was smaller said that people were afraid to go to Mòn Initil because that's where in the olden days the slaves who had escaped the old Abitasyon Pauline had gone to hide, and some of them had never made it out. The bones of our ancestors, Madame Louise had

said in her croaky voice, still litter the grounds of Mòn Initil, and their ghosts still haunt its trees.

In the daytime, though, and from the water, Mòn Initil looked harmless, even inviting. The ground was naturally terraced so the trees were neatly lined up in rows, each one taller than the last. The Anthère lighthouse was ugly in the daytime, and sometimes, with the sun shining overhead, it was all rocks sticking out of cement when it did not look washed out altogether. But at night, especially nights when someone was missing or dead, it was lit up like a super moon. And it glowed.

She had never been up to the top of the Anthère lighthouse, in the gallery, but she imagined that if ever she were to go, it would be to say good-bye to her father if he were lost at sea. It would be to light a lamp or swing a flashlight one night, hoping that he would see it from the water.

"A few moments earlier and it would have been me," her father had told her that very morning. And what would she have done if it had been him? Where would she have gone if the fabric vendor had said no yet again? Who would have taken her in for the rest of her life? There were the relatives in the mountain village, her mother's people, who showed up at Christmas sometimes with yams and breadfruit, which they knew she liked. But aside from that, she never saw them.

They would appear again and she would have to follow them up to the mountain and she would have to leave her school and the one or two children in her class who spoke to her. But would she see her father again? He was giving her away to the fabric vendor, the woman whose breasts were the first she had suckled, as he liked to remind everyone. Why hadn't he just given her to this woman after she had suckled her breasts? she wondered. She would have known no other life. She would have used her first word to call this woman "Manman." She would have cried for her when she was sick. She would have pouted at her when she was scolded. She would have held her hand on the way to and from school. She would have known the woman's dead child as her sister and she would have had a sister to mourn, rather than a mother. It might have been all the same. She would not have remembered much about the sister either. All she would know would be the empty space that this sister would have occupied, without being able to define it. She had no idea what it was to have a mother rather than a string of motherly acts performed by different hands: the aunt in the mountains—who'd had her the first three years of her life, the neighbors, including Madame Josephine, who'd motion for her to come out of the sea when she'd been in there too long. Her father often took her to the cemetery to visit her mother, but if it had been up

260

to her, if she had had a say, they would have been visiting her mother at sea, because her mother would have been buried at sea. It was clear that her mother had liked the sea. Both her mother and father must have loved the sea to have given her that name. If only he spoke more, her father. If only he would share with her the pieces of her mother he had enjoyed. If only those pieces of her mother could be placed in a box for her to open every day. One moment would suffice, one important moment that involved more than the word "Vini" that she'd heard him tell people about.

"It was my wife's last word and it was to Claire," he liked to say. "And yet by the time Claire came her mother was already gone."

The way he told the story always made her feel like someone who had shown up uninvited somewhere, as if she shouldn't have come. As if her mother's death were her fault. Other times he seemed so happy that she was here. She could sometimes see him watching her while she was doing her homework. He would pretend he was repairing a net or sharpening a stick into a toothpick while sitting on his cot across the room, but he would be watching her, as though he were looking for something, something he could never find. Maybe he was looking for her mother. The women who combed her hair, the vendors whose products she picked up and laid down, all said

that she looked like her mother. "Like two drops of water," they said. She must walk like her mother too, and when she was a woman, a true Madame, when her adult voice came in, would she sound like her mother too? Or would she continue to confuse with her presence the people who had known her mother? Maybe they would take her for her mother, when her body was filled in, when her chest had fully grown, when she became a woman.

Now she would have a mother, but not a mother whom she looked like. Only for one moment, for one word ("Vini"), had she had the mother she looked like anyway.

While playing wonn, when she held hands with other girls, either at school or on the beach, when they swayed their arms up and down before taking off in their circle, when they were deciding which way to play or which song to sing, she would always think of the same song. Sometimes she suggested it and it was shouted down, and other times she kept it to herself, and whatever the other girls were singing, she would sing that one particular song in her head. She even sang it when she jumped rope, when no one was singing anything. And whenever she sang it, it was as if someone else were there with her. When there were five other girls playing, if she moved faster than anyone else, she would see seven shadows on the ground.

Lasirèn, Labalèn
Chapo m tonbe nan lanmè
Lasirèn, The Whale
My hat fell into the sea

The other girls didn't always like this song because it was not a real wonn song. It was a fisherman's song. Although the melody was cheerful, the words were sad. You never got back things that fell into the sea. She was surprised that the granmoun, the adults, were not singing this song all day long. So much had fallen into the sea. Hats fell into the sea. Hearts fell into the sea. So much had fallen into the sea. So much could still fall into the sea, including Msye Caleb, who fell in that morning, and all the men like her father who went there to look for fish. She was always afraid that one day she might have to sing that song every moment of every day. Not about a hat, but about her heart, about her father. And this is why she sometimes wished the sea would disappear. If the sea disappeared, she would miss its ever-changing sounds: how it sometimes sounded like one long breath. And sometimes like a cry. She would miss thunderclaps and how the lightning that came with them momentarily brightened the farthest-out reaches of the sea. She would also miss the sea's colors: the turquoise in the distance and its light-blue ripples up close, the white foam at the peaks of the waves. She would

miss the surge of high tide and the retreat of low tide, the milky or rosy clouds of dawn and the orange mists of sunsets. She would miss driftwood, sea glass, seashells, especially the baby ears and buttercups. She would miss throwing stones into the sea and seeing how far they would go. She would even miss the slimy seaweed that the sea spewed out, more during the warmer months of the year. She would also miss smelling the sea, which sometimes reminded her of wet hair. Sure, if the sea disappeared, there might be no fish to eat and she might not be able to lie on her back in it and look up at the hills from the water and sometimes see the magic of how it could be raining up in the hills and be perfectly sunny where she was. But maybe if the sea disappeared her father wouldn't have to go there anymore, and the crazy waves might not get him like they got Msye Caleb. There were more seas elsewhere, and if he left her, he might go to these other seas. They might be even stronger, crazier, more powerful seas than the one outside her front door. But in those other places he might have a bigger boat, one that was big enough for the two of them to live in, and she might be able to go with him wherever he was going and there they would live together where the crazy waves would not get them. And maybe if she sang this song all the time it would keep bad things from happening and it would keep her father from

leaving, and if he stayed, from dying in this sea. But during those times when she went in and lay on her back, her face aimed at the sky, while he was in another part of this sea, someplace where she could not spot his boat, she hoped that if the sea disappeared at that moment, she would disappear with it too, and she wouldn't have to miss him and he wouldn't have to be sad and she wouldn't have to wonder all the time where he was chèche lavi, looking for a better life. But what if there was no better life? How could he not know this? How could granmoun, grown people, not understand such things? How could they not understand everything?

She had somehow tonight convinced the other girls to sing the Lasirèn song for the wonn. It was her birthday, she had told them. She was seven, she had told them. The oldest girl let her pick the song. They'd groaned when she said it, but they knew it was coming and they were prepared, and as the adults gathered around to mourn Msye Caleb, she and her friends sang that song until they were hoarse, circling until they were dizzy. And though she wanted to stop after a while, she did not want them to stop and not begin again with the same song, so she tried to hang on. It was the best seventh-birthday gift they could give her.

When Madame Gaëlle arrived, Claire somehow knew that she'd interrupt their game. And sure enough, as soon as they saw Madame Gaëlle,

the other girls stopped circling and took the opportunity to escape from Claire and her song.

She could tell by the look on Madame Gaëlle's face that she had something in mind. Madame Gaëlle wanted something from her. And the only thing she had that Madame Gaëlle might want was her. It was also what her father wanted, for Madame Gaëlle to have her. At first, she was frightened by Madame Gaëlle's approach, at the careful way she moved in her direction. It was unusual too for a lady like Madame Gaëlle to be out in a fancy party gown with her hair rollers and with slippers on her feet. Something about Madame Gaëlle's mission must be pressing. At first Madame Gaëlle seemed to creep up on her, then she hovered over her, as though she were building up enough courage to ask a simple question that other adults often asked her, "Is your papa here?"

She had to look up into Madame Gaëlle's face to answer. She didn't want to, but she had to because of the sounds of the waves and all the people visiting Madame Josephine, and whenever she was nervous her voice wasn't so loud anyway, so Madame Gaëlle wouldn't be able to understand her unless she was looking straight into Madame Gaëlle's eyes.

She wished she could explain to Madame Gaëlle before answering that she was not trying to be disrespectful by looking into her eyes. She

knew that looking into an adult's eyes was as disrespectful as whistling in public or making ugly remarks about someone's mother. So instead of speaking, she nodded her answer.

Madame Gaëlle walked away, over to a big rock, then motioned for her to come and sit on another rock, next to her. She looked past Madame Gaëlle, wishing that her father could see them from wherever he was. She had not seen him for some time, but seeing her and Madame Gaëlle together would bring him running over for sure.

Before starting the wonn, she had hidden her sandals near the rock where Madame Gaëlle was now sitting. Maybe this was some sign. Maybe her sandals had chosen Madame Gaëlle. Her father would certainly see it as some kind of sign if she told him that Madame Gaëlle had come to sit where she had hidden her sandals. Maybe she should be saying something now. But she didn't know what to say and Madame Gaëlle didn't seem to know what to say either, because Madame Gaëlle didn't talk for a long time, but Claire could feel that Madame Gaëlle was watching her the way her father watched her. She took her time slipping on her sandals, not knowing how to make Madame Gaëlle's staring and not-talking stop. Then she heard Madame Gaëlle say, "I knew your mother."

Of course Madame Gaëlle had known her

mother. Everyone in town, it seemed, had known her mother. Everyone, except her. She knew this the way she knew everything else, by hearing bits of things adults said to one another when they didn't think she was listening. Besides, her mother and Madame Gaëlle's daughter were buried together in the same part of the town cemetery where she had gone that very morning.

But wait. Was Madame Gaëlle going to tell her something about her mother that she'd never heard before, that extra thing she often wished her father would tell her? Had Madame Gaëlle wrapped a piece of her mother, an invisible piece, in an invisible box, that she now wanted to open for her to visit? Were her mother and Madame Gaëlle friends? Is that why Madame Gaëlle had nursed her that one time, making Madame Gaëlle, as her father liked to say, her milk mother? She wanted to hear more. What could she do to hear more? She raised her head and looked directly into Madame Gaëlle's eyes. It was not disrespectful if it was urgent, if you wanted something and couldn't ask. It was not disrespect. It was curiosity. It was like Madame Josephine, who, because she could not speak, had to look in the faces of all people, even the white doctors at Sainte Thérèse when they were trying to talk to her about her leg. But white people didn't care if you looked into their eyes—that's what the people who'd seen them up close at

L'hôpital Sainte Thérèse said. The white people there actually wanted you to look into their eyes. That's how they claimed to know you were being honest. So she was now looking into Madame Gaëlle's wild, mournful eyes and she was pretending that Madame Gaëlle was one of those white people who didn't care if you looked into their eyes, even as a stream of words came pouring out of Madame Gaëlle's mouth.

"Your mother had sewn so many things for you," Madame Gaëlle was saying, but in a jumble, as if to herself. "She had sewn little dresses for you even before she was pregnant with you." Then Madame Gaëlle said something about God. No, not God, God's hands. Her mother, Madame Gaëlle said, had stolen her from God's hands. "And then you were born," Madame Gaëlle said, her voice clear now. And the revenan talk, Madame Gaëlle was saying she didn't believe in that. But she believed in birthdays, she said, and she wished Claire bòn fèt.

Claire wanted Madame Gaëlle to keep talking about her mother. But Madame Gaëlle stopped talking. Instead Madame Gaëlle smiled, showing some perfect-looking and long white teeth. Then, as though this were a revelation even to herself, Madame Gaëlle said, "Your mother *was* my friend."

Since people said that she and her mother looked so much alike, maybe that's why Madame

Gaëlle wanted to be her friend too. And why her father wanted her and Madame Gaëlle to be friends and for Madame Gaëlle to take her.

Tell me more, she wanted to say. Please tell me much more. Open that invisible box with the invisible mother and let me see what is inside. But Madame Gaëlle did not say more. Her smile faded and her face dimmed as if something puzzling were coming into her mind, and she frowned as though the thing that had entered her mind were something that she was trying to make sense of, that she was trying to understand. And Claire now imagined that there might be a similar look on her own face, because she too was trying to figure out whether Madame Gaëlle was now upset. Or maybe Madame Gaëlle was thinking about her daughter. Madame Gaëlle smiled again, as if something had been decided in her mind, and Claire suspected that perhaps Madame Gaëlle's smile was meant to keep her from worrying, and maybe her father had been watching them from somewhere, because at that moment he rose out of the shadows and suddenly he was standing over them, and his shadow covered Madame Gaëlle's body.

Her father had been drinking a little, most likely with the other fishermen around the bonfire. He didn't drink often and never drank a lot, but when he drank he was never happy. She knew most adults got happy when they drank kleren. They

laughed and danced by themselves and told jokes. But her father became even quieter when he drank. He became sadder too, as sad as when he was standing at her mother's grave.

Her father's feet seemed to be failing him, as if he were tired of standing over her and Madame Gaëlle, and he sat down on the sand between them. Her father and Madame Gaëlle each seemed to be waiting for the other to talk first, so Claire went back to tugging at her sandal straps and picking tiny grains of sand out from beneath her toenails. While her father had his face turned toward the lighthouse and the hills, Madame Gaëlle said, "Tonight, I take her."

Could it be as simple as that? One day she was her father's daughter and the next she was Madame Gaëlle's? And could this really mean that her father was going away for good and that she would never see him again? Would he even come back, like her relatives from the hills, to bring her yams and breadfruit at Christmas?

Her father seemed surprised to hear that Madame Gaëlle was looking to take her that very night. Maybe that's how it was when you got something you'd always wanted but thought you would never get. Maybe her father would be just as shocked when he went somewhere else to live, only to find that chèche lavi, the life he had spent so much time looking for, was no life at all without her.

She tried her best to fight back her tears, kept her hands to her sides as long as she could so her father and Madame Gaëlle would not see her wiping those tears, but the tears came anyway.

"Why now?" her father asked. But why not now, if he was planning to give her away anyway?

"Now or never," Madame Gaëlle said. And Claire wondered what this meant. Was this the last time the three of them would be together?

Claire looked past Madame Gaëlle and her father, over at the crowd of people still gathered around Madame Josephine. Most of them had known Msye Caleb, just as most of them had known her mother.

She wondered whether her mother would have been able to do what her father was doing, if she would have had the courage to give her away like this, to someone else. She knew of both fathers and mothers, fishing families, who had given their children, both girls and boys, away. They had taken their children to distant relatives in the capital to work as restavèks, child maids or houseboys. Others had taken their children to the white people at Sainte Thérèse and the white people had put the children in orphanages. Some of those children were taken to the capital and other places and were never seen or heard from again. They became other people's children in other lands that they'd never even known existed.

At least she would be staying here, and if her father didn't leave, if he gave up on chèche lavi elsewhere and stayed in Ville Rose, she could visit with him now and then. He would have more time for visits too, because if she was living with Madame Gaëlle, he wouldn't have to work as hard. He wouldn't have to worry about her as much.

"Claire Limyè Lanmè Faustin." Her father was trying to get her attention. But he didn't even need to call out her name. She was already listening for any word, every word from him. But she did not want to look at him. She did not want to see him sad. She did not want to make him sadder. She thought she heard tears in his voice when he asked Madame Gaëlle, "You will not change her name?"

This is why he had said her full and entire name. He wanted to remind Madame Gaëlle of it. Claire Limyè Lanmè Faustin. This would always be her name.

And what else, Claire wondered, would he ask Madame Gaëlle to change or not to change about her? She might never sleep in the same place as her father again. Would they even visit the cemetery on her birthday?

Her father was now saying something about a letter he'd given to Madame Gaëlle. Maybe the letter would explain more than he had been able to. Maybe it would make her understand

everything. But no words could ever do that. She knew that because even if, like Msye Caleb, she could write the most wonderful letters, she could never write a letter that could explain how she was feeling at that moment.

It was then that she raised her hand. She thought she would pretend she was in school pointing her index finger up to the sky to get their attention. That way, she wouldn't have to look at either of them.

They would also realize that she was always going to be a good girl, that she wasn't going to fight them or disobey, that she would always do what they said. But even if she was going to live with Madame Gaëlle, she wanted her things. She wanted her school notebooks and her uniforms, and even if Madame Gaëlle had fancy beds in her house, she wanted at least the quilt that draped her cot, the quilt her father said had belonged to her mother. So she kept her head down and her hand raised and she told them that she wanted her things, "Bagay yo."

Rather than speaking, her father looked in the direction of the shack and pointed to it with an index finger, showing that he agreed she should go get her things.

She wanted to walk the long way, through the crowd, for this was surely her last walk to the shack when it was still hers, but she sensed that both her father and Madame Gaëlle were in a

hurry, that they wanted to get the entire thing done with, so she walked quickly, and soon she was opening the unlocked door and peeking inside the shack. But it was pitch-black inside, as dark as when she would wake up in the middle of the night needing the latrine and was too scared to get up even to use the chamber pot. But it wasn't her fear of the dark that prevented her from going all the way in. That darkness was already familiar to her. She knew her way through it.

What kept her from going in was feeling like she had been kicked out, like her home was no longer hers. So she looked back to where her father and Madame Gaëlle were sitting and she noticed they were no longer following her with their eyes. Instead they were each looking at different parts of the beach, trying not to look at each other, so she took advantage of that moment when she knew she was on each of their minds, but in different ways, and she pulled the shack door closed and ran.

She ran through the alley that snaked between the shacks, up to the coco de mer palms at the entrance of a path that led to the lighthouse. Her sandals became entangled in some ylang-ylang creepers that bordered the trail where sandstones turned to hill gravel, then mountain rock. She was relieved when, at last, the trail curved and made an incline up toward Anthère Hill.

Most of the houses on Anthère Hill had high

concrete walls topped with bottle shards, conch shells, and bougainvillea vines. The bougainvilleas, she knew, grew so easily, so fast, that they crossed individual walls, creating unintended canopies. The canopied and uncanopied trails zigzagged up toward the lighthouse and Mòn Initil.

The higher she climbed, the breezier it got and the brighter the stars became. The moon seemed larger, more silver than white. The air was much cooler and the sound of the waves faded, though it did not fall away completely. The only voices she now heard were coming from the lighthouse and from the paths between the houses. Muffled conversations were punctuated by giggles from people who sounded as though they were tickling one another.

She heard a dog bark. That bark was echoed by another, then another, until a chorus of barks from large-sounding dogs had been started. Dogs barking—especially big, fat-sounding dogs—always meant you were not welcomed. She heard yardmen's voices hushing the dogs, talking to them as though they were people, telling them to calm down. To be sure she wouldn't be seen, she headed toward the dark, empty houses at the edge of the hill, the newer and larger houses that were occupied only a couple of weeks a year.

She stopped to catch her breath, leaning against the last wall before the hill abruptly ended at a cliff. The wall felt cool against her arm and

smooth too, as though it were on the inside of a house. From up there, the view was clear as always, and she could now see part of the beach. She couldn't see her shack or the palms behind it but, even with her eyes closed, she would have been able to point in its direction, along with the bungalow where Msye Sylvain lived with his wife and twelve children and grandchildren. When he wasn't out at sea, Msye Sylvain sold pen tete, breast-shaped bread, which he and his brood baked in a clay oven that was even now flaming.

She couldn't see her father or Madame Gaëlle just then, but she knew where Msye Xavier, the boat builder and metal forger, was, because from the hill the sparks coming from Msye Xavier's tools looked like tiny fireworks. She saw Madame Wilda, who weaved her nets in a low chair behind her house by candlelight. She also saw Msye Caleb's place, because the girl who stayed with Madame Josephine was cooking something, and the girl was illuminated by the cooking fire and the lamp hanging from a post in the outdoor kitchen. Claire saw the white-clad, ghostlike silhouettes of Madame Josephine and her friends from church. These familiar people and the fires that made them visible to her, these points of light, now seemed like beacons calling her home.

But no, she was not thinking of going back.

Suddenly there were more lights. More people were coming forward with lamps. Then one person (her father? was that his voice?) called out her name. Then many others called her name too.

There were so many people calling her name that their voices made their way all the way up the hill to her.

She could hear the men on the gallery of the lighthouse calling out her name too.

She almost answered.

Could this be a song? she wondered. Could her name being called out by dozens of people be a song?

Could it be a new song for her next game of wonn?

For a circle of one.

> Yo t ap chèche li . . .
> They were looking for her
> Like a pebble in a bowl of rice
> They were looking for her
> But no, no, no, she didn't want to be found.

She continued uphill until she found herself on a flat plot of land behind one of the empty Anthère Hill mansions. The land seemed as though it had just been cleared by fire. The earth was still warm beneath her sandals.

Her father liked to say that in a few years Mòn Initil would no longer be useless or initil since

very rich people had figured out that they could burn it down, flatten it, and build their big palaces there. Soon it would have to be called Mòn Palè, or Palace Mountain.

She could no longer see the beach, so they wouldn't be able to see her either. She stood for a long time, alone, in the middle of that newly scorched field. Her name was being called from the lighthouse by two or three men whose voices she could easily identify if she thought long enough about it, but she was no longer even tempted to answer.

Maybe they'd think that, like Msye Caleb, she was lost at sea. Her father would be the most worried about her being lost at sea, although he would hide it. He wouldn't show his worry to his friends and neighbors. And not to Madame Gaëlle. But he would no longer have to worry. She would go away. She would go away on her own. She would go where he would never think to come and find her. Like the fugitives in Madame Louise's stories—les marons—she would hide inside what was left of Mòn Initil.

She would be the girl at the foot of the sky. She would find a cave large enough inside Mòn Initil to live in, and at night she would lie on beds of ferns and listen to the bats squeal and the owls moan. She would dig a hole to catch rainwater for drinking and bathing. And she would try very hard not to disturb the marooned spirits who had

found refuge there before her. She hoped that there would be no snakes because she was afraid of snakes, though she could learn to live with them if she had to.

But she wouldn't spend all her time there; she would come out every day to watch the beach. She would watch the fishermen go out at daybreak to lay their nets, then return at midday or late in the afternoon. When her father would look up at Mòn Initil from the sea, he would be looking at her without realizing it. He would be sad, but maybe he wouldn't leave the beach or Ville Rose. Maybe he would stay, just as he had when she was living with her mother's family. He might stay close by, waiting, hoping for her to return one day.

She'd heard some of the fishermen's wives say that the spirits of those who'd been lost at sea would sometimes come ashore to whisper in their loved ones' ears. She would make sure he felt her presence too. She'd sneak down at dusk to collect fallen coconuts and grab salted fish left out to dry and she'd stop by and say a few words in her father's ear while he slept. That way she would always be in his dreams. She would go away without really leaving, without losing everything, without dying.

She stood in the middle of the scorched field for a long time, imagining this life as a maroon. She waited for the voices from the lighthouse to die

down, until she heard none at all, then she walked past the wildflower field around the lighthouse, and back down through Anthère Hill, to the edge of a much lower butte so that she could see the beach once again.

She was hoping to see her father, hoping to catch one more glimpse of him before she went back up the hill to make her total retreat into Mòn Initil. Then wouldn't he be sorry.

From the lower butte now, she could see that most of the lamps had disappeared, as had the people carrying them. The bonfire had been put out. There were no more lights to be seen, except the moon and the stars and Msye Sylvain's clay oven and Msye Xavier's forging tools and Madame Wilda's candles and net and Madame Josephine's outdoor kitchen lamp. Everyone else, it seemed, had gone in for the night. Or into their own darkness.

Maybe they wouldn't miss her after all.

A warm burst of air brushed past her, rising, it seemed, at that very moment, from the sea. It reminded her of a sensation she sometimes had, of feeling another presence around her: of noticing only one branch of a tree stir while the rest remained still, of hearing the thump of invisible feet landing on the ground, of seeing an extra shadow circling while she was playing wonn. She would sometimes feel the gentle strokes of fingers traveling up and down her

back, then lingering ever so lightly at the nape of her neck. She couldn't always pin down the moment these things would start, then stop, so she would call them rèv je klè, waking dreams.

She'd had these types of dreams for as long as she could remember. Soon after they occurred, she would search for signs that something, someone might have actually been there. She would search the ground for footprints, flower petals, sparkly feathers from angel wings. And usually there would be nothing.

But just then, as she was looking down from the butte, she saw Madame Gaëlle running with a lamp in her hand and her shiny, silver-looking gown glowing in the moonlight. And when she saw her father, brightened on the edge of the water by Madame Gaëlle's lamp and satin gown glow, and when she saw other people approaching them with their lamps, forming a circle as if they were a sun, something felt different.

In the middle of the lamp circle, half of which was now in the water, she saw someone pull a man in a red shirt out of the sea. Like a dying fish, the man's body jerked about. Madame Gaëlle and her father were standing together in front of him.

The man reached up, grabbing both her father's and Madame Gaëlle's legs, nearly pulling them both down on top of him. Her father pulled himself back, regaining his balance. Madame

Gaëlle fell forward on her knees, landing on the sand near the man. Who was he? she wondered. Could it be Myse Caleb, whom the sea had taken this morning? No. He was gone, they had mourned him, and this man was too wide to be her father's friend.

She thought she heard people shouting her schoolmaster's name: "Ardin! Ardin!" as if to wake this man from the sea.

She started running farther down the hill, past the jacaranda trees, down to the gravel path, then back through the ylang-ylang vines. Then she stopped on a hibiscus-covered precipice to look down once again. She saw her father and a few other men bend down and join Madame Gaëlle on the sand. They grabbed the man's waist and turned him on his back. Then she saw Madame Gaëlle lower her face and put her mouth on the man's mouth, as though to kiss him.

Her father turned back to face the shacks on the beach. He was moving his arms wildly, as if to call for more lamps, more people, more help. Or maybe he was simply feeling helpless, feeling just like she was now, afraid.

More people started coming and more lamps. So many people now that they were blocking her view and she could no longer see the red-shirted man, Madame Gaëlle, or her father. She continued down the hill, running so fast that she slipped on some loose gravel stones and fell. She popped

back up, then started running again, leaving her sandals behind.

She ran and ran, down toward the alley of coconut palms behind her home.

Fòk li retounen . . .
She had to go back

She thought this too could make a good song for the wonn.

She had to go home
To see the man
Who'd crawled half dead
Out of the sea

She had to go back and see her father and Madame Gaëlle, whose own sorrows could have nearly drowned them. She had to go down to the water to see them take turns breathing into this man, breathing him back to life. Before becoming Madame Gaëlle's daughter, she had to go home, just one last time.

Acknowledgments

I am grateful to the John D. and Catherine T. MacArthur Foundation for the fellowship that gave me the time to attempt this book and so much more. Thanks to my family in Léogâne, those gone and those still there, for introducing me and reintroducing me to the sea.

Mèsi, Fedo, for things that it would take a lifetime to list.

I owe so much to Nicole Aragi and Robin Desser for their love and guidance over nearly two decades now. Thank you, Jennifer Kurdyla, for your time and patience.

The excerpt from the poem "Le Soleil and Les Grenouilles" is from *Les Fables de la Fontaine* (Livre 6), available in various editions. The English translation is mine.

Additional Copyright Information

A Note About the Author

Edwidge Danticat is the author of numerous books, including *Brother, I'm Dying*, a National Book Critics Circle Award winner and a National Book Award finalist; *Breath, Eyes, Memory*, an Oprah's Book Club selection; *Krik? Krak!*, a National Book Award finalist; *The Farming of Bones*, an American Book Award winner; and *The Dew Breaker*, a PEN/Faulkner Award finalist and winner of the inaugural Story Prize. The recipient of a MacArthur Fellowship, she has been published in *The New Yorker*, *The New York Times*, and elsewhere. She lives in Miami.

Center Point Large Print
600 Brooks Road / PO Box 1
Thorndike ME 04986-0001 USA

(207) 568-3717

US & Canada:
1 800 929-9108
www.centerpointlargeprint.com